HOVERING DEATH

I leaned close to the helicopter's window and looked out over the ocean. "What's that?" I asked Chesterton. I pointed to a small, apparently deserted island, where a primitive shelter sat in ruins.

"Pirate's Island. Just a bit of rock where—"

Suddenly it felt as if a crushing blow had struck the helicopter. We dipped sharply to the right.

I was aware of Chesterton struggling with the controls as the craft floundered, losing altitude. His left hand groped for something by his door—the lever?—and without warning, my door dropped open. With the helicopter tilting precipitously, my door flapped wildly in the wind and I looked straight down at the rocky island. Only my seat belt prevented me from plunging hundreds of feet to my death. Staring down in horror, I had a vertiginous sensation of falling.

"Hang on!" Chesterton cried. He reached a hand to my chest as if to grab a handful of clothing and hold me in the craft. But, jerked about as he was by the violently rocking helicopter, his large hand clapped onto the edge of my seat-belt latch.

To my horror, the latch released. Both strap and buckle fell away, dangling uselessly at my right side, banging violently against the outside of the helicopter. . . .

The Booklover's Mysteries
by Julie Kaewert

UNPRINTABLE*

UNBOUND*

and

coming soon

UNSOLICITED

*Available from Bantam Books

UNTITLED

A BOOKLOVER'S MYSTERY

Julie Kaewert

BANTAM BOOKS

NEW YORK TORONTO LONDON SYDNEY AUCKLAND

UNTITLED: A Booklover's Mystery
A Bantam Crime Line Book / November 1999
Crime Line and the portrayal of a boxed "cl"
are trademarks of Bantam Books, a division of Random House, Inc.

ISBN 0-553-57717-4
Published simultaneously in the United States and Canada

Bantam Books are published by Bantam Books, a division of Random
House, Inc. Its trademark, consisting of the words "Bantam Books" and the
portrayal of a rooster, is Registered in U.S. Patent and Trademark Office and
in other countries. Marca Registrada. Bantam Books, 1540 Broadway, New
York, New York 10036.

PRINTED IN THE UNITED STATES OF AMERICA
OPM   10   9   8   7   6   5   4   3

For Elizabeth

Untitled

CHAPTER 1

*A room without books is like a body without
a soul.*

—CICERO

Finding the world's rarest book in my library that Sunday afternoon was a bibliophile's dream. But now I'd give anything if I *hadn't* caught a glimpse of its hiding place behind my bookshelves. For while that outwardly charming volume fascinated and delighted the bibliomaniac world, it held dangerous secrets—secrets that not only ignited hostilities that had simmered for a millennium, but took from me everything I held most precious.

On that unforgettable afternoon I sat at my desk in the library, scrawling American addresses on ivory wedding invitation envelopes—hundreds of them. Sarah Townsend, my intended, had insisted my handwriting was infinitely preferable to that of the commercial calligraphers she knew. I wasn't sure I agreed, but anything for Sarah. A few hundred envelopes? Delighted, my love.

It was also infinitely preferable to the nasty task of home maintenance that awaited me outside. One of our ancient oaks, which had been ailing for several years, had keeled over against the house in a violent gale the previous week. It was still perched there, waiting to cause a new disaster. I'd intended to get to it that weekend, but . . .

The doorbell rang. I checked my watch as I rose and went to the door, stretching luxuriously. Four o'clock on a Sunday afternoon. The *Sunday Times* was still strewn about the sofa in pleasant disarray, its rumours of deepening hostilities between America and Iraq as remote as those faraway deserts. Even the lesser evil of a flu epidemic in London seemed remote, with the roses blooming and the birds singing outside the open French doors. Ah, but life was good here at the Orchard, long the family home of the Plumtree clan. The oak could wait. And it was time for tea.

I swung open the door, enjoying its characteristic creak on the old hinge.

"Max!" I exclaimed. "What a pleasant surprise. I was just going to put the kettle—"

"Sorry, Alex." My brother pushed past me, all business, into the hallway. "I need to borrow a book, if you don't mind. Sorry to disturb."

"Not at all," I murmured. I closed the front door and followed him into the library. I was used to Max's brief enthusiasms, his frequent small emergencies. I understood him well: He was simply a more concentrated version of myself. Emotionally, Max was more mercurial; physically, he was smaller and darker. He went straight to the shelf of reference books.

I watched him, as I leaned against my desk. "I've just been addressing the invitations for the Nantucket ceremony," I began to explain.

"Ah," he said distractedly, clearly not hearing a word I'd said. The vows I would take in little more than two months were not uppermost in his mind.

"I read in the paper this morning that aliens contacted the Queen. They spoke through her corgis at a polo match in Windsor Great Park."

"That's nice," he muttered, continuing to search through the richly stocked shelves—a bit wildly, it seemed to me. He was certainly in a flap about something.

"Not there," he said. "*Damn!* A client of mine—an anonymous one, funnily enough—said he'd already tried Maggs. They couldn't help him. So if *I* could, it'd be a coup. And I *know* we had that volume here . . . that heraldry volume Dad was forever showing us. I won't *sell* ours, of course, but at least my client could see it. And," Max said with exaggerated emphasis, quite pleased with himself, "if I have to meet with him, I can find out who he is. The book was a private issue, you know, a Dibdin Club edition. I have the impression he's after a more modern volume than the one we have, but I can't exactly remember the date of ours."

"Yes, I know the one you mean. It must be here somewhere." I went to a different wall of shelves to help him look; we had a very relaxed system of ordering our books, which allowed us the thrill of a treasure hunt each time we looked for an uncommon volume. And a Dibdin edition *was* a treasure . . . the Dibdin Club was the most prestigious group of bibliophiles in all England. Each year, one member chose an exceedingly rare volume from his or her own library and reissued it for the other members. It was a bit like a printing society, only less bourgeois and far more private. The Dibdin stopped just short of royalty, and its members held the loftiest titles—and books—in the land.

"Ah-ha!" Max cried, triumphantly snatching a large volume off the shelf.

"What's that?" I asked, squinting at the bookshelves. I went across to my brother, suddenly intrigued.

"*Really*, Alex!" Max rolled his eyes in exasperation. "I

know you're busy with the wedding, my boy, but the world does carry on. I just *told* you it was the Dibdin edition on heraldry, which I'd—"

"No, no, sorry. I mean what"—I bent down to reach to the back of the shelf—"is *this*?"

I knelt and lifted out several other books, placing them on the floor. Then I studied the wall behind the bookshelf more carefully. At this hour and season the sun was on the shelf directly; normally, I would have drawn the curtains by now to shield the spines from excessive light. "I do believe," I said, following a rectangular outline cut into the wood with my fingertips, "that there's something here."

I pushed on the rectangle, and it sprang outward toward me, opening on a hinge at its left edge. "I don't believe this," Max said incredulously, kneeling next to me and breathing down my neck. "Dad had *another* safe in the shelves?"

I wanted a torch; it was dark in the space, and I didn't fancy sticking my hand inside without knowing what was there. But I couldn't wait. I reached in and found that the area was quite small, perhaps twelve inches wide by eight deep. My fingers met with a hard object that felt very much like—why was I surprised?—a book. I pulled it out. Max and I found ourselves staring at a smallish volume, perhaps eight by six inches and half an inch thick.

"What are *you* doing here, then?" I said under my breath to the book.

Having something just short of an obsession with antiquarian books, I knew instantly that this was not any old volume. Its covers were upholstered with wine-red-velvet fabric. The covers and book itself were bound together with leather thongs; the binding of a very old book indeed—an incunable, in fact, a book from the cradle period of printing in the late fifteenth century. Book collectors positively salivated over such books, and often paid a great deal of money for them. Most were carefully preserved in museums.

Max and I exchanged a glance.

There was no title in the velvet on the front cover. I turned the book over and saw that the back cover was blank as well. The spine, too, was utterly devoid of print or decoration. Carefully, I lifted the cover to discover pristine, creamy-white rag paper. Rag, unlike modern woody stuff, held up miraculously well over the centuries without so much as discolouring.

"Good Lord," Max murmured as we stared down at the words on the page. "This is incredible. Look at that black letter—and you can see that they dampened the paper, which made a very deep impression. Alex, this is *unquestionably* an incunable."

"You're right. And look at the binding—definitely English. They've put the straps and clasps from the bottom up instead of the continental bottom down."

On the fine page before us, set in thick Gothic black-letter type, were the words:

DOMINUS SERVET VERITATEM ET VIRUM QUI EAM SCRIBIT

The remnants of my school Latin struggled to organise themselves into a translation. "*God preserve the truth, and the man who* writes—or *prints?*—*it.* . . . most unusual," I said.

"Mmm," Max replied. I knew he'd noticed, too, that there was no forematter, no early pages listing author, printer, or binder. Nor was there any date, though the heavy black-letter print and primitive printing process told us the book was likely to be fifteenth century. Just the rather dire Latin verse, followed by several blank pages.

Eagerly, I turned another page and found more black ink. The dark Gothic words opposed a breathtaking woodcut print of a knight in armour. A coat of arms ornamented the cloth covering his chain mail. He stood facing the reader, sword and shield in hand, features hidden by the metal helmet, and I noticed that a tiny four-poster was one of the symbols in the design on his chest. As best I could translate from Middle English the print opposite the woodcut of the knight, it said:

> *This is the story of the Royal Order of the Bedchamber, the loyal group of men who have pledged their lives to protect the King over the last three hundred years. We wish to tell the Order's history, and important historical facts known for centuries only to members of the Royal Order of the Bedchamber. These facts have never before been revealed, and were preserved by word of mouth within the Order until Giovanni Boccaccio became acquainted with a member of the Order, was captivated by the story, and wrote it down in 1371. We have printed it now thanks to the miracle of the printing press. We pray that no offence will be taken by His Majesty, King Edward IV, from our effort to record this magnificent truth.*

So the book I held in my hands was an account of the daily activities of the knights of the Royal Order of the Bedchamber, evidently the king's closest and most loyal protectors. I'd never heard of them, but that didn't mean they couldn't have existed. I looked at Max. "Late fifteenth century, then, if the reigning monarch was Edward IV. But why would he take offence? It almost sounds as if the author *expected* the king to be displeased."

Max shrugged impatiently. "Let's have a look through the rest."

I turned through the remaining pages. The book contained only sixteen leaves; the last featured a stunningly detailed illustration, again from a woodcut, of a small four-poster surrounded by curtains. A knight knelt next to the bed dramatically, dripping dagger drawn at his side, a rampant lion with a crown in its teeth posturing aggressively on the coat of arms on his chest.

The pattern in the fabric of the bed curtains consisted of so many cross-hatchings that at first glance my eye imagined a multitude of nearly microscopic letters jumbled together and crossed by fine lines. When I looked more closely, I couldn't distinguish any letters at all. Holding the book a bit farther away, I blinked and looked again, trying to sort out the tiny patterns my eye perceived.

Not letters after all, I decided, but merely a design of overwhelming detail and precision, not to mention beauty. I turned back to the beginning to read the book's text. There was really very little print; a huge initial capital letter began the scant lines of text on each page.

> It is the duty of each Knight of the Order to make the King safe, to guard his Bedchamber while he is sleeping, to taste his wine, water and mead before allowing him to drink. All Knights of the Order are sworn to give their lives before allowing any harm to come to His Majesty.

I turned another page.

> For this reason the Knights of the Order are considered the bravest and most faithful of the realm. Because the King is appointed by God to reign over His people, the Knights serve God as well as the King. And so the tale I am about to relate is all the more tragic, because a Knight failed in his duty to both God and King.

The book went on for a bit here about the traditions of the Order, the specific duties of the knights and how they were carried out. I could hear Max breathing aloud as he too read. Then there came a fascinating bit about King Richard the Lion-Heart and the Crusades:

*One of the most worrisome periods for the Knights of
the Order was the Crusades. The Knights found themselves deeply suspicious of Saladin, the sultan of Babylon with whom Richard established a firm friendship
and even a truce in the Second Crusade. Every day the
Knights expected the Saracen to commit some act of
treachery toward their King, but this never came to
pass. The unlikely friendship between the two rulers extended so far that King Richard offered his sister
Joanna's hand in marriage to Saladin's brother, Al-
Adil, as a peace offering. In the end, it was King
Richard who grew tired of waiting for Saladin to deliver
certain monies and the True Cross of Christ as agreed.
It was our own King who broke the truce and slaughtered Saladin's people.*

I read on, fascinated at this view of history through the
knight's eyes. Several anecdotes later, I found a stunner:

*Legend has held for hundreds of years that Richard the
Lion-Heart died of a crossbow wound from a common
poacher, after a disagreement with a peasant about some
old coins the peasant had unearthed. This is not true; we
wish the truth to be known. His Majesty lay abed for
some time, recovering from his wound, which had unfortunately festered. As the noble Knight of the Order of the
Bedchamber watched from behind the bed curtains one
night, ever vigilant on behalf of his monarch, the Master
of the Order crept in to the room.*

*Now, there was no reason for anyone to enter
his Bedchamber at that hour unless they meant
him harm. But the Master of the Order of the Bedchamber
was much trusted and not a little feared, as it was known
he had a violent temper, and his close relationship with
His Majesty had never been doubted. True, his lands
had been revoked with his title that spring over some*

*perceived lack of loyalty, but the Master of the Order
had seemed repentant for whatever had caused his
penury and humiliation.*

*The Knight watched from behind the bed as the Master
advanced and searched the Bedchamber for members of
the Order such as himself. Seeing no one, and neglecting
to look in the one spot the guarding Knight occupied, he
proceeded to genuflect and kneel silently at the King's
bedside.*

*Then, as the Knight guarded His Majesty silently from
behind the curtain on the far side of the bed, he perceived
that the Master of the Order made a subtle movement.
While the Knight noted it, he did not reveal himself to
see, as it did not seem violent and he surmised that the
Master had merely been genuflecting. Shortly thereafter the Master rose, genuflected once again, and left
the room.*

*When the Knight came round the bed to check on His
Majesty, the King seemed oddly pale. The Knight looked
upon him closely and realised that his spirit had passed into
the next world. After telling the account you have just read
to his vassal outside the door, the Knight impaled himself
on his sword and was found on the floor beside the King's
bed, dead. May God have mercy upon us all.*

"History rewritten," Max breathed. "Amazing!"

At that moment a breeze blew in through the open
doors, ruffling the pages of the book and my hair. In the
next moment the wind sucked the doors outward again
and slammed them closed. Their wooden edges banged
together, then drifted back open. The afternoon was once
again balmy and still.

We exchanged another look. I could see Max felt as I
did; we'd uncovered something utterly extraordinary.

•   •   •

The next day found us hurrying for the first time to Diana Boillot's private treasure room. Her little office was buried deep in the bowels of the British Museum, down a subterranean hallway few knew existed. Soon her office would be relocated to the new British Library, near St. Pancras, but she'd told us she would be just as happy to stay in the museum. Only a handful of people knew Diana worked there; both she and the museum preferred it that way. In her hidden grotto she restored and cared for some of the most precious books in the world.

My brother and I negotiated the last of half a dozen turns in the rabbit warren that was the deepest level of the museum, and at last came to a wooden door tall enough to admit a fully grown elf. "Diana Boillot, Restoration" had been stencilled on the door in gold paint. This subterranean kingdom seemed worlds away from the sunny Bloomsbury streets above, thronged with tourists, and the offices of Plumtree Press—the family publishing company I run—just around the corner. I raised my hand and knocked twice.

The door swung open; warm light from Diana's ceiling and table lamps dispelled the gloom of the dank corridor. "Max! Alex! You survived the maze. Come in." The scents of fresh paper and leather washed over us, and Diana's flowing red hair shone like flame. Stacks of ancient volumes surrounded her on sturdy shelving lining three walls, waiting to be made good for another few centuries.

Walking into Diana's paradise of books was a bit like Lucy and Edmund stumbling through the back of the wardrobe into Narnia. It was beautiful, thrilling; a dream come true.

She laughed at our expressions. "I know. I'm the luckiest woman alive. Sit down, sit down! The morning's been endless since you called, Alex . . . I nearly died of suspense. I'll just clear some space here. . . ."

Diana nodded at two tall stools for us opposite her work table, then lovingly removed a book from the table and placed it flat on a shelf behind her. Its cover was what the book trade knows as basil, an eighteenth-century material made of heavily glazed sheepskin, in the usual dull crimson hue of ledgers and other books of record. It had been clamped shut; no doubt she'd just glued something with her flour-and-water paste, known to be especially kind to books over hundreds of years. Diana had once told me that corrosive chemical adhesives had done more damage to books than anything else. I myself had seen enough glue and sticky tape, applied by well-meaning amateur restorers to vellum and paper alike, to make me cry.

Max and I took our seats, gazing hungrily at the books surrounding us. Max recovered first. "Thanks again for taking time to see us, Diana."

"Not at all," she replied, coming back to the table, her eyes shining in anticipation. She rubbed her hands together. "Let's see your book!" I reached inside my book bag and pulled it out. She took it from me almost reverently, inspecting the cover before opening it. "Perfect condition. Looks as if it's never been in circulation. Definitely fifteenth century . . . lovely job . . . I'd say we're looking at one of the top binders. English. You can tell by the way the strap's on backwards—But you know that. Sorry."

She opened the book and turned pages until she came to the first illustration. The breath caught in her throat. "What an exquisite woodcut! The *detail* . . ."

She turned through the pages for a first cursory examination, and after squinting at the design in the bed curtains on the last page turned back to the beginning. She read the Latin inscription on the first page, turned another page. She frowned and looked up at us. "How very curious. It almost seems as though the printer and binder . . . not to mention the author . . . *wanted* to remain unknown."

"Yes. I wondered if perhaps they were worried that the

king might be angry at having his private Order of the Bedchamber details made public—you know, like Prince Charles's valet writing a tell-all of life inside the palace."

"Mmm. I suppose so," she said. "I was just contemplating checking the museum catalogue, and Hain"—indispensable reference books of antiquarian book collectors—"but since there's no title or author . . . not even a printer . . ."

We all eyed the book, hopelessly intrigued. Nothing like a good puzzle . . . and certainly nothing like one involving incunabula.

"Aside from its anonymity, Diana, the real significance of this book is that it tells a new story about King Richard's death. Here . . ." I showed her the pages. She read.

"The historians are going to love this." Diana tilted her head. "Would you mind if I rang Bartholomew Boswell? I wonder if he might know something about this."

"Good idea. Why not?" Max said.

I nodded. I knew Bats Boswell, the curator of rare books at the museum, only by reputation as an expert on antiquarian books, and of course by his surname. All London hung on him as the sole surviving relative of *the* Boswell. Women had thrown themselves at him for years, hoping to acquire his last name by marriage.

"Good. Hang on." She pressed four numbers on her phone and said, "Hello, Pat. Diana here. Is Bats in?" A pause. "Wonderful. Thanks."

It was testament to her status at the museum that Boswell was immediately on the other end of the line. "Listen, Bats," Diana said without preamble, betraying her excitement, "Alex and Max Plumtree are here in my office. They've discovered a rather interesting little book—we wondered if you'd care to come down and have a look." She smiled at us and winked. "Good. We'll be waiting."

"He's fascinated," Diana told us as she hung up the phone. "He loves a new discovery. And he does seem to know things that aren't in the reference volumes—no one knows how he does it." Turning her attention back to the book, she asked, "Would you mind if I read through the whole thing quickly, just until Bats gets here?"

"Of course not. By all means," Max said. We followed along as she read the brief text, losing ourselves in the beauty of those heavy black letters and the primitively printed illustrations. It seemed barely moments before there was a knock on Diana's door.

"Come in," she called. There was rattling at the door-knob. The door shook but remained closed. "That lock," she said, rolling her eyes. "There's a trick to it." She lifted up sharply on the doorknob, then jerked it to the right. The door opened to reveal Boswell, who had the appearance of a surprised owl. He was a small man, fussily dressed in bow tie, striped shirt, and dark suit. Round spectacles gave him his wide-eyed look.

"Must have that fixed," the curator grumbled, fiddling with the troublesome doorknob. "Hello, Diana. Max, Alex—delighted to meet you."

We shook hands and returned the good wishes. Diana handed the book over to him, offering him her tall stool. He sat and studied the cover, then the binding, then the opening pages. It is true that people who love books inspect them in an invariable ritual, like connoisseurs of wine. We've all seen oenophiles first inspect the colour of the wine, then swirl to determine viscosity, sniff, sip, and finally draw in air over the liquid to intensify the taste. Bibliophiles, on the other hand, inspect the condition of the cover and binding, check the forematter for vital dates and names, sniff for mould, make a visual inspection of the printing job, feel for the general condition of the paper or vellum—a telltale lack of crispness would indicate that it had been washed, making it less pristine and therefore slightly less valuable—and then usually repeat their inspection of forematter and cover.

The book Boswell was inspecting was more unusual than most, not only because of its obvious age, but because of its lack of title and information about pedigree. Date of publication, author, printer, binder . . . in old books, these were essential clues to value and importance.

"Good heavens," he said at last. "You don't suppose . . ." He appeared so taken aback, so full of something beyond casual surprise, Diana shot us a questioning look. *We're on to something big,* it said.

"You don't suppose what?" I asked Boswell.

He looked at me distractedly. "Well, it's just this bit about Saladin . . . For ages there's been a rumour in book circles that there was an untitled book—originally written by Boccaccio, containing some damning secret about the Saracen emperor Saladin. You know how Boccaccio, writing in the fourteenth century, always took it for granted that West and East came in contact frequently— if violently—because of the Crusades. In fact, in his life, Christendom might still have owned some small part of the Holy Land.

"Anyway, the *Decameron*—his most famous work, written at the time of the Black Death in Florence—contained stories about East and West as if they were neighbouring villages. I've heard it said that there was some volume that contained a story so horrible about Saladin that when the fifteenth-century emperor of Persia heard of the book, he sent a message to King Edward IV warning him to dispose of every last copy, or prepare for another holy war.

"Naturally, the king didn't want to do battle with the Persians. So he decreed that every book must be destroyed, and its author, printer, and binder must die. But Boccaccio was long dead, of course, anyway, and the printer and binder were never discovered. All the books were said to have been burnt, but"—he blinked rapidly, intensifying the owl-like impression—"I wonder. Perhaps all but *one* were destroyed."

"What a coincidence! We've just issued a modern English-language edition of the *Decameron* from the Press, edited by Margulies Whitehead." My mind ran through the details I'd retained from the preface; I hadn't read the entire book. The work contained one hundred stories told over the course of ten days—thus the book's title. The stories were, according to my friend and author Margulies, fun, often frivolous yarns about love and human nature. Boccaccio was a contemporary of Petrarch's, a predecessor of Chaucer's—but somehow he'd never become as famous as the others.

"I don't think there's anything terrifically damning about Saladin in the untitled book," I said, looking to Max for confirmation. He shook his head. "Just that Richard I offered his sister to Saladin's brother as a peace offering during the Crusades. But perhaps that wasn't widely known in the fifteenth century. It's certainly in all the history books now."

"Hmm. Gives one pause, all the same." Boswell hesitated, adjusting his glasses and licking his lips. Then he seemed to come to a decision. "Would you excuse me while I make a telephone call? I'd like to consult with someone on this. I'll be back straightaway." He began to back towards the door, still clutching the book. It was at that moment, when we all found ourselves staring at the small volume as if it were the Holy Grail, that I first worried about its safety. Boswell stopped as if he sensed my concern. Smiling sheepishly, the curator handed the book back to me.

"Sorry. You'll want to hang on to this! Back straightaway," he repeated, and bumbled out the door.

Diana crossed her arms, a suspicious look in her eye. "What was all *that* about?"

Laughing, Max said, "Where does he hear these wild stories? I'd love to know his sources."

"You know," Diana said thoughtfully, "you might wish to have some facsimiles made of this. The museum would love to have one, if you decide to keep the original. We might even have some funds for the project, considering the significance of the material."

"That's an excellent idea," I said, thinking. I'd seen a facsimile of the Domesday Book, and of the Ellesmere Chaucer. They were remarkably realistic. The duplication of those books had greatly enhanced people's understanding of history; millions had been able to discover the past through them in travelling exhibits, instead of the few hundred who might gain access to a special collections room.

"In fact," Diana said, "I'd like to take some photos of the book's pages today. It won't hurt the book, and I could study it a bit more after you've gone. If you don't mind."

"I'll make a start now—we might as well do something while we wait for Bats."

"By all means," I said, and Max concurred.

Diana turned on a bright light using a switch on the wall. Then she rolled over an apparatus that suspended a camera over the book, and began to shoot each page. Halfway through, she commented, "Bats is taking his sweet time with his phone call, isn't he?"

"Mmm." I looked at my watch; it had been twenty minutes.

"I'll have a zinc plate made for each page, using the photographs. Then we'll simply print your book," Diana explained. More time ticked past as we watched her finish the job, roll the photo apparatus away, and disassemble it. Then she took the spent rolls of film and slipped them into her handbag. She'd only just patted it contentedly with a smile at us, rather as if she'd swathed a baby safely in a bunting, when Boswell was with us again.

He knocked and then fussed with Diana's doorknob. She opened it for him with her little trick and a cheerful "Hello, Bats" on her tongue.

But everything had changed. The happy companionship of sharing the discovery of a long-lost book had vanished, and in its place were hesitancy and guilt. Boswell had difficulty looking any of us in the eye, and I do believe it was a bead of sweat I saw decorating his upper lip. Behind his ultra-cool, supercilious facade I sensed fear.

"I'm frightfully sorry," he said. "I've just got off the phone with my experts. I'm afraid it *has* been established beyond all doubt that *all* the original books were destroyed. But it seems that from time to time a forgery does come to light. . . . I'm sorry to say that while yours is a fine specimen, Plumtree, it almost certainly falls into the latter category."

All the same, I was curious to note that he picked up the volume again and, while pretending to leaf through it, felt rather furtively along the inside back cover. I watched his face carefully but couldn't tell if he'd found anything beneath the red velvet.

"Nonetheless, a—er—forgery from so long ago is quite an artifact in itself." He licked his lips and looked from me to Max. A thin rivulet of perspiration trickled down his temple; he'd licked the bead off his upper lip. "Would you mind awfully if we kept your book and studied it for a bit? Perhaps have Diana make a facsimile?"

Something was awry. My eyes strayed to Diana; I saw her mouth twitch: *No*, she was warning. *Don't let him have it.*

"I—ah—"

"Bats," Diana intervened matter-of-factly, "what's the desperate hurry? We can let them enjoy their book for a bit." She smiled at Max and me as if in sympathy. "Well, at least your little find had its flirt with fame." She stepped toward the door. "Thanks anyway, Bats."

But the famous Boswell wasn't having any of it. Ignoring her obvious attempt to end the interview, he said stiffly, "Alex—Max. A find such as this—even a forgery—does confer a certain obligation on you to share it with the public. And frankly, it's much too valuable for you to safeguard on your own. Might I suggest you let us keep the book for several weeks for an evaluation?"

I studied the sheen of sweat on his face, noted the narrowing of his eyes. I didn't even consult Max. Playing the innocent buffoon, I answered, "Mr. Boswell, my brother and I have only just found this. Why don't you let us pretend it's the real thing for a bit longer? Then we'll consider turning it over. I'll ring you in a couple of weeks. All right?"

He looked concerned, but—too late—seemed to recall the importance of remaining casual about the whole affair. I could almost hear the cogs whirring. "Yes, yes, of course," he said finally. "I'll just have to contain my curiosity until then. Makes for a bit of excitement on an ordinary Monday, doesn't it?" He stood awkwardly for a moment longer, still not moving towards the door. "Er—will you notify anyone of your discovery?"

"I thought I might consult some authorities on history; naturally, I'll share it with my bibliophile friends. But I hadn't considered a public announcement of any kind. Why do you ask?"

"Oh! No reason, no reason at all. Merely curious—it comes with my job." With a nervous smile, he bade us civil but damp good-byes. I was interested to notice that his hand fumbled a bit for the doorknob as he left.

Diana closed the door behind him and waited, catching our eyes and putting a finger to her lips. Was Boswell standing outside the door, listening? It was several moments before we heard his footsteps recede down the marble-floored hallway. She said, "If this book's a forgery, I'll eat my paper stock. He behaved *very* strangely."

"Fake or not," I said, "I do think it's important for you to make a couple of facsimiles. The very fact that such a book might have existed is fascinating, given the rumours about it."

Max nodded. "I agree. If Diana's right, and the book *is*

authentic, the museum might like one to display. If not, it would still be convenient to have a copy or two."

"I'll be happy to make the facsimiles. It might take some time though—perhaps a month or two. I'm overloaded at the moment. But you never know . . . I might hit another bout of insomnia." She tapped her long, slender fingers on the work table and frowned. "I really don't understand why Bats would prevaricate. I had the distinct feeling he was hiding something from us. I've never known him to be quite so . . . *clever* before."

"Hmm," I said. "Did you see the way he felt inside the back cover? It *was* a bit surreptitious."

Diana nodded. She picked up the book again, felt carefully with her fingertips where Boswell had, and shrugged. "I'll see what I find. Sometimes there's an identifying mark that authenticates a book; perhaps he was checking for it. I don't want to muck it up though; we'd better wait." She glanced at the clock on her wall. "Damn. I've a meeting upstairs with Boswell's boss. Sorry," she added.

We rose to leave as she did, but before she opened the door for us, she put a hand on my shoulder.

"I want you to know that I'm going to take very good care of your book." To my astonishment, she turned, wrapped it in soft tissue and bubble packing, and tucked it in the huge shoulder bag she seemed to take with her everywhere. She patted the bag. "I'm not taking any chances with this one. I'll ring you when I'm done."

As we rode the lift up to the ground level of the museum, Max sighed heavily. "I'm famished. How about a quick sarnie over the road?"

"Excellent idea." My stomach rumbled as we headed toward the Museum Tavern, conveniently located opposite the museum on Great Russell Street. I thought I heard footsteps from behind hurrying toward us, but when I turned to look, I saw nothing. A huddle of Japanese tourists was standing just inside the museum entrance, staring upwards in awe as if they were in the Sistine Chapel. We walked past the guards and through the door to the outside. Stepping into the bright sunlight only intensified my feeling of good fortune: the book, the wedding, and, to top it all off, the glory of an English summer.

Max's thoughts apparently mirrored my own. He breathed a contented sigh. "Fantastic, isn't it? Coming across a book like that in our own library. Just when you think you've seen it all . . . how on earth do you suppose it ever wound up at the Orchard?"

Again I turned, thinking I heard someone very close behind us as we descended the steps outside the museum. Nothing. One funny little man lost in his British Museum brochure, shuffling along with his nose in the leaflet. Bats's odd behaviour had given me the willies.

I forgot about him and concentrated on getting across busy Great Russell Street. We arrived at the outdoor tables of the Museum Tavern just as a gaggle of sun-worshippers reluctantly got up to leave. I rested my leather book bag on the table to claim it, and debated whether to intervene on behalf of the bee I saw drowning in the remains of an abandoned half of cider. Just as I scooped the struggling insect out of its drowning pool, a harried pub employee came to clear away the used glasses and swipe his damp cloth over the table. The bee struggled to the edge of the table and safely launched itself before the cloth could get him.

"Busy day for you," I said, noticing the sweat on the waiter's brow.

"The tourists don't make it any easier. Autumn won't come soon enough," he said, and was gone.

"Poor chap," Max said. "I'll get some sandwiches and drinks. What'll you have? The usual?"

I nodded, and he disappeared inside the pub. He would bring a granary bread ham-and-cheese sandwich and a pint of bitter for me, roast beef in a French roll and a Perrier for himself. It was very pleasant indeed the way

Max and I got on these days; we hadn't always been on such good terms. I sank into one of the pub's plastic chairs and set the empty book bag on the seat next to me. The pavement was thronged with a torrent of tourists, not to mention all the usual inhabitants of Bloomsbury. It took one of these rare, perfect days to bring everyone out for lunch.

I was gazing at the street when a bee—my bee—buzzed past towards an adjacent table. I half-followed it as it landed, only to see it abruptly swatted away by the table's occupant, a man roughly my own age. His most memorable features were a two-day stubble and a thick, beery look.

"Ah! So 'ere is the important meeting you 'urried off to!" a familiar French-accented voice teased from behind me.

I grinned and turned from the unpleasant man next to me. My deputy managing director and best friend's wife smirked down at me, eyes sparkling. I stood and pulled out a chair for her. "Lisette! Join us. I've quite a story to tell you. Max is just inside fetching—"

Plastic scraped violently against the pavement behind me. Whipping my head round at the noise, I saw Beer-Belly's hand snatching the handle of my black leather bag. He was on his feet, already on the go with it. But as he whirled away from me, I'm certain I saw him do a double take at the bag. He shook it as if to determine if there was anything inside.

I dived at my bag with a shout, taking the man with me to the ground. My table and his crashed to the pavement, scattering a flurry of plastic chairs topsy-turvy. The man fell heavily, and I heard a horrible crack as he tried to break the fall with the hand gripping the book bag. Pub patrons scrambled to their feet and tried to get out of the way. Beer Belly cried out as I tried to wrest the bag from him. He yanked at the strap stupidly, viciously, like a pit bull. It was absurd, a schoolboys' fight.

It wasn't until the pub boy shouted "Hey! You there!"

and came at a run that the man released his grip. The would-be thief scuttled into the gawking crowd, his right hand held protectively in front of him, then took off down Museum Street. He moved with surprising speed, considering his paunch.

I picked myself up along with my hard-won book bag, and began apologising to Lisette and the startled pub guests. The place looked as if a hurricane had struck. Lisette and I righted the overturned tables and chairs with the help of the indignant pub boy. "We've never seen this sort of thing before, not here," he muttered. "Bloody tourist season."

Just then Max came out with our drinks and saw the mess. He grinned at Lisette. "Alex, can't I leave you alone for five minutes . . ." he joked, then twigged that something was wrong when he saw our expressions. "What? What's happened?"

"Some 'orrible man tried to pinch 'is bag!" Lisette huffed. "I was talking to Alex, and that thief 'ad it 'alfway out of the chair by the time I saw what was 'appening. Alex, are you all right?"

I nodded. "I think I might have hurt him though. I heard something crack, perhaps in his wrist, when I pulled him down to the pavement."

"Serves 'im right," Lisette pronounced.

As we sat down again, Max looked at me with an unspoken question. Had the thief really been after a rather decent leather bag? Or had he been perhaps after something far more valuable?

The look of surprise on the man's face when he first lifted the bag told me he'd been expecting something a bit heavier . . . the Order of the Bedchamber book, perhaps?

I shook my head and shrugged, not wanting to alarm Max. But between Bats Boswell's strange behaviour and this attempted theft, I felt the first faint tingle of alarm.

CHAPTER 2

Thus, right from the outset of the Decameron, *the
author juxtaposes the work's three central themes
(Love, Intelligence, and Fortune), and suggests
that the trials and tribulations attending the first
can be assuaged or avoided by the application of
the second or the intervention of the third.*

—G. H. McWilliam, Boccaccio scholar

An hour later I'd waved good-bye to the receding
tail lights of Max's black BMW, and was doing my
best to concentrate on the financial forecasts for the coming year. I'd invited Max inside Plumtree Press for a brief
visit; our family publishing company's offices in Bloomsbury's Bedford Square, the traditional publishing centre
of London, were barely a street away from the museum.
But now it was time to get back to work.

My father had started the tradition of planning for the
coming fiscal year in early June. It was before summer
holidays, after the spring list was launched, but before the
autumn rush. It was also tradition that the Plumtree publisher take charge of this process himself, broadly outlin-
ing the plans and letting our accountant produce the
detailed official documents.

At my notebook computer I typed a stunning yet completely realistic figure into one of the spreadsheet cells—

our expected sales in the academic division for the coming year. The financial success of both the academic and trade fiction lines was startling—sometimes even a bit frightening. Such rapid growth could be positively dangerous. In the last three years our income had doubled. The accountant and I had called in a consultant to advise us on how best to reinvest the profits.

But disquiet over the man at the pub distracted me, as did the intrigue surrounding the Order of the Bedchamber book. How had the volume come to be hidden in our library? And *why* had it been hidden? I could barely wait to tell my bookish friends about the volume, and about Boswell's bewildering reaction to it. By a wonderful stroke of luck, that very night was the monthly meeting at the Athenaeum with my small, private group of bibliophile friends. Above all, I was eager to tell Ian Higginbotham, my father figure and partner at the Press. Ian seemed to know something about everything. I had just ordered myself to stop dreaming and finish the financial forecast, when the phone rang.

"Alex Plumtree," I answered.

"Ah. At last! Alex Plumtree." The man's outrageously posh accent transformed these enigmatic words to *Et laarst! Ellex Plahmtreh.*

"Yes?"

"Forgive me. It's just that I had rather hoped to reach you today. I'm delighted to find you in."

I waited. *Who on earth?*

"You don't know me, Plumtree, but I know you. Actually, knew your father. I'm Charles Trefoyle—and I have the privilege of informing you of your election to the Dibdin Club."

I was too stunned to reply. I? A lowly Plumtree, a member of the most revered book club in England? The one composed of earls, dukes, and lords in possession of England's finest private libraries? The international brokers of hidden power?

How very strange that the obscure Dibdin Club had come up in conversation just the day before in our library as Max searched for his heraldry volume. Everything I'd ever heard or read about the aristocratic bibliophile's group flooded to mind: their reputedly excessive dinners, the "venerable purple stream" of wine that flowed at their meetings, their sought-after private reprints of old and nearly extinct books. I sat forward in my chair. This had to be a joke.

"Plumtree? Are you there?"

"Yes, of course. Sorry. I'm—well, I'm a bit surprised."

Trefoyle chortled. "Thought you might be. I wanted the pleasure of ringing you myself. Nothing like a cracking good shock, eh? Now, then. No doubt you're aware that we meet every year on the anniversary of the Duke of Windlesham's sale in 1812. The seventeenth of June."

That was the Saturday of the coming weekend. They certainly didn't give new members much warning. My oak tree would go right on leaning against the house for another seven days, it seemed.

Unless I was right and this was indeed a prank.

Perhaps sensing my reaction, he went on. "This is an extraordinary circumstance, Plumtree. We called an emergency meeting to decide who should take Croxley's seat. Everyone agreed it should be you."

I recalled a *Country Life* article that explained that the Dibdin Club had just forty-four members at any one time. The only way for a new member to be admitted was for someone to die. Lord Croxley's obituary had appeared in the *Times* the week before. The flu plaguing London was particularly dangerous for the elderly, and the octogenarian peer had succumbed.

"Well. I'll be sending you details of the weekend in the next post," my caller continued. "I'm host this year—we'll meet at the castle. Do come on the Friday afternoon; we'll have a bit of fun clay-pigeon shooting before we begin. Does that suit?"

"Y-yes," I stammered. "Wonderful. Thank you so much, sir." I really didn't shoot at all well, although my father had taken me for lessons in my teens, claiming it was something everyone should know. I hadn't fired a gun since—though I'd had one in my hand quite recently. I'd nearly been forced to use it to save my life. And the closest I'd been to Castle Trefoyle was to ride past it in awestruck silence on a childhood holiday in north Cornwall. I still remembered gawking at the rocky eminence that seemed to jut out of the oceanside boulders, towering over the crashing waves. Trefoyle was one of the most renowned collectors in Britain. Other than that, and his castle, I knew little of him.

"Cheerio, then, Plumtree."

And he was gone, leaving me to ponder this sudden and inconceivable ascent to the vertiginous pinnacle of bibliosociety.

I entered the dark, panelled room of the Athenaeum on the stroke of eight o'clock that night. Three men sat round a smallish table, sipping drinks. They were Ian Higginbotham, my mentor; Wollcraft Cholmondeley, an academic expert on incunables from Oxford University; and Robert Lovegren, a bibliophile and philanthropist who worked for the Order of St. James in Clerkenwell. Ian and Lovegren were trusted friends; Cholmondeley was a much-admired authority.

But my stomach still turned a somersault every time I saw Ian and Lovegren together. A book-related adventure that spring had drawn both of them into its dangerous web and was all too fresh in my mind. The attempted theft of that afternoon came back to me in a rush, and I felt a familiar twinge of fear.

"You look as though you've seen a ghost, Plumtree," Robert Lovegren teased.

I laughed as I moved round the table, clutching an unpretentious foolscap envelope. In it were prints of the pages Diana had photographed. With the sort of enthusiasm that endeared her to book lovers everywhere, she'd processed the film that very afternoon. She'd brought the photos round personally, keeping the negatives and a set for herself.

"Well, for goodness' sake, don't keep us in such suspense," Graeme Abercrombie groused as he slunk into the room through a concealed door. We met in a private room at the rear of the club for Graeme's sake; he happened to hold the highest office in the land and preferred not to walk through the front entrance. "What have you got?" The prime minister seated himself as I took the remaining empty chair opposite him.

Ian, who'd been out that day speaking to a group of academic book publishers in Oxford, twiddled his thumbs—as much indication as he ever gave of impatience.

"All right," I said, barely able to conceal my excitement. This was such stuff as book lovers' dreams were made on, in the noble phraseology of the Bard. "Max was looking through the Plumtree Collection, searching for a heraldry reference book to show a client. And behind the volume we found a book, in a chamber someone had made behind the wall. These are photographs of its pages."

My friends were instantly fascinated. "It's a shame I don't have the book itself to show you," I continued, "but I thought it wisest to leave it with Diana Boillot at the museum to have a facsimile made. As it happens, it's a good thing I did—someone tried to snatch the bag I'd used to carry it to the museum. It's a perfect fifteenth-century find, bound with oak boards and leather thongs and a bottom-to-top clasp—so it's definitely English. The boards are covered in red velvet. Interestingly enough, the book is untitled. The author, printer, and binder are anonymous. No date of publication either. But it records the history of the Royal Order of the Bedchamber. I'd never heard of it before, but then, I'm not much of a mediaeval scholar."

I thought I saw a muscle tighten in Ian's jaw, but couldn't be sure.

I passed round the colour prints, saw my friends lingering over the print and illustrations. Ian seemed captivated by the penultimate illustration, which showed dragons and other monsters lurking at the windows, and a serpent coiled on the floor.

"I've read the text," I said. "The most notable thing about it, besides the previously secret details of the Order, is its claim that Richard I, the Lion-Heart, was murdered by the Master of the Order—presumably this particular knight, kneeling by the bed with a dagger opposite the story on the last page. Of course, there's no way to know if the story is true.

"Bartholomew Boswell, the head curator of rare books at the museum, claims to know a legend about the book." I related the story to them. "But there's very little about Saladin in the text, which is the odd thing. Just a rather innocuous mention. At any rate, Boswell rang another expert, who told him ours is almost certainly a forgery, that all the original books are known to have been destroyed. But I'm not so sure. The paper looks right for the late fifteenth century, as do the printing process and the binding. But I suppose it's possible it was a *contemporary* forgery—one printed at the time of the controversy."

The room was absolutely silent. My friends loved this sort of tale.

"Personally," I concluded, "I think one copy survived."

"Plumtree!" Lovegren's eyes were practically popping out of his head. "How can you be so *calm* about this? If the book's authentic, it's a national treasure! A historic find! I shouldn't wonder you'd feel a bit uncomfortable having it in your library at home in the Orchard. It's worth an absolute fortune. Every biblioklept in Britain will be bashing in the panes of your French doors."

"I know it," I answered. "I haven't quite worked out

how to handle that. Oh—there's something else too; after Boswell made his phone call, it seemed to me that he studied the inside of the rear board intently, as if he expected to find something there. The velvet is glued over the board; here." I showed them the photograph Diana had taken of the inside of the back board.

Cholmondeley spoke. "If the identities of the printer and binder were so vital, considering that Edward IV wanted both executed, perhaps Boswell was looking for the equivalent of a 'binder's ticket.' In the eighteenth and nineteenth centuries, binders would attach this ticket to one of the top outside corners of a front endpaper. Some binders put them on the inside lower corner of the back pastedown endpaper. But your book would pre-date that practice."

The prints were making the rounds slowly; no one wanted to give them up. "Remarkable," Cholmondeley pronounced as Lovegren reluctantly passed them on to him.

Graeme frowned. "Why do you think Edward IV should have been so angry about this book—angry enough to behead everyone associated with it? It doesn't look so very damaging—just the king's nightly rituals, really, and, of course, the news of Richard's murder."

"According to Boswell, the emperor of Persia threatened war if Edward didn't destroy all the books and those associated with them," I said. "It could be, too, that Edward felt these were intimate secrets. Perhaps he saw their publication as a gross betrayal of confidence. I plan to consult an expert on the history of the period; perhaps that will shed some light on it."

"I wouldn't want to offend the Iraqis today." The PM shook his head grimly. "I'm not telling any secrets when I say that things are getting more tense by the moment— for the Americans *and* for us. They've thrown out the UN arms inspectors again."

Graeme's solemn words took us all aback. He was so

unpretentious and easygoing, I often forgot the awesome office he held. The burdens of his position, I thought, must be crushing.

Then, as if he realised he'd got a bit too serious, he smiled. "The Royal Bedchamber . . . the mind boggles. Some very intimate secrets indeed might have been revealed. Nothing salacious, then?"

I shook my head. "No lurid tales about unexpected female visitors to the Royal Bedchamber, sorry to say. Perhaps their loyalty in that area was absolute."

Cholmondeley looked thoughtful. "If Richard the Lion-Heart were murdered, it would dispel one of the great legends in the history of English monarchy—that of his death from a common poacher's bow. It would also cast a new light on his brother John's succession."

"These woodcuts!" the PM exclaimed. "They're magnificent . . . the *detail* . . . What a prize, Alex."

Ian alone sat quietly. I saw disquiet in his eyes. He never failed to give the impression that he'd long known the secrets of the universe, and he seemed eerily aware of the subtlest nuances of my life. Long ago I'd decided he was the anonymous author who had given Plumtree Press its first bestseller, and plunged me into the first of an apparently endless succession of book-related intrigues.

What did he know that he wasn't telling me?

I nobbled Ian as the others were leaving and asked him if he'd mind staying for a moment.

"Not at all—I've all the time in the world, my boy. Something else has happened, hasn't it?" He knew me so well, it was disconcerting.

"Yes. I don't quite know what to make of it. Earl Trefoyle rang me at work this afternoon. Ian, you're not going to believe this—but evidently I'm the newest member of the Dibdin Club."

If Ian was surprised at my news, he didn't show it.

With the unearthly calm that both frustrated and awed me, he said, "Alex, the Dibdin is a great honour. It was your father's fondest dream to be a member. And you're very young. . . ."

His voice trailed off, and I wondered if he was thinking what I was. Perhaps I had been asked into the club at an early age to make up for the fact that my father hadn't been. I'd never known that my father had dreamed of Dibdin membership.

"I hope you're pleased," Ian said.

"I am. *Very* pleased. But I can't help feeling that I'm—well, I'm not exactly a logical choice, am I? Let's face it. No relation to the royal family, no title, no immense holdings of land, a small albeit fascinating library . . . the only criterion I meet is that of not being in trade."

"Isn't it remarkable that they've stuck to that old rule? It's all right to publish books, but how shocking and un-seemly that anyone should *sell* them." Ian gave a little snort of a laugh, and with elaborate casualness, glanced at his watch.

"You know, Alex, if you've time, you might pop round the flat with me for a nightcap. I've some old materials on the Dibdin . . . at one point I did a bit of research on printing societies, especially the Scottish ones, for the Athenaeum group. The Dibdin came into it peripherally, though strictly speaking it's not a printing society." He tossed off the words so carelessly that I knew it was desperately important that I accompany him.

"Thanks, I'd love to."

He gripped my shoulder for a moment. "Congratulations, Alex—I'm really very pleased for you."

I drove him to Malet Street in my car. His recently re-done flat still smelled of paint and varnish, but all the comfortable old furnishings had survived.

"Sit, sit," he said.

I plonked down on his well-worn sofa, feeling very much at home. He poured me a small whisky—not out of miserliness, but because he knew I wouldn't want much at that hour—and busied himself gathering papers out of a cupboard.

"Here is the sum total, nearly, of my knowledge of the Dibdin Club. You can take these things home with you if you like—I don't need them any more."

He placed them all in a file folder and set them on the table in front of us, then joined me on the sofa. As he sipped his drink, I sensed he was considering the best way to say something important. Unlike most of us, Ian always thought about what he said before he said it. I waited, listening to the traffic thundering past on nearby Gower Street. Eventually he spoke.

"You know, Alex, the Dibdin Club is quite an unusual organisation. The members are eccentric but extraordinarily well-read. You've probably heard about the Duke of Windlesham's estate sale in 1812."

I nodded.

"Then you know that it was the sale of Boccaccio's *Decameron*, printed by Valdarfer in 1471, that fetched the astronomical sum of two thousand pounds. Just imagine what a big splash two thousand pounds was in 1812! When Dibdin, a bibliographer, heard of it, he decided the purchase deserved a celebration in the book world and assembled a gaggle of bibliophiles for a notoriously indulgent dinner. Thus began the Dibdin Club, and the tradition of dining extravagantly on the anniversary of the 1812 sale. An odd little man named Joseph Haslewood chronicled the meetings of the Dibdin in a collection of articles he entitled *Dibdin Dissipations*."

I'd heard this story, though not in such a detailed version. One of my authors, Margulies Whitehead, had only the previous week proposed a book related to Dibdin Club history: a fictional biography of Thomas Frognall Dibdin, including some fascinating incidental papers left him by Haslewood. "Rather remarkable, isn't it, that we've just printed that new edition of the *Decameron* edited by Margulies Whitehead?"

Ian smiled as if he were enjoying a joke and was waiting for me to catch on. Was he intimating it *wasn't* a coincidence that we'd just published Whitehead's authoritative new translation of Boccaccio, with its three translations in one format? But what would that mean? Had the Dibdin Club been honoured by Plumtree Press's reissue of the noble tome, and so invited me to join? Good heavens, I thought. Literature was so inextricably woven into the events of my personal life that I could barely tell where one left off and the other began.

"Makes me wish I'd read the *Decameron*—I'm ashamed to admit that I haven't," I said. Ian's division of the Press, the academic side, dealt with scholarly works like Margulies Whitehead's. I sometimes felt quite detached from that bread-and-butter side of the business. "We didn't study Boccaccio in school, and somehow I missed him in university as well. But I did read Margulies's preface; it was quite informative. Really, I'm going to have to sit down with it one of these days."

"Mmm," Ian said. "A bit of background is useful. But there's something I'd like to show you now you're a Dibdin member. Wait here a moment, will you?"

I studied the photo on the wall of Ian and his daughter, Sarah's mother, on their yacht at Nantucket—the *Carpe Diem*. My Sarah's eyes were so like her mother's—slanted slightly upwards so that she always seemed to be smiling. And green, like the ocean. I would ring Sarah at her parents' when I got home; it would be early evening in Massachusetts. Thank God she was coming in a few days, though my little junket to Cornwall was going to cut into our time.

"Here we are," Ian said brightly. "It's time you had this."

He held out a large volume. I knew immediately, from

the oak-board cover and the obvious age, that this was an extremely valuable book—and that was before I realised what it *really* was. I set my drink down on the table in a hurry and wiped my hands on my trouser legs to get rid of any dampness.

"You're not serious, Ian," I said, accepting the book as he passed it into my hands. The cover of the book was vertically grained solid oak bound with woven thongs. In gold paint, across the front, were the following letters in decorative Gothic script:

IL DECAMERONE
GIOVANNI BOCCACCIO

"Yes, I am serious. Quite serious."

"Ian! But this has to be . . . it's . . ." I looked up at him; he understood what I meant to say.

"Yes. It is. One of two known Valdarfer Boccaccios in the world—although the existence of this one is only rumoured. Your father never told anyone he had it. In fact, no one knows that this Boccaccio—your Boccaccio—is even in England. For goodness' sake, don't let on. It's a joy to own as a secret, but it could ruin your life if you made it public."

"*Why?*" His warning seemed rather dire.

"Because you'd be surprised what people will do for a book this notorious."

The boards of the precious book were about twelve by eight inches wide, perhaps slightly more. The text itself was two inches thick, and the backstrip holding the pages together was white alum-tawed pigskin.

I lifted the cover, and found a page brightly emblazoned with a coat of arms; in silver, on a background of deep blue—azure, heraldic experts called it—were a sword, a Maltese cross, an open book, and a small tree studded with dark fruit. At some point, this copy had belonged to a noble family.

On the next page, I saw the remarkable print on the equivalent of the title page: *Christopher Valdarfer, Milano, MCDLXXI.* I turned another page and noticed that the creamy white paper crackled as I touched it; it had a lineny feel, and a slight roughness that would allow a collector to call it "crisp." I bent my head to the page and smelled only a wonderful inky mustiness—an indication that the volume hadn't suffered any attacks from mildew or damp. Remarkable, after five centuries.

Books didn't get any better than this.

I turned another page. The text began here; I saw that the type was a simple, slightly round roman face with a curious swooping capital Q. The impression of the print was strong, even, and dark; red and blue ink filled in the initial capital letters. "Rubricated," a collector would say.

"But, Ian—"

"Yes. I know you don't read Italian." His eyes shone as he made light of my objections. Ian was nothing if not gracious. "You can read Margulies's version for content. But your father did want you and Max to have this one day. He said it went with the Order of the Bedchamber book—presumably because both were rumoured to have been written by Boccaccio, just as Boswell told you."

"My father *knew* about the Bedchamber book?"

Ian nodded but said nothing.

"Why on earth did he hide it away?"

"I think he was worried about its safety, considering its value. Same with the Boccaccio. My profile was always considerably lower than your father's during his life; he felt it would be safe with me. And so it has been. Frankly, I've been hoping you'd go ahead with your plans to install a security system at the Orchard. Until you did, it seemed safer to keep it here. You won't find a lovelier book anywhere, even considering your new find."

What an odd world it is, I thought as I turned the pages carefully on one of the most rare, prized books in existence anywhere. I looked through the pages as Ian sat at my side. It was like a ceremony, an accession to the throne of the kingdom of books. Ian had just handed me the sceptre. I turned the sacred pages one at a time. But at the next to last page I came upon an oddity: a stiff, yellowed papyrus-like piece of paper had been inserted, loose. It had been cut into a sort of latticework, a bit like a lace doily but with irregularly curved patterns. The holes in the page were minute.

"What do you suppose this is all about?" I asked, lifting out the sheet. "Bookworms?"

"Not exactly," Ian answered, all seriousness. "Not many people know about this, Alex. Your father said that bit of paper could well be the most valuable characteristic of this book, so for heaven's sake don't throw it out, thinking it's a bit of twentieth-century rubbish. Only one of the two Valdarfer Boccaccios in existence—yours—has it. No one knows its purpose, but it makes the book a great treasure."

Evidently he felt the need to change the subject. "Now. What about the Dibdin Club members? Do you know any of them?"

"I know *of* them, of course," I said. "There's Margulies—I'm glad to know at least one member fairly well—and I've met Sir Harold Westering and Lord Peter Albemarle on occasion at the odd book do. In fact, I wrote an article about the merging of their companies for the *Bookseller*. And I know *of* Trefoyle. But otherwise I'm rather in awe—the Duke of Chesterton, for instance, and all those other dukes and earls and marquesses. Oh, yes, I do know Colin Jones-Harris."

The lack of enthusiasm with which I pronounced this last name told Ian volumes. Jones-Harris was the worst of his kind, in my opinion: a womaniser, a drunkard, a Hooray Henry to the last. A pity his name *wasn't* actually Henry, I thought.

"You're not impressed by all that tea?"

I shook my head. Jones-Harris was heir to the world's greatest tea fortune. Some of his family's tea had been thrown overboard in the Boston Tea Party. But none of it compensated for the fact that he was a hopeless degenerate. All that would have been all right as long as he didn't hurt others, but he'd done many an unkind deed to trusting and over-impressed females.

"The Dibdin is renowned for the eccentricity of its members," Ian pointed out.

"Hmm, you mean the Duke of Beckham, who runs round in his bedroom slippers all the time?"

Ian chuckled. "I just don't want you to be surprised when you go for the weekend. No doubt you're aware that the sexual preferences of some of the members lean to the—er—unconventional." He coloured slightly; this was uncomfortable for him. "The book crowd has always been a bit that way, you know. And throw pots of money into the equation . . . well, these people can do exactly as they please. There have been rumours over the years about certain ladies of the night, shall we say, visiting the club at the anniversary meetings. And, of course, there's the drinking . . . the Dibdin is famous for it."

Ian tried to look casual as he went to his desk for a piece of paper. He plucked a pen from the desk and returned to his armchair. "They've never published membership lists, you know, though there was an article in *Country Life* several years ago that gave the current accounting. All right. You've already mentioned Colin Jones-Harris, Sir Harold Westering—he's the vice president this year, I believe—Lord Peter Albemarle, and the Duke of Beckham, with his bedroom slippers. Earl Trefoyle rang you, you know who he is. . . ." He jotted down the names. "Then we've the president, the Duke of Chesterton, and, of course, the Archbishop of Canterbury."

"Really! I'd no idea."

"Mmm. And young Lord Ashleigh—he's sixty-five,

mind you, but he took his father's spot in the club the year before last. The Ashleighs used to own the other Valdarfer Boccaccio."

Ian didn't know all the members, but soon I had nearly forty of the most notable—and notorious—men and women of England listed on the sheet of paper before me. As I studied it, and remembered what Ian had told me about them, I wasn't certain I wanted to have a confab with this particular group. But surely they were a harmless bunch of eccentrics. . . .

"I should go, Ian. Work tomorrow." I stood, cradling the Boccaccio carefully.

"Wait a moment," he said, and went into his kitchen. I gathered the papers he'd given me about the club and tucked them under the precious book. When he returned a moment later, he was unfolding a large cream-coloured plastic carrier bag from Debenhams.

"Ah, thanks," I said, enjoying this small deception we were about to inflict on the people of London. "Who would ever guess?" He held it while I gently set the book and papers inside. "And thank you"—I looked him in the eye—"for everything, Ian."

On the doorstep, he once again placed a hand on my shoulder. "Be careful," he said quietly.

As I waved good night and set off toward my car, I wondered . . . was he warning me to be careful about the book? Or the club?

CHAPTER 3

[In Boccaccio's Decameron*] three separate levels of reality are identified: author, narrators, and narratives.*

—G. H. McWilliam, Boccaccio scholar

And so I found myself settling down on the sofa at the Orchard an hour and a half later, thumbing through an inch-high stack of papers on the Dibdin Club while casting frequent glances at the Debenhams bag I'd placed reverently under the coffee table. The top page in Ian's file consisted of a 1930s-looking art nouveau–style heading that read "Dibdin Club Publications." I turned the page and found the name of the club in black letters, followed by RULES AND REGULATIONS AS AMENDED.

Curious, I read on:

I.   The Club shall consist of forty Members including the President, Vice President, and Treasurer.

That had now grown to forty-four.

II.   Every Member shall contribute a Book to the Club.

I looked up from the list and thought. Now I had two magnificent books to offer the club; I couldn't reveal that I had the Boccaccio, or at least that had been my father's and Ian's advice. But perhaps I could use the Bedchamber book. . . .

III.   Every Member shall pay a Subscription of Six Guineas to the Account of the Dibdin Club at the Bankers for the time being, upon his election, and subsequently on the first of January in each year. The Subscription for Members elected before the year 1895 to remain at Five Guineas.

Eighteen ninety-five! This really *was* an antique copy of the rules Ian had found.

IV.   The sum thus raised, or a competent portion of it, shall be expended, under the direction of the Printing Committee, in printing some inedited (sic) manuscripts or in re-printing some book of acknowledged rarity and value; and generally for the purposes of the Club.

V.   The total number of copies printed of each Work shall not exceed one hundred, and it is hoped that those who present books to the Club under Rule II will not pass, even if they consider it necessary to reach, this limit.

VI.   Every Member who has paid his Subscription shall be entitled to two copies of each Work printed at the expense of the Club, and these copies shall be distinguished by the engraved title and shall have the name of the Member printed in red ink. The Printing Committee may print an extra copy on vellum for the President.

VII.   The name of the Member in the second copy shall have an asterisk prefixed to it. The remaining copies of each Work shall be delivered by the printer to such Members, whose subscriptions are not in arrears, as may apply for them, upon payment of the sum fixed for each work by the Printing Committee. The sum so received shall be carried to the account of the Club and applied to its general expenditure.

VIII.   Every Member shall write in his second copy of the Work the name of the Person or Public Society to whom he may present it.

Interesting, I thought. So at least according to these old rules, there was provision made for books to be presented to libraries and other institutions. Skipping over some tedious details, I arrived at the section covering meetings.

XV.   One General Meeting of the Club shall be held in the month of April or May. The President shall be empowered to call at his discretion other General Meetings, at such times as he may deem expedient, for the election of Members, and for the transaction of the general business of the Club.

XVI.   The Anniversary Meeting of the Club shall be held on the 17th of June, or at such time and place as the Club in General Meeting may determine; when such Members as are able shall dine together.

XVII.   Candidates for election must be proposed and seconded by two Members, and their names shall be entered in a book kept for the purpose.

XVIII.   Notice of any vacancy which may occur shall be given to all Members in the notice convening any meeting, or at least one week before such meeting, and at the same time a List of proposed Candidates shall be circulated among the Members. Should the number of Candidates exceed the number of vacancies, Members shall be requested to return the lists, marking the names of those Candidates whom they wish to have priority. No Candidate shall be balloted for whose name has not been so circulated, nor when there are more Candidates than vacancies shall any other Candidate be balloted for at any given meeting than those which have obtained priority in the marked list.

XIX.   In the ballot two black balls shall exclude, unless fewer than seven Members are present, in which case the election must be unanimous.

I shifted uncomfortably at the thought of my name making the rounds for evaluation, prompting forty-three eminent men and women to consider their opinion of the Plumtree moniker. My name had been in the papers far too often since I'd taken over the Press five years ago, and not always in a flattering light. It seemed highly unlikely all forty-three other members would have approved me. Still, some no doubt knew of me as I knew of them.

Margulies Whitehead would almost certainly have voted for me. Not only had we grown to be friends, but publishers hold a strange and disproportionate power over their authors. I must confess, Margulies's proposal for a book about Dibdin held more interest for me now than before I'd been asked to join the Club.

On the other hand, the very thought of what opinion Sir Harold Westering and Lord Peter Albemarle might have of me was disturbing. It was extremely difficult to imagine they'd have voted for me. I rubbed my weary eyes, almost wishing I hadn't expressed my opinion quite so forcefully in the article I'd written for the Publishers Association newsletter the previous month. The ancestors of Lord Peter and Sir Harold had founded some of England's most famous book-buying institutions. The Albemarle name had stuck fast to rare books; the Westerings had sold their nationwide bookshop chain to an American concern called Books & three years ago. Now, of course, the elderly bookish peers were so far distanced from actual trade that their names really were the only link tying them to those enterprises . . . otherwise even *they* wouldn't have been allowed in the club.

Books & had initiated a new venture with Albemarle's, prompting my outspoken article. The American chain had purchased Albemarle's, on Albemarle Street, from Lord Peter's descendants. Books & had created its first flagship store by knocking through the wall between its giant new shop—complete with gourmet coffee bar—and the rare-book institution next door.

Flying in the face of the age-old tradition of snobbishness at Albemarle's, the large chain hoped to introduce more people to the joys of old books and fine editions. There would be an Albemarle's attached to every major city's Books & in England; the corporate bigwigs weren't yet sure how that would play in America. One small, selective alcove would remain the preserve of discriminating collectors and people in the trade. And what had once been the most exclusive shop in England would shift its stock downwards to include affordable old books and reproductions for the masses. American editions of Wodehouse and second printings of old Dick Francis novels would soon figure surprisingly large in the Albemarle stock, I imagined.

I put the papers down, and with a groan recalled my visit to Albemarle's last year. I'd gone in search of a John Donne volume of love poems for Sarah's wedding present, knowing that it might take some months to find one in the proper condition. Still, when I walked into Albemarle's, all eyes shot in my direction. The state of my attire was taken into careful consideration by the fussily attired shopkeeper and was clearly found wanting. With a frown, the delicate man had approached me, as if to ask what someone of my obviously lowly status was doing in his shop. Even Lord Peter Albemarle—let alone Wimsey—wasn't as snobbish as that pasty-faced bloke had been. He said, still looking me up and down, "Was there—er—something . . . ?"

An unbecoming five o'clock shadow suddenly felt scratchy on my face; I was horribly aware that the crease in my trousers was no longer as precise as it had been at seven that morning. And, even less forgivable, not only was I not wearing a suit, my tie bore the unmistakable mark of the pasta sauce I'd splattered on it at lunch.

Reminding myself that I had as much right as anyone else to be in that shop—perhaps more, since my family had been publishing books for at least seven generations—I'd replied, "No, I don't think so, thank you. I'm looking for a gift."

With a snide smile, he bowed his head with ridiculous formality and returned to the antique sales desk. He continued to watch me from his massive bunker with ill-concealed disdain.

Partly as a result of this experience, I had slanted my article in favour of the merging of Albemarle's and Books &. I'd written something to the effect that opening up the world of old and rare books to a wider clientele could only be a good thing, while acknowledging the difficulty of welcoming change in institutions. I expressed approval that Books & was allowing Albemarle's to retain its original name and character, so that its individuality was preserved. In theory, I wrote, their merger was a laudable "bring-culture-to-the-masses" idea.

I hoped Lord Peter wouldn't hate me for that article.

His family, especially the younger folk who had decided to involve themselves in the family business, thereby forever excluding themselves from the Dibdin Club, had been up in arms over what they called the hostile takeover by Books &. The young Westerings, it was said, no longer spoke to the young Albemarles.

I wondered if Lord Peter and Sir Harold were on friendly terms. My mind boggled at the thought of the two of them spending an entire weekend at Castle Trefoyle together . . .

. . . with me.

I sighed and turned back to my reading. The rest of the rules applied to getting out of the club and accepting resignations. As they looked a bit dull, I put them aside in favour of Haslewood's *Dibdin Dissipations*, a collection of outrageous tales of the excessive club meetings by the club busybody and secretary. I'd just picked them up, when the telephone rang.

"Alex?" A female voice whispered my name. At this hour I'd have thought it would be Sarah. But the pronunciation was all wrong. Nor was it Lisette; no French accent. Nicola, then, my new trade editor at the Press?

I sat up. The papers slid off my lap into a jumble on the floor.

"Nicola?"

"No." The soft voice was intense. "Alex, listen, it's Diana."

"Why are you whispering? Are you in danger?"

"No—yes—I'm not sure. I heard something outside the door a minute ago. Alex, someone's been trying to get your book—" I heard a whimper.

"*What?* Diana, what is it?"

"He's rattling at the window—in the side street—" A sob travelled down the line.

Dear God, I thought. "Okay. Have you rung the police?"

"No, I—"

"Stay on the line—I'll ring them on my mobile. What's your house number?"

"Twenty-nine."

"Right. Just hang on."

I dialled the emergency number and dispatched the troops to Diana's. The 999 operator insisted I stay on the line.

"Are you still there?" I asked Diana.

"Yes. Thanks. I—I wasn't thinking clearly." She gulped, clearly on the verge of panic. The fact that she was at that very moment quite close to someone who might want to do her harm sent gooseflesh crawling up my arms.

"The police will be there before you know it. Stay on the line with me, okay? Don't make a sound."

A whimper came from Diana's line. "Oh, God! He's broken the window!" she sobbed, and I passed this on to the police dispatcher. Then, with immense relief, I heard the discordant tones of a police siren over Diana's line. In a quavering voice, she reported, "He's running away—he's getting away!—through the back garden. Oh, thank *God*. The police are at the door—I see them—Alex, I'll ring you later."

Click.

I paced from one end of the library to the other for forty-seven minutes before she called back. I jumped at the phone when it rang.

"Thank you, Alex. If not for you . . ." Diana's voice was shaky, but she was trying to put a brave face on it.

"What a horrible ordeal, Diana. Shall I come round?"

"No, no—not all the way from Chorleywood! But—it's very sweet of you. He's gone, ran off as I watched from the window. It looked as if he had a bandage on his arm, or a plaster cast. Quite stout, too, for running so fast."

With a start I recalled how quickly the beer-bellied man at the Museum Tavern had lumbered off, and the crack I'd heard when he crashed to the ground.

"You won't believe what *else* happened this evening, Alex." I heard the *clink* of a decanter or bottle on crystal. "This is what I first rang you about, before I realised how immediate the threat was. After bringing you those prints, I must have left you close to half past five, then I taught my evening class."

She paused to take a sip of her drink. "Well. Afterwards, I stopped back at the museum to check on a book I'd washed. I always check at that critical point, in case the paper's drying too quickly or not quickly enough. Sometimes the process goes bad." She took a deep, shuddering breath. "As I came down the hall to my office, I saw a light from underneath my door. Someone was in there! In *my office*! And I'd locked it. Absolutely, I'd locked it. I *always* do. Any one of those books would be a tremendous loss."

My heart sank, but what had happened wasn't Diana's fault. I waited for her to tell me my book was gone.

But I was wrong. "Don't worry about your book—I've had it with me all the while. He *was* looking for it, I'm certain. I watched and waited, and you'll never guess who came out of my door."

"Not Boswell!"

"*Spot* on. Now, why else would he be in my office? And do you know what he said when I nobbled him as he sneaked out?"

"I can't imagine."

"That he was trying to fix my wonky doorknob! Of all the absurd excuses! Even *he* seemed embarrassed." She snorted disdainfully. "I told him the next time he wanted to come into my office, he should ask me. I *know* he wanted your book, Alex. I could feel it. It's the real thing, of course. He wants the original more than he can bear."

"I think you're right, Diana." I sighed. "I've had a slightly cloak-and-dagger day myself." I told her about Beer Belly and his aborted theft. "And now that you mention the man running away with a cast on his arm, I'm quite certain it's the same man."

"Good God," she said. "They *are* after the book. And I have it here."

I knew what I had to do. "I'm coming down, Diana. I can take the book to the Press and stay there for the night. No one will think to look there. Expect me in forty-five minutes. Okay?"

"Yes, okay. I'll be watching for you. And thanks, Alex—you're a darling."

I rang off, already thinking that I could use the drive to London to talk to Sarah. I was suddenly desperate—beyond desperate—to hear her voice.

Before I left the room, however, the Debenhams bag caught my eye; I felt the staggering weight of responsibility for preserving one of the greatest treasures of the world. The Valdarfer Boccaccio, of all things, in my library!

"A safe place," I muttered, looking round the room. "A safe place . . ." Then I thought of the hidden cupboard in which we'd found the Bedchamber book. No one would ever know to look there. As I hurried to the bookshelves and tucked the Boccaccio into its hiding place, carefully replacing the books again in front of the hidden door, I told myself I really would have to purchase an alarm—and quickly.

But first to rescue Diana. I climbed into the Golf and was off to Kensington. Before the car was out of the lane, I'd punched in Sarah's number in Massachusetts.

"Alex! I was just talking to Ian. He said you have exciting news."

I relished the rich, deep timbre of my fiancée's voice. Definitely cello rather than violin, or even viola.

"Sarah, my *love*. I'm so glad you're in. I miss you far too much."

She sighed. "Me too." With the wedding approaching, it was growing even harder to be apart. Despite the intervening ten weeks, it was characteristic of Sarah that she was determined to remain cheerful about it. Besides, she

was coming in just four days for almost a whole month.
"Well? What's the news? Ian wouldn't tell me."

"You're not going to believe it, darling. Have you ever
heard of something called the Dibdin Club?"

"Yes . . . you showed me the article about it in *Country
Life*, remember?"

"Did I? Well. Earl Trefoyle, the president of the Club,
rang me this afternoon. For some reason, they've made
me a member." I thought of Sarah's long, glossy dark hair,
and longed to run my fingers through it. I saw the intensity of her intelligent green eyes, the heavy eyebrows that
accentuated them.

"Alex, that's marvellous!"

"Yes, I suppose it is. I'm stunned, if the truth be
known."

She laughed, a full-bodied chuckle. "I'm glad to
know the club has such good taste. My opinion of them
is improving: I assumed they were a stuffy, inbred old
bunch. Are you going to tell them about the book you
found?"

"Mmm, I suppose I will. Something rather interesting
has happened there." I turned off Long Lane at the edge
of Chorleywood and entered the M25 racecourse.

"Oh?"

I told her about taking the book to Diana, and Boswell's
legend. I also told her about his revised opinion, his peculiar reappearance at Diana's office, and the intruder at
Diana's house.

"Wow," she said. "The legend's fantastic. But I don't like
the idea of normally mild-mannered curators sneaking
about, trying to steal your book." She was silent for a moment. "You'll have to put in that alarm system now, won't
you?" She knew I'd dreaded that day intensely. But even
in rural Hertfordshire, homes weren't as secure as they
used to be.

"Mmm. On the other hand, perhaps I should give the

book straight to the museum for safekeeping." I didn't tell
her about the Boccaccio Ian had given me. Nor did I
mention the attempted theft at the tavern. She'd only
worry.

"Well. I can hardly wait to see it. Any other news?"

"Just that I'll be away for the weekend at Castle Trefoyle—it seems a shame, since you'll only just have
arrived."

"Don't worry—we have the rest of our lives. And Alex,
I hope it's *wonderful*—more than you expect. Really,
you'll probably have a lot in common with the other club
members."

I laughed. "Thank you, darling. You're very kind. But I
think it would be more accurate to say that I'm a lot *more*
common than the other club members."

"Very droll. Just remember you're half American. At
least half of you should be appalled by thoughts like that."

She was right. My American mother had always taught
us to value people according to their substance, not their
name or title. It's just that the Dibdin was so at one ex-
treme of society. . . .

"Besides, Alex, you're ten times the man any one of
them is—the only one who doesn't know it is you. It's one
of the reasons I love you so much."

"Sarah." I sighed, trying to ignore the almost physical
ache of missing her. "Oh, my love. I'm desperate to be
your husband. Please take care of yourself until *I* can—"

For some unfathomable reason, my phone went dead
at that moment. I checked the battery and tried immediately to redial her number in the States. The only result
was an extremely irritating engaged signal.

Exasperated, I snapped the phone off and threw it
onto the seat next to me. I hated being cut off from
her . . . it reinforced the impression that our lives were
held together by the merest thread, which could be sev-
ered at any moment.

I told myself not to worry and as I drove focussed on

the extraordinary events of the day. Why would the curator of rare books at the British Museum, a *Boswell*, for heaven's sake, try to steal a rare book about the Order of the Royal Bedchamber? It didn't make sense. It all dissolved into a muddle: Earl Trefoyle's voice braying *Et laarst! Ellex Plahmtreh* . . . the beer-bellied thug's hand creeping toward the book bag . . . Diana's whispered voice over the phone line . . . the break-in at her window.

As I pulled up at Diana's house, I told myself there must be a sensible explanation. Men like Boswell didn't hire thugs to steal incunables.

Did they?

Diana answered the door and let me in quickly. She looked exhausted. She was still wearing her pea-green-linen trousers and jacket of the morning, but they, too, looked tired. Even the takeoff angle of her ski-jump nose seemed a bit less perky than usual.

I gave her a quick hug, smelling the sweat of fear on her as I did so. Poor woman . . . and all for a book. "I'm so sorry, Diana. What an ordeal."

"I can hardly believe it," she said shakily. "Bats Boswell? It's *absurd*!"

"I know. Still, we can't ignore what's happened. Where's the book? I'll take it and leave you to get some rest. Oh—and I'll ring Boswell's office right now, leave a message on his voice mail saying I've put the book in a safe deposit box or something. We need to get him off your back."

"Here," she said, and lifted her bag off the side table by the door. She pulled out the bubble-wrapped book and passed it to me hastily, as if eager to be rid of it. I couldn't blame her, I thought as I tucked it under my arm.

"What's the number for Boswell at the museum?"

She told me. I entered it on my phone, which now seemed to be working perfectly, then waited through his voice-mail message. "Mr. Boswell," I said cheerfully. "Alex Plumtree here; I wanted to let you know that I placed the incunable in a safe deposit box this afternoon. I know you were worried about it, as I was. It should be quite safe now. Good-bye."

I gave Diana a look as I turned off my phone. "That should keep him at bay." She looked forlorn. "Will you be all right? Is there anyone I can ring to stay with you?"

"Not unless you're available." As soon as she said it, she laughed and apologised. "Don't mind me, Alex, I'm just tired. Only joking. Really."

But something had changed ever so subtly; we both noticed and were embarrassed by it.

"What about that window? Didn't you say it was broken?"

"Yes, but the police were very kind. They boarded it up for me and moved a few things in front of it. No one will be getting in there tonight. I'll have it fixed properly tomorrow."

I didn't like it. It didn't seem right to leave her there, vulnerable—because of me. Then I had an idea that would solve both our problems. I smiled.

"Actually, if you don't mind, I think I'll call my private security company. You'd be surprised how often I need a security firm in this business. They can send someone to stay here for a day or two, until we see what's what. Would that be all right?"

She looked immensely relieved. "Well, *yes*! But if it's too much trouble . . ."

"Of course not." I made the call and waited with her, accepting her offer of a brandy.

"I'm sure you've thought," she said, "about the sequence of events this afternoon."

"What do you mean, exactly? Cheers," I said, taking the glass from her.

"Well, somehow the phone call Boswell made when he left us totally changed his view of the book; turned him from a head curator to a common thief. When he couldn't get you to give *him* the book, Boswell expected his thug to collect it from you at the pub. When the thug noticed there was no book in the bag, he told Boswell, who decided I must have it."

"Mmm. I hate to say it, but I think you're right."

Diana huddled in a corner of her sofa like a child. "I wonder," she said weakly, "how far they'd have gone to get it if you hadn't rung the police. And why they want it so desperately."

On that disquieting note we sipped our brandy. I didn't know the answer to either question, but I reassured her repeatedly that she need worry no longer. Boswell knew she didn't have the book.

The tried-and-true representative of the security firm was there in half an hour, ready to stay for as long as it took. When he and Diana were introduced and sorted out, I left clutching the book, asking them both to keep in touch. The bodyguard gave me his implacable look, the one that said *You know I'd die before I'd let anything happen to her*, and patted the bulge under his jacket. I nodded my thanks and left satisfied. He rammed home the lock on the door behind me.

Considering the events of the day, I walked quickly to the Golf, got in, and locked my doors. I kept an eye on the street behind me as I pulled out from the kerb, but no one followed. All the same, I took an indirect route to the office and drove round the oval of Bedford Square twice before parking the car and going in.

I left the lights off at the Press—no point in arousing suspicion—locked the door behind me, and climbed the majestic staircase in the hall. It was satisfying to know my way perfectly in the dark. It came of having spent a great deal of time in the building from the age of three. I made my way to my office, tucked the book at the back of a drawer in my filing cabinet and locked it. After cleaning my teeth and removing my contact lenses, I returned to my office, stretched out on the sofa, and finally closed my eyes. I was bone-weary.

But after a moment, they popped open again. Troubled thoughts set my heart racing as wildly as if I'd just run a mile. It wasn't merely that Diana had been in grave personal danger . . . or that I had been so at the pub, though all that was bad enough. But in view of the excessive and violent interest in my untitled book, I couldn't help wondering if it had anything to do with my invitation to join the Dibdin Club.

Even as I thought it, I could hear Sarah laughing. "You're very good at thinking of reasons why you don't deserve your accomplishments," she would say, shaking her head. "Remember your gold medal on the racecourse at Vail?" She'd made sure I would never forget it; the moment I'd matched the time of the NASTAR pacesetter and won a gold medal, I'd been convinced there was something wrong with their timekeeping device.

Still, finding the book *and* receiving an invitation to join the Dibdin Club in the same week did seem an unlikely coincidence.

Was it *also* coincidence that Margulies had just finished one book about the Dibdin Club—the Boccaccio edition—and had proposed another . . . the Dibdin biographical novel with the Haslewood stories? Had my invitation to join something to do with Margulies Whitehead's publications at Plumtree Press?

Either way, it touched a nerve. I'd learned my lesson in the past: Too many coincidences meant trouble. Lots of it.

As I listened to the old building settling round me, I drew comfort from the familiar old place. Authors had lived in the rooms that were now our offices; Bloomsbury's literary salons had flourished in the ballroom. New fiction had been born here; many works had achieved immortality in the form of academic texts that lived on through endless editions. And some, in the natural way of things, had died a quiet death and gone out of print.

Plumtree Press had seen the full gamut of book-publishing experience. But never until that night had it housed a book with so much power to change the world—particularly *my* world.

Unaware of this, I dozed at last.

CHAPTER 4

Boccaccio explores in unusual detail the possible twists and turns of a narrative. . . .

—G. H. McWilliam, Boccaccio scholar

A loud bell went off near my ear. I sat up quickly, confused. A familiar print of The Bookworm on my wall, the blurry foreground of my desk, swam into view. Ah, yes. I'd slept at the Press. The telephone was ringing.

I am very nearly blind without my glasses; I groped for them and stuck them on my nose, then reached for the phone.

"Plumtree Press," I answered, trying to sound awake. What time was it? I squinted at my desk clock; held it up in front of my eyes. Seven-thirty A.M.

"Alex! Thank *God* you're there! I've been sick with worry."

It was Max. He did sound almost ill. No wonder; the hour was much too early for him to be awake and functioning.

"Why? What's the matter?"

"I'm so sorry, Alex—it's the Orchard. There's been a

burglary. The milkman found the front door standing open this morning, thought it suspicious, and rang the police. I thought—when you weren't there—well, I didn't know what might have happened."

The Boccaccio!

I was wide awake now. "I'm fine. But last night Ian gave me—*us*—an extremely valuable book. I put it where we found the Bedchamber book. Would you please go and look for it?"

"But—"

"Please, Max! I know—I'm sorry I forgot to tell you. *Please* just go and see if it's still there."

"All right," he said, sounding injured. I listened to the sound of his footsteps moving away and bit my nails. Several moments later his footsteps came back again.

"Good heavens, yes, Alex. But don't tell me that's *your* Valdarfer Boccaccio! That's one of the most valuable books in the world!"

"I know it is. And no, it's not mine—it's *ours*. Ian said Dad wanted him to give it to us when the time was right, whatever that means. Evidently it travels in a pair with the Bedchamber book. But Ian said the Boccaccio should remain a secret—because of its value, I think."

"Right." He thought for a second, but his joy overcame the momentary thoughtfulness. "Jolly good thing you hid it like that! Well *done*, Alex. Just imagine what might have happened if we hadn't left the Bedchamber book with Diana!"

I cleared my throat. "Actually, Max, we didn't." Dropping my voice, I said, "It's here with me now, at the Press. In the back of my filing cabinet, to be precise. Diana had an intruder last night; we think he was after the book." I told him about it, and about my call to Boswell telling him the book was in a safe deposit box.

Max was aghast. "Evidently I've missed a great deal in the last twelve hours. You might have *rung* me, you know." He thought for a moment. "So you think someone—

well, Boswell, presumably, really *is* after the book! The attempted theft at the pub wasn't just coincidence. Alex, promise me you *will* put it in a safe deposit box. As soon as you can. The moment the banks open."

"Mmm." My response was deliberately noncommittal; I wasn't about to lock up that book without enjoying it a bit first.

Fortunately, he seemed to take my acknowledgment for agreement. We discussed the minor inconveniences of the break-in, namely the broken panes in my library that Robert Lovegren had predicted the very night before, and Max promised he would hire someone for the repairs. We rang off.

I decided the book was safe enough for the moment in my filing cabinet. I tidied up a bit with some fresh clothes out of my office cupboard, and padded down the hall to the loo to apply toothpaste and a razor. The day was drizzly, I saw. So much for the beginnings of summer.

Ten minutes later I was digging into real work in the form of familiarising myself with a new standard contract for the trade division; our lawyer had recommended certain changes. But I hadn't been at it for more than half an hour, when Max rang again.

"Alex." He sounded quite cheerful. "You're not going to believe this! I've just checked my e-mail, and we've been approached by an anonymous party . . . who wants to purchase the Bedchamber book."

"Why am I not surprised?" If they couldn't steal it, they'd have to buy it. It would be fascinating to learn who the anonymous buyer was.

"You're not thinking that Boswell's just trying a new tack, are you?"

I didn't answer.

"Alex, you've become quite a cynic."

Sadly, I realised he was probably right. "How do you communicate with your mysterious buyer?"

"I don't, of course. He—she?—is represented by Maggs."

"Ah." Clever. Maggs Bros., one of the most respected book dealers in the world and purveyor of books to the Queen, was discreet as a Swiss bank. We'd never find out who was behind the offer.

Max made an exasperated noise. "You can be incredibly infuriating, Alex. Aren't you even going to ask how much they're offering?"

Ah. An offer of massive proportions would explain the manic edge to my brother's voice.

"No."

"I'll tell you, then. Half a million pounds."

I nearly dropped the telephone. It wasn't that half a million pounds, or the half of it that would belong to me, would make much difference in the enjoyment of my life. But it was so far out of the realm of a reasonable price that it told me someone truly was willing to go to extraordinary lengths to get it. Who wanted our book so badly? And *why*?

"You have no idea who the buyer might be?"

"No. My friend at Maggs made it quite clear in his message that under no circumstances would the identity of the purchaser be revealed. So it must be someone quite public who needs to hide."

"Why not say we're not interested at present, but might be at a future date? That would leave our options open."

My brother sounded relieved. "Good. My thoughts precisely. Why close the door?"

Too much had passed between us to go unacknowledged; an unmistakable, uncomfortable silence followed that neither of us could ignore, though it lasted only an instant. Two hundred fifty thousand pounds—my brother's half—was not an insignificant amount in the upkeep of a large house like Max's.

"Well. Back to work, eh? We'll talk again soon, Alex."

"Right. Thanks."

On top of whatever else we hadn't said, I was keenly aware that I'd so far avoided any mention of the Dibdin Club to Max. It was certain to gall him, as he'd been the one to throw himself wholeheartedly into antiquarian bookselling several years ago, not me. I didn't know why bibliophile society ignored Max, possibly it was his lack of involvement in its charitable committees and professional organisations. Or perhaps I merely attracted more attention as the proprietor of Plumtree Press. Whatever the reason, I knew their neglect hurt him already. My election to the Dibdin would only exacerbate his sense of rejection.

Half an hour later, I was only one clause further into the contract than when Max had rung. My mind insisted on returning to the anonymous pursuers of the Bedchamber book. I checked my watch; half past eight. I gave up on the contract and dialled Diana's home phone number.

"Diana," I said. "How are you?"

"Fine, thanks," she replied, sounding quite cheerful. "It's been a great comfort to have your bodyguard here. I don't think I'd have slept at all without him."

"How would you like to find out who was trying to break into your house?"

"I'd love to—but we already know that Boswell was involved—don't we?"

"Exactly. And we can use him to find out who he rang yesterday while Max and I were in your office, who told him to say the book was a forgery. Remember? Before that he was perfectly normal. I think whoever he called told him to obtain the book at any cost. Either the unknown party or Boswell tried force first at the pub, and then again at your house. When he came up empty-handed, he set about trying to purchase the book through Maggs, via Max. Anonymously."

"Really!" she exclaimed.

"For half a million pounds."

The momentary silence at her end told me she well understood the significance of this. "Whoever wants it is dead serious, isn't he? So how do you propose we find out who it is?"

"Telephone records. Itemised calls are a godsend. Here at the Press, we circulate the bills from BT, partly so people can see if they've been charged for calls they didn't make, and partly so we know who's been ringing the boyfriend in Indonesia once too often. I know it sounds frightfully Draconian, but it was our accountant's idea, and it has saved us quite a bit. A wasteful publishing house is a dead one. Do you think you could get hold of the bills at the museum?"

"I don't know . . . but it's an excellent idea. I'll try."

"I'm going out of town on Friday . . . if you find out anything after that, ring me on my cell phone, all right?" I gave her the number. "Diana," I said as an idea dawned, "would it be possible for you to make a rough facsimile using the photos you took yesterday? I know it might not be like the Ellesmere Chaucer facsimile, but—well, could you?"

"Of course," she replied. "You'd be surprised what I can do with those photographs. They're all I need to make a set of zinc plates to print with."

"That's great. Just one for the moment, and perhaps more later. If someone *does* get this book away from me, I want to have a copy."

"I understand perfectly; I'll begin right away. Let's think of it as my wedding gift to you. You probably saved my life last night."

"Diana! *I* got *you* into the mess, remember?"

"I remember. But I also know that no one else would have cared enough to get me *out* of the mess. Thank you, Alex."

After we rang off, I was reassured by the thought that a copy would be made. But before I could get back to checking the contracts, the phone rang again.

"Alex? Margulies Whitehead here. Listen, I know you're busy, but Van Vanderbilt is in from San Francisco to confer with me on his Dibdin papers. He says you're friends from university! Small world. We wondered if you'd care to join us for dinner tonight."

I grinned. Theodore Aloysius Montmorency Vanderbilt and I had shared many a boat ride up the Connecticut River together, rowing with the Dartmouth heavyweight eight. For obvious reasons, we called him Van.

"That would be marvellous—thanks."

"And congratulations are in order, I believe. I'm glad you've become a member of the club, Alex."

"Me too, though I still find it hard to believe."

He chuckled. "You're probably the most deserving member alive. How does half-past seven sound, at that place on Greek Street?"

"Perfect. The Chateaubriand, right?" I'd taken him there in signing the Boccaccio edition a year and a half ago.

"Mmm," he said. "Good. See you then."

I'd no sooner hung up than the phone gave its enervating twitter—again.

"Alex Plumtree," I answered with more than a little irritation.

"Alex. Graeme here. There's something I need to speak to you about immediately. If you could come over to Number Ten, I'd be grateful."

Rarely had I heard my friend sound so grim. "Of course," I said, and barely managed to stop myself from asking what it was about.

"Good. I'll tell them to expect you."

I hung up the phone and sighed, glancing at my watch. Not quite nine o'clock. So much for work this morning. I pulled on my jacket, told Dee, our receptionist, I didn't know when I'd be back, and hailed a taxi in Tottenham Court Road. As I told the driver our destination, I noticed in the rearview mirror his curt nod and quick evaluation of me. Settling back in the seat, I puzzled over what Graeme might possibly want. What could *I* do for *him*?

I was no closer to an answer as I disembarked in Whitehall twenty minutes later. The phalanx of uniformed guards let me through, and an assistant ushered me upstairs to the now-familiar study of the PM.

"Alex. Thanks for coming so quickly. Coffee?"

"No, thanks."

Graeme dismissed his assistant with a nod, and sank onto a sofa as if he were carrying the weight of the world. "I'm sorry to have inconvenienced you, Alex, but I've been advised not to discuss this over the phone. I'm afraid we have a problem that requires your immediate assistance. I do hate to ask it of you."

I sat opposite him. "Not at all, Graeme—you know I'd be delighted to help." I grinned. "Unless you want me to publish another political book." But my joking reference to our adventure of that spring didn't bring a smile, and mine quickly faded as I perceived the depth of his seriousness. My father's old friend normally went to great lengths to maintain a sense of humour.

Reluctantly, he raised his eyes to meet mine. "I don't know how word got out about your book on the Royal Order of the Bedchamber. But it has. And the book's suddenly acquired international significance. You know that the Iraqis have refused to cooperate with the United Nations weapons inspection programme."

I nodded.

"Well, now they're claiming that the Americans are deliberately antagonising them to draw attention away from the President's scandal. And because they know we're allies of the Americans, they feel we're cooperating. Alex, they find the very existence of the Bedchamber book intolerable. They think we're deliberately flaunting its existence to antagonise them."

"The *Iraqis*?"

"It's ridiculous, of course. Even my experts can't work out why they should care about the book."

"But how did they even hear about it?"

Graeme shook his head. "News travels fast in the antiquarian book community; you know that."

He was right; and to think all this had started with Boswell. I felt an irrational anger towards the man. "It can't be that reference to the truce with Saladin," I marvelled, incredulous.

The prime minister shook his head. "I can't imagine. I saw your prints at the Athenaeum; there's nothing offensive in the book. Still, the Iraqis have offered to stand down if we hand over the book to them." He met my eyes. "I hate to ask it of you, Alex. But if it can stop this mess in Iraq—"

"Of *course*," I said. "Of *course* I'll give them the book . . . I've got it back at the Press. It just doesn't make any sense." I'd been right to ask Diana to begin on the facsimile right away. Where would I be if she hadn't taken those photos?

"Given the importance of the volume, I think it would be best if we sent you back in a car and had you bring the book straight back yourself. Sorry for all the travelling to and fro, but it's no good sending a courier in this case." He stood and went to his phone. "A car for Mr. Plumtree, please. To the Press and back immediately." Turning to me, he said, "Thanks, Alex. And I am sorry."

I'd been dismissed. I was escorted by a young man in a well-cut suit down the stairs and through light drizzle into a waiting car. As we oozed away from the famous residence, tyres whooshing in the thin film of water on the pavement, I pondered this latest wrinkle in the bizarre life of the book of the Bedchamber.

Rack my mind as I might, I couldn't recall anything damaging to Saladin in the story . . . just that he and Richard had established a truce and become quite friendly. So friendly, in fact, that Richard had been willing to cement the bond by marrying off his sister to Saladin's brother. But surely there was nothing damaging in that; royals of all sorts intermarried, and always had.

I hated to part with the book. But if it was so vitally important . . . realistically, I had no choice.

But how extraordinary that people on the other side of the world had already heard about our book! Besides Boswell, the only people who knew were Diana, Graeme, Ian, Wollcraft Cholmondeley, and Robert Lovegren. All were above reproach. Cholmondeley was the only one I didn't consider a close personal friend, but I respected his integrity. The blame must lie with Boswell and his mysterious consultant. More than ever, I wanted to know who he'd rung the morning before.

The driver pulled to a stop in front of the Press and was out of his seat and opening my door before I knew what was happening. "I'll wait here, sir," he said.

I thanked him, jogged up the steps of the Press, stuck my head in to Reception to tell Dee I was back for a moment but would be popping out again, and took the plum-carpeted staircase two steps at a time. Then I went straight to my office and began to unlock the filing cabinet. The instant I touched it I knew something was wrong.

I'd left it securely locked the night before, but now it slid open easily at my touch. Fearing the worst, I jerked the drawer open until it was fully extended: The book was gone. The space at the rear of the drawer, behind the other hanging files, gaped in a silent scream. In desperation, I groped along the bottom of the drawer. I lifted out half the files and checked beneath them, unable to accept that the book was not there. I slid the files to the other end and stared in disbelief at the metal bottom of the drawer.

It simply wasn't possible. The only person I'd told was Max. Max wouldn't steal our book from me . . . would he?

I dashed round the corner into Lisette's office. "Have you seen anyone here besides us?"

She frowned. "Only the man from the printer company. Why?"

Damn! There should not have been a man from the printer company. For once, there was nothing wrong with my laser printer. "What did he look like? How long ago was he here?"

Lisette realised from the look on my face that this was serious. She rose from her chair and came over to me. "I'm so sorry, Alex. I don't know how long 'e was 'ere—when 'e was finished, 'e let 'imself out. Shuna"—she called to our editorial assistant—"ring Dee, see if she knows 'ow long ago 'e left. . . ." Lisette turned back to me. " 'E was dark-skinned, Middle Eastern, perhaps—dark hair, dark eyes, under six feet tall. 'E was wearing a cover-all—a repairman's uniform. Or so I thought."

"Thanks," I mumbled, and hurried toward the door.

"Alex!" Shuna called after me. "Dee thinks he left about twenty minutes ago."

"Right." Damn my carelessness, I thought, heading for the staircase and taking the stairs two at a time. I should have expected this. The thief might have even heard me telling Max where the book was over my phone line. I wouldn't ring Graeme with the bad news on my phone, then—and to use my mobile phone would be to invite eavesdroppers.

The waiting chauffeur saw me coming and stepped out of his car, picking up signals that something was wrong. "I need to ring the prime minister," I told him. "May I do it from your car?"

Picking up the phone, he said, "It's encrypted," and dialled the number. When I had Graeme on the line, I said immediately. "It's gone."

"*Gone?* Just since you left it an hour ago?"

"I'm afraid so. A man came in while I was out, ostensibly to repair my laser printer. It's a bit spooky; someone knows my office well enough to know that my printer's usually up the spout. But it wasn't broken today. Graeme,

I should tell you—someone broke into the Orchard look-ing for it last night. And early this morning an anony-mous buyer offered to purchase it for half a million pounds. I don't know if all this activity is coming from one source or many."

Two, then three seconds passed. He didn't respond.

"Shall I ring the police?"

"No," he said. "I'll get my people on it; this has to stay quiet." He sighed. "I dread telling the Iraqis. They won't believe us, of course."

"I'm sorry, Graeme."

"Me too. But we're going to find out where that book is and get it back. I'll be sending some people over." *Click.*

Ashamed of having let down my country and my friend, I handed the phone back to the chauffeur. "No need for me to go back with you," I said. He nodded. I walked back up the steps, feeling as dreary as the day. The drizzle had given way to leaden grey skies.

Back upstairs, I told Lisette that people would be com-ing to ask about the theft, and asked her to help them. I decided not to tell Shuna and Lisette anything more about exactly what had been stolen; it might be safer for them that way.

Within the hour, as I sat rereading the fourth clause of that morning's abandoned contract for the twelfth time without making sense of it, a small swarm of men in suits descended upon us. Some sort of prime-ministerial pri-vate police? I wondered. These were things we never read about in the papers.

From Lisette they got a description of the man, and one of them went off immediately to question the firm we engage for our too-frequent printer and photocopier repairs. Another began to develop the thief's face with the identification kit on his portable computer screen as Lisette told him everything she could remember about the man.

"That's 'im!" she cried suddenly, startling me. I studied

the face on the screen; the man had a strong cleft in his rather small chin, close-set brown eyes, and a thick helmet of curly dark hair. I'd never seen him and I doubted I ever would. He could be at Heathrow by now, gone for good.

When Graeme's men were finished with us, I wandered back to my office. Lisette followed me. "Don't be so discouraged, Alex. Besides, 'ow could you know 'e would steal this—whatever it was? It is not your fault."

"Mmm."

"Don't give me your *'mmm,'*" she teased. "If I had a pound for every—"

The phone tweeted; one ring for an internal call. Lisette reached for it. " 'Allo." She gave me a look as if to say *well, well, aren't we posh*. In her best imitation of an upper-crust British accent she said, "Yes, Dee, if Earl Trefoyle is in Reception, I think you 'ad better bring 'im right up. The conference room, yes?" She looked to me for confirmation; I nodded.

What on earth was Earl Trefoyle doing here? Now? Surely *he* didn't have something to do with the Bedchamber book . . . perhaps he was the mystery buyer!

Dee appeared just ahead of Earl Trefoyle at the door. They couldn't have been more in contrast; she was trendy London, dressed all in black, with her usual militant black boots laced up the front. Trefoyle was Jermyn Street from head to toe, every inch the country squire in his London best. Except, I couldn't help but note, for the toes of a pair of running shoes—bright white with lime-green and neon-orange stripes—which stuck out from beneath his tailored trousers. His old school tie met his belt buckle perfectly beneath a dapper navy blue jacket. His face had the ruddy look of someone who was often out of doors, and his blue eyes danced with alert intelligence. The overall impression was of a very young man in a seventy-year-old's body.

"Lord Trefoyle," I said, hand outstretched. "What a pleasure."

He gripped my hand firmly. "Thanks for seeing me, Plumtree. Sorry for the intrusion." He looked at Dee, and she knew she'd been dismissed. I closed the door behind us.

The earl took in his surroundings, obviously evaluating the conference room. It was on the small side, true enough, but I was proud of the antique cherry-wood table and its hand-rubbed patina. The framed prints on the wall were centuries old; he took them in with a smooth glance. "Plumtree, you might think me overcautious, but I think we'd best go somewhere else to talk. I understand your phones may be tapped." He pronounced it *tepped*. "Heaven only knows what other gadgets they've installed."

We strolled down to the pub just behind the Press. I found myself hurrying to keep up with the earl. My legs are so long that I'm forever having to shorten my stride and slow down. But the earl, a full six inches shorter than my six foot five, definitely seized the lead. He opened the door of the pub, and it was like walking into a party. The sound of laughter and loud conversation spilled out into the grey day like bubbling champagne. As we stepped inside, the packed, pleasantly ordinary pub felt cosy, loud, and quite safe.

"What can I get you, my lord?"

The earl looked round him as if unaccustomed to frequenting pubs. Then he smiled gamely. "Pint of bitter, thanks, Plumtree. And please, let's not stand on ceremony. Call me Trefoyle. I'll go in search of a table."

I came away from the bar with two pints; oh, well, I thought, it wouldn't be the first time I'd had a liquid lunch. I found the earl just taking possession of a table for two in its own little nook, perfect for a confidential chat.

He smiled his thanks. "Cheers. Here's to your first Dibdin weekend," he said, and sipped at his beer. I acknowledged the toast and waited for him to continue. "I won't keep you in suspense," he said. "Graeme rang me about this book that seems to have disappeared. As it hap-

pens, I know the legend about it. It *is* quite a treasure—
the only one of its kind left in the world, I believe, and
written by Boccaccio and printed in the fifteenth century
besides. Not to mention its history of being banned by
the king and supposedly destroyed. It's actually difficult
to imagine a more attractive book."

His blue eyes held mine without straying. "I've no idea
why our friends in the Middle East are so keen to acquire
it, and I have numerous contacts in the region through
book-collecting circles. Graeme tells me he's seen the
prints of the book's pages, and there is nothing more than
an innocuous mention of Saladin."

"That's right," I said.

He leaned towards me across the table. "Alex, I think
that whoever is so terrifically interested in this book
might belong to the Dibdin Club. You've no idea of the
enthusiasm of these collectors—I shouldn't be surprised
if the thief brought the book this weekend, unable to resist leaving it behind. Graeme will help us to get the book
back if we can work out who's taken it. The weekend
won't be as carefree as you might like, but such are the
burdens of inheriting the world's rarest volume."

I took a sip of bitter to hide my astonishment at this
turn of events. "What makes you think it's a member of
the Dibdin Club?"

He nodded as if he'd expected my question. "Graeme
told me about Boswell's call to his mysterious expert
while you were at the museum. The truth is, Alex, the
book-collecting world is a very close-knit community at
our level."

Our level? Was he putting me in the same category as
himself and the Duke of Chesterton?

"Relatively few of us know enough about books to be
in a position to advise Boswell. But those of us who do
are in the Dibdin."

"I see," I said. It did make sense.

He smiled. "Graeme tells me you have experience in such matters. Plucking the bad apple out of the barrel, I mean."

Inwardly, I groaned. Outwardly, I smiled. "I suppose that's true."

"Well." Earl Trefoyle stood. "I won't take any more of your time; see you on Friday afternoon. No, don't rush, enjoy your pint. Cheers, Plumtree."

I watched his back disappear through the doorway. I felt I'd been caught up in a tidal wave, swept along like a bit of flotsam. But at least the opportunity to ferret out the thief would make me feel I wasn't completely powerless.

My first Dibdin weekend, I realised with a thrill of fear and anticipation, promised to be anything but a quiet country house party.

I did manage to get through the new contract by the end of the day. But for the most part my Tuesday had been sacrificed at the altar of the Bedchamber book. Everyone had left the office by the time I sighed, slid into my jacket, and went to meet Van and Margulies at the restaurant in Greek Street. As I locked the front door of the Press, I felt strangely vulnerable for a moment. Why, exactly, I couldn't say ...

... And then it came to me as I strode across the paving stones. In my experience, when people wanted a book as badly as our mysterious thief-buyer wanted mine, it was because they wanted its contents to remain secret. There was something in the book that was damaging to someone—now Graeme said the Iraqis thought it damaging to *them*, which was still a mystery to me.

But perhaps there was also someone else. . . .

As I walked up Bedford Avenue to Tottenham Court Road, the leaden skies finally could hold off no longer. A steady drizzle began. I hadn't brought my umbrella, but it wouldn't hurt to get a bit damp. I hurried along frenzied Tottenham Court Road and crossed Oxford Street into Charing Cross Road, thinking I would have to put the disaster of the afternoon behind me at dinner with Van and Margulies. It wasn't their fault that I'd left an irreplaceable incunable in my file drawer, susceptible to theft.

When I stepped into Manette Street, the traffic noise dropped by a few thousand decibels. With the subsequent turn into Greek Street, my surroundings became positively tranquil. I was fond of this quiet backwater of Soho, where you could all but forget you were surrounded by a teeming megalopolis. As I approached the Chateaubriand restaurant, I saw two figures ahead of me on the pavement, battened down as far as possible with hats, turned-up collars, and brollies. One was tall—Van—and the other shorter and plump, Margulies.

"Van! Margulies!" To my surprise, the two men didn't turn or respond but kept right on—accelerating their pace. They steamed ahead until they turned down Bateman Street and disappeared. I shrugged off the encounter—or lack of one—and pulled open the door of the restaurant. It was peaceful and candlelit inside.

"Alex!" my old friend called out, standing and waving at me. Van and Margulies had already been seated at a private table in the rear. I gratefully handed my dripping coat to the maitre d' and hurried back to them. Van, gaunt and haunted-looking as a modernday incarnation of the old Bloomsbury Lytton Strachey, gave me a European double-cheeked kiss. With a start of surprise, I realised that the rather delicate grace I'd always noted about him had blossomed into flamboyant homosexuality. As we sat again, I thought I detected a note of intimacy in the glance that passed between Van and Margulies.

Margulies beamed like a pleased pussycat, plump and urbane in his cravat. My fellow Dibdin Club member was of an unusual breed: He was a third-generation literary scholar who'd deviated from family tradition by becoming political in his middle age. Now he was an outspoken Labour Member of Parliament, keen on abolishing hereditary peerages in the House of Lords. But he'd never given up his literary criticism, or his decade-long quest to produce the definitive edition of Boccaccio's *Decameron*.

I'd thought he was unrealistic when he'd come to me two years earlier with the project: He wanted the two best-known English language translations—one Elizabethan and one modern—side by side, with scholarly commentary. But by the time I passed the project on to Ian on the academic side, I'd seen the wisdom of Margulies's approach. Both translations were important in their own ways: one captured the flavour and humour of Boccaccio without remaining completely faithful to the text; the other was accurate to the last word.

"I've been regaling Van with tales of what a gifted publisher you are, Alex. Anyone who will bend so far as to publish the Boccaccio edition I proposed to you is truly a genius."

"Never trust an author who's trying to sell his next book," I joked. "Good to see you, Margulies. And as for you," I said, turning to Van as the waiter poured the wine Van had already selected, "what brings you to London?"

Van raised his eyebrows at Margulies. "It's his next book on Dibdin. Margulies either had to come to San Francisco to research it, or the other way round. I opted to come to London and bring copies of my Dibdin papers for his perusal. It's not every day someone recognises the importance of Thomas Frognall Dibdin—though I understand that you will soon become aware of the man's gift to bibliophilic society, if you aren't already. Congratulations on your election to the Dibdin."

"Thanks." The waiter brought us menus, but. Margulies and I waved him away. "Your speciality for all of us, please," I said, and confirmed this with a glance at my friends, who nodded emphatically.

"What exactly do the Dibdin papers consist of?" I asked Van.

"I bought them, as you may know, because of my family's long-time membership in the Dibdin Club of San Francisco," he replied. "The San Francisco club is, of course, very interested in the English club, which it imitates to some extent. Since Dibdin founded the original Club, he's quite the notable. And then there are some very interesting papers he inherited from Joseph Haslewood, that colourful character who chronicled the Dibdin Club meetings—rather irreverently, I might add.

"The most fascinating thing in the Dibdin papers, I think, is a bit of Haslewoodiana listing the legends about lost books Haslewood heard of over his years of association with the Dibdin Club. He itemises twenty-one lost books to which are attached legends: Some are rumoured to have existed but are supposed lost; others were seen by past Dibdin Club members but were destroyed by fire or other tragedy. Fantastic stuff, wait till you see it, Alex. You're going to be wild for it for your bibliophile series."

I couldn't help but wonder if the Bedchamber book was on Haslewood's list . . . who would know about such treasures better than the chronicler of the Dibdin Club?

"Er . . . I hate to get specific when we're out for an enjoyable evening. But do you happen to remember anything about a book about the Royal Order of the Bedchamber on Haslewood's legendary list?"

Margulies's face lit up. "Absolutely! Tell him, Van."

"Well." Van leaned forward, clearly surprised that I'd heard of the book. "Haslewood even has a note in his list—and I might point out that I have the sole existing copy of this list, in my private collection—that he fears for his safety in noting the Order of the Bedchamber book's existence. Evidently it was a real thorn in the side of *royalty*, in particular." He lifted his wineglass, his eyes

on the red burgundy, and took a sip. "He died not long after, you know. And who can say what that might mean?"

I'd found out what I needed to know; I didn't want to
ruin the evening. I nodded at Van, turned to Margulies
with a smile. "When do I see your proposal?"

"After I go through everything Van's brought and survive this weekend's extravaganza—I'd say, oh, the end of
next week."

"Consider me interested. Here's to the Dibdin-
Haslewood novel, then." I raised a glass to my friends.

"Cheers," they responded, and the rest of our evening
was spent recalling happy times and cementing existing
friendships. But by far the best thing about it was that
amidst the companionship and good food, for a comforting
two hours, I actually forgot about the Bedchamber book.

CHAPTER 5

The Devil came to the Tamar and stood
wondering whether to cross over into Cornwall.
"No, I won't risk it," said he. . . .

—CORNISH LEGEND

Early Friday morning, I woke with the awareness that this was no ordinary day—and not just because I was taking the day off from work. I sat up against my pillows and took stock. Life had gone on for the last two days despite the fact that no progress had been made on the missing book, and nearly half my employees—including Lisette and Ian, as of yesterday—were at home with the flu. The necessity of finding the book thief at the Dibdin weekend hung over me like a persistent black cloud; I found myself unable to imagine how it might all be resolved.

But at times the sun broke through. Sarah would finally arrive that morning—by car from Heathrow, since she insisted I should not get up at an ungodly hour to meet her six A.M. flight. I smiled. We would have several hours together before I had to leave for Castle Trefoyle. The Dibdin weekend was a most unfortunate interruption of our time together, but Sarah seemed more thrilled about my inclusion in the club than I was. We would, after all, still have weeks together after I got back—and a lifetime after that.

My mind was further eased by the fact that my security company and I had agreed upon an extensive alarm system for the Orchard, the installation of which Sarah had volunteered to supervise later that afternoon.

By tonight Sarah would be safe. The Valdarfer Boccaccio too—although in the meantime, I felt fairly secure about its hiding place in the Bedchamber book's former home.

I rolled out of bed, stuck my specs on my nose, and made for coffee. Having forsaken my drip percolator for a *cafetière* meant a slightly longer wait, but it was worth it. I boiled the kettle, got the coffee steeping, and went to the front door for the paper and the milk. A bird flitted out from under the pediment above me as I opened the door; I followed it as it dipped and winged its way into the bright summer morning. It all looked deceptively peaceful, quite in contrast to the week so far, and all the more beautiful because of it.

The expanse of lawn we used to roll and mark for a tennis court extended before me like a plush green carpet; my trees and hedges exploded with verdant foliage. There is nothing quite like the long-awaited arrival of summer in England. The countryside conscientiously mists itself for nine months of the year to achieve such green lusciousness; as a result, each picture-perfect day is prized. The sky was a perfect robin's-egg blue—divine weather for what now loomed ahead as a slightly ominous house party on the north coast of Cornwall.

I unfurled my copy of the *Times*. The smell of inky newsprint, bringing its associations with small, everyday pleasures and world events alike, struck my nose with pleasant intensity. As I went inside and banged the door closed with my hip, I saw that the flu epidemic was now front-page news. It had reached disastrous proportions, killing the elderly at a frightening rate. Businesses, schools, and public departments alike were suffering from employee absences as a result of the virulent bug. A box on page one publicised free jabs from the Department of Health, and listed locations along with phone numbers to ring for more information. The plague revisited, I thought. Some things never change.

As my eyes moved down the page, I recalled that plagues had actually brought us great literature: John Milton had moved to nearby Chalfont St. Giles to escape the plague, and finished *Paradise Lost* there. Giovanni Boccaccio had written the *Decameron* during the plague in Florence, and in fact had used the epidemic as a device to set the stage for his work. The *Decameron* opened with a group of young people fleeing to the countryside to escape the horror and death all around them; they distracted themselves for the next ten days by telling one another amusing stories.

I pushed down the plunger on the coffee carafe, poured the steaming brew into a mug with full-cream milk, and sipped gratefully as I read on.

The modern-day plague was disturbing enough ... but equally dangerous was the escalation of hostilities in the Middle East. I wondered just how much the Bedchamber book actually had to do with the situation; it remained unmentioned in the press.

An eighteen-point headline, *WAR IMMINENT IN IRAQ,* revealed the seriousness of the matter in the estimation of the *Times* editors. Another series of attacks on the massed UN peacekeeping forces by the Iraqis, and in-kind attacks by the Americans, made it appear that the problem was not about to fade away. Below that article was a separate piece about recent terrorist attacks on American civilians, thought to have been committed by the Iraqis. A bomb had been found on a flight from Los Angeles to New York, fortunately before take off. An explosion had ripped through a restaurant in New York City, killing five and injuring several dozen. And a parking garage near the Civic Center in San Francisco had collapsed as the result of a bombing, killing two. Aside from evidence indicating that the attacks were consistent with Iraqi methods, their timing coincided with repeated threats from the Americans to admit the arms inspectors or prepare for the consequences. Little doubt remained that the Iraqis were responsible.

Great Britain and America were massing their air, sea, and land forces in preparation for the conflict. Both Western nations desperately wished to forestall the confrontation, having come under considerable domestic fire several years before over the loss of troops in the Gulf War. But the Great Satan of the West was not only the military enemy of Iraq, it was the target of generalised cultural hatred. Regular burnings in effigy of the American president and Graeme Abercrombie made for vivid and frightening television news. An Iraqi spiritual leader calling himself the Great Teacher had emerged and rallied his people against America and Britain, using fervent faith to inspire hatred.

I shook my head. History really did go round in circles. Not only the plague, but the Crusades—holy wars in the Middle East.

When I'd finished two coffees, toast, and the *Times*, it was time to pack for Castle Trefoyle. I wanted to be finished with that task by the time Sarah arrived; it was already eight A.M. She might be here within the hour.

The Dibdin weekend required clothes I didn't normally wear; I'd had to make an emergency trip to Jermyn Street to acquire the requisite evening dress for Saturday night. I filled my suitcase with the resplendent new black clothing and freshly cleaned and pressed shirts and trousers. It wouldn't do to look sloppy for this group— many of them actually had valets to keep them faultlessly pressed and starched.

I thought, then, about the prints of the Bedchamber book pages Diana had given me. Now that the actual book had been stolen, I wanted at least to be able to look at the prints. And since there was another set, not to mention the negatives, I decided it wasn't a very great risk.

I reached deep into my cupboard for the scruffiest, most disreputable piece of luggage the world has ever seen: the waterproof bag I carried in my former career as a leader of flotilla sailing holidays. I opted for it not because it would impress my fellow club members, but because it had qualities they could never imagine. The Dibdin members would simply have to endure my abysmal taste in luggage.

Sticking my arm as far as it would go into the faded blue hulk, I unfastened the absolutely convincing false bottom—essential, Father had said, in my circumstances with the flotilla cruises. He'd been right; my yacht had been ransacked many times, and while the tape players and American jeans had gone, my passport and money had always remained intact. The thought of thieves at Castle Trefoyle was incongruous indeed. But considering the sensitive nature of the prints, if I took them with me, I couldn't leave them in plain sight.

I dashed downstairs and retrieved the prints in their plain envelope. I tucked them gently into the depths of the bag, then replaced the false bottom. I threw the remaining necessities into the sailing bag, along with Margulies's edition of Boccaccio—in case I found a spare moment to read. I was ready to go—except for one last thing. I plucked Sarah's framed photo off my bedside table and tucked it under the top layer of soft clothing. Now I was ready.

I stepped into the shower and thought of my plans for the half day with Sarah. We'd discussed the possibility of her driving down to Cornwall with me for the added time it would give us. But she didn't want to fritter away the weekend alone there, waiting outside the castle keep, when she had things to do in London. Nor did it make sense for her to make the trip twice, to be my chauffeur. In the end we'd reluctantly decided to part ways for the weekend.

Closing my eyes, I ducked my head under the stream of hot water to rinse the shampoo out of my hair. Before I realised what was happening, the door to the shower slid open and closed again. Strong arms closed round my chest.

Sarah! I twisted in her arms to face her, delighted to see her beaming through the mist. My heart gave a leap as I bent to kiss her, shampoo mixing with the water and her lips. I put my arms around her and lifted her up in pure joy, turning around several times in wordless celebration.

It was the best shower of my life.

Afterwards we dried each other off. In her rich, deep voice she began to relate a story about someone she'd met on her flight, and as she spoke I feasted my eyes. I couldn't get enough of looking at her; it was if I'd been starved for months. Sarah's beauty was, of course, derived from the sum total of her character and manner as well as her appearance. Every word she spoke, every act she initiated, demonstrated her integrity and strength. From experience, I knew that she was loyal, and brave, and probably a good deal more intelligent than her fiancé.

But no one could deny that Sarah's exterior was stunning as well. She was striking in a tall, leggy, muscular way. While very feminine, there was no fragility or hesitancy about her, and an early widowhood followed by years of a brilliant international investment banking career had brought her independence and maturity in abundance.

"Alex? Did you hear anything I just said?" The smile in her voice told me she knew exactly where my mind had been.

"Sorry, darling. Obsessed with your ineffable beauty. Here, let me comb out your hair."

"Mmm. Thanks. Tell me more about this book, and why you think it was stolen."

I took up a comb and started at the bottom of her dark tresses, working my way up. "It's very much a mystery. But I've thought of several reasons. At first I thought perhaps the Iraqis had stolen it, which would have solved all our problems, in a way. But we know now that didn't happen. Someone might be desperately greedy to have it for personal reasons—the way I feel about you." I gave her a kiss. "Book collectors do become obsessed by these things. Or it's possible that the thief might be threatened by its contents somehow." I finished with her hair and touched her cheek. "One other crazy idea came to me, but I think it's unlikely. . . ."

"Tell me."

"Well, I suppose it's possible that someone knows Iraq wants the book and doesn't want them to get it. Perhaps someone *wants* this war."

"They'd be insane," Sarah declared. "And I find it hard to believe that a person with any one of those motivations could be a member of the Dibdin Club."

I shook my head. "It's just that these are the people who know the most about books in England, especially incunables like the Bedchamber book. I wouldn't expect that one of them would actually have the book there, of course; they'd be smarter than I was and lock it up right away. But I might be able to probe a bit and find out who *knows* about the book, though I don't expect easy results."

"No. I suppose not. But if anyone can do it, Alex, you can." She moved behind me and started to massage my shoulders.

I sighed. "Whatever would I do without you?" I turned and looked into her deep green, almond-shaped eyes.

"You'll never have to find out," she promised me.

We got dressed eventually and went down to the kitchen for tea, chatting on about the plans afoot in Massachusetts. I was astounded by how much preparation it took to carry off a wedding, especially the sort her family traditions dictated. How fortunate for us all, I thought, that it fell to the bride's parents to make the arrangements. I would be hopelessly unequal to the task. Sarah and her mother seemed to have everything in hand quite effortlessly, from music to flowers to the dinner for hundreds afterwards, on the lawn sloping gently down to the beach. What I appreciated most was the way they approached the plans: They actually seemed to enjoy it all.

"I'll be able to finish the invitations while you're away," she said, cradling her Bateman's tea mug. She was the only one who ever used the small pottery souvenir of our visit to Rudyard Kipling's National Trust home; she'd been enchanted by the author's picture-perfect English country house. "It'll give me something to do."

An hour later I had to say good-bye; she sent me off with a kiss and a hug and the important reassurance that she would be thinking of me. "Just promise you'll be careful," she said. "Who knows what sort of character this thief might be. . . ."

For some reason that reminded me what I had forgotten. "Hang on! I almost forgot the shotgun."

Sarah looked distinctly taken aback at this; she'd never seen or heard about my father's gun before. When I came out carrying it in a canvas zip-up case, she said, "Now I *really* want to hear you'll be careful."

I laughed. "Not to worry, we shoot up at the sky, not at each other. You be careful too, my love. Don't take any chances, okay?"

She waved off my concern. Tenderly, I put two fingers under her chin and lifted it until she looked me in the eye. "I'm serious, Sarah. Even though the book isn't at the house anymore, and no one knows about the Boccaccio, remember there was a break-in here just a few nights ago. Make sure the alarm works before you let the security firm leave."

"I will, I will! Now *you're* the one worrying! Everything will be fine. Oh, and I'll probably look in on Grandfather tomorrow; he might want some company. So don't worry if I'm not here when you call—and don't feel you *have* to call. Try to enjoy yourself this weekend, Alex, at least a little."

One more kiss, and I reluctantly loaded my gear into the Golf and climbed in. She smiled beatifically as I waved; I watched her in the rearview mirror as I crunched down the drive.

I was a fool to leave her.

Speeding down the motorway to the West Country, I felt strangely out of place, having forsaken both Sarah and work. But such, I told myself, must be the rigours of membership in the Dibdin Club. My Golf GTI purred down the road; a cloak of well-being settled on the day. Really, I told myself, there was nothing to worry about—the Press wasn't about to go under because I was taking a Friday off, and my future wife still loved me. I'd survived perfectly well before discovering the Bedchamber book; I could certainly live without it. The only really disturbing thought was that I might have prevented loss of life if the book hadn't been stolen. But diplomatic efforts might yet resolve the conflict—and I might still recover the book.

I watched the grim terraced houses of suburban London give way to commercial and then rural Berkshire. I couldn't help reflecting on the packet I'd received from Earl Trefoyle the day before. The professionally printed timetable for a weekend-long extravaganza spelled out more meals and sporting opportunities than anything else. Upon arrival that afternoon there would be shooting, followed by tea, an hour or so of free time before aperitifs in the library, then dinner at eight.

Saturday would consist of a similar parade of gustatory and recreational delights: a breakfast buffet from eight to eleven o'clock; the annual business meeting from eleven to one; lunch at one; sailing from two to four; tea; helicopter flights until it was time to change for aperitifs in the library; then dinner once again. The Saturday-

night dinner would be the renowned Dibdin extravaganza. Tradition held that the party continue far into the
night, aided by the venerable purple stream Haslewood
so gleefully publicised in his *Dibdin Dissipations*.

Sunday morning would bring an outdoor breakfast
buffet immediately before a brisk ride on horseback
known as a point-to-point—a steeplechase course with
obstacles used in hunting. June was far from hunting season, however, so I could only guess that the Earl wanted
to give us a fun, competitive ride. My hunting-jumping
skills were a bit rusty, but I did enjoy riding. The experience of my childhood and adolescence hadn't deserted
me entirely; my parents had kept ponies at first, then a
chestnut mare, for my brother and me until we'd left
home. Lisette and George kept a horse in the fields opposite their house in Heronsgate, and were generous in letting me ride him. I'd also ridden in the odd hunt over the
years—not live fox, but scent only—which was not so
very different from the jumping and obstacle-breaching
of a point-to-point. I assured myself optimistically that I
would survive.

Two hundred miles flew by. Upon reaching a sign
telling me that I had crossed the River Tamar and entered
Cornwall, I made a point of detouring far enough off the
main road to find a Cornish pasty. I'd been anticipating
one ever since learning that I'd be driving to Cornwall. As
I sat at an outdoor table at the small pub, I relished the
warm dough enfolding meat, potatoes, turnips, onions,
and whatever indistinguishable ingredients made the
filled pastry so comforting and satisfying. When I finished the first, I indulged in another and enjoyed it just as
much. Then I returned to the Golf to complete the short
journey to Castle Trefoyle.

Upon entering the town of Trefoyle, just past Tintagel
on the rugged north coast, signs directed visitors to the
castle. I followed them, eventually turning off into the

drive. It led through miles of green parkland, until at last I arrived at the visitor's car park. Castle Trefoyle was an awe-inspiring sight, a jewel of grey rock suspended over the foaming sea. My first thought was to wonder if the sea would sweep it away one day, although it had already managed to cling to land for seven centuries.

A small, tasteful sign in gothic type directed "Dibdin Club members" along a small driveway to the right. Earl Trefoyle had told me that a special route would be marked to direct us. Following instructions, I drove down the road until a chain suspended between two black-painted posts blocked my way. I looked into the walled courtyard lined with cars before me as a uniformed man approached, courteous but enquiring.

I rolled down my window. "Alex Plumtree. With the Dibdin Club."

The man smiled and unfastened the chain from its post, stepping aside to let me past. "Welcome to Castle Trefoyle. If you park just in there, Mr. Plumtree, his lordship will be out to greet you."

I nodded my thanks and drove towards an empty space against one wall of the stone courtyard.

"Plumtree!" I heard, having barely turned off the ignition. The jovial shout came from behind me, where the elderly but athletic Trefoyle was taking his duties as host seriously. As I climbed out of the Golf, he strode towards me, both arms extended. Trefoyle had obviously finished a round of golf not long before; he was kitted out in tweedy plus-fours.

"Wonderful, wonderful to see you again. Welcome to Castle Trefoyle." The elegant gentleman, blue eyes sparkling at our secret, put one hand on my back. With the other he took my hand and squeezed it. "So glad you could get away today. You'll have a chance to get acquainted with the other members." He said this in a conspiratorial tone that told me it would be useful. "Pleasant journey, I hope?"

"Very pleasant indeed. Quite a change from driving a desk—and I might even escape the flu."

He chortled, brimming with good humour and energy. "Wonderful, wonderful. Quite right. Let me show you where you'll be staying. Then we'll go straight to the shooting range, if it suits you."

"Of course," I said, picking up my sailing bag and suitcase, locking my car—out of habit—and hurrying after the earl.

"And remember, no standing on ceremony. Call me Trefoyle."

"Right. Thank you." I tried not to smirk at the familiar joke in which the lord says to the commoner, *Let's not stand on formality. You may call me Lord.* But Trefoyle was not at all the stuffy sort. He was surprisingly normal, considering his privileged background.

Abruptly, he stopped at the door to the castle and pulled a foil packet out of his trouser pocket. "Kendal Mint Cake?" he asked, unfolding the tinfoil and proffering it while taking a dry white chunk of the sweet for himself. I remembered the stuff from holidays to the Lake District; it was hardly my favourite.

But I wouldn't offend my host. "Thank you," I said, accepting a small chunk.

Just as rapidly he folded the packet up again, dropping a dusting of white powder, and shoved it into his pocket as he moved through the heavy oak door.

I followed him into a dark hallway, then through it into a magnificent stone great hall. An immense fireplace occupied one entire wall of the room, which I estimated was perhaps one hundred feet long—longer than many homes. Oriental rugs covered the granite floors, and ancient torch-holders still hung on the walls.

The place certainly had the feel of a Dark Ages castle— dank chill, stale air, and deep darkness. The gloom was dispelled at intervals by lamps on top of priceless coffers and tables. The temperature was at least ten degrees cooler inside these stone walls; I shuddered to think what winter felt like here. Perhaps the earl could centrally heat the place now, but seven or eight hundred years ago, it must have been brutal.

"This is the best I can do with the old place, I'm afraid," my host threw over his shoulder apologetically. "But at least we have electricity and ensuite bathrooms for all the rooms."

"It's magnificent," I commented, passing a suit of armour as I followed Trefoyle up a miniature scale stone stairway. As I practically tiptoed up the tiny stairs, spiralling round behind Trefoyle, I felt a thrill that alarmed me. It was unmistakably the thrill of being included where others had been excluded, a feeling of pride and ego.

Stop it, I warned myself.

Upstairs, we travelled down a narrow hall past door after door of heavy oak—I lost count at fifteen. It was most oppressively dark, though here, too, table lamps made a vain effort to bring warmth and light. My host chattered on amiably. "We refurbished the plumbing and heating again last year. Really, I was most unpleasantly surprised at the lack of competent contractors. Don't you find it difficult to get good people?" He twisted round to look at my face, though he didn't slow his pace. There was something both tragic and endearing about his assumption that we all had castles to keep up.

"Yes," I replied matter-of-factly. "We did some repairs and redecorating about five years ago. I remember my mother saying it took all her time just to keep the workmen on the job. She made them lunch, tea, cakes—anything to keep them at the house."

"Well, that's it," he agreed, finally slowing at a door. "Once they're off to the pub for lunch, you've lost them. Now, mind your head," he cautioned.

"What a spectacular room!" I exclaimed, ducking through the barely six-foot doorway after him. Summer light poured in through leaded-glass, diamond-paned windows, filtered by the foliage of massive oaks outside. The light illuminated a small four-poster and enough antiques to populate a suburban shop. A magnificent tapestry covered most of one wall.

"I'm so pleased you like it. Do make yourself at home. I'll have Hawkes unpack for you while we're shooting." He reached for a pocket and drew out a hand-held radio.

"Oh, no," I said, hoping my panic at the thought of anyone rummaging in my sports bag didn't show. The prints were hidden, but . . . "Not necessary at all. Really, I didn't bring much." I shrugged.

"All right, then. Shall I give you a moment, or would you like to follow me out to the shooting area?"

"I'll come with you now." I laughed. "I might never find my way otherwise." I unzipped my father's gun out of its canvas case and slipped a box of cartridges in my pocket.

"You'll be surprised. By the end of the weekend, you'll be feeling quite at home here."

As Trefoyle led me back outside, he put a friendly arm round my shoulders. He had to reach a bit to do it. "Now, Plumtree. I don't want you to worry one bit. I know how it is when you're the new boy, as it were. But everyone is absolutely delighted to have you in the club. We all admired your father immensely." I noticed he was careful not to make reference to my "mission" there that weekend, although his tone implied a certain familiarity that I suspected would not have been there otherwise. "Ah—I see we're all here."

We'd rounded a hedge to find six men and a woman facing us with guns over their arms. Although the shotguns were uncocked and hung backwards as if broken over their elbows, I found the sight a bit startling. A kindly looking man with a paunch and a bulbous red nose stood holding a cigar, the aroma of which I had smelled long before he'd come into sight. I knew he was Sir Harold Westering; his photo had appeared in the paper on occasion. The elderly man near him looked as fragile and refined as Westering was red-faced and robust. I immediately recognised him as Lord Peter Albemarle, a fellow oarsman. He was well known through his outspoken participation in the House of Lords, and of course from the bookshop that bore his name. I was relieved to see Margulies in the group; he immediately smiled and waved. A sleek woman with shoulder-length, silky blond hair tied back with an Hermès scarf glared at me: Countess Thornbury, Lady Desdemona Hart, notorious friend of various royals of my approximate age. The other two were young men I didn't recognise.

Every last gun-toting Dibdinian was dressed to the nines in tweedy made-to-measure shooting clothes. I tried not to think of my khakis and striped shirt, open at the neck. At least, I consoled myself, the shirt had been made by Turnbull and Asser.

You're doing it again, Alex . . . you're becoming a snob.

As Trefoyle and I strode across the last few yards to meet the others, I couldn't shake the feeling we were marching toward a firing squad.

"Alex Plumtree, meet your fellow Dibdinians," Trefoyle boomed good-naturedly. "Osgood Forsythe, Denis de-Chauncey, Sir Harold Westering—good God, Westers, do you have to smoke that thing every blessed moment?—Lord Peter Albemarle, the Countess of Thornbury. And, of course, you know the Honourable Margulies Whitehead."

"Delighted to meet you all. Good to see you again, Margulies."

"This is one of the many traits I admire in Alex," Margulies said. "He can sit at a desk all week and then play golf, ride, and shoot with the best of them. How do you do it?"

"To say nothing of his rowing exploits," Lord Albemarle said. The aged peer, despite his delicate appearance, rowed for Leander in a senior eight. I'd seen him at Henley and other regattas. There was steel under those chiselled cheekbones.

"Or his bestsellers," the countess said. "I've begun seeking out the new section some of the bookshops are starting, featuring books published by Plumtree Press. What an extraordinary list! You're to be congratulated. Literary, yet entertaining." There was a note of irony to her voice, but I chose to interpret it as a personal idiosyncrasy.

"You're much too kind. And I'm afraid it'll be all too obvious that I haven't shot for quite some time."

"Well. Shall we get on?" DeChauncey seemed eager to heft his gun. His bored tone hinted at his displeasure with the barrage of attention I'd received.

"Right," Trefoyle said, rummaging in his pocket. "Kendal Mint Cake, anyone?" He pulled out his packet and took a bit. Everyone demurred, apparently used to his habit.

He crunched up the packet again and thrust it in to his pocket. "I'll just get Hawkes started in the tower, then."

I did know enough about clay-pigeon shooting to understand that there was an automatic throwing apparatus in the small stone tower that stood to one side, in front of us. When a marksman shouted "Pull!" someone pressed a button to send the bit of clay catapulting into the air. If this was anything like other informal shoots I'd attended, we'd take it in turns to shoot at the clay pigeons.

Trefoyle had given Hawkes the thumbs-up and moved away to the edge of our little group. "All right! Lady Desdemona!"

"Pull!" she cried, achieving remarkable volume. The clay disc flew into the air, making a whooshing noise like a bird's wings. She stroked the air with the gun as if it were a paintbrush, following the motion of the pigeon. She pulled the trigger, and the clay disc exploded into dust. After a second successful shot, she emptied out the spent cartridges, shoved them carelessly into her pocket, and reloaded. She disposed of four more clay pigeons, then opened her shotgun and stepped back.

"Pull!" deChauncey shouted, then wheeled instinctively to shoot at what came hurtling through the air. Even as it flew past me, I was aware that it was wildly off course, judging from the first five pulls. The gun roared.

"Gah!" came an anguished cry. In disbelief, I looked at the source of the sound and saw Osgood Forsythe writhing on the grass. Blood was soaking through the sleeve of his lightweight tweed jacket.

"Good Lord!" Trefoyle exclaimed, and ran to where Forsythe lay. "Hawkes!" he bellowed. "Ring for an ambulance!"

Hawkes appeared at the door to the tower, pale-faced, ready to do the earl's bidding.

"No," Forsythe said through clenched teeth. His eyes were closed in agony. "If someone could just drive me to the surgery . . ." He began to struggle to his feet, badly shocked. No one made any effort to help him. Having seen a surprising amount of carnage in my anything-but-sedate publishing career, I was relatively at home in the situation. I stepped forward and put a hand under Forsythe's good arm, helping him up.

"Forsythe, I—" DeChauncey seemed desperate to say something but couldn't get the words out. Grey-faced himself, he looked as if he might topple over before his victim did.

"I know," Forsythe muttered, still gripping his bloody arm. "Don't worry about it."

Trefoyle took over then, ushering Forsythe to where the cars were parked in the courtyard. Trefoyle turned and looked daggers at the mournful deChauncey, who followed them at a distance—rather pitifully. I thought I caught a significant look from Trefoyle in my direction too, as if to say, *Take note of this, Plumtree.*

"Hardly surprising, is it?" the countess said under her breath to Lord Peter Albemarle. Albemarle, beside me, made no response.

I was beginning to think I'd imagined her strange remark, when Sir Harold said, "Now, Lady Des. Mustn't give young Plumtree here the wrong impression."

She turned and regarded me through half-closed eyes. There was a hardness to her face that was off-putting despite her relative youth—late thirties, I guessed—and sleek blond, blue-eyed good looks. "Well, I think young Plumtree here is capable of drawing his own conclusions. Quite capable." With that she threw me a look that was at once flirtatious and contemptuous. "Young Plumtree actually hasn't a clue about what's happening here, has he?"

I gazed at her levelly, saying nothing.

Lord Albemarle frowned into the middle distance. "That pigeon," he said, "didn't come from the tower. It was way off the normal trajectory. Lady Desdemona, your pigeons came from over there"—he waved his hand to the north, and the sea—"and that last one came from the opposite direction. I suppose deChauncey saw it out of the corner of his eye and instinctively shot—but it was low, and some of the pellets struck Forsythe instead."

"Matter of fact, any one of us might have been hit," Sir Harold pronounced. It came out as, *Mettrefect, enny wahn of us might hev been hit.*

"But deChauncey has no *reason* to shoot *us*, Sir Harold," the countess snorted.

At that moment Hawkes returned from helping Trefoyle and Forsythe to the car and began to lock up the tower.

"What the hell do you think *you're* doing?" the countess demanded somewhat shrilly.

Hawkes froze, then turned to face her. "Er, I assumed that since—well, the earl—"

"Get back in there, man. We've only just begun."

I was nearly as stunned as poor Hawkes. Lord Peter and Sir Harold glanced at each other and merely shrugged. Equivocally, Lord Peter said, "Well, I suppose we might as well carry on. . ."

Hawkes closed his mouth and trudged back inside the tower.

"You're next, Plumtree," the countess said to me, a challenge in her voice. I cast a glance after deChauncey: He stood forlornly at some distance, watching the Range Rover speed out of sight down the long drive.

"Pull!" I shouted, and missed the first shot. But somehow, I managed to hit the next pigeon, and my fellow markspeople nodded with approval. DeChauncey rejoined us, and we continued for almost an hour. Fortunately, there were no further mishaps with the shotguns. All the same, I couldn't help but wonder why the countess was so convinced deChauncey had shot Forsythe deliberately.

The very thought that it might not have been accidental made me want to get away from all of them . . . and their guns.

CHAPTER 6

*There arose certain customs that were quite
contrary to established tradition.*

—GIOVANNI BOCCACCIO, *DECAMERON*,
FIRST DAY: INTRODUCTION

Relieved, I followed the group inside. Hawkes, looking a bit overwhelmed by the events of the afternoon, took our guns to clean them. To my surprise, when
we entered the room where tea was obviously to be
served, judging by the massive silver samovar there,
Forsythe and Trefoyle had already returned from the
surgery. DeChauncey rushed over to him.

"Forsythe. I'm so sorry . . . I simply don't know what
could have happened. . . ."

Forsythe smiled kindly at him. "I think you're worse
off than I am, old boy. Charles, get him a wee dram, won't
you?"

"Perhaps we could all use a bit of something," Trefoyle
said under his breath, and crossed to a drink trolley set up
across the room.

"I was quite embarrassed when I arrived at the
surgery. There were only a few pellets, and they weren't
very deep. Please don't think of it again, deChauncey."

I admired Forsythe for this public acquittal of the man who'd shot him. But deChauncey remained anguished despite the absolution. Trefoyle had poured him a potent gin and tonic and now delivered it to him with an encouraging pat on the back. "Sit down, deChauncey. Relax."

Woodenly, deChauncey sat. And drank.

"I know everyone's preferences but yours, Plumtree," Trefoyle said, "but let me guess: whisky, neat."

"Amazing," I said, though I knew his trick. It had been my father's drink. Trefoyle was right in thinking I'd inherited my father's preferences.

He chortled and poured a triple measure. So this was the nature of tea with the Dibdin Club, I thought. As I lifted the crystal tumbler to my lips, a uniformed servant appeared in the doorway.

"My lord," he said, and stepped aside. A small crowd exploded into the room, led by the Duke of Chesterton, whose ancestors had long held the presidency of the Dibdin Club. I immediately understood the bustle and hush that accompanied the newcomers. These were a dozen of the most influential people in Britain. Chesterton was widely acknowledged to be more royal—and certainly more English—than the Queen herself.

Dame Cleopatra Kirk swept in, making a beeline for the countess. Dame Cleopatra was a brilliant historian who now blended history with romance and adventure to create bestselling fiction. She was sixtyish, clever, and engaging, and had received her equivalent of a knighthood ten years ago. Each member who drifted in through the doorway had a similar title and equally notable background.

"Well, well," Trefoyle boomed, hurrying to meet them. "Your helicopter made it here safely, I see. Hope it wasn't too crowded at the landing strip?"

"Not at all. Delightful journey—lovely little aerodrome you have here." The portly Chesterton, heir to one of the world's largest petroleum companies, chuckled. "Hello, everyone. Ah, this must be young Plumtree."

I smiled in acknowledgment, took his proffered hand.

"Welcome," Chesterton boomed. At nearly my height of six feet five and twice my bulk, the duke exuded power and confidence. His handshake was firm. "You are most welcome." Then Trefoyle was quizzing him about his new French state-of-the-art aircraft, and the room erupted with the enthusiastic greetings reserved for close friends who rarely see one another in private.

For the moment, though I stood with them in a tight circle, I was left alone to wonder why they all called me *young* Plumtree. Perhaps what Ian had said about my early election being a posthumous apology for having bypassed my father was true.

As I watched the group mingle, I noticed an air of—I struggled to put a finger on it—almost sacred respect for one another. Perhaps this was to be expected, when the top stratum of England's bibliophiles gathered in one room. Here they could be themselves, could say and do what they might be roundly criticised for elsewhere.

They were safe amongst themselves.

After a moment, Trefoyle brought the Duke of Chesterton over and left to get the esteemed president a drink. "Nothing like tea with the Dibdin, is there, Plumtree?" The duke looked directly into my eyes, seeming to search for something there.

"No, there isn't." I laughed, lifting my glass. "It's a very great honour to be here, Your Grace."

"Call me Chesterton, for heaven's sake. Sit next to me at dinner tonight, won't you? I'll mention it to Charles."

"Thanks very much. I'd like that."

Trefoyle returned with his drink, then he was off to greet the others. I sipped my whisky and watched. Dinner at the right hand of the Duke of Chesterton. What next?

For the next forty-five minutes I felt I was on a reception line as one member after another came to greet me. Dame Cleopatra coquettishly batted her mascara-laden eyelashes at me and suggested that someday we might collaborate on a project. I said, quite honestly, that I'd love to—hers was just the sort of intelligent fiction I liked to publish. "Sweet boy," she said, and drifted off.

The Duke of Ashleigh was next. "Delighted to have you as a member, my boy," he said.

I thought if one more person called me a boy, be he fifty or eighty, I'd scream. But instead I said, "Delighted to be here, sir. This is a privilege I'd never contemplated."

"Sit down, sit down," he murmured, looking weary. I knew that his father, the ninth Duke of Ashleigh, had died the previous year at the ripe old age of eighty-five. "Young" Ashleigh was at most sixty-five or so. But he didn't look at all well as he settled himself into an easy chair next to me. "Small aircraft and I don't agree," he whispered confidentially, as if to explain his appearance. "Now then, my boy. . . ."

I gritted my teeth.

"What do you know of the history of the club?" Had Ashleigh planted himself next to me because he wanted to stay in one place for a bit, or because he really had something to tell me? Perhaps he'd been appointed to school me in Dibdin Club history.

"I know about its origin from the Duke of Windlesham's sale, and the Boccaccio, and Dibdin and Haslewood. And I've seen a bit of the *Dibdin Dissipations* as well."

The duke gave me a long, slow nod of approval and reevaluation, as if this had been more than he expected. I refrained from telling him, of course, that Ian had given me the Boccaccio. I did think, however, of the modern edition by Margulies that I'd brought in my bag. I hoped to read it after dinner; perhaps even after tea.

The project had been Ian's, not mine, as the volume was published by Plumtree Press's academic division rather than the trade division. Still, the very thought that I could put an M.A., Cantab. after my name and actually publish books while having managed to avoid reading

Boccaccio's classic of Italian literature was enough to make me flush. I desperately hoped the elderly gentleman wouldn't want to discuss the book, which had inspired Chaucer to write a certain set of extremely popular tales about travellers.

"Good, good," he said. "You'll learn more about us as time goes on. Now then. I've heard a good deal about the Plumtree Collection. I was a friend of your father's, you know, and I remember how modest he was about your very creditable library. What was it, now—the something-or-other Chronicles?"

"The Malconbury Chronicles," I replied. "Yes. I suppose that's one of our gems. They were inscribed by the monks, and illuminated with a particularly striking shade of blue derived from a root that grows only in East Anglia, near the Malconbury Priory."

"Lovely. I should like very much to see them," the elderly duke intoned. "I also remember hearing about your Dartmouth Bible, of course technically the Douai Bible. What do you think you'll choose when it's your turn to print something for us?"

"Mmm, I'm not sure." I pretended to equivocate, while eagerly sensing my first real opportunity to bring up the Bedchamber book. I decided to throw my cards on the table with abandon. "I found something rather special just recently—*literally* found it, behind some other books on the shelf."

"Good heavens, that sounds intriguing," the weary duke said, his eyes flashing even as his jowls seemed to droop further. "What was it?"

"It doesn't have a title, actually, but it's a history of the Royal Order of the Bedchamber, a little-known chivalric order begun by Richard I. The book does appear to have been printed in the late fifteenth century, in England, though it was written in the fourteenth—by Boccaccio, as legend has it. At least that's what Boswell at the British Museum claims. He also says there is some intrigue about the book; that evidently King Edward IV wanted to prevent its publication. He even threatened to behead the printer and binder, but he couldn't determine who they were. Until now it was thought he'd destroyed all the copies."

"Fascinating. *Absolutely fascinating!*" he said with extraordinary attentiveness. His accent transformed those dramatic words into *Ebsly fessenetting!*

"Yes. It was . . . unfortunately, it was stolen from my office several days ago."

"No!" Ashleigh was aghast. "You're *joking!*" He seemed genuinely appalled at this turn of events.

It might have been my imagination, but there seemed then to be just the merest hint of a momentary unnatural silence in the room. The duke cleared his throat, and the hum of voices resumed quite naturally.

Ashleigh looked ready to question me further on the matter, but Osgood Forsythe came to join us just then. When we paused to welcome him to our discussion and ask after his injury, he launched into questions about Plumtree Press and its publications. I noticed he'd changed into a different jacket, sans pellet holes and blood.

"It's quite an honour to have you among us, Plumtree. You probably know that all of us here had great admiration for your father. No finer man. Didn't seem to have the usual faults of the rest of us, eh, Ashleigh?"

The duke shook his head, very sadly it seemed to me. "No. No indeed."

"Anyway," Forsythe continued, "I follow your list quite closely. I think it's marvellous the way you've been able to build a substantial trade list so quickly. How long since you took over from your father?"

"Five years now," I said, scarcely believing it. "A few of the titles have been more than a little problematic, but I suppose that's typical. The public seem to have embraced a literary-history–oriented list with surprising alacrity."

"Shouldn't be surprised if Dame Cleopatra would want to work with you. Right up your alley, no?"

"Yes, indeed." In fact, I did entertain the hope that Dame Cleopatra would be interested in collaborating on a forthcoming title, but knew better than to take her earlier comment too seriously. Authors were often unrealistic about their abilities, and her agent would probably be unwilling for her to leave her long-time giant of a publisher. The giant certainly could pay her more than Plumtree Press could, though we had begun to excel at producing particularly beautiful books, set in special typefaces to suit the subject matter, and using more than the average number of initial capitals and similar embellishments. We also used fine acid-free paper when the book warranted it. Some authors preferred beautiful books to money.

"Margulies has just edited a wonderful academic volume for us," I ventured to say, trying to direct the conversation to something of more definite interest to them. "No doubt you've heard about the Boccaccio edition he's been working on for the last decade—the only one to include both the Elizabethan translation and his own modern one."

"Yes, indeed, but I didn't realise it was finished." Forsythe glanced at the scholar as he sat adjacent to us, chatting with the countess and Sir Harold Westering. I found myself wishing that Westering would cease and desist with the cigars—the stench made me feel ill. Margulies felt Forsythe's gaze and looked over, clearly aware that we were talking about him.

I made my best effort at a smile. "We're hoping to sign him for another book, this time a novel for our trade division fictionalising the life of Thomas Frognall Dibdin." Then I saw my opportunity. "And, as a bonus, he plans to put an appendix of Haslewoodiana in a literary guise—including a list of supposedly legendary, long-lost books."

"*Really?*" the Duke of Ashleigh exclaimed in as excited a tone as he ever achieved. "Why, this *is* intriguing. Why on earth didn't you tell us sooner?"

Forsythe and Ashleigh looked at Margulies at the same time, as if their heads had been pulled by a string.

"But this is *outrageous*," Forsythe said good-naturedly. "I'll have to give Margulies hell for not telling us. Why's he being so secretive? But wait—this would be his first work of fiction, wouldn't it?"

"Yes. No doubt that explains why he hasn't mentioned it." I felt a pang of regret at having revealed Margulies's intentions too early, perhaps before he was ready. But he'd seemed quite eager in London; after all, he'd brought Van Vanderbilt all the way across the Atlantic for the purpose. "Fiction is quite a different art. Most academic authors tremble in their boots at the very thought."

"Yes. I see. Work in progress." Forsythe and Ashleigh exchanged a glance. It seemed to me that the normally blasé Forsythe was struggling for calm. He sat back in his seat very deliberately. "So what sort of thing did that old troublemaker Haslewood bequeath to the esteemed Dibdin?"

"Actually, it's quite fascinating: You know that Haslewood was always compiling lists of wildly obscure observations. Supposedly, this included his list of legendary books rumoured to have once existed. I haven't seen it myself; it's never been published."

Conversation again came to a grinding halt. My own voice echoed in the room with the last words to have been spoken, *never been published* . . . Was everyone again terrifically interested in what I had to say, or was it mere coincidence?

Forsythe raised his voice and said in Margulies's direction, "Why didn't you tell us, old boy? Listen, everyone! Whitehead has found some tract of Haslewood's in Dibdin's papers, listing legendary books that might once have existed but with no surviving copies. Plumtree here is publishing it as part of Whitehead's fictionalised life of Dibdin."

Margulies shot me a look that perfectly blended horror with regret and as swiftly hid his feelings. Smiling with admirable calm at me, he said, "And there could be no finer publisher." He licked his lips. "Hadn't I mentioned the Haslewood list, really?"

More silence. Then, as if to cover whatever awkwardness existed about Margulies's work, Chesterton spoke up. "I have news from San Francisco," he boomed, and the large group became one intimate circle.

Contributing to this feeling was the fact that Hawkes and a young woman in a black uniform with white collar and cuffs had been topping up the drinks. They'd done it with such subtlety that I'd hardly noticed, but now my suspicious side had realised everyone assembled in the library had probably consumed three or four drinks. The servants were so skilled that they kept track of what we were drinking and simply took the empty glass out of our hands as they slid a fresh one in. In fact, I wondered if I'd have been quite so forthcoming about the Bedchamber book and my publishing plans if I hadn't had two drinks already myself, with a third in my hand. It was insidious, this sort of pampering.

Chesterton was going on about the Dibdin Club of San Francisco. Apparently, this was a heated issue for the club, as members all over the room had begun huffing indignantly among themselves the moment he brought it up. "They've refused to change their name, and are threatening a lawsuit. Imagine! And *we* were the original club. They didn't even *begin* until 1925."

"Interlopers," muttered someone.

"Frightful Colonials," said Ashleigh.

"Ignoramuses," said mild Lord Albemarle.

"*Precisely,*" Chesterton confirmed. "I think we should have a go at them."

"Hear, hear," said the men and women who populated the House of Lords.

I was surprised yet again that I actually knew something about this subject. Van Vanderbilt had long been a member of the San Francisco club. In fact, his great-great-grandfather had been a founding member. He'd mentioned, late in our dinner at the Chateaubriand, that the American publishing house Elm Knoll Press was urging him to turn an article he'd written on the subject for *San Francisco Magazine* into a book. I'd told Van over brandy that I'd like the option to publish it in the UK. He'd laughed. Sure, he said. An *option.*

If the club knew what I'd planned, they might be more than a little upset, considering their animosity towards the San Francisco group. In fact, now that I was a member, could I in all good conscience publish Van's book?

My internal debate was interrupted when Trefoyle, our host, stood and took the floor. "Might I suggest we discuss this at the business meeting tomorrow morning? Drinks and dinner in just an hour," he said, glancing at his watch.

I was aghast. More to follow, hard on the heels of what we had just put away?

The august members of the Dibdin Club rose reluctantly. They bid brief good-byes to their friends, and, to give them credit, to the newest member. The room emptied rapidly. I followed an instinct to climb one of the ladders that rose to the gallery surrounding the room on the upper level. Elegant arches topped copious shelves housing half as many books again as the awe-inspiring ground floor. Somehow the less accessible books were more tempting; they were certain to be less famous, and perhaps more familiar than the ones downstairs that I didn't dare touch.

I'd barely gained the gallery floor when I heard voices return to the library below. "What Trefoyle had in mind I can't imagine, even if he *can* help us produce the yearly editions."

The voice was indignant. Was it Forsythe? I couldn't be

sure. . . . Good Lord. Were they talking about me? Producing yearly editions? Suddenly I was loath to reveal my presence and embarrass us all.

Another voice piped up. "And that dreadfully indiscreet nattering on about the Royal Order of the Bedchamber— that's no laughing matter. Some of us had family in the order. It's an ancient chivalric tradition, not some new opportunity to publicise the Plumtree family library. He simply doesn't *realise.*"

"No. Not our sort at all, is he?" It was a female voice— since there were only two in the group, it was easy to identify the Countess. "And where are we to meet when it's Plumtree's year, out at that ghastly little Orchard in Hertfordshire?" She spat out a less than savoury expletive. "I'd rather spend the evening in Wapping."

I felt my heart sink. What kind of people *were* they? I'd heard the same voices, honey-sweet, welcoming me to their club, making friendly conversation less than an hour before. It came as a most unpleasant surprise that in addition to my other responsibilities, Trefoyle had lured me into the Dibdin to act as its resident publisher. The silence I'd heard upon mentioning the Royal Order of the Bedchamber book *hadn't* been imagined.

But what had I expected? Why *would* they have invited me to join the Dibdin Club? Unless . . .

I'd thought it actually had something to do with my family and its library. But all along I'd been aware that the invitation had come from Trefoyle only *after* I'd found the Bedchamber book. I'd told myself that Margulies must have spoken on my behalf, but now saw the bald-faced truth: my membership in the club was related to my former possession of the untitled book.

The group shuffled out of the room. I found myself seething. Cowards; *hypocrites.* Did I want to associate with these people? I climbed down the ladder again, much subdued, and wandered out of the far door into the garden. I strode past tidy rows of shrubbery and still-spectacular displays of rhododendrons. Walking faster and faster, I narrowly avoided colliding with Trefoyle, who looked a bit guilty as he stepped out from behind a tall yew hedge, munching on his Kendal Mint Cake.

"Plumtree! You take your exercise at a brisk pace, don't you?" He glanced backwards, as if to see whether someone was still there. I heard rapid footsteps moving away from us, behind the hedge. "I say, I *am* impressed. I can never find people who keep up with me."

I knew that he'd said it just to let whoever else was in the garden move away. "Yes. Particularly when I'm—Trefoyle." I stopped. It took all my self-control to compose the next sentence. "I need you to tell me: Was I invited to join this club, one, to help publish your yearly editions, two, solely to ferret out the thief of my politically vital incunable, or, three, to honour my family, our publishing house, and our collection?"

Looking down at the ground, he chewed on his lower lip for a moment. Then he met my eyes squarely and spoke, his voice resigned. "Why do you ask me this now?"

"Several members chatting in the library, who didn't know I was in the gallery. I'd rather not name names."

"So like your father, Plumtree." He sighed deeply. "Please, join me."

We began to walk towards the sea, its rumble against the rocky shoreline growing louder by the second. "I won't deny it: I told the group it wouldn't hurt to have a book publisher in our ranks. But that was mere window dressing, Plumtree. First of all, you've earned the right to be here, between your publishing success and your family collection. And we all regret not inviting your father to join before his death. He was next on the list, you know. So you would have been invited with or *without* the Bedchamber book coming to light."

We walked on.

"Now that you know the truth about the Bedchamber book," Trefoyle went on, "you might say you have twice the reason to be here. *And*—I hadn't really intended to come out with this just yet"—he gnawed on his lip again—"the truth is, Plumtree, I need your help to sort out another frightful muddle. . . . I don't suppose you remember the newspaper accounts of old Ashleigh's death?" Trefoyle asked, looking up at me.

Startled, I said that in fact I did. "Horrible, as I recall. He died of a stroke during the last club dinner, didn't he?"

Trefoyle shook his head. "That's the story the ex-editor of the *Times*, a friend of ours, was able to get into the paper. Actually, he didn't die from natural causes."

I stopped, turned to look at him. Now we stood a shadow's length from the sea. Its roar was deafening. "What are you saying?" I shouted.

He moved his mouth closer to my ear. "Plumtree, someone here killed old Ashleigh. And I've reason to believe another murder will occur—this weekend."

CHAPTER 7

[He] is too fond of books and it has turned [his] brain.

—LOUISA MAY ALCOTT

Trefoyle's face was grim. Again he sighed, and motioned to a bench nearby. "It's the Valdarfer Boccaccio. People are obsessed by it. They'll literally *kill* to get it. Old Ashleigh was the last to own it before passing it on to his son." Trefoyle stared out at the violent sea. The setting seemed all too appropriate for what he was suggesting.

"But for some reason, after his father's death young Ashleigh sold it immediately to Osgood Forsythe. No one really knows why; perhaps he couldn't bear the sight of the thing anymore. But here's the main point: You saw what happened today at the shooting party. I fear for Forsythe's life. You wouldn't think that normally sane men could behave in such a way, but, you see, deChauncey's ancestor competed with Chesterton's ancestor to purchase the Boccaccio and other significant bits of the Duke of Windlesham's library in 1812."

He shrugged. "Perhaps in some way he is out to capture the Valdarfer *Decameron* once and for all. I think deChauncey's become a bit unbalanced, though I've always found him an immensely likable and sporting young man. But he's come upon hard times. He hasn't the money to buy the Boccaccio legitimately, even if Forsythe would sell. So you see."

Good God! I saw why Ian had recommended I keep quiet about my Boccaccio. I shook my head. "But surely even if Forsythe died, the Valdarfer edition wouldn't go to *deChauncey*. It doesn't make any sense. And, if you suspect such a thing, why haven't you rung the police? Or sent us all home again?" I wanted to say, *What on earth do you expect if you allow a madman to roam the premises with a loaded shotgun?*

Trefoyle sat up and spoke urgently. "As you know, we've something important to accomplish here that requires everyone's presence. Any one of them—particularly deChauncey, considering his current instability—might have the book we need. And putting the police in the middle of it would only hamper our efforts. Plumtree, you've acquired an—er, a reputation—for dealing with this sort of thing. Please. Help me keep tabs on this lot. Keep an eye on deChauncey, won't you, and for God's sake, protect Forsythe." He blinked back tears, and I found myself putting a hand on his shoulder.

"I'll do what I can, of course." I felt a bit overwhelmed by my various responsibilities, and not a little afraid. These people were one signature short of a full book. Ian had mentioned eccentricity, but . . . "Will we be able to meet and talk about this during the weekend?"

"Yes. I'll come and find you; we'll have an excuse to talk while I show you my collections tomorrow. And I daresay you'll learn a good bit at dinner tonight." He stood reluctantly, as if his duty as host called.

I got to my feet too. "I'll do what I can."

"I know you will."

"Are you going back . . . ?" I gestured toward the castle.

"In a moment, yes. You go ahead."

Thus dismissed, I left him alone, staring down at the waves crashing relentlessly onto the rocks.

Back in my room, I closed the heavy wooden door securely behind me and turned the lock. I flopped on the bed, fervently wishing that I didn't have to endure *more* drinks and then dinner with these people. Murderers? Thieves? People who shot their friends—supposedly by accident—for the sake of an old book? Prominent citizens who falsified newspaper reports? People who firmly declared me beneath them but still wanted to use me?

I dug for Sarah's framed photo in my bag and found it. Her face radiated joy, while at the same time showing the depth of the pain she had suffered. Her heroism, not only in the face of losing her first husband, but in the way she had twice saved my life in dangerous situations, regularly reduced me to a sentimental heap of emotion. And she'd stayed with me through many more unlikely circumstances, all of them arising from my publishing career.

I shook my head, placing her picture on the bedside table, and began to pace. How had I managed to embroil myself in yet another deadly mess?

I stopped, facing the tapestry, and saw that the antique piece featured the unlikely image of a woman, barebreasted and rather wild looking, with two goats. The customary leaves, rabbits, squirrels, and birds decorated the edges of the needlework.

Goats? Was this some myth I'd missed in my public school days?

I shook my head. A glance at my watch told me that in twenty minutes I was expected to appear for aperitifs. I groaned, very much aware that I was still feeling the effects of "tea." I decided to take a moment to check on my

Bedchamber book prints, and felt down to the bottom of my overnight bag. The comforting crackle of the paper envelope reassured me that the prints were safe beneath the false bottom. On the way out of the bag my fingertips brushed Margulies's modern Boccaccio, and on a whim I pulled it out. Perhaps I could absorb a story or two before the next round of overindulgence.

I skimmed his editor's note quickly before beginning, noting again that the *Decameron*, written in 1354, contained one hundred stories told over ten days by a group of young men and women who had fled the deadly plague in Florence. They'd gathered at a house—a palace, actually— in the Italian countryside to seek refuge and entertain one another after the horrors of the pestilential city.

With a little smile, I thought that it was not unlike what the Dibdin Club's meeting here at Castle Trefoyle was meant to be—a refuge from London, offering fellowship and recreation for the members. My smile faded, however, as I thought of the flu plaguing London at the moment. Reality was coming a bit too close to fiction again.

Too often—three times in as many years—I had found myself living out classic bits of literature. I know it sounds ridiculous—impossible, even—but these episodes always held very real and drastic consequences for me. Worse, they'd proved to be tragic, and even deadly for others. The strangest thing about these dramatic manifestations of literary works in my life was that they seemed somehow, at their root, a benign and logical consequence of my actions within my chosen profession. I'd come to see them rather philosophically as a bit of judicious editing of my life by the Senior Publisher in the Sky.

I began to skim some of the "Novells," or stories, told by the friends as they enjoyed the countryside on the first day. The tales, fairly short, were really quite entertaining. Lots of mistaken and hidden identities, pirate ships, and fortunes reversed—not merely once or twice, but as many as nine times. Most led to the same conclusion: an honourable person, if he or she behaved virtuously, would triumph through adversity. As long as honour was upheld, then property was restored and integrity publicly acknowledged. True love and faithfulness were always richly rewarded.

I flipped through the pages until I found myself at the sixth story of the second day. Margulies's footnote at the bottom of the page told me that in the well-known but anonymous translation of the seventeenth century, "roebuck" had mistakenly been translated as "goats."

Incredulous, I raced through the rather touching story, which apparently featured the woman in the tapestry now hanging in my bedchamber—one Madame Beritola, whose children had been stolen by a band of pirates. They left the poor woman literally adrift, alone, on a ship. The vessel eventually was washed up on an island, where, her breasts still full of milk from nursing her baby, she suckled the roebucks to relieve some of her grief over the lost human kids.

I let the book fall back onto the bed. Staring at the tapestry, I got a distinct crawling feeling on the back of my neck. At that moment I wanted very much to escape from the room, and in fact the castle and the club altogether. But one didn't simply walk away from a Dibdin Club anniversary weekend—even if this one seemed extraordinarily and increasingly complicated. So, cursing my reluctance to depart from accepted social practice, I dressed for dinner and descended the ancient, royally red-lined stairs. Squaring my shoulders, I entered the library and told myself to bear up.

Colin Jones-Harris, an acquaintance of my own age, stood with a clump of members I had not yet met. He gestured to me to join his group. I didn't know Jones-Harris well, but had seen him often at the Athenaeum. It was commonly known that he was heir to a fortune amassed over hundreds of years from importing tea. Colin had never done a day's work in his life in the tea company; he devoted himself exclusively to carousing and womanising.

An after-tea contingent of roughly twenty-five men had arrived, making up the majority of the Dibdin Club. I knew many on sight from photos in the newspapers and so forth, but very few personally. I glanced across the room and saw the famous old gentleman whose family had practically started banking in Britain, the Duke of Beckham. Unable to help myself, I stole a glance at his feet. Bedroom slippers even with his evening dress, just as the legend had it.

Small candles had been set out about the room, presumably to illuminate the hors d'oeuvres on the tables. The library roared with hilarity and lively chatter. A string quartet played chamber music in the gallery, but it was barely audible over the raucous laughter and raised voices.

Charmed by the energy of the gathering, and the inescapable beauty of the surroundings, I'd nearly reached Jones-Harris's little conversational knot when Hawkes sidled up with yet another neat Scotch. Seeing the *no, not again!* expression on my face, he spoke discreetly into my ear. "I thought you might like to try our still ginger beer, sir. Looks ever so much like Glenfiddich."

Relieved, I thanked him warmly. As I did, I had an idea. "Hawkes, do you have a moment?"

"Yes, of course, sir."

I leaned towards him; he was perhaps eight inches shorter than I was, which made confidential conversations difficult. Still, the noise in the room would easily cover my words. "Can you tell me anything about what went on at the shooting party? We all noticed that the pigeon deChauncey tried to hit came from a different direction."

"My thoughts precisely, sir. I'm glad you asked. I did

find something rather strange that makes me think someone planned the 'accident.' I'd like to show you—but I can't do it just now. If I might take the liberty of finding you at a more opportune time . . ."

"Yes, of course. I'd be grateful. Thanks very much, Hawkes."

"Plumtree," Jones-Harris said, gripping my arm and pulling me once again into his circle. "It won't do at all to fraternise with the servants. Meet Turnbull, Marchmain, and Hindleford." He was slurring his words a bit, but seemed steady enough on his feet. I smiled and nodded at the new acquaintances.

"All right, Jones-Harris? Partaking generously of the venerable stream of Haslewood's legend, I see," I teased him. "Looks as if you've already had quite a good party."

His eyes widened in childlike wonder. "Had? *Had!*" He guffawed helplessly. His friends, too, also looked ready to collapse with hilarity. Drink sloshed out of their glasses and onto the carpet beneath our feet. As Jones-Harris waved his gin wildly, I stepped aside to avoid smelling like a distillery.

"Plummers, don't you know, old boy, my literary lad." Wiping tears from his eyes, he said, "The best is yet to come! The famed Dibdin Damsel is here for our pleasure. Even a slave to virtue like you needs a final fling before he ties the knot." Looking round at his friends, he confided, "He's getting married in a few months."

All made a big show of looking grim on my behalf and offering consolation and sympathy. Turnbull alone looked actually happy for me. *Turnbull,* I thought. Good heavens. The name brand of the gin that had oiled the cogs of Britain for centuries—the very sort Jones-Harris was sloshing over Trefoyle's priceless rugs.

"She makes the rounds all night," Jones-Harris continued confidentially. "She'll come straight in to your room unless you leave your necktie on the doorknob. Which, of course, you'd be *insane* to do."

I began to perceive that he was serious. The lecherous smiles on the faces of the men to whom he'd introduced me, with the exception of Turnbull, who looked slightly uncomfortable, convinced me that there was indeed a Dibdin Damsel.

Now that Jones-Harris had started, he couldn't be stopped. Each comment he made drew a greater cheer from his cohorts. "'Sa different girl each year. The bloomingest of Bloomsbury, that's the criterion. The *bitch* o' the *bookmen!*" he crowed, the fog of alcohol in his brain persuading him he was an alliterative genius. "The *best* of *breasts!*" He and his companions seemed ready to collapse. I wondered how they'd make it through to dinner. All round us, groups were surprisingly rowdy, and the noise level quite high. No one seemed to pay particular attention to us.

As I sipped my ginger beer, Jones-Harris seemed to enjoy a brief flash of renewed lucidity. "Plumtree," he leered. "Fancy a bet?"

"What about?" I'd been around enough drunks to last a lifetime, between university in America and the flotilla holidays I'd led in the Agean.

"Your fiancée."

I snapped to attention, looked him straight in his bleary eyes. "What on earth do you mean?"

He smiled drunkenly. "I'll bet I can bed your sweet Sarah between now and your wedding."

What he said was so unexpected, so shockingly tasteless, I was at a complete loss for words. The very thought was not only disgusting but impossible: Sarah would beat Jones-Harris to a bloody pulp before she'd become his Dibdin Damsel. My next impulse was pity for such a sadly pickled brain.

"Jones-Harris, you're totally sloshed. You don't know what you're saying."

"We're on, then," he said quite clearly. Before anything further could pass between us, however, the gong sounded for dinner.

My drunken companions evaporated as if by magic, and Chesterton stood beside me. He looked positively legendary in evening dress. Judging from his similarity to portraits of his ancestors in the National Portrait Gallery, he might have been any one of them, visiting from the past.

"I say, Plumtree. You seem to know virtually everyone in the Dibdin already. Well done, my boy."

"Just a few old friends . . ."

"Well, I daresay you didn't know who belonged until you arrived here today." He straightened his tie and ushered me out of the library. "We don't publicise the membership, you know. Little enough privacy as it is these days, what?"

"Indeed." I looked down at the carpet that lined our path to the great room, intent on avoiding the duke's eyes. Anyone in England who could read or watch television knew that certain embarrassing photographs had come to light illustrating the duke's penchant for not only women but deviant practises, mostly aboard his yacht or on his island estates. Such was the aristocracy that this was accepted as normal; he and his sort felt that it was the paparazzi with their telephoto lenses who were at fault. I could accept the man at face value, understand that he had a great deal to offer, and was merely afflicted with a bit of moral weakness. Still, I was embarrassed for him—and I'm sure he felt it.

"Ah. Here we are." Chesterton solicitously took me to the head of the table and indicated the chair to his right. Surely he didn't mean me to sit in a place of honour above Trefoyle. But just then our host drew opposite and stood behind the chair to the left of Chesterton, smiling broadly.

"You're certain you want me to . . ."

Now it was Chesterton who wouldn't meet my eyes. "You will sit there, Plumtree," he commanded.

"Right," I acquiesced, and stood taking in the room as my fellow members assembled.

Miles of narrow, mediaeval table extended the length of the room. The wood was so old and well buffed through half a millennium of use that it looked like polished leather. Again, small candles lit the table subtly but effectively, and low clusters of orchids and gardenias, obtained at heaven knew what expense, adorned the table. I saw that it had all been designed to foster conversation among the members; no lofty candelabras prevented one member seeing another. The string quartet had moved itself into one corner of the great hall, and began playing as I sat. Silver charger plates with the Trefoyle crest, a golden trefoil on a background of deep blue, decorated each place. At a glance I could see that the cutlery was heavy sterling; the fork was large and substantial enough to make a sturdy garden tool.

"Hmm. Looks as if all forty have arrived. The customary excellent turnout," Chesterton said to Trefoyle.

"Yes. The four who are absent are either out of the country or down with flu." Trefoyle picked up his freshly filled glass of white wine as he eyed the table of men and women assembling in his hall with proprietary pleasure.

"Tell us, Plumtree," Chesterton said while a waiter filled my glass. "I've been eager to learn whether you're really the paragon of virtue the book world paints you."

I laughed. "Paragon I'm not, but I'm no fool. I've found the most brilliant, gorgeous, delightful woman in the world, and I'm not going to give her the least excuse to leave me."

Trefoyle and Chesterton exchanged what appeared to be

a sarcastic glance. I felt a ripple of suspicion. A combination of the way I'd been so deliberately put in this place, and the attitude of the two men gave me the impression that some sort of programme had been set for me that evening. I had a feeling they were carrying out a *plan* rather than a casual conversation.

"We all felt that way once, didn't we?" Chesterton asked Trefoyle, and drank greedily from his wineglass. When he set it down, the wine steward materialised at his side to refill it. I guessed that this must be an essential requirement for service at Dibdin Club events: solicitousness at the sight of an empty glass.

The fish course was placed in front of me, smoked salmon and toast triangles generously adorned with caviar; still we stood, waiting for the others to find their places.

"People don't realise what my true situation is," Chesterton sighed, looking longingly at his smoked salmon and the enticing pile of salty beluga roe. "They know only what they read in the paper. But my autobiography is coming out next year—from Kreidenfeld and Mickelson, your neighbours there, I believe, in Bedford Square, Plumtree. I am getting on in years, you know. The press has made such a hash of things lately, it's up to me to tell the real story."

"I'd be fascinated, if you're willing to tell us about it," I offered. People loved to talk about themselves, and I loved to listen. Besides, few lives in England had been as privileged or as notorious, as Chesterton's.

"Oh, do, Chesterton. Go on," urged Trefoyle.

The duke put down his glass and sighed. "All right, then. But first I've club matters to attend to. I believe we're all here at last. Archbishop? Would you do us the honour? By the way, have you met young Alex Plumtree?"

I looked to my right and saw, to my great surprise, that I was standing next to the Archbishop of Canterbury. "So sorry, Your Grace," I mumbled, horrified that I had ignored the churchman, having been caught up with Chesterton and Trefoyle. "What an honour."

"A pleasure," the esteemed archbishop pronounced with great dignity. I wasn't sure if he meant it would be a pleasure to say a blessing on the meal, or that it was a pleasure to meet me.

He rose, and as he did, the table fell silent. "Gracious Heavenly Father, we thank You for Your great goodness to us. We thank You for the magnificent books with which you have charged us, to preserve forever as England's own. We thank You for this gathering of like-minded bibliophiles, and ask that we might be worthy of Your blessing. In the name of our blessed Saviour, Jesus Christ, Amen."

I was struck by how unusual it was to have an unabashedly Christian blessing in what had become an increasingly secular society. Perhaps this was a tenet of the Dibdin Club I wasn't aware of, or simply another strong tradition.

As the archbishop sat, amidst mumblings of "Amen" from around the table, I felt a movement on my left. With an effort, the illustrious president of the Dibdin Club pushed back his chair, rose, and unrolled a sheet of paper that had been tied with a scarlet ribbon. Unrolling mine quickly, I saw it was headed "The ordre of the Tostes" and was printed in an imitation of gothic type. A subheading read "To give a freshness to ancient lore." I suspected we were about to reenact the toasts of years gone by.

Chesterton raised the wineglass that had been replenished yet again and cleared his throat. The diners, seeing their leader standing with his glass, rose and held their glasses out in front of them. I followed suit. Fascinating, I thought. Toasts before dinner? The Dibdin Club obviously had its own traditions.

"The immortal Memory of John, Duke of Windlesham—of Christopher Valdarfer, Printer of the *Decameron* of 1471—of Gutenberg, Fust, and Schoeffer; the Inventors of the Art of Printing—of William Caxton, the Father of the British Press—of Dame Juliana Barnes, and the St. Albans Press—of Wynkyn De Worde, and Richard Pynson, the illustrious Successors of William Caxton—of the Aldine Family, at Venice—of the Giunta Family, at Florence—The Society of the Bibliophiles, at Paris—the prosperity of the Dibdin Club—the Cause of Bibliomania all over the World—and the preservation of England's own books for Herself."

"Hear, hear!" came the chorus. I joined in, though I wasn't certain I understood the final toast. The preservation of England's own books for Herself? It sounded like the peculiar phrase in the archbishop's prayer. I remembered it because it had seemed so strange: *the magnificent books with which you have charged us, to preserve forever as England's own*. And why only England, not Great Britain?

But in the next moment I'd decided that he'd been referring to the private libraries of all the assembled members, which in fact did encompass the bulk of England's fine specimens.

"If you look under your charger plates, you'll find a menu for tonight's dinner. We have copied with several small exceptions the menu for a Dibdin dinner on the night of 17 June 1818 at the Albion. As you can see, your host insisted upon an extraordinary dining experience for both evenings of our gathering."

The party sat down again, more serious than before. I pulled out the menu and studied it. My jaw dropped.

FIRST COURSE.

1818: Turtle. 1999: Smoked salmon with beluga caviar.

1818: Turtle Cutlets.

1818: Turtle Fin.

1999: Lobster.

1999: Prawns.

Turbot.

Boiled Chickens.

Ham.

Sautée of Haddock.

Chartreuse.

1818: Turtle. 1999: Salmon.

1818: Turtle. 1999: Swordfish.

Tendrons of Lamb.

Fillets of Whiting.

Tongue.

Roast Chickens.

1818: Turtle Fin. 1999: Halibut.

1818: Fricandeau of Turtle.
1999: Crab.

Cold Roast Beef on Side Table.

Whitebait.

SECOND COURSE.

Venison.

THIRD COURSE.

Larded Poults.

Tart.

Cheesecakes.

Artichoke Bottoms.

Jelly.

Prawns.

Roast Quails.

Roast Leveret.

Salade Italien.

Creme Italien.

Peas.

Cabinet Pudding.

Tourt.

Roast Goose.

I tucked the menu back beneath my plate. I hadn't guessed that the evening would have such a formal structure, nor that it would be rooted in tradition down to the toasts and the menu. But it all fuelled my impression that each moment had been carefully planned. Even the shooting party and the "tea" had had a calculated air about them, despite the accidental (?) shooting. What a feat for Chesterton and Trefoyle, I thought, to manage such a vast, eventful party with apparent effortlessness.

Chesterton settled himself again in his seat. As he did, I suddenly saw him in a different light. With his face so serious, even grim, he gave the impression of a deeply tired and discouraged man. The glow from the candles illuminated the fleshy bags under his eyes. A layer of puffiness seemed to pad his features. No doubt the duties of the patriarch of England's most distinguished family weighed heavily on Chesterton, not to mention the publication of his indiscretions in lurid colour magazines, and leadership of the Dibdin Club. And that was to ignore the toll his gourmandising and tippling took on an aging and obviously sedentary body.

Still, the noble features of the family that had spawned one of Britain's greatest prime ministers, not to mention great military heroes of the past and untold generations in the House of Lords, remained. In the next moment he was smiling, his well-practised grin dispelling the exhaustion and dissipation I'd seen an instant before.

"So, you want to hear my story, do you?" He shovelled goodly hunks of smoked salmon onto a triangle of toast, piled on lots of caviar, and popped it all into his mouth. I recalled a passage from Haslewood's *Dibdin Dissipations* lent me by Ian, a quotation of a servant that seemed to apply to the Dibdinians: *Sir, they eats with a woraciousness that is wery extonishing.*

"I'd very much like to hear it, Duke."

"Go on, then, Chesterton, don't keep us waiting," Trefoyle said.

The duke began by speaking to the archbishop. I was mildly disconcerted, as the conversation had begun between the two of us. But it was hardly surprising, I supposed, since the archbishop outranked me in every conceivable way.

"One word describes the story of my life: *misunderstood*. If my publisher would have accepted it, I'd have used it for the title." Chesterton took another swig of wine. "I know you've all heard about my so-called treachery in matters of buying and selling. Foreclosing on debts, unfaithfulness to my wife. But in my autobiography, written with the help of young Ms. Garthwaite at Kreidenfeld & Mickelson, I'm going to set the record straight. Imagine my frustration at being so grossly misunderstood in one matter after another. It all stems from the average man's jealousy of anyone with my surname."

"Tell us about that scandal in the *Times* last year, what it was really about," Trefoyle urged.

"Hmmph!" Chesterton huffed. "Yes, the press has been a large part of all this. I offered to purchase the failing racing stables of a couple that I knew from my steeplechase days. They and I knew the fair value of the property and the livestock, which they duly accepted. But when the day came to close the deal, all of the really valuable horses had vanished—roughly half of the twenty. As I walked round the stables before going to the house to close the sale, one of the stable lads told me the best horses had been sold the day before.

"So, while I was surprised, I knew they were in desperate straits. I didn't say anything, because it would have seemed rude to accuse these old friends of any sort of treachery. So I knocked off a good many thousand pounds from the price and wrote them the cheque as promised. On the spot. They took it, signed the papers, and the stables were mine. As I was leaving—after a very convivial drink in the study, I might add—they noticed the amount of the cheque, saw it wasn't for the amount agreed upon, and started behaving as though they were very offended. I stated the obvious, that the valuable horses, nearly half the stock, were gone! Why on earth would I pay for horses I would never see? They never explained why they had sold the horses, which they jolly well knew were to've been included in the transaction."

The waiter came, and one by one exchanged our salmon plates for turbot in a sauce, altering the cutlery as required.

Chesterton continued. "They were absolutely indignant. My old friends ran to the papers immediately with the story that they'd been tricked—taken advantage of by the wealthy and unscrupulous Chesterton. My *old friends!* Of course I didn't embarrass them further in their desperate financial situation by defending myself. I just let it go. *Noblesse oblige* and all that. And that's only a start."

"How frightfully impressive. I don't think I've ever heard a story of greater restraint and kindness, your grace." The archbishop looked at Chesterton with admiration. "You don't mean to say that *more* of this sort of thing has happened to you?"

"Indeed I do," Chesterton said a bit self-righteously. The waiter refilled his glass, and the duke seemed to sit up a bit straighter in his chair. "No doubt you've heard of the alleged mistreatment of my wife?" He looked pointedly at me.

I could only nod, my mouth full of fish. I had, of course, heard the sensational story. His wife had appeared at the local constabulary near their country estate, beaten black and blue. She claimed Chesterton was responsible and demanded that the adulterous fiend be locked up straightaway. The scandal was so lurid, it was difficult to forget. Most of the nation was of the opinion that he'd triumphed because he had more money than she and therefore a better barrister, but I suppose none of us really knew the truth.

"I'll tell you what *really* happened." He took a large bite of fish, chewed enthusiastically, and washed it down with the inevitable. "My ex-wife, God bless her soul, has a—well, there's no pleasant way to put it—a *mental* problem. I've kept it quiet for forty years. The children have never breathed a word. But it was one hell of a cross to bear, I can tell you. Sorry, Archbishop."

"Not at all, my dear man. Go on." The churchman inclined toward Chesterton, practically leaning over my plate in his eagerness to hear more. He was so close, I caught the scent of his shampoo.

"Well. My wife had the idea that people were out to get her—paranoid schizophrenia, I believe it's termed. We had it diagnosed when she was still quite young, but she wouldn't accept the diagnosis. She never took her medication."

"Good heavens!" The archbishop had abandoned his meal entirely.

"At times I've wondered if the heavens *are* in fact good," Chesterton said in wry riposte. "But late in life I have come to believe more than ever in God's existence and beneficence. At any rate, on the night in question, she came at me with *knives.*"

The archbishop dropped his garden-tool fork; it clattered onto his plate.

"Anyone with a bit of sense would've noticed that after she appeared at the police station, no one saw me for weeks. I claimed to be seeking privacy at the country house, but actually she'd injured me so badly, I didn't want to humiliate her. In defending myself, I'd hurt her as little as possible while preserving my life. Eventually, a tall cupboard fell on her—she was trying to tip it over on *me* as I lay nearly unconscious on the floor. That was how she received the bulk of her injuries."

"Gracious Lord!" the archbishop exclaimed.

I couldn't imagine the proper way to respond to all

this, and so took refuge in sipping my wine. The waiter came and removed our turbot, offering a choice of boiled chicken and sautéed haddock, or roast chicken and Chartreuse. I'd actually been looking forward to the ham, which according to the menu was a valid choice at this point, and the waiter saw the question in my eyes.

"I'm sorry, sir, there was some difficulty in procuring the ham."

"*What?*" boomed Chesterton. The waiter shrank back. "I told the countess what to order weeks ago."

"I know, sir. You'll have to take it up with her. Something about nothing but hens . . ."

Chesterton and Trefoyle looked at each other significantly. Clearly this meant something to them. Chesterton was the first to recover, and blustered, "Such incompetence, and at this level! No ham . . . Please excuse me, I'll be back in a moment." He rose, again with difficulty. He was obviously tipsy as he strode down the table to where the Countess sat in animated conversation with Osgood Forsythe. Chesterton had a whispered, intense confrontation with her and stalked back to us, his face red.

Naively, I wondered if there was always so much drama at Dibdin Club dinners.

"It's all right, Chesterton," Trefoyle said soothingly when his friend returned. "It's a fine meal. No one could possibly notice anyway, with all this wine in them. Only Plumtree has been moderate enough, and, I might add, clever enough to notice."

I should have just taken the chicken, I thought.

Chesterton shot Trefoyle a look as he seated himself again. "Yes. Quite."

Seeming to sense that Chesterton was going to tell no more fantastic stories just then, the archbishop tactfully changed the subject. "Did you hear about the Spenser going to the Saudis last Friday?"

"You're joking," Trefoyle said. "Where were *we?*"

I couldn't seem to follow what they were saying. Did the Saudi-Arabian government buy a book by Spenser from the British Museum, perhaps at an auction that they would have liked to attend?

"We can't catch them all, *damn* them," Chesterton said so quietly that I wasn't certain he'd said anything of the sort. He tucked disgustedly into his boiled chicken. After one bite, he demanded the waiter take it away. "But Plumtree doesn't want to hear about all this," he said loudly. "Tell us. What of this Order of the Bedchamber book we've been hearing about? Such a loss. Any luck in recovering it?"

"No," I answered. I carefully kept my eyes from straying to Trefoyle. "But the authorities are working on it . . . and we have an idea who might be responsible."

The duke hesitated briefly. "You do? That's marvellous. Whom do you suspect?"

"I don't want to name names, of course, but I believe it's someone who understands the historical significance of the volume. A great deal of trouble was taken, repeatedly, to obtain it—unfortunately the last attempt succeeded. I've no doubt we'll have our answer quite soon. My only real worry is about the book's condition when it is returned."

Chesterton buried his nose in his wineglass, and the archbishop piped up. "I understand the book claims Richard I was murdered."

"Exactly right, Your Grace." Word certainly travelled fast in these circles. No article had appeared about the theft of the book; we hadn't rung the police after the theft because the PM had wanted to keep control of the situation himself. And though the break-in at Diana's had got in the paper, she hadn't told them the title of the book she'd brought home from her work. Still, all these men knew the book's story. Fascinating.

"Do you mind my asking how you've heard about

the contents of the book?" I tried to make the question sound innocent.

"Er—well, let's see," Chesterton said calmly. "I believe my friend at Quaritch told me—or was it Maggs?"

Ah-ha! Was Chesterton our mysterious buyer? If he was, he certainly stayed cool under questioning. Or had he really just had a chat with the book dealer?

The archbishop looked thoughtful. "You know, I can't recall where I heard it. . . . The book's caused quite a sensation, you know—everyone's talking about it."

I didn't really suspect the archbishop of having anything to do with the book's disappearance; I simply couldn't picture the Church of England despatching burglars disguised as laser printer repairmen to steal books.

Trefoyle looked at me, careful not to hint at our shared knowledge with eyes or gestures. "Things have a way of working out, Plumtree. You'll see. Thieves, no matter how intelligent, always make mistakes. I have no doubt you'll get your book back, and quite soon."

And that was the extent of our discussion on the subject.

Dinner wore on, course after course. I was exhausted, not only by Chesterton's dramatic tales but by my own attempt to convey a confident knowledge of who'd taken the book. I realised that this put me in a tight spot, as the thief was going to be inclined to silence me. But at least I would know, then, who it was.

I also found it difficult to make entertaining chit-chat, especially under the circumstances. Usually I preferred silence as the safest route, but they kept trying to draw me out, and I didn't want to appear awkward. We talked about Plumtree Press, some of my own misrepresentations in the news media, and my father's accomplishments.

Finally, after four and a half hours, dinner was over.

•   •   •

My relief was immense when Chesterton led the procession to the garden for—what else?—after-dinner drinks. The cool sea breeze was quite refreshing after the lengthy meal and an incessantly refilled wineglass. I couldn't say I was surprised at the extent of the tippling so far; I'd read in the *Dibdin Dissipations* just how many bottles of wine per member were consumed at club dinners. It had stuck in my mind that sixty-two bottles of wine had been purchased to serve twenty men—and that wasn't including the volumes of beer and ale that many of them preferred. The tolerance these men and women displayed for alcohol was truly amazing.

As Trefoyle passed me on his way into the garden, he said close to my ear, "Remember, watch Forsythe. Don't let deChauncey get at him. I'm counting on you, Plumtree."

I ambled over to where Forsythe stood. DeChauncey wasn't far off, and to my dismay seemed to be eyeing Forsythe.

"Ah, good evening, Plumtree," Forsythe said.

I smiled. "How's the arm?"

"Fine, fine. In a few days I'll never know it happened."

"I hear you're the proud owner of the Valdarfer Boccaccio," I said. "From what I hear, it's quite the coveted item." *If only he knew*, I thought.

He stiffened at my mention of the book. "Yes, the Boccaccio is mine, but I fail to see why everyone must discuss it incessantly. I'm extremely proud of it, as you can imagine, and a bit worried, considering your own recent experience."

"Mmm. It's what we all dread. From the moment news of my find went out on the grapevine, someone was after that book. They tried theft twice, without success, and then attempted to buy it legitimately. In the end, they stole it after all."

Forsythe shook his head. "What's the world coming to?"

"The strange thing is, I don't think it's a common criminal. I'm quite sure I know who it is—and it's someone who knows a great deal about books, and understands the full historical significance of this one."

"You mean the fact that Richard the Lion-Heart was murdered?"

"Um, could be." I smiled. Having dangled my bait, I thought perhaps we should discuss his situation with deChauncey. "Trefoyle's worried about you, you know." I glanced at deChauncey, who lurked nearby. "Perhaps you should watch your back. I've been keeping an eye out for you."

"How absurd!" Forsythe said coldly. "That shooting accident was, if anything, arranged by someone to make deChauncey look bad—and it's all because of this ridiculous rumour that he's after my Boccaccio. I don't want to hear another word of it. And I don't need *you* to look after me." He excused himself abruptly and sought greener pastures.

Well done, Alex, I told myself. I'd managed to drive him off in less than five minutes.

I wasn't sure I shared Forsythe's confidence that someone had framed deChauncey. Who knew what effect a few drinks and the late hour would have on a man with a loose screw?

DeChauncey stood in a circle with the bedroom-slippered duke and two others I didn't know. Conversation had become quite difficult; most of my fellow members were falling-down drunk. Still, I stuck with my job of keeping an eye on the Forsythe/deChauncey situation and even had a brief chat with the Duke of Beckham, who regarded me as if I were dirt beneath his smooth leather soles.

After an hour, deChauncey was casting puzzled looks in my direction. After another hour, his glances had grown distinctly less friendly. It was after two in the morning when he finally took me aside, looked me in the eye, and told me off.

"Look, Plumtree," he said, slurring his words a bit. "Just because I run the most prestigious art museum in London doesn't mean I'm the only person in the Dibdin worth hanging around." Then he lowered his voice, speaking with clenched teeth. "And I'm not gay, no matter what you've heard. I *certainly* didn't think you were. So why don't you just *bugger off*!"

As he stalked away, I felt utterly humiliated. To make matters worse, Chesterton's personal secretary, an insipid-looking young man with overactive sweat glands and long strands of hair combed forward over his bald spot, had overheard deChauncey. He winked at me, smirking, as he moved off.

But humiliation was only part of it. I was torn. I had promised to keep Forsythe from coming to harm, and Trefoyle was depending on me. I'd seen the earl looking worriedly in my direction ever since dinner, sometimes nodding approvingly. I couldn't throw Forsythe to the wolves for the sake of my ego.

Three A.M. came, then four. I had chatted at some length with nearly everyone by then. Hawkes came over with a glass of golden liquid and said, "I'll show you what I was talking about in the morning, all right? It's a hand-throwing tool that someone must have used to launch the errant pigeon. I can't leave until everyone else does. Here—I thought perhaps you might enjoy a *real* whisky at this point."

"Yes, please," I said. I realised that for deChauncey to have an excuse to shoot the stray pigeon, he had to have a partner. Who'd been at the far end of the line, closest to where the clay disc had come from? Who would have launched it? Trefoyle had been there as far as I remembered, but . . .

My speculations were disrupted by a glimpse of

Osgood Forsythe retreating into the castle with his arm around the countess's shoulders. He'd be safe for the night.

"Thank *God*," I breathed, taking a sip of my whisky.

Next to me, Hawkes looked a bit taken aback. "It was nothing, sir. Anytime at all, sir."

CHAPTER 8

Sure as death.

—GIOVANNI BOCCACCIO,
IL FILOSTRATO

H alf-past four in the morning. No wonder I felt so gruesome. Yawning, I loosened my tie, stripped off my jacket, and gathered up toothbrush and toothpaste to perform my evening—or, rather, morning—ablutions.

But as I turned, I was startled to see a woman in my bedroom. She hadn't knocked, she hadn't said a word, but when I turned round, there she was—unclothed and wrapped in a huge white sheet.

"Clarissa!" I exclaimed. Clarissa Garthwaite was a friend from the Young Publishers Society—the woman Chesterton had just told me was editing his memoirs. She ruthlessly wielded her red pen as a highly respected copy-editor at Kreidenfeld & Mickelson.

It was difficult to believe that this nearly naked woman with blond hair falling loosely about her shoulders was the same person. I'd never seen Clarissa without her hair in a severe bun, her feet in sensible shoes, her figure concealed in a navy-blue suit. Though my mind was working at half speed, it didn't take long to figure out what she was doing there: She was the Dibdin Damsel whom Jones-Harris had anticipated so gleefully. No one could have been less expected in that role.

Exhausted as I was, I'd forgotten to hang the necktie from my door.

I massaged my forehead with my fingertips, anguished at this gross misunderstanding. "Clarissa, you don't understand. I'm about to be married, I wouldn't, couldn't possibly . . ."

Then I noticed how very distraught she was. Her face was a frightening shade of grey, and her eyes looked glassy.

"Hang on," I said. "Here. Sit down." I grasped her badly shaking arm through the sheet and guided her to the edge of the bed. Putting my arm around her, I tried to still her shuddering form. Poor woman . . . what she must have been through that night. She'd clearly come to me for help. What had Chesterton done to make her humiliate herself in this particularly horrible way? Perhaps threatened the loss of her job at Kreidenfeld & Mickelson?

"Clarissa, what is it?" As if what she'd been asked to do wasn't bad enough.

"M-Margul-ies," she stammered, making a heroic effort to get the words out. She pointed vaguely toward my door. "He—he d-died while . . ." Silently, she turned to face me and stared into my eyes.

She might as well have told me that Castle Trefoyle was falling into the sea. Shock about Margulies and pity for Clarissa struck me in equal measures. Absurdly, it occurred to me that Van would be furious about Clarissa, considering what I'd picked up at the restaurant the other night. "Dead!" I exclaimed. "Are you certain?" I gripped her hand to stop her pointing tragically towards the hallway; it was ice cold. I rubbed it between my two warm ones.

She nodded her head dumbly.

"Have you told Earl Trefoyle? Rung for an ambulance?"

"You don't know . . . It wasn't supposed to be . . . like this. . . ." She stared at me as if in a trance. Her words faded into a whisper.

I was losing her. "Clarissa." I stood and shook her gently. She stumbled and fell into my arms. Poor girl. "I need you to help me, Clarissa. Tell me why you haven't told the Earl, called for help?"

"I can't . . ." she whispered. She began to hyperventilate. *Dear God*, I thought. I gripped her arm hard enough to make it hurt a bit, and saw her look at me with surprise and fright.

"Now, listen, Clarissa. Do you have your own room here?"

She stared and nodded, her mouth open.

"Let's get you back there." Every second that passed might be spent resuscitating Margulies, but I couldn't just run out on her in this state, leaving her alone.

She nodded again, like a terrified child. I ran to the wardrobe and pulled my bathrobe off the hanger, a warm, hooded gift from Sarah with my initials embroidered on the plum towelling. After wrapping Clarissa in the thick garment, I guided her into the hallway.

"Where's your room?"

She pointed straight ahead; I hurried her in that direction.

"And Margulies's?" She pointed back down the hall on the left.

Chesterton's personal secretary was just passing into his room slightly ahead of us. As we hurried towards him, he leered at me and raised his eyebrows, smirking at my initials on Clarissa's breast.

"Listen, we need your help," I told him. "One of the members is ill. Can you take Clarissa to her room?" I left her with the unwilling man and dashed in the direction

Clarissa had indicated. There was a door ajar where she had pointed; I pushed it open with my elbow. My friend lay sprawled across the bed, nearly naked, his face too white. I fumbled with my inexperienced fingers for the pulse in his neck. At first I thought I felt something, but my heart was pounding so hard, I couldn't be sure it wasn't my own bounding pulse.

I began CPR, thinking of the advice I'd heard never to stop trying until help came. *Come on, Margulies, come on,* I urged my friend as I pumped his heart and breathed for him.

Hawkes appeared at my side. "I've rung for the ambulance; Chesterton's secretary said he'd tell Earl Trefoyle and the others.

"I'll have a go," Hawkes volunteered. Gratefully, I let him take over. I was spent. As I watched him work on my friend, it suddenly struck me that Hawkes was a very capable man. He was strong and extremely fit as well, qualities I hadn't noticed in him before.

Hawkes and I had traded twice more before we heard the bustle of ambulance men up the stairs. They strode into the room, and one of them pushed Hawkes aside. "We'll take over now, sir," he said as his colleague began checking for vital signs.

The colleague shook his head. "No point. He's gone."

The first streaks of dawn were appearing through the windows and a bird sang incongruously. *This can't be happening,* I thought. *It can't be real.*

"Are you certain?" I panted. I couldn't believe they had decided to give up so quickly. I went to my friend and placed my fingers on his neck. Nothing.

"We must find his Lordship," Hawkes told me. On the way out, we saw Chesterton's private secretary, who'd watched our futile attempts. "Didn't you ever find Earl Trefoyle?" Hawkes asked impatiently.

The obnoxious man shook his head and offered no excuse.

"Would you please stay with Margulies until we return?" I asked him, then turned to the ambulance men. "Please—please just hang on for a moment while we find Earl Trefoyle."

Hawkes led me off down the hall. At the very end, he knocked on a door and opened it without waiting for a response. A bit cheeky for hired help, I thought, even under the circumstances. Trefoyle sat at a round table in a sitting room, flanked by windows that overlooked the grey ocean. Stars and daylight were both still visible; I had the feeling I was caught in a bizarre time warp that surrounded the castle.

Chesterton, the archbishop, and Desmond Delacroix sat round the table with the earl. From all appearances, they'd been having a serious discussion. Why were they all assembled there at this ungodly hour? When Trefoyle looked up and saw us, he didn't seem startled at our interruption.

Chesterton stood quickly and crossed to an alcove behind the men, hidden to us, where he disappeared from our sight. It sounded as if he closed a door. Hawkes cleared his throat and glanced at me, almost as if to see whether I'd taken notice of Chesterton's activity. Chesterton came back and stood near Trefoyle; all watched us expectantly.

"I'm afraid we have bad news, sir," Hawkes said.

"Good God. What?" Trefoyle looked at me. His eyes asked, *Does this have something to do with the Bedchamber book?*

I shook my head ever so slightly, once. "It's Margulies Whitehead. I—it seems impossible, Trefoyle, but he's dead."

Immediately the quiet castle was transformed. At Trefoyle's instruction, Hawkes rang the local constabulary and a trusted local physician. Trefoyle, the other men, and I went straight to Margulies's room. They'd pulled a blanket over his face—Clarissa had taken the sheet.

Trefoyle took it all in at a glance and asked briskly, "How? What happened?"

"Heart attack, I'd say," the ambulance man said, filling out a form on a clipboard.

"But—" I objected, then stopped short. Margulies had certainly been a good candidate for a heart attack. It was just so difficult to accept that he was dead. And everyone but Hawkes, Clarissa, and I seemed disturbingly nonchalant about it.

The ambulance men were ready to go; Trefoyle asked them to please wait until Dr. Mortimer arrived. They both seemed to understand what this meant. "Hawkes, go down and watch for the doctor, will you?" Trefoyle said. It all seemed very strange to me . . . I wondered if, when people died, Trefoyle was always so dispassionate. Hawkes went down and returned quickly with the doctor and police constable.

"Mortimer. Burns. Thanks so much for coming," Trefoyle said, greeting the elderly doctor and constable, both clearly friends, at the door to Margulies's room. "Can you have a look at him, and tell us what you think . . ."

The elderly physician tottered over to the shape of my friend's body. "I'd say he died of cardiac arrest." He shook his head. "I'm sorry, Charles."

There was a moment of silence out of respect for this pronouncement. In the silence, Clarissa came to mind.

"Doctor, a woman was with our friend when he had the attack . . . if you wouldn't mind taking a look at her? I think she might be in shock," I said, feeling not a little stunned myself. I stole another glance at the shape of my friend under the blanket. It was impossible to believe he was dead.

He nodded. "Where is she?"

I showed him to her room and respectfully left them alone, then trudged back to Margulies's room in a daze. There, barely twenty minutes after the ambulance had arrived, they were carrying my friend out on a stretcher.

I might have been irrational, but it was all much too hasty for me. "Wait a moment," I asked the ambulance men. "Will tests be performed to establish the cause of death?"

"We already know it was a heart attack." I jumped as Trefoyle appeared, as people so often seemed to do in that castle, just behind my shoulder. "Dr. Mortimer confirmed it."

"But can he be *absolutely* certain? Did they check to see whether anything else—"

"My dear boy. In Cornwall, when someone dies of a heart attack, that's the end of it. This isn't London."

It was all wrong, somehow. Everything in me was crying out that they should stop. I had the ghastly feeling that Trefoyle and even the doctor wanted, *expected*, Margulies to have died of a heart attack.

"I'm going with him," I declared, striding out to join the two stretcher-bearers.

"I'm sorry, sir! That's not allowed," Burns objected, gripping my arms rather viciously.

"Not—!" I fought against the constable.

"Now, Plumtree," Trefoyle said, dismissing the constable's forcible restraint with a little gesture. I shook the man off me, outraged. "I know you were friends with Margulies, that he was even one of your authors. But I also think you're a bit overwrought. A terrible thing has happened. It is difficult to fathom. I think you should go to bed and rest."

Rest was the last thing I could do. Without thinking, I ran to Margulies and ripped the blanket off his face. I reached my hand to his neck again to feel for a pulse.

But there was none. He was cold. He was absolutely, inarguably, dead.

Strong arms again gripped me, pulling me away roughly from my friend. It was the constable, Burns. "Sir! This is *not allowed*!" he bleated.

"He's all right," Trefoyle said. "Leave it with me." The earl came as if to take my arm, and I shrugged him off.

I stalked off to Clarissa's room to check on her, though

I was eager to get back to my own room and lock the door securely. The doctor was just leaving her as I entered.

"Ah, there you are," he said. "I've sedated her. I think she'll be all right tomorrow. Must've been a ghastly shock." I looked in at Clarissa, and seeing that she appeared to be sleeping, followed the doctor out and closed the door behind me. I still felt outraged by the way Margulies's death had been . . . *accepted.*

"Doctor," I said at the top of the stairs.

He turned back from the top step to look at me, his eyes hooded with fatigue.

"My friend might have been a touch overweight, and perhaps out of condition, but he's young for such a sudden death. How can you be so sure it was a heart attack?"

The doctor shrugged. He wasn't unkind; but he didn't seem at all concerned by my friend's death. In his line of work I supposed I might have expected as much. "It's always hard to believe it of our own friends," he replied. "A genetic weakness, perhaps? An unaccustomed level of physical activity?"

Was that a ghost of a smile beneath his seriousness?

"Believe me, young man, it's not as unusual as you might think."

I felt myself redden. The man knew exactly what had gone on that night. He turned and continued down the staircase. As I headed down the hall to my room, feeling dazed, I heard Trefoyle as if from far away. His distorted voice, through echoes and missed words, said something that sounded like ". . . upset? . . . too much?"

But I heard the doctor answer quite clearly, "He'll be all right. The lady was surprisingly distraught though; gave her something to help her sleep. Might want to have someone check on her later."

Surprisingly distraught? Wouldn't, *shouldn't,* a person be extremely distraught if someone died in her arms?!

I stood still, listening for a time, until the doctor left the castle. Then I hurried into my room, quickly closing and locking the door.

Something odd, and decidedly sinister, was afoot. They'd got Margulies's body out and away from the castle so fast. *Too* fast? I sank onto the edge of the bed, seeking the source of the niggling feeling that it was all wrong. Then it struck me. Clarissa. Shouldn't the constable at least have questioned her, considering she was alone in the room with Margulies when he died? God knows I didn't want Clarissa implicated for murder; clearly she hadn't *killed* Margulies. But was it normal practice here not to investigate a sudden death? Why?

Then I realised what a fool I'd been. Of *course*! This entire region—certainly the town of Trefoyle, probably a good deal of the north coast of Cornwall as well—was indebted to, or at least desirous of cultivating goodwill with—the powerful Earl Trefoyle. The feudal system still functioned quite well here, as it had for centuries. The doctor—and the police—would jolly well say and do as Trefoyle told them. But why on earth should Trefoyle, of all people, want Margulies dead?

Footsteps sounded outside my door, then a gentle knock. I didn't answer. The footsteps went away again; I sat without moving.

At long last I picked up Sarah's picture and studied it. I couldn't ring her at this hour. I wasn't going to wake her to cry on her shoulder . . . though she would want me to.

Thoughts assailed me then, as if the very thought of Sarah had cleared my mind. Trefoyle had asked me to protect Forsythe, fearing that deChauncey might harm him—even kill him—in his desperation to possess the Valdarfer Boccaccio.

But it hadn't been Forsythe's life that was in danger at all. It had been Margulies's.

Had Trefoyle deliberately misled me? There was something else . . . something Trefoyle had told me earlier that made me think that was so. . . .

Enlightenment didn't come. Exasperated, frightened, and exhausted, I stretched out across the bed. My modern Boccaccio edition still lay open to the Novells of the first day. Staring at nothing in particular, my eyes came to rest on the summary of the first story.

Wherein is contained, how hard a thing it is, to distinguish goodnesse from hypocrisie; and how (under the shadow of holinesse) the wickedness of one man, may deceive many. Messire Chappelet du Prat, by making a false confession, beguyled an holy Religious man. . . . And having (during his life time) bene a very bad man, at his death, was reputed for a saint, and called Saint Chappelet.

I remembered the archbishop saying that Chesterton should be called a saint, after he'd transformed himself in our sight, becoming an exemplary man in the space of roughly an hour. Was I seeing parallels where none existed, my English literature-oriented brain imagining things?

Or, I thought, blinking my tired eyes, did life consist of the same little dramas, deceits, and misfortunes over and over again? Perhaps it was no coincidence that my experience here was conforming to the stories of Boccaccio. Still, the virus in London and the plague; the goat lady tapestry; and now Saint Chesterton. Though, of course, the duke wasn't dead yet . . .

. . . and Margulies was.

All of a sudden the thread that had escaped me earlier seemed within reach. Old Ashleigh, Trefoyle told me, had been the last to die. But what if it *wasn't* because he owned the coveted Boccaccio? What if it was something else entirely? And what if Margulies's death was tied to that same purpose?

Ashleigh ... Lord Ashleigh, William Convers. The only thing I knew about him was that he'd been in the House of Lords, and championed some unconventional cause long before it was popular. ...

Think, Alex, think. I rubbed my hands over my face. What did the deceased Lord Ashleigh have in common with Margulies Whitehead apart from a love of books? Margulies had been a "New Labour" MP, so they were both in government. Margulies's causes had been higher standards in comprehensive schools and better early child care for disadvantaged children. Recently, he'd taken up the New Labour cause of studying the House of Lords with the intention of abolishing hereditary peerages.

That was it! I sat up again on the bed. Lord Ashleigh, too, unlikely as it might seem, had thought hereditary peerages a shocking anachronism. Hadn't he wanted, in effect, the abolition of his son's own inherited position?

Was there a political terrorist in the ranks of the Dibdin Club? And could it be Lord Ashleigh's own son?

It was only eight o'clock. Still early for Max, on a Saturday ...

I dialled Max's number.

He picked up the phone and breathed into it but didn't say anything.

"Max?"

"Hmm? Maddie?"

Poor Max, I thought. His angelic wife was still away tending her sick mother in Spain. He was quite disoriented without her.

"No, sorry, it's Alex. I am sorry to wake you so early, Max, but this weekend's turned out to be rather eventful. I need your help."

"Right." He yawned·into the phone. "Of course."

"Could you please get into your computer and look on

the Web site of the campaign to abolish hereditary peerages? I need to know if Margulies Whitehead and Lord Ashleigh, the one who died last summer, were both involved. I'm quite sure, but if you could confirm it . . . And one more thing."

"Hang on . . ." I knew he was making notes. His memory functioned remarkably like a sieve. "All right."

"Could you get into your antiquarian bookseller's database and find out how many Valdarfer Boccaccios there are—dating from 1471, I believe—and who owns them? The last *three* owners, in fact, if you can. Ring me back any time on my mobile phone, okay?"

"Right. But, Alex, you sound awful. What's going on there?"

I told him briefly about Margulies, deciding not to go into further detail about the eerie Boccaccio similarities, or the bizarre customs of the Dibdin Club.

"I just need to sort a few things out, that's all," I finished.

"I'm sorry it's turned out this way," Max said, yawning again despite himself. "I'll ring you later." *Why was it* that Clarissa and I were the only ones who seemed the least bit disturbed by Margulies Whitehead's demise?

I ended the connection only to hear a gentle rapping on my door. "It's Hawkes, sir. Your early morning coffee."

I got up and went to let him in. "Thanks very much, Hawkes. Not much of a night's sleep, was it?"

"No, sir." He placed the tray on a small round table near the door and pushed the door closed behind him. Actually, he looked surprisingly fresh, though I knew he couldn't have slept either. His eye fell on the open Boccaccio on my bed. He didn't leave immediately, but stood rigidly next to the tray he'd just delivered. I waited.

"Sir, Earl Trefoyle told me that you were helping to keep us all safe here." The obvious fact that one of us had just died on the very first night of the weekend not only made his statement absurd, but reminded me painfully of my failure in my duties. "Er, sorry," he said, glancing down.

"Not at all. But—I might have asked Trefoyle earlier—surely the rest of the weekend will be cancelled now that there's been a death?"

"No, sir. I'm afraid not. The weekend always goes on, regardless of accidents or tragedies. It's always been done this way. Tradition, you know."

A terrible certainty struck me then: Margulies's death, if Trefoyle's suspicions of deChauncey were correct, was unlikely to be the *only* death of that weekend. At that moment I wanted nothing more than to get in my car and drive away at high speed, back to Sarah.

But I couldn't. It wasn't right to leave Trefoyle alone with this mess now that he'd given me part of the responsibility. And if more deaths occurred, I would be responsible for not helping to forestall them. Besides, there was the damned Bedchamber book to think of. I would have to see this through.

Hawkes was watching me.

"Sorry. Go on, Hawkes."

"Yes, sir. Well, what I wanted to tell you about was a hand-throwing tool. For the clay pigeons."

My face must have looked blank.

"For the shooting party, you know, throwing the pigeons into the air. The automatic thrower is in the tower, but sometimes people use a manual tool—a hand-throwing device."

"Ah, got you," I said. "Is that unusual?"

He looked at me with something approaching pity. "Remember we discussed that the pigeon deChauncey shot seemed to have come from a completely different direction?"

"Yes, yes, of course. Now I remember. Sorry. It's been quite a night."

"I know, sir. Well, as for the hand-throwing tool, I've

never seen it out before. Normally, it's stored in the base of the throwing tower. I just thought it might have something to do with the accident yesterday."

"Yes."

"You see, I have a private spot in the garden where I go to write. I'm a bit of an amateur novelist, I'm afraid. There's a yew hedge all round, and every day in the very early morning I work a bit on my novel . . . That's where I found the hand-throwing tool."

Having been told by most of the people I meet that they've a novel in them, or under way, I recognised instantly what he wanted. His information about the throwing tool, and the mention of his novel, was merely a thinly veiled bid for publication. He'd given me valuable information, and in exchange he wanted me to consider his book.

"Why don't you send me your synopsis when it's ready? I'd be fascinated."

"Really? I'd love to. Thanks ever so much, sir." He turned toward the door.

"Hawkes."

"Yes, sir?"

"I don't suppose you'd be interested in continuing in your role as an extra set of eyes and ears for this weekend . . . ?" Why not enlist him as a fellow spy? I thought.

He positively beamed. "I'd like nothing better, sir. Thanks ever so much." He bowed quickly before backing out of the doorway.

I poured a cup of coffee from the small pot provided on the tray and added full-cream milk. Lifting the cup from its saucer, I drank gratefully, but then stopped short. A small folded square of white paper sat on the saucer where the cup had been. Hurriedly, I set the cup down directly on the tray, sloshing milky coffee onto the white linen place mat, and picked up the scrap of paper. Opening it out, I saw that it was far from a friendly hello.

LEAVE BY NOON TODAY OR SHARE YOUR
FRIEND'S FATE

The note had been written in block capitals, in ordinary black ballpoint ink. I had no way of knowing who had written it, and whether they meant that Margulies had been murdered. I supposed sharing his fate didn't mean anyone had actually killed him . . . but I wasn't sure. It was possible that Hawkes himself had written the note, though instinct told me to trust him. Or perhaps Hawkes had seen someone; I could ask him later.

I crumpled the note and tossed it in the waste-paper basket I wasn't about to leave—there was something bizarre about this club and the deaths at its yearly functions, and I wasn't going to let more people die. Not only that, but it was essential that I found out *who* had the Bedchamber book. I had a lot to do in the next eighteen hours, and it was absolutely vital that I did not fail.

Showered, freshly dressed, and angrier than ever, I made my way out to the garden to find Hawkes's private writing area and the hand-throwing tool. A brisk offshore wind blew; clouds hung over the land farther inland, but the breeze had cleared them away from Castle Trefoyle. Savouring the salt air, I moved in the direction Trefoyle had led me the day before to meet the shooting party. I knew the throwing tool couldn't be far from where we'd shot.

I rounded the hedge where we'd met the others and noticed it was boxwood. There was one just like it on the other side of the shooting area; I'd check them both. Walking around the boxy shape of greenery, I found a narrow opening and stepped into the square of hedge. I saw at once that this was where Hawkes wrote. A weathered lap desk sat on the ground, and near it, a chunky wooden tool consisting of two slabs of wood joined by a hefty spring. I knelt by it, trying to work out why the culprit would have left it lying about and couldn't help but notice little white crumbs all round it. Kendal Mint Cake.

I thought again about what the rogue thrower had intended. If a pigeon flew up from the side, as this one had, a marksman's instinct would be to react and shoot at it. Just as deChauncey had. But if deChauncey had wanted to kill Forsythe, would he *really* have shot him in front of half a dozen people? And exactly *who* had sent the pigeon flying on its unfortunate trajectory? Trefoyle had been at the end of our line, closest to the hedge. But as far as I could remember, he'd been there watching too. Chesterton and the others hadn't yet arrived in Cornwall.

I still recalled the shock on deChauncey's face when he realised what he'd done; the way Forsythe himself suggested Trefoyle get deChauncey something to drink when we came in after shooting. It was hard for me to believe that deChauncey had deliberately shot a man who, though he possessed a much-coveted book that once belonged to him, was a friend and fellow Dibdinian.

The cell phone in my jacket tweeted. "Yes."

"*Alex!* Are you all right?"

"Of course. Why?"

I could hear Max breathing into the phone. "You've *got* to stop doing this to me."

I hadn't heard my brother sound this distracted since he'd met his wife. If only she weren't away at the moment . . . there was an edgy, high pitch to his voice that I didn't like. He sounded almost hysterical.

"Doing what? What is it, Max?" I asked cautiously. I'd spoken to him barely five minutes ago; surely nothing monumental had happened in the meantime.

"You—oh, I—" He cleared his throat; I imagined him trying to compose himself. "Alex, you didn't tell me about the alarm in the house. I went over and set it off, and the security firm came. They thought I'd broken in. I had to ring Martyn to come and vouch for me."

"Oh, no. I'm so sorry, Max." I could understand why

he was so upset. "I forgot to tell you. But Sarah should have been there . . . wasn't she?"

I heard an unnatural instant of silence on the other end of the line. "Uh—no. No. She wasn't there. It's all right. Really, it's all right, it's just that—" If I didn't know better, I'd think he was dissolving into tears.

This wasn't at all good. He'd made it three years now off drugs and alcohol, but he *had* been acting a bit strange ever since Madeline had gone to Spain.

"Max, do you need me to come home? Please—tell me what's wrong."

"*No!* No, don't come home. I just need—Alex, it's the Bedchamber incunable. I—I need it."

Good God. I'd forgotten to tell Max it had been stolen, I'd been so wrapped up with my own life . . . and he'd been away Wednesday and Thursday at a book fair in Brighton. Our lives, having converged over the Bedchamber book the previous weekend, had gone their normal separate ways again.

But why on earth should he need the book so urgently?

"Max, the book was stolen, actually, from the office. I had it locked in my filing cabinet, but someone knew where to look." I had to make a decision quickly whether or not to tell him about the prime minister's request for the book, and my assignment to find it. No; sadly, I judged, I shouldn't tell him. He wasn't reliable enough.

I listened as my brother breathed right into the phone again, too rapidly.

"Max, won't you just tell me, please, *why* you wanted the book just now?"

"I can't." Another near-whimper. "But *I'm* all right, really I am. It's not that." He made an almost audible attempt to pull himself together. "I suppose I'm making too big a fuss over this. It's just that some of the collectors' group in Chalfont St. Giles are getting together, and I thought I might show them."

"Ah." His story didn't ring true.

"Where are the photos Diana took of the pages?" Now his voice was surely too casual.

"I think I'd better come home. I've got them here, Max. It was silly, but I brought them. I just wanted to be able to look at them."

"I understand." He sounded tragically wounded. "Don't come home—really, don't. I'll do what I can here, then. Thanks, Alex."

"Wait! What did you learn about Ashleigh and Margulies?"

"Oh, that. You were right," he said dejectedly. "They were both outspoken in the campaign to abolish hereditary peerages. And as for the Valdarfer Boccaccio, it has the most tangled provenances imaginable. One of them is owned by Osgood Forsythe, formerly by Lord Ashleigh. And the owner of the second is unknown. In fact, it's only rumoured to exist. Ours, I presume."

"Fascinating. Thanks, Max. Ring again if you need me, for any reason, won't you?"

"Yes. Yes, of course." It sounded as if he dropped the phone as he replaced the receiver, then fumbled as he set it in its cradle.

Something was badly wrong at home . . . as it was at this bizarre outpost on the Cornish coast. I had to think. . . .

I stared at the angry waves. Looking up at the castle, I saw its noble outline projecting high above the rocks, then followed its profile down to the gigantic boulders of its foundation, where it was assaulted by the sea. White-capped waves slammed against the rocky base of the structure as if determined to destroy it.

And beneath those whitecaps, I thought, there were still greater depths and swells. Beyond them were the pull of the moon and the forces of the earth's gravity, controlling their tides. For millions of years, the moon, the earth, and the oceans had been plainly visible to all. Yet no one had discovered their interrelationship, their secret pact to move and work together, until quite recently.

I knew, somehow, as I stood gazing at the castle rising out of the turbulent sea that there was a similarly secret synergy here at Castle Trefoyle. Something was at work just beneath the surface, all of its parts visible to me and yet unknown. Already, I knew something someone wanted to keep in the dark. But I despised ignorance; it was no excuse. I would probe and probe in the hours remaining to me here, gathering all the intelligence I could. The links between the many parts of the whole would become apparent . . . they must.

As I walked back to the castle, I felt my shoulders sink for a moment. As with the oceans and the moon, people important to one another can be quite distant. Separate, even. Look at Sarah and me, I thought ruefully. I'd loved her for eight years, known that we belonged together. Now we were finally joining together for life, and still she was hundreds of miles away. I tried to shrug off this discouraging thought, reminding myself that after all, the connection between the oceans, the earth, and the moon had eventually been established for all time.

When I entered the great hall, I saw no other living soul. Dibdinians who partied the night away didn't rise with the sun, obviously. And it had been far from a normal night . . . though most of my fellow club members had lain comatose through the tragedy of Margulies's death.

A full English breakfast buffet had been set out on the massive sideboard, kept warm in chafing dishes. I took a plate bearing the Trefoyle crest and helped myself to everything from kippers to ham. Then I carried it all to a seat far, far away from the one I'd occupied the night before.

I couldn't help imagining, as I studied the smooth leatherlike surface of the massive table, the knights gnawing joints of meat and swilling mead and wine there, while their animals shared the warm refuge of the great hall with them. At least there had been some improvements since the Dark Ages, I thought, if not in the actual nature of men. The similarity of my experience that weekend to Boccaccio's stories proved that beyond all doubt.

Dear God, how could I possibly survive another dinner at that table, that very night? At least it would be the last for a whole year, I thought, if I remained—or survived to remain, according to that morning's threat—a member of the club. Well, I'd survived threats before, I told myself by way of consolation. Still, there was the definite feeling I should be watching my back. The suits of armour holding their jousting poles didn't help diminish the feeling of constant and deadly threat.

In the light of day I could see that the hall's ceiling was hung round with banners, tattered and torn, clearly from real battles somewhere in history. Some of them actually appeared to be stained with blood, though I hoped it was rust. I didn't know the significance of many of them, but was willing to bet Trefoyle did.

I was still staring up at them when Trefoyle himself joined me—though once again, I didn't hear my host approach until he was just behind my shoulder. I jumped as his voice boomed behind me, and a bite of kipper went down the wrong way.

"Interested in heraldry, are you?"

As I rose, coughing, to respond, it struck me as more than odd that his first greeting made no reference to the shared horrors of the night before. Surely the death of one of his fellow club members and guests troubled him as deeply as it did me. But the aristocracy of England was nothing if not eccentric, not to mention unfailingly trained in the stiffness of the upper lip. Max half-jokingly referred to this quality as "emotionally challenged." Every British public school boy learned early on that he didn't dare scream as the prefect held the flame to his wrist.

Besides, I knew this might be our only chance to talk about progress and plans regarding the Bedchamber book. "Yes—but I'm afraid I know very little about heraldry."

"I should show you Chesterton's book, issued for the club last year. Actually, it was old Ashleigh's—but he died before he could get it out. Young Ashleigh took hold of the project for a bit, but in the end gave it over to Chesterton . . . some difference of opinion. It's the most magnificent, masterly colour pageant of historic heraldry ever to grace the pages of a book. A labour of love, you know. Took old Ashleigh twenty years," he said, "to assemble all the information. Mind you, very few of us remain who have any idea of the significance heraldry once had."

We began to climb the royally carpeted stairs towards his private quarters. "Do you know, Plumtree, your own ancestry? Your own coat of arms?"

"No coat of arms, I'm afraid, but I'm quite familiar with the previous eight generations—names, dates, achievements, et cetera."

"Then you're in for a surprise," Trefoyle said mysteriously, continuing in silence.

When we reached the open door to his private sitting room, he walked to an alcove, where Chesterton had disappeared the night before. He'd closed a door, I remembered, from the sound of it. Now Trefoyle opened what I presumed to be that same door. It was small, arched, and wooden, like the door to my room down the hall.

"Mind your head," he warned, closing the door behind us, and led the way into pitch darkness. After hesitating for an instant, I followed him blindly, not knowing where the next footstep would take me—perhaps down a flight of stairs, or into a stone wall. Trefoyle made no comment whatever about the nonexistent light; perhaps there was some dim illumination that my faulty eyes couldn't perceive.

My vision was absymal at the best of times; I'd recently

learned that I had a rare progressive eye disease, the result of which I preferred not to consider. Even wearing contact lenses, it was nearly impossible for me to see in dim light.

So as I blundered down the narrow passageway after Trefoyle, I said not a word, well schooled to maintain silence in the face of discomfort, and even danger. I groped for the walls and sensed rather than saw—as blind people are said to do—Trefoyle moving downward rather than on the level. I heard him say, "Mind the—" but it was too late.

I heard an *ooof* from Trefoyle as I pitched into him and tumbled down the last few feet of what I instantly learned was a sharp little stone staircase, like the others in the castle. Cut in a spiral, the staircase was not pleasant to fall down—even though I was very nearly at the bottom of it. The edge of each step cut into my sides, legs, and arms. My head crashed into the solid wall of stone, after which I saw stars.

I was vaguely aware of Trefoyle fussing with keys in a lock and opening a door next to us. The next thing I knew, Trefoyle was standing over me, looking concerned, with dim flickering light behind him. I blinked, getting my bearings, and sat up from where I was on the floor. Max would have had a good laugh at my instinctive apology. "Sorry, Trefoyle. Must've missed a step."

"I say, you've a great lump coming up on your forehead. Are you quite all right?"

"Fine, fine," I said. But when I began to take in what lay behind Trefoyle and the open door, I thought perhaps the bump on the head had knocked me silly.

Before me stretched a massive great tunnel of a room with a ceiling barely higher than my own head. It extended at least fifty feet into the distance, and every inch of it was covered with antique globes standing on the floor, and maps displayed in cases on the walls and in glass-topped tables. In fact, it was a veritable ocean of

globes, hundreds of them. The effect was one of an innocent fascination indulged to the point of mania. The
globes all looked extremely old, but even my untrained
eye could tell the maps were even older, and no doubt extremely valuable. A series of gauges along the walls indicated an extensive climate-control system, presumably to
control the damp.

Gazing at all those man-made images of the world, I
felt the same prickling of fear I'd sensed at breakfast. I
also felt and heard a rumbling, something like I imagined
an earthquake would be. Trefoyle was watching me.

"Yes," he said. "We're quite near the sea right here.
Those are breakers you're hearing." He sighed, apparently
with satisfaction. "You're in my private treasure room,
Plumtree, one even the servants don't know about. In
fact, only several of my closest friends are aware that it exists. Dragged you in here first as it's closest to the bottom
of the stairs. Thought I'd see how badly you'd injured
yourself."

I felt uncomfortable with his phrasing, as if it wouldn't
really have mattered to him whether I'd died from the
fall. I thought of the note under my coffee cup that
morning.

"At any rate," he continued, "I'll count on you not to
broadcast its existence."

"Of course," I assured him, gazing at his private museum. "It's fantastic."

"Isn't it?" he agreed. "Regardless of what happens to
me, my collection will survive to remind the world of the
truth: England, because of families like the Trefoyles and
the Plumtrees, once ruled the world."

It was then that I realised I had fallen into very deep
waters indeed.

CHAPTER 9

My library was dukedom enough.

—William Shakespeare

I'd be interested to know something," Trefoyle said, turning to me. "Because you attended university in America, you're a fascinating aberration."

Well, thanks very much, and so are you, I thought. It struck me that perhaps this outwardly normal and likeable man was suffering from delusions.

"Are you aware that England, hand in hand with the Church, once ruled the civilised world?"

I struggled for a diplomatic answer. "Are you referring to the conquer of Acre and the Holy Land in the time of the Knights Templar?" I trawled for the remains of my sixth-form history and came up with a bit more. "Saladin and the Christian soldiers—all of that?"

He nodded, with a satisfied smile. "I should have known that *your* ancestors would educate their boys. You've no idea the respect I had for your father . . . no idea." He seemed to lose himself in thought for a moment. "Yes, indeed, Plumtree. I *knew* you were one of us."

Somewhat amazed by his reaction to my awareness of a rather basic bit of history, again I waited for him to go on. I might learn far more than I ever expected to this weekend, I thought.

"The heart of the world, Jerusalem, was once ruled by us, together with the rest of the Church. My forefathers—and yours, obviously—were there when Richard the Lion-Heart made a truce with Saladin. Sadly, they were also there when the truce broke down."

He began to walk into the sea of wooden worlds, gently setting one and then another spinning, until all around us images of the earth were whirling. The effect was decidely eerie, a man-child playing with an all-too-adult toy.

"Come and look, Plumtree. People didn't make globes until they'd discovered the world was round, of course. Ptolemy figured it out in 150, but as you no doubt know from your American education, in 1492, when Christopher Columbus sailed, some of his countrymen were still afraid he would fall off the edge of the world. But here"—he stretched out his hands lovingly—"is the first known globe in the world. At least all the best experts think so. Made in the early twelfth century."

He gazed fondly at a small dark globe perhaps twelve inches across. It rested on a simple wooden stand, concave to accept its shocking curve, on top of a small table all its own. "Go ahead, Plumtree. Look at the Middle East, the cradle of Judeo-Christian civilisation, on the very first globe."

Bending down over the small, too-dark sphere, I fought to make out the Middle East in the dim light. I could vaguely perceive the familiar coastal outlines of what I knew to be Saudi Arabia, and then present-day Israel, Syria, Turkey, and the surrounding areas. They were way out of scale; things warped according to the sensibilities of their time, like the elongated figures in an El Greco painting. But I couldn't make out the writing.

"Sorry, Trefoyle, I can't seem to—"

"Oh. Here. You'll need a magnifier to read it." He passed me a large magnifying glass, which I held over the area. There, in faded but legible script, someone had painted *Terrae sanctae victae pro Christo*—*the Holy Lands, won for Christ,* in Latin. These words surrounded pinpoints labelled Jerusalem, Acre, Constantinople, Alexandria.

"Yes, I see," I murmured. "Remarkable." Fascinated, I began to search for Europe on the globe, curious as to precisely who ruled whom when it had been made. Trefoyle startled me by ripping the glass out of my hand, then using it to gesture dramatically towards the other globes in the room.

"Most people don't even know these days—young, common people, I mean—that Christianity ever ruled the world. Now we have NATO, the European Union, the United Nations—but *then* the world was united in faith under God. Warring kingdoms came together to fight for their ultimate King."

It was quite a thought, I had to admit. But, while I am a Christian, it struck me that it didn't leave much room for anyone who didn't share the same faith. Besides, Christianity had never actually ruled the world. The Western world, perhaps, yes . . . but vast parts of the world remained unexplored and undiscovered in the Middle Ages. Besides that, China, India, and much of the rest of the known world certainly were not then and never have been Christian. I didn't point out these facts to Trefoyle; he might have struck me down with his magnifying glass in a fit of holy pique. Strange, I thought; he'd never impressed me as the religious type—hearty and welcoming, surely, and not unkind. But not exactly oozing loving-kindness and understanding.

In the next moment, I understood why.

"Well," he pronounced with an air of finality. "All these *worldly* records of temporary political power on the earth show just how fleeting the reign of a pretender can be. Look at this one—the Union of Soviet Socialist Republics—and this globe next to it, made three years ago, with the independent states. Eh? All of that happened in the blink of an eye. Now there's trouble there too. And look how blithely we once painted a nation on our globes called Czechoslovakia.

"No, I'm not about to admit defeat for our side. And I'll bet you're not either, are you, Plumtree?"

I shook my head, trying not to be awkward, but also not understanding his precise meaning. If he meant would I give up my faith, no. I would not. But I was thinking that he'd forgotten the other sad half of history: all the tragic injustices committed in the name of faith, such as the slaughter at Acre by Richard the Lion-Heart's men. Far more good than bad had been done in the name of God, but that judgement might depend on where you stood. At the very least, one might say that Trefoyle had a selective memory where history was concerned.

"Now, then. Enough of that. I brought you down here to show you my Dibdin collection, and Chesterton's heraldry book in particular. Here, you'd better take this." He handed me a battery-powered torch, turned down what I now realised were gas lamps in the globe room, and ushered me out the door. My body protested, the bruises and bumps I'd acquired on my way downstairs complaining insistently. Trefoyle fussed with keys and a lock as I waited behind him in a narrow hallway, clearly chipped out of the rock. It was damp but not dripping; a tasteful Oriental runner made a path down the centre of the stone floor.

I found it extraordinary to be virtually under the sea, or at the very least right next to it. Trefoyle made no comment as he moved ahead of me to a door down the hallway on our right. Singling out a key from the large bunch still in his hand, he began to unlock the next door. I focussed the beam of my torch on the lock to help him see.

"Thanks awfully, Plumtree. Helpful sort of chap, aren't you? Ah. Here we are." He swung open the door and stepped aside to let me in, turning up the gas lamps with a control by the door. As the light grew stronger, I blinked, awestruck. A richly patterned Oriental silk carpet covered the stone floor of a room only about twelve feet square. Three walls held fully stocked bookcases covered by glass doors, and a round cherry-wood table in the middle had just one chair next to it, a comfortable soft leather one. Again, climate-control indicators showed that the moisture level was being monitored. It was the most beautiful, intimate jewel of a library I'd ever seen. Here, clearly, were the books closest to his heart.

"It's splendid, Trefoyle."

"Sit down, sit down," he urged, waving me into a chair. "This is my Dibdin library. As you know, the club's been going now for one hundred and eighty-seven years. At one book a year, and in the early years sometimes there were more, that's more than two hundred books." He saw from my face that I understood the value of a complete collection of Dibdin Club books.

"*All* of them?" I asked.

"Every last broadside from the early dinners," he answered. "And more besides, such as Haslewood's original handwritten manuscript of the *Dibdin Dissipations*."

"I had no idea! And the book-collecting public doesn't know a complete set exists!"

He smiled. "My friends are not eager to publicise my collection. They understand it's a very *private* matter."

I took the hint.

"Yes," he sighed, moving over to the shelves nearest the door. I assumed the most recent books would be kept there if the shelves were arranged chronologically. "There's been a Trefoyle in the Dibdin from its inception, just as there's always been a Chesterton. And a Jones-Harris, for that matter. I saw last night that you and Jones-Harris are already friends."

Acquaintances, I wanted to correct him, but it served no purpose. I nodded.

"His father and I were the closest of companions. He—Jones-Harris's father—was one of us too, you know."

Us? Did he mean Dibdin Club members? He kept using the expression, but I had the distinct feeling it applied to more than our little book club.

"Shame his son didn't follow in his footsteps," he finished. "They very rarely do, you know; that's why I'm so pleased about you."

Again, I wasn't sure exactly what he was pleased about. He closed the glass door on the right-most cabinet and approached the table with a large leather-bound book which he handled with something approaching reverence. "This is Chesterton's offering from last year. Old Ashleigh's heraldry book. Really a magnificent work. I've never understood why young Ashleigh didn't want to see it through—something about a disagreement with Chesterton over some detail or other." He leafed through the first few pages and stopped at the list of Dibdin members. "See? Chesterton's name is listed in red, as the publishing member. The rest of us are listed in black."

I studied the page with interest.

"Normally, only the president's copy is printed on vellum, but Chesterton said that while he was going to the trouble to produce one for himself, he'd make one for me as vice-president." Clearly this pleased him.

The book was indeed gorgeous; one hundred magnificent full-page colour plates had been lovingly mounted on the vellum at the centre of the book, framed on both sides by vellum pages printed with text. I doubt that more than a dozen books a year, for whatever reason, are printed on vellum. Just as the history of the world has passed out of modern awareness, so have the printing arts. Only a few people remain who know or care, and apart from the odd small, specialist book publisher, the bulk of them probably consist of Dibdin members.

Trefoyle turned to the body of the book. "Here, I'll show you my family heraldry. It's so extensive, Chesterton gave it a page of its own. You can see how it evolved: In the tenth century, it was the trefoil, of course—this sort of modified rose; an oak tree with its roots showing, known in heraldic terms as 'eradicated'; and, of course, the cross, all of it gules on a field of argent."

Gules, I surmised, was red, because what I saw in his crest was red on silver, or argent.

"By 1100," Trefoyle continued, "the sword had been added. In 1200, this castle was added. It didn't change again until 1850, when my great-great-grandfather petitioned to add the book symbol."

I marvelled at Chesterton's creation. Although he didn't tell the story of the changes in heraldry, the images were extremely vivid and beautifully reproduced. I wished my friend Amanda Morison, the fine-art printer, and Diana could have seen it.

"Just think, you'll receive a copy of all Dibdin books from this day forward, including the one I'm presenting everyone with tonight at the banquet. It's a surprise," he confided, anticipating the inevitable question. "After two hundred years your family will have this many as well."

I smiled up at him. "I really appreciate you showing me your private library, Trefoyle. Very generous of you."

"Oh, we're not done yet, my boy."

I felt my hackles rise, and it wasn't merely the "my boy." He made it sound as if he had an agenda, as Sarah would say, for bringing me down there.

He was turning pages in the book. "Right, I thought so," he said. "Here's your page."

My page?

I stared down at the image before me, hardly able to believe my eyes. The coat of arms was the same as the first page in the Valdarfer Boccaccio Ian had given me, signifying that my own family—if I could believe Trefoyle and the book before me—had it bound. In the upper right-hand corner was a Maltese cross; opposite it, a sword. A compact plum tree not unlike the one I used for our Plumtree Press colophon graced one lower corner, and the ever-present open book the other. Last revised in 1489, Chesterton's brief printed notes explained. The timing made sense; my family of printers and publishers had included the book after the cradle, or incunabula, period of printing, in the fifteenth century.

The technical description at the bottom of the page read *"Plum tree, issuant from a mount vert, fully fructed, all proper; sword, Maltese Cross and open book, all argent on azure."*

I glanced up at Trefoyle as he stood over me. He placed a hand on my shoulder. "You know, at one point your father had decided not to tell you boys about your noble history, about the title and lands Richard the Lion-Heart bestowed on your ancestors for their service in the Crusades. I can't comprehend why your older brother hasn't assumed his rightful title of Earl. At any rate, I'm glad your father came to his senses before he died. A real tragedy, his death. One of the finest men I've known. I can see now that at some point he did tell you."

But as far as I knew, he never *had* told me. Then, as I stared at the page, I thought I understood what my father hadn't wanted me to know. From the sword and the cross together, I could assume only that there had indeed been Crusaders in my family line. My father had certainly not told me. Nor had my grandfather or great-grandfather, both of whom I'd known. My father had made it a point, for some reason, to show me the Dibdin heraldry book of 1925—the one Max had borrowed the previous Sunday. Quite a coincidence, that, now that I thought of it . . . or perhaps not. I knew for a fact there hadn't been a Plumtree page in the 1925 volume. Perhaps my grandfather had arranged with the author to have our record expunged, and my father showed us the book to persuade us we *didn't* have a noble history, in case someone like Trefoyle brought it up one day.

So why did this newly issued book of Ashleigh-Chesterton origin contain our name? I'd never seen the coat of arms before; we had no flags or arms of any sort round the Orchard. Evidently, Old Ashleigh, or Chesterton after him, had rediscovered it and included it. My father was no longer alive to intervene.

Trefoyle must have taken my silence for great delight. He clapped me on the back and said, "Beautiful, isn't it? I must say, from an esthetic point of view, I do prefer your coat of arms to mine.

"Here, have a look at Chesterton's," he said, turning the pages carefully back from "P" to "C." "Yes, here it is. Look at that unusual coat of arms . . . the lion rampant, argent on gules, with the crown in its teeth. Nothing quite like it anywhere else. But then, you know how powerful the Chestertons are . . . more royal than the royals, you might say."

I nodded, unable to take my eyes off the page, not only stunned by what I'd learned about my own family but by Chesterton's family coat of arms.

For the Chesterton coat of arms was the same unmistakable combination worn by the knight in the Bedchamber book, who knelt with dagger in hand by the king's bed. The crown in the teeth of the lion was unmistakable. The Bedchamber book had revealed another secret: A *Chesterton* had killed Richard the Lion-Heart!

I began to suspect that I was unravelling not only a modern-day mystery, but one from the Middle Ages also.

Trefoyle closed the book and replaced it. "Now then. I'd best get back . . . good heavens!" he exclaimed, looking at his watch. "It's nearly ten-fifteen; the annual business meeting begins at eleven. I must fly. But just think, Plumtree," he said casually, putting the book away on the shelf and closing the glass door over it. "Your family might have concealed its heritage and renounced its lands, for what reason we may never know. You may still claim it. But one day all of Trefoyle might be yours too, if you prove yourself worthy. I have no heir, you know. Someone must carry on."

With that he led the way upstairs, and I wordlessly followed him with the torch, reeling from the bizarre succession of facts I'd learned and their uncertain relationships.

Why was he confiding in me about his lack of children? And why would he consider me a suitable heir?

And *one of us* . . . I was beginning to think he meant some sort of fellowship of ex-crusading families, of which I'd just learned I was a member. I'd had a hint of a longer Plumtree history when I'd discovered last year that the mediaeval hedges on our land had been planted in a series of interlocking Ps. In order to have mediaeval hedges, identifiable by the minimum of seven particular species combined, my ancestors must have lived there to plant them. Our family home, while nearly three hundred years old, certainly wasn't old enough to suggest that we'd been there for the bulk of a millennium.

And the Chesterton coat of arms on the murderous knight . . .

Trefoyle was speaking again as we ascended the staircase. "We wear business suits for the meeting, don't know if I told you. Most of the old sots don't even struggle out of bed until just before eleven. That's why we serve coffee and pastries."

"Right," I said. "Thanks." My voice sounded vague and distant, even to me. *Pull yourself together,* I warned. I had to get some information, and quickly. "Er, Trefoyle, about the Bedchamber book. Any thoughts on how we should proceed?"

He shook his head. "You're doing magnificently. I've heard the hints you've been dropping in conversation, that you know who's taken your book. An extremely daring, and effective, way to go about it, dear boy—drawing the culprit to yourself. Nothing less than I would expect from the descendant of a crusading knight. But I hope you're prepared for the consequences . . . the guilty party will almost certainly try to do you harm. Still, you'll know who it is. I'll be keeping an eye out for you, never fear."

I wasn't sure if his words were more reassuring or disturbing. "Someone's actually already threatened me—put a note on the early morning tray. It warned me to leave by noon or, and I quote, 'share my friend's fate.' "

Trefoyle seemed to start, but then resumed his steady pace. "Progress, then," he murmured. "Do be careful, Plumtree."

"Thanks, I will. There's just one more thing—"

"Yes, of course, my boy. Go on." He kept walking, effortlessly climbing the staircase I'd tumbled down earlier. He probably kept fit by making this trip at least once a day.

"I'm thinking of poor Margulies. Isn't it odd that we suspected someone *else* might die last night? As it turned out, Forsythe was quite safe. And deChauncey was very put out to have me hanging round him all evening. We had words about it."

"Did you?" He chuckled.

"I just wondered . . . why did you think deChauncey wanted to do away with Forsythe, when there is another copy of the 1471 Valdarfer Boccaccio in existence?"

Naturally, I didn't tell him the copy was mine.

Trefoyle stopped dead in his tracks, just short of the top step. "*Another copy?*" For a moment I thought he might overbalance and sweep me down the stairs again. I clutched the rope strung along the side and put up my other hand to catch him, just in case. "My boy, where on earth did you hear that? It's impossible! There's only ever been one copy known." Was that fear I heard in his voice?

"My brother, as you may know, is an antiquarian book dealer. He heard of it somewhere." Not, strictly speaking, an untruth. Max had heard of it from me.

"Who owns it?" His voice was sharp.

"No one seems to know."

He looked me in the eye. "Well. That rather changes the balance of power in the book world, doesn't it? I'm frightfully sorry, my boy, to have caused you embarrassment with Forsythe and deChauncey. I was so certain . . . and after that shooting incident yesterday . . ." He trailed off. "I owe you an apology. Sorry, Plumtree. Sorry." Much subdued, he said nothing more when we reached the doorway and entered his sitting room; he simply wandered off into what appeared to be an adjoining bedroom. I took that as my cue to return to my own room and change.

Still forty minutes before the meeting . . . I decided to see how Clarissa was getting on. I knocked gently at her door, thinking she might still be asleep, but received no response. Quietly, I opened the door, and was astonished to see that the bed was not only empty, but the sheets had been stripped off. The carpet looked as if it had been freshly hoovered, and the roses and bud vase from the night before—morning, rather—were gone.

Perhaps she'd awakened, felt better, and gone off under her own power. But I was frustrated; I'd had so many questions to ask her about what had happened that night, and how she'd come to be the Dibdin Damsel. I would ask Hawkes if he'd seen her leave.

No one else was about as I went to my room. But I thought they'd probably all be down for the earl's library tour; it wasn't every day that one had the opportunity to see one of Britain's greatest private collections. And they didn't even know about the jewel in the cellar, I thought.

I flopped on my bed. The effects of a sleepless night were beginning to take their toll. For just a moment I began to drift off, then took out my cell phone and entered my home number. An interminable pause followed while I waited to hear the first ring. At last it came, then another, and two more. Finally, the answering machine message began. I hung up. I'd ring again when Sarah was there. I sighed and decided to call Diana at home; perhaps she'd had some luck with the phone records.

"Alex!" she exclaimed. "You're not going to believe this!"

"Yes?"

"I got the records yesterday—I told my friend who manages the business side of the museum that I was worried there might be some personal calls I need to pay for. He said I was in luck, because they now kept track of calls by extension, and the records are available to his closed account at all times over the computer with BT. I said I'd made some from Bats's office, and he gave me those too." She paused, pleased with herself. "I have the number of the person Bats was on the phone to the day he saw your book! I dialled it myself, of course, the instant I got to a phone. But it's someone with a terrifically posh voice saying, '*hair-lair?*' and nothing else. I made up a cover story about a book being ready for him at Maggs—terrible of me, I know—but he said, 'Who is this?' rather indignantly, and rang off. So I've the feeling it's an unlisted line, for his personal use."

A shame she hadn't got his name. Still, it was a start. "Nice work, Diana. What's the number?"

She rattled off a series of digits; I recognised the London prefix, 0171, but nothing else except an odd coincidence—the number was made up entirely of the digits 0, 1, and 7. I scribbled it down on a notepad bearing the Trefoyle crest.

"I'll keep working on it, Alex. I quite enjoy the play-acting side of it. . . ."

"Marvellous. Diana, this is really helpful. Are you all right?"

"Thanks to you. You're a noble sort, you know, Alex."

I winced at her choice of the word "noble."

"Not at all. You've saved the day, making the facsimile and now this."

"Oh! The facsimile. I nearly forgot. It's done. . . . I'm assuming you need it there. I don't want you to argue— I've despatched it to you at the castle by courier. Expect the packet later today."

"Did you—"

"Yes, yes," she interrupted. "Of course I camouflaged it. You'll see. And it's all done up in brown paper. No one will ever guess what's in that box . . . or, rather, if they do, they'll be wrong."

I laughed. "You're beginning to sound as paranoid as I am. I'll let you know what happens here. Thanks a lot, Diana."

"Enjoy yourself, Alex—cheers."

She was gone; I replaced the phone. I didn't want to hang about in my suit, so I put off dressing until the last minute. Margulies's modern Boccaccio edition still lay open on the bed. Ah, yes, I thought. The last one I'd looked at was the story of St. Chappelet, manifesting himself this weekend as St. Chesterton. Shaking my head, wondering again if they were playing some very obscure literary joke with all these distant parallels to Boccaccio, I scanned the page.

The third story of the first day concerned a dilemma faced by the Sultan of Babylon, Saladin, whom I had by coincidence (?) mentioned in the globe room with Trefoyle not half an hour earlier. In the story Saladin had squandered the fortune he'd earned and won, and decided to go to a wealthy Jew named Melchisedech to ask for a loan. But the Sultan knew he'd have to be clever, and decided to trap the moneylender with a trick question. He asked Melchisedech which of the three great religions was truest, that of the Jew, that of the Saracen, or that of the Christian? Melchisedech, a very wise man, saw that Saladin was trying to back him into a corner. So in response he told this story: Once upon a time there was a wealthy man who told his sons that whichever one of them possessed his ring at the time of his death would be his heir.

The ring passed down through many generations this way, until the time came for a father to pass it on to one of three excellent, worthy sons.

"The good man," the story went, "who loved no one of his sons more than the other, knew not how to make his choise, nor to which of them he should leave the Ring: Yet having past his promise to them severally, he studied by what means to satisfie them all three. Wherefore, secretly having conferred with a curious and excellent Goldsmith, hee caused two other Rings to bee made, so really resembling the first made Ring, that himselfe (when he had them in his hand) could not distinguish which was the right one."

The wise Melchisedech finished, "In like manner, my good Lord, concerning those three Lawes given by God the Father, to three such people as you have propounded: each of them do imagine that they have the heritage of God, and his true Law, and also duely to performe his Commandements; but which of them do so indeede, the question (as of the three Rings) is yet remaining."

In the end, Saladin had so much admiration for the man that he asked him as a friend for the money, and Melchisedech gladly granted it out of mutual respect.

Another happy ending. I *liked* happy endings. As I put the book down, I mourned the loss of good old stories such as Boccaccio's. Today, for the *Decameron* to be declared a literary classic, all of Boccaccio's storytellers would have had to perish from the plague they'd fled, after first detailing each agonising moment of their demise and raging about the absurdity of life. I liked Boccaccio's message of hope.

Something else occurred to me: Boccaccio had written this quite complimentary story about Saladin in the *Decameron*; his story in the Bedchamber book about Saladin and Richard's friendship also seemed positive. *So why did the Iraqis assume the Bedchamber book held some dastardly secret?*

I sighed and checked my watch—fifteen minutes till the meeting. Time to get dressed and go down for some coffee. I'd need it.

Dressed for my first Dibdin Club business meeting in my new suit, I descended the too-familiar spiral staircase. I wore a Sulka tie Sarah had bought me; my shoes gleamed, my belt buckle sparkled. And the goose egg on my forehead had begun to turn black and blue.

It earned me several respectful glances as I queued for coffee at the urn, though no one dared ask. For a moment I fought the urge to laugh; it occurred to me that my bedraggled (if expensively dressed) colleagues and I looked like nothing so much as down-and-outs lined up outside a soup kitchen, waiting for the day's ration. The duke in his bed-slippers only intensified this impression as he shuffled along with the rest of us. I smelled strong liquor on nearly everyone's breath: hard to tell if they'd been indulging again recently or were still pickled from the night before.

To his credit, Chesterton, as president, opened the hundred and eightieth-anniversary business meeting with a moment of silence for "our fallen member, Margulies Whitehead." An unfortunate choice of words, I thought, though well-intended. Chesterton looked a bit rough about the edges himself. His thick stand of grey hair stuck straight up in several places, as if he'd barely hoisted his bulk out of bed in time to stagger to the podium. I wondered that his "man" hadn't tamed it for him.

"Archbishop?"

The archbishop rose and offered a touching eulogy for Margulies; I wanted to add that they would all have loved his forthcoming book about Dibdin with its memorabilia of the club of ages past. I wondered just how far Margulies had got with the Dibdin papers. The archbishop resumed his seat.

"Shall we begin?" Chesterton said, clearing his throat. "To business. There are three pieces of news." Unfortunately, I chose that moment to make a trip back to the urn for a second cup of coffee. Sheepishly, I heard him say, "First, our newest member is Alexander Plumtree, of Plumtree Press, whom you may already have met." He smiled at me as I raised a cup in acknowledgment from the coffee urn. "Introduce yourself to Alex before the weekend is out. Perhaps he'll publish that novel you've always meant to write." Scattered laughter from those who were still awake, a glib smile at me from Chesterton.

"Second, I would be delighted to offer helicopter flights before dinner for those of you who like that sort of thing. Be at the castle's hangar at five o'clock, straight after tea, if you're interested."

I very much wanted to go; helicopters had always fascinated me. I only hoped Chesterton wouldn't be drinking all day before flying the thing.

"And finally to finances. Your bills for the year, including this weekend, will be on your beds when you return to your room, according to club tradition. The club currently has a balance of eight thousand nine hundred pounds.

"Now, I know we're all eager to get on with the presentation of the Castle Trefoyle library. Trefoyle?"

Our host stepped up and welcomed us all to his library. "I've chosen several of my favourites to show you today. Afterwards, I'll invite each of you to come up and inspect them at this front table." He paused, then held up a thick, brown-leather-bound book that drew several gasps from the crowd.

"It can't be!"

"The Valdarfer Boccaccio?"

"Surely not!"

I could feel my cheeks burning, and thought of my own copy. Where had he got *this* one? Or was it Forsythe's?

Grinning smugly, Trefoyle continued. "I'm delighted

to announce that I was recently able to purchase this from a dear friend—not Forsythe, although, of course, he is a dear friend. The price, for your information, was precisely half a million pounds."

You clever old coot, I thought, remembering how shocked he'd acted on the staircase when I'd told him there were two Boccaccio volumes. The half-million-pound figure was all too familiar; was *he* the would-be mystery buyer of the Bedchamber book? For a horrible instant I wondered if Max had sold him *our* Boccaccio in my absence, but then I noticed its cover did not have the rubbed spot ours did on the upper right-hand side.

"But *I've* the only surviving copy!" exclaimed Osgood Forsythe, incensed, rising from his seat. "Where did you get *that*?"

"No need to take offence, my good man." Trefoyle looked surprised at his friend's reaction. "I purchased it on the condition that I wouldn't reveal the seller. It in no way affects the value of your copy."

"But it's impossible! Everyone knows that—"

"I've the other," Lord Ashleigh said.

My mouth fell open. *Four* Valdarfer Boccaccios?

Everyone turned to gape at Ashleigh as if we were mesmerised spectators at a Ping-Pong match. I looked back at Forsythe in time to see his jaw drop.

"The *other*!" he exclaimed, exasperated. "But everyone knows *I* have the only . . ." He trailed off, sounding confused. "Legend had it there may have been just one other, with that odd piece of paper in the back, but no one's ever seen it. . . ."

My ears burned. So my paper was rumoured to exist. Again I wondered at its purpose and origin.

"Show it to me, Ashleigh." Forsythe had recovered, and was more furious than ever. "Mine is in my room, as is yours, I'm sure. No one could come to an anniversary meeting of the Dibdin Club without bringing his Boccaccio."

"All right," young Ashleigh said mildly, rising. "Excuse me. I'll be back straightaway."

Forsythe, wild-eyed, stalked off.

A buzz filled the library, and Trefoyle refused to meet my eyes. I'd told him about the other Boccaccio, and he'd acted surprised.

Wait a moment . . . three books. Three rings. Three faiths . . . the debate over which one was true. It was happening again.

Gossip prevailed until the two men returned to the room, the normally calm and civil Forsythe looking daggers at Ashleigh, and at Trefoyle too. Both men stepped up to the front table with their host and displayed their books for all to see. It did appear that each of them possessed a Valdarfer Boccaccio. Apart from the rubbed spot on my copy, they looked exactly like mine overall— except, I had to say, mine appeared to be in slightly better condition.

"Desmond? Would you be so kind?" Trefoyle asked. Desmond Delacroix was the resident authenticity expert, a well-respected antiquarian-book dealer who'd acted as consultant for the British Museum. Had Boswell perhaps rung *Delacroix* that morning Max and I had met with Diana? It was worth considering. He'd identified some forgeries a decade or so before, and had become a national celebrity, written up in the Arts section of the *Sunday Times.* The famous old man tottered up to the front table, apparently a bit flustered about the controversy. With the summoning of Delacroix, there was no question that Trefoyle was heading straight into the issue of potential forgeries. There was fear on Forsythe's face, but Ashleigh and Trefoyle seemed amused.

In a quavering voice the old book expert instructed, "Please place the books on the table in front of you."

I saw the wisdom of this; if each man stood by his book, there could be no argument which was his after the inspection. Delacroix lifted the first, no mean feat for a man of his age and frailty.

The dignified members of the Dibdin Club had begun to strain to see this drama unfold from their seats. The more brazenly curious began to stand, apologising to their neighbours while completely obstructing their view. Casually, they drifted up towards the book expert, then stood watching with hands in their pockets or arms folded. Naturally, I followed suit, and in the space of three minutes we had clustered round the three volumes and the four men like bees around a honeypot. Chesterton remained at one end of the table, as if to referee the event.

Delacroix turned the first page of Ashleigh's copy, inspected it, and remained silent. He bent closer, then took a magnifying eyepiece from his pocket. Without saying a word, he turned the next page. This, too, he inspected, then turned to the first story of the first day. Once again he lowered the glass and his eye toward the page. Then he straightened and proclaimed, "This is an authentic Valdarfer Boccaccio. May I see your provenance please?"

Ashleigh reached into his breast pocket and drew out a yellowed, thin slip of paper. He handed it to Delacroix.

"I see." The old man opened it, read it, then returned it to him, saying, "This is in order. I believe I was present at the transaction."

"But it can't be!" Forsythe expostulated, seething. "I bought mine from his father! He can't have had *two*."

"Why on earth not?" Delacroix rejoined, amused. "Have you confided to us everything you own?" He paused for effect, and in the stillness a slight palsy in one hand made it look as if he were shaking a finger at Forsythe. "If one Boccaccio is desirable, are not two even more so?"

It was clear that Forsythe wished to comment further, but found himself unable to do so. Delacroix's logic was irrefutable. Besides, the old man, with his mild manner, had already won our hearts and trust.

Delacroix inspected the second book as he had the first, declared it to be authentic as well, and asked Forsythe for his provenance. Forsythe thrust it at him, throwing a nasty look at Ashleigh, who smiled at him pleasantly. As I watched, what had been a thin film of sweat gathered into a droplet that ran down Forsythe's temple.

"This is in order," Delacroix stated mildly, and moved on to the third book—Trefoyle's. This, too, he declared to be authentic. There was hushed awe among the rest of us as this news sank in. Three Valdarfer Boccaccios in this very room!

"Your provenance, please, Trefoyle."

Our host motioned the old man to lean across the table, cupped his hand around Delacroix's ear, and whispered something into it. Then Trefoyle reached into his pocket and drew out an even more ancient-looking document than Ashleigh's. Delacroix took this, opened it, holding it low and close to his chest, then looked up at Trefoyle, startled.

"This is most certainly in order," he declared, sounding stunned, and extended his shaking hand with the document to Trefoyle.

"They're all authentic," he announced. "There are three surviving Valdarfer Boccaccios."

Plus one for good measure, I thought.

Forsythe bleated, "But—but what will we do? I—mine was—"

"My dear boy," Delacroix told him gently. "Don't tell me you haven't ever read the *Decameron*."

Forsythe looked both confused and confounded.

"The third story of the first day," I said softly. "The three rings."

Delacroix slowly turned to look at me; Trefoyle fixed me with hawklike eyes.

"Just so, young man," said Delacroix.

"You *bastard*!" Forsythe screeched, radiating hatred in my direction. "You scheming, literary *bastard*!"

At that point a large-boned man arrived and "escorted" Forsythe, clutching his Boccaccio, from the room. "You'll be sorry! You can't do this!" We heard his cries as he was half dragged out of the library, down the hall, and away to God knew where.

Suddenly, in the hush of the library, we found ourselves looking a bit wide-eyed at one another round the table, very much awake and utterly sober.

It was Trefoyle who broke the silence.

"Good. Well, then. Shall we carry on?"

CHAPTER 10

*The conversion of fantasy into the realm of the
possible is what constitutes the Decameron's
peculiar dynamic.*

—G. H. MCWILLIAM, BOCCACCIO SCHOLAR

T he remainder of the "business gathering" was un-
eventful compared to its first half hour. Still, the
delights of Trefoyle's library were many. He showed us the
books the world envied: a coloured *Nuremberg Chronicle*
in German, heightened in gold and bound in contemporary blind-stamped pigskin; a lovely Aldine *Hypnero-
tomachia* untrimmed in original Venetian calf; and Dame
Juliana Berners's *Treatise of Fishing with an Angle*, printed
by the great father of English printing, *Caxton!*

Trefoyle even possessed a book no one had seen before: a previously unrecorded Mainz Catholicon in oak
boards with the original clasps still present. Seeing these
precious books was, for me, a near-religious experience.

I kept wondering what my fellow members would say
if they knew about his private collection beneath us. I was
rather surprised that Trefoyle kept the treasures he'd just
shown us up here and not down in his treasure room; but

there is no explaining why collectors prize one volume over another.

At the stroke of one o'clock, our host announced that it was time for luncheon, which would be taken in the garden. As I followed my fellow club members out to the manicured lawn, flanked spectacularly by both sea and castle, I spotted Hawkes near the door.

"Hawkes," I said, taking him aside. "What happened to Miss Garthwaite?"

"What do you mean, sir?"

"I mean, her room was empty when I went to look in on her this morning. Has she gone?"

"Yes, sir. The—er—Dibdin damsel always leaves the next morning before people are about. And in this case she was particularly eager to get away. I took her out to the driver just after I saw you this morning. She was quite upset. And who can blame her?"

I shook my head. "Thanks, Hawkes. I wish she'd come and spoken to me about it—we're friends. Did she say anything more about last night?"

"No. She was quite reticent."

"I see." I noticed then that Trefoyle was looking straight at us from where he stood on the lawn. It seemed to me that he was smiling. "Oops," I said, turning to Hawkes. "Hope I haven't got you in trouble. See you later."

I moved towards the tables, leaving Hawkes to his position by the door. It was obvious that since morning the castle staff had been extremely busy. Seven round tables covered in pristine white cloths, decorated with centre-pieces of roses, were strewn decoratively about the lawn.

"May I join you for lunch?" Sir Harold Westering asked. He seemed to be hovering near my shoulder. Had he heard me talking to Hawkes?

"Please do." I wondered if perhaps the senior members of the club had schemed to make me feel welcome, with each taking care of me at one event over the course of the weekend. Or, my suspicious side postulated, perhaps they had set up a rota to *observe* me? Trefoyle himself had taken me in hand at the shooting party; young Ashleigh at tea; Chesterton at dinner; and now Sir Harold at lunch. Who, I wondered, would be charged with me tonight at the anniversary dinner?

As we took seats at the table nearest the sea, the scent of salt spray was strong, and breakers crashed onto the nearby rocks. The servants fussed, spreading table napkins in our laps and pouring wine. It was a bizarre if suitably dramatic setting for treachery and death. I cast about for Forsythe, but didn't see him at any of the tables. Sulking in his room, perhaps.

I worried a bit at having drawn Sir Harold, wondering if perhaps he would take this opportunity to have a go at me about my *Bookseller* article. But so far I hadn't sensed any hostility in him or Lord Peter Albemarle—either towards me or between the two of them. Perhaps the two elderly gents were so far distanced from their businesses at this point that they no longer regarded them as their own.

Or perhaps they were only camouflaging their desperate hatred of me with cast-iron wills.

As I made introductory meal time chitchat about the weather with Sir Harold, I found myself marvelling at the extraordinarily complicated rules that applied to English upper-class social interaction. In normal company, there were layers upon layers of subtle signals that each conversational partner looked for in the other: education, where and when; background, who and what; with an automatic dismissal of anyone newly arrived, foreign, or simply boring by virtue of discussing religion, politics, or children. This all happened subconsciously, the habit of a lifetime, a subtle, continuous evaluation, a dubious skill passed by osmosis and breeding from generation to generation.

This gathering, therefore, was truly exceptional. Rarely

did one find so many people of such similar education, background, and sensibilities in one place. One would never hear such brazen statements in Dibdinian society as "When I was up at Eton" or "When I was up at Cambridge." Everyone here had attended similar institutions. With none of those qualifications to establish, there was a feeling of kinship, of closeness through shared experience and understanding. But I was well aware that all this tended dangerously toward snobbishness. It was the "we" apart from "they" that made me uncomfortable.

As Sir Harold and I commented on such acceptable topics as the climate, the view, and a passing yacht, I was secretly amused that neither of us referred to the three Boccaccios revealed at the meeting. In the completely unacknowledged game of conversational one-upmanship, it was understood that to refrain from mentioning the events of the morning would be to display a truly impressive degree of imperturbability.

So naturally, the most breathtaking event in English book history for years—decades—was utterly ignored by those of us who had witnessed it. This could have happened, I reflected, only in England. Had Max been there, he'd have got up on his chair and shouted "IT HAPPENED! LET'S TALK ABOUT IT!"

I smiled at the thought as I raised the first wineglass of the day to my lips. It was a Provençal rosé, perfectly suited to what I saw from my menu would be prawns, sea bass, lobster in wine sauce, and salade niçoise. How appropriate: a meal from the sea, eaten at the water's edge.

A waiter placed a decorative display of giant prawns before me. Trefoyle gave us permission to begin by taking the first bite himself, and Sir Harold followed. I tucked in.

There was certainly no lack of conversational material to span a luncheon with Sir Harold; not only would I need to bring up the Bedchamber book to him and drop a hint about knowing who the thief was, I could ask him about his fascinating charitable cause. While his ancestors had been outspoken against returning the Elgin marbles to their rightful home, Sir Harold had taken a slightly different tack. He'd earned a reputation for trying to keep England's treasures from benign but persistent cultural marauders such as the Americans, Saudis, and Japanese. Together they'd exported so much furniture, books, and historical artifacts from the sceptred isle that it was a wonder anything remained. Sir Harold's Committee for the Preservation of English Artifacts was regularly in the news.

"What is your committee working on at the moment?" I asked, sincerely interested.

His mouth open in a startled O. The plump prawn he'd speared fell back onto his plate.

What had I said?

In the next instant, however, he recovered. Without referring to his obvious surprise at my mention of the committee, he said in his courtly way, "Very kind of you to ask, Plumtree. The fact that you have done so confirms my desire to have you as a member."

"I would be honoured," I said, trying to hide the true extent of my surprise. It *was* quite an honour to be invited to join Sir Harold's committee. Although I already had my finger in a dozen charitable pies, I was more than willing to plough a little time and money into purchasing back some of England's finest books and other antiques. It would also, perhaps, put me in a better position to probe for information on the Bedchamber book.

"One of our most innovative—and successful— efforts," Sir Harold continued, "has been to influence the Government to legislate against the wholesale export of our past. It might sound draconian, but believe me" —he shook his head—"it's needed. We're finding an extremely sympathetic audience at Westminster amongst the Conservatives."

He sat back as the waiter replaced the empty prawn plate with one containing a mound of sea bass in a greenish sauce. Making a humourous face for my benefit at the colour of the sauce out of sight of the waiter, Sir Harold forked up a bite. With a lift of his eyebrows, he nodded grudgingly.

"Looks frightful, tastes fantastic," he pronounced.

"In that case, I'll risk it."

"You've risked quite a lot, haven't you, starting that new trade list at the Press? I've been watching it. It's really taken off."

I swallowed a bite of fish, in a sauce that tasted purely and pleasantly of coriander, surprised that Sir Harold had taken note of my modest trade list. "I suppose it was risky," I said, "but sometimes a risk is necessary."

The sun dipped behind a cloud bank, abruptly changing the warmth of the afternoon to chill, and extinguishing the vivid colours of sea and sky. Surprised, I glanced up; I hadn't seen the clouds approaching.

"I don't suppose you'd be willing to use your contacts at Westminster to help the committee?"

I admired his directness. He knew the prime minister and I were friends.

"I would be happy to mention it to Graeme; it seems the sort of thing he'd enjoy being a part of—in a personal rather than an official capacity."

"Good, good," Sir Harold said, his nose reddening and his bonhomie growing by the moment. "I'll contact you about our next meeting. Quite a few of us are here today. Trefoyle, you know, is actually president now. He has skills the rest of us only read about in Ian Fleming novels. Believe it or not, they come in quite handy sometimes." He picked up his wineglass and drank, obviously enjoying his own little private joke. I might have been wrong, but I thought the wine might have affected him a bit.

"What sort of James Bond skills?" I was intrigued, considering the side I'd seen of Trefoyle that morning.

"Oh, don't mind me. Talking too much, that's all. Shouldn't have said anything. Hush-hush, you know." Sir

Harold studied me then as if seeing me for the first time. "I say! Has anyone ever told you that you look remarkably like that new Bond chap in the films?" He struggled for the name, then looked triumphant. "Pierce! Or is it Price?"

I laughed and shook my head, privately reliving the evening Sarah and I had run into the "new Bond chap" at a premiere in Leicester Square. When the film star had caught a glimpse of me, he had come over and performed an impressive bit of mime, pretending he was looking in the mirror as he stood opposite me. Sarah and I had laughed and gone for drinks with him afterwards.

"I could use a few Bond skills of my own now that this book of mine has been stolen."

"Yes, I heard about that," Sir Harold said, growing immediately serious. "Any progress on finding it?"

"Well." I leaned a bit nearer him. "I do have a theory, but I hate to cast aspersions on anyone until I know for sure. . . . I think I'm about to gain the bit of evidence I need—here this weekend."

He raised his eyebrows. "You don't say! A member of the *club*?"

I tried for a smug look and nodded.

"Good God!" Sir Harold exclaimed, and lapsed into silence. Shortly after that, he lit the inevitable cigar, and the other members at the table distracted us from each other. The man on my right, Turnbull, whom I'd met with Jones-Harris the night before, had heard of my sailing exploits. Would I care to go out on Trefoyle's yacht with him after lunch? I eagerly accepted, thinking that I wouldn't turn down any opportunity to talk with members of the club. I told him that I did, however, want to get back in time for the helicopter flights—another chance to hobnob with Chesterton and others, though I didn't tell Turnbull that. Besides, I'd been looking forward to it ever since Trefoyle had sent me the programme for the weekend.

"Fine, fine," he said, and we agreed to change our

clothes and meet down at the private harbour in half an hour. Replete with prawns, wine, sea bass, lobster, salad, and finally liqueur-drenched strawberry tart followed by coffee, I managed to haul myself back to my room. But on the way there, I thought of Forsythe again, with a pang of worry. What if deChauncey had got to him? DeChauncey had been at lunch; once Forsythe had been escorted from the library, he had never reappeared. I asked a servant if he knew which was Mr. Forsythe's room.

"Fourth on the right from the top of the stairs, sir," he replied.

How on earth did they remember? I hurried to the room and knocked on the door. A moment later it opened; a quite normal-looking, very much alive Forsythe blinked at me from inside. "Yes?"

"I didn't see you at lunch, just hoped you were all right."

He smiled. "Very kind of you, Plumtree." He glanced down the hallway in both directions. "Listen, don't take our antics here too seriously, all right? Really, it's not all as bizarre as it seems. Trust me. Now, go out and enjoy yourself. I'll see you later." To my surprise, he winked, then closed the door in my face.

I wandered back to my room, shaking my head. Once safely inside, I turned the lock. As I turned away from the door, a bright flash of green caught my eye. On the table before the fireplace was a quarter-inch-high stack of A4 pages tied with the eye-catching ribbon, neatly word-processed. On the top sheet were the words, in Palatino:

Synopsis of
A Kingdom by the Sea
by Harold Hawkes

He hasn't wasted any time, I thought, sitting down at the chair before the acrid-smelling fireplace. I wouldn't have time to read the pages carefully now, but years of wading through the slush pile of unsolicited fiction at the Press had taught me to skim with great rapidity. I never entirely disregarded a manuscript that came out of the blue; one unsolicited gem had become my first trade bestseller.

But Hawkes's manuscript brought me up short. The book he proposed was clearly a thinly disguised roman à clef of his time in the service of an esteemed nobleman. It was an exposé of the most scathing sort, one that cruelly revealed all his master's weaknesses, peccadilloes, and, as it turned out, crimes. Hawkes didn't use the name Trefoyle, but the character was clearly the earl.

I soon learned that Trefoyle had been hauled into court years before for dallying with a choirboy from the castle church. Though it was illuminating, that titbit wasn't half as extraordinary as what followed.

Hawkes's synopsis portrayed Trefoyle as a madman obsessed with a militaristic form of religion that included ruling the world through military might. The author reported secret comings and goings through sea entrances beneath the castle, and mysterious meetings in the wee hours in the subterranean rooms beneath the earl's bedroom suite, next to the sea. The shadowy characters who arrived at the harbour by night, Hawkes reported, were members of an almost extinct brotherhood consisting solely of descendants of crusading knights.

I let the synopsis fall out of my hands and into my lap. Some of the pages slid onto the floor.

Good Lord! What if it were true? It was even more bizarre that such a scenario had actually occurred to me when Trefoyle had related his tale about the Crusades and my family arms. But it had seemed so unlikely as to be ridiculous. What if he meant to include *me* in that bizarre brotherhood?

And what if Margulies's death had something to do with all this? Could Trefoyle's odd suspicion of an attempt on Forsythe's life be related too?

Forcing my eyes back to the page, I saw that the story ended with an almost believable suggestion that Trefoyle, using pleasure boats that came and went from his harbour, was sending arms to mysterious allies of some sort in the Middle East—where, exactly, Hawkes didn't say. His goal? The deranged earl planned to conquer the Holy Land again for Christendom.

It struck me that I would be in one of those pleasure boats, at that very slip, in moments.

It also struck me that if Hawkes knew about all these activities, perhaps he'd been a part of them and couldn't be trusted. That might explain his coolness before lunch when I'd asked him about Clarissa; but then Trefoyle had been watching us.

This weekend was growing stickier by the moment.

I stood and threw off my suit, donning khakis and a polo shirt for sailing, along with my prized Top-Siders from Massachusetts. I didn't know whether to feel sorry for Hawkes for imagining such a farfetched set of circumstances, or for myself for having believed I could trust him. From what I'd seen yesterday, his story was *just*, perhaps, possible. But what did Hawkes hope to accomplish by writing it down, even seeking publication? Perhaps his synopsis was a cry for help. He'd seen wrongs committed, obsessions indulged at terrific cost to others, and was taking a stand. Perhaps, because I'd asked him to help me that weekend, I'd been chosen as *his* accomplice. The stuff of mystery novels, I thought. But it was just possible. . . .

In the next moment I had a vision of masked modern-day Crusaders in skin-tight diving suits instead of chain mail, and laughed aloud at my gullibility. Surely it was much too unlikely. It was just a story, someone's idea of an adventure story.

Get a grip, Plumtree.

Much relieved, I glanced round the room, ready to dash to the harbour. Sarah's picture next to the bed caught my eye. Pulling out my phone, which I'd already fastened inside a Velcro-closing pocket of my windbreaker, I pressed in her number.

The line was engaged. I wanted to scream. Rarely, since our engagement, had so much time passed without us speaking. The continued lack of contact brought back a flash of the uncomfortable feeling I'd had the night we'd been cut off, specifically my unspeakable fear that something would happen to her now our wedding was so close.

I tried Max, concerned about his earlier state of mind. Busy too. Good. I chose to hope they were talking to each other and stuffed the phone back into my pocket.

As I travelled down the staircase and through the downstairs corridor, I heard a television turned on at high volume. I followed the source of the noise, and found myself in the downstairs drawing room. Trefoyle, Chesterton, Delacroix, and Westering were riveted to a Sky station newscast.

"... and war looks inevitable this afternoon as British and American forces mass with the United Nations peace-keeping force against Iraq. The agreement for arms inspections in Iraq by the UN will, Secretary General Mofi Danan says, be enforced. Danan, Foreign Secretary Dowe, and the American secretary of defence have issued statements expressing their firm commitment to enforcing the agreement. Diplomatic efforts continue, but so far there seems to be little progress. ..."

Trefoyle cast a grim glance at the rest of us in the room and shook his head once, regretfully. I took this as supporting evidence that Hawkes's synopsis was pure bunk. If Trefoyle *wanted* war in the Middle East, he'd be thrilled about this. Our host switched off the set with a button on his remote control and said, "Let's hope they can get that mess sorted out . . . quickly. In the meantime, let the revels resume!" He gave a determined smile and shooed us outside to enjoy ourselves.

I caught him on the way out. "Trefoyle."

He turned, preoccupied. "Hmm—oh, Plumtree. Yes, my boy. Come in here." He led me into what must have been his private study; a desk faced the door, with still more shelves jammed with books behind it. One particularly attractive antique globe stood next to it. "What is it?" he asked, closing the door behind us.

"I couldn't help but wonder what you were proving with all those shocking Boccaccio copies. Why did you pretend to be surprised when I told you the rumour about one other besides Forsythe's?"

He smiled a rather cold little smile. "Two reasons. Neither of which I can tell you just now."

We stared each other down for a moment; neither of us looked away.

"Let's just say, Plumtree, that we're in much the same position. Just as you're pretending to know who has the Bedchamber book to smoke out the thief, I'm playing a little game with the Boccaccios. Fair enough?"

For just an instant I considered telling him; then my natural reserve took over. There was a reason Ian had told me to keep it quiet, and this could be it. What if Trefoyle *suspected* that I had the Boccaccio with the unusual piece of paper in it, and had been trying to get a reaction from me?

"Fair enough," I said. "I suppose. Where did you get the other Boccaccios, if you don't mind my asking?"

"Aged facsimiles, skillfully produced, of course. Forsythe's *is* the only real Boccaccio here." With that, Trefoyle strode to the door and opened it, passing through brusquely and leaving me alone in the room to ponder what had just happened. I studied the desk, books, and walls, stopped short at a photograph of Trefoyle and Graeme shaking hands on Trefoyle's yacht, the *Crusader*. If I didn't know better, I'd think Graeme had set up this entire weekend at Trefoyle's to recover the Bedchamber book. But nothing had led me to believe that the plans for the event had been hasty or unusual; at least no one had referred to a change of plan. Perhaps it really had been Trefoyle's year to host the anniversary weekend all along.

I left the gloom of the office and went quickly outdoors. Turnbull would be waiting. Hurrying down to the yacht harbour, the sky blue once again but the wind challengingly gusty, I saw Turnbull removing the sail cover aboard the *Crusader*. Helping him was the muscular young man who'd restrained Forsythe in the library earlier. I assumed the stranger was one of Trefoyle's hired crewmen, as his cap bore the Trefoyle crest.

As I stepped on board, Turnbull smiled a greeting and came to meet me, letting the crewman raise the sail. "Sorry I'm a few minutes late," I said. "Trefoyle had the television news on inside. The situation doesn't look good."

"Ah. And Trefoyle in particular has reason to worry," Turnbull said, seating himself at the tiller.

"Why is that?"

"No one's told you about Trefoyle's dealings with Iraq."

I thought of Hawkes's book and Sir Harold's comments at lunch. "What dealings?"

Turnbull squinted into the sun, eyeing our route out to sea. "Trefoyle doesn't talk much about it, but everyone knows. He has dealings of some sort with them, dating from the time his forefathers lived over there. Not business, of course, but diplomatic, or humanitarian causes. The rumours are always vague, but everyone knows. He's a personal friend of some of the religious and political leaders of the moment. . . . Remember the Gulf War? They flew Trefoyle in to talk to Saddam Hussein, all very hush-hush, and before we knew it there was a truce— which was reneged upon, of course. Still, he understands them." He smiled at me and shrugged.

It was rather a wild day at sea, the dream of every experienced sailor. The wind caught our sail and yanked us away from the harbour. The muscular crewman trimmed the sail expertly; Turnbull and I took turns at the tiller and enjoyed intermittent snippets of conversation.

As we flew across the water with the fresh breeze, which at the same time made me wonder about a helicopter flight through such unpredictable gusts, Turnbull complimented me on a book in our trade list that had recently hit the bookshops. I'd written a rather personal introduction to the book, as it was my father's account of his solo sailing adventures in the South Seas. It had already received orders far beyond what I'd expected.

Turnbull was at the tiller. The temperamental wind had now waned to the point where we had no breeze at all, and the crewman let the sails luff, watching for a puff of wind. Turnbull announced he was going to get a mineral water, and did I want one. I told him yes, and looked up to watch a seagull as it sailed overhead. The crewman took the tiller while Turnbull went below.

At that moment the yacht seemed abruptly to change direction, without warning. I never actually saw the crewman move the tiller, but the boom whirled round in my direction with terrific speed and force, the unfastened lines whizzing through their cleats. The deck rocked wildly. Perhaps if I'd had any sleep at all the night before, I'd have responded more quickly. I heard rather than saw the metal cylinder of the boom swinging straight towards me and, despite the years of my life I'd spent aboard yachts, didn't duck far enough, fast enough.

If I hadn't ducked at all, it might have been far worse. As it was, the heavy cylinder knocked me at forehead height, unfortunately for the lump already there. As I flew overboard, my last thought was what rotten luck it was to have it hit in exactly the same place.

Suddenly I found myself underwater, disoriented. The Trefoyle crest swam into view somehow, or the impression of it. Then I imagined I was struggling to stop the waiter pouring wine down my throat. He was holding my head, keeping me from escaping. The harder I fought to escape the stream of liquid, the harder he tried to hold me in it.

Then I realised that Turnbull and the crewman were in the water with me, trying to help me back up to the surface. My head popped up above the water, and Turnbull and the crewman surfaced next to me. We were treading water in our very own little Bermuda Triangle in the yacht's shadow, gasping for breath.

"You really went flying," Turnbull panted. "Are you all right?" He winced as he studied my forehead.

"Clumsy of me. I'm sorry."

"Let me get back on board first," the crewman said. "I'll put out the steps."

Turnbull and I let him swim ahead of us the few yards to the yacht. As he threw out the steps, his ring glistened in the sunlight. I climbed up, my head aching, and caught a glimpse of Trefoyle's crest unmistakably engraved on the signet ring's gold surface.

The crewman, it seemed, saw me looking at his finger— my powers of subtlety were dulled at that point—and abruptly slid his hand behind his back. Fascinating, I thought. Accident or incident, the threat of that morning's note had come a bit closer to being fulfilled.

We started back, all three a bit subdued, to land. The wind had picked up again, and between the bright sun and the brisk breeze, our clothes began to dry stiffly on us. Turnbull talked the crewman into letting him trim the sail, and we enjoyed the incomparable thrill of heeling to thirty degrees. By the time we arrived at the harbour, the delight of the outing had far overwhelmed the inconvenience of the mishap—or whatever one might call it. I did, however, vow not to leave my back turned to the crewman again.

"Sorry for the fuss," I apologised to both of them as we climbed off. "And thanks." The crewman shrugged impassively; Turnbull waved it off. "Coming over to the helicopter pad, Turnbull?" I asked.

He laughed. "No. Don't tell me *you* are!"

I looked at him questioningly.

"Are you *daft*?" Turnbull shouted. "In this wind? Don't you want to go in and take some aspirin tablets or something?"

"It's not as bad as all that," I assured him. If I went and sat in my room, I'd never work out anything. Besides, the child in me quite fancied a ride in that noisy machine.

Turnbull shook his head and clapped me on the back as he hiked toward the castle in his damp clothes. "See you later, then," he said.

But by the time I'd made my way to the hangar, the first flight had already gone. The Chesterton family arms, rather like a royal warrant insignia, graced the side of the large forest-green aircraft in gilt paint. I watched as the helicopter moved up and away over the glittering water, the wind snatching away and then intensifying the powerful roar.

"No matter," Lord Peter Albemarle told me. He, too, watched the impressive craft move away, shielding his eyes from the sun with a pale, freckled hand. "He'll be back for another go. Westering tells me you're joining us on the committee, Plumtree."

"Yes." I turned to look at him. "Good of you to have me. I have an artifact of my own I'm trying to keep from harm at the moment."

"I've heard about your stolen incunable," Lord Peter responded, shaking his head. "Shocking. I've also heard you know who's taken it. Not a common thief, eh?"

Good. Word was getting round.

"No, I don't think so. Still, I think it will all be resolved quite soon."

We watched the rotors beat the air, the wop-wop of the blades fading. "An hour ago Chesterton said he wasn't sure we could go up; someone up at Tintagel reported wind shears. It seems to have improved a bit since then," Lord Peter said doubtfully.

"Quite unpredictable today."

I decided not to tell him about my freak experience with the wind—if that was what it had been—out on the yacht. But it was unquestionably an unsettled afternoon. Patches of dark-bottomed clouds sailed across the sky, instantly changing the sunny day to a grey, colder one as they had at lunch. It was not unlike my state of mind. One moment I thought Hawkes's novel was a secret indictment of the respected Earl Trefoyle, the next I thought it was pure fiction—only to learn that it was partially true after all. One moment we were becalmed, and the next I was flung overboard by a fluky swing of the boom.

And there was the threat under my coffee cup. I considered the incident on the yacht . . . I simply couldn't be sure whether it had been an accident. Aside from my strange feeling of being held underwater, and my association of that feeling with the Trefoyle crest, I had no reason to think it had been deliberate. And it made sense that after I'd fallen in, instinct told me to keep water from flowing into my lungs.

Besides, who could have engineered such a thing? The crewman *had* been standing on the other side of the boom, at the tiller. It was just possible that when he'd swung the tiller round, he might have helped the boom fly in my direction . . . but the crewman worked for Trefoyle. And Trefoyle was on *my* side.

Right?

For an instant, I did consider returning to my room and forsaking the helicopter flight. But as the elegant chopper headed back toward the hangar, I was reminded of my task. I forgot my doubts, eager for the chance to learn more about Chesterton—the man whose ancestor had murdered King Richard I.

The helicopter landed with all the noise, wind, and excitement I loved about the aircraft.

"Plumtree! There you are. Welcome aboard," Chesterton bellowed, ushering his previous passengers away from the wind blast. "Ah, Westers! You'll have to put out that blasted cigar, old boy!" I turned to look behind me on the crushed-shell path and was pleased to see my recent luncheon partner. We greeted each other with smiles as he pulled the cigar out of his mouth and crushed it beneath the handmade heel of his shoe. "And Lord Peter. Splendid passenger list." Lord Peter smiled and saluted Chesterton.

Chesterton ushered the deceptively fragile-looking Lord Peter into the craft first, as the oldest of our group. Perhaps Chesterton had never seen the latter powering his scull at Henley; he wouldn't have treated the older man quite so carefully. Sir Harold climbed into the backseat next to Albemarle, and Chesterton indicated that I should sit next to him in the front. Surprised at being allowed the best seat, I clambered aboard and strapped myself in, noting that I had a stick and pedals just like Chesterton's.

Chesterton hopped into the pilot's seat, indicated that we were to put on our headphones so he could talk to us en route, and checked to see that our seat belts were fastened. A bank of complicated-looking instruments bulged into the cockpit between Chesterton and me; I noticed two identical sets of indicators. Two engines, I guessed.

"It was a bit choppy on the last outing," our pilot said into his headset microphone, "but I think we'll be all right. It's a marvellous way to view Trefoyle's paradise. I like to leave the doors open—ten times the fun, and a much better view."

No doubt, I thought, and checked my seat belt with a thrill of fear.

He grinned and lifted off, then, slowly, straight up. I

watched as his feet moved pedals on the floor, and his left arm pulled up on a hand-brake type of lever. The stick was just in front of him; he adjusted it very slightly as we went. It struck me that flying a helicopter must be quite challenging, with three controls to manage simultaneously. When he'd pulled up on the hand-brake–looking lever, the roar of the machine had increased; I guessed it controlled the throttle. The stick, I knew, determined direction, but I had no idea what the pedals were for.

"Chesterton," I said into the microphone just in front of my mouth. "What do the pedals do?"

"Rudder, my boy. In the tail. Keeps the whole chopper from spinning round with the torque of the rotors." He smiled over at me, appreciative of my interest. I was happy to note the duke seemed absolutely sober. "This is a Froggie helicopter, an Aerospatiale. Bit of trivia for you, since you seem interested: The Frogs make their rotors go in the opposite direction to every other helicopter in the world." He gave a bark of laughter.

I smiled and looked out my open door. Even through the padded sound-dampening material of the headphones, the twin turbines and the rotors were deafening. The sound was thrilling in an instinctive, gut-wrenching kind of way—like the involuntary flutter in your stomach when a plane flies low overhead. I felt another tingle of near-fear as we rose above the castle, past the Maltese cross still mounted on its uppermost tower. Then we swung out over the ocean as the previous load of passengers had done. We were floating in what amounted to a glass bubble, suspended quite unnaturally over the ocean by several backwards-spinning strips of metal.

I leaned close to the window and looked out over the sea. "What's that?" I asked Chesterton, speaking again into the button microphone in front of my mouth. I pointed to a small, apparently deserted island on which a primitive shelter sat in ruins.

"Pirate's Island. Just a bit of rock where—"

Suddenly it felt as if a crushing blow had struck the helicopter. We dipped sharply to the right.

I was aware of Chesterton struggling with the controls as the craft floundered, losing altitude. His left hand groped for something by his door—the lever? With the helicopter tilting precipitously, I looked straight down at the rocky island. Only my seat belt prevented me from plunging hundreds of feet to my death. Staring down in horror, I had a vertiginous sensation of falling.

"Hang on!" Chesterton cried. He reached a hand to my chest as if to grab a handful of clothing and hold me in the craft. But, jerked about as he was by the violently rocking helicopter, his large hand clapped onto the edge of my seat-belt latch.

To my horror, the latch released. Both strap and buckle fell away, dangling uselessly at my right side, banging violently against the outside of the helicopter in the wind. Still, I seemed anchored to my seat by the force of the rotors struggling to pull us upward. But the thought of the island and ocean below, and how very far I was above them, made me dizzy. I *felt* I was falling . . . I groped for something to hang on to and reached for the strap of the seat belt.

Everything might still have been all right had the air not struck us another violent blow. This time the wind hit the helicopter from above with a sharp impact, as if the massive flat palm of a hand had swatted us down and to one side. Before I knew what was happening, I was sailing right out of the seat. I clutched blindly at the doorframe on my way to oblivion. The wind was a screaming, violent force, whipping me about like a blade of grass, fighting to pry me from the craft. I hung on for dear life as the massive hand swatted the helicopter again; my right hand was knocked down and to the side; my knuckles rapped painfully hard against the rim of the floor. Desperate, I extended my fingers and latched on. And so I came to be literally hanging from the helicopter, attached to it by sheer force of will as Chesterton fought to right his craft. Below me, the sea rippled in sparkling wonder, looking miles and miles away. I tried not to think about falling. I wouldn't fall. I couldn't.

The rotors began to make a sharp slapping sound as if they weren't used to rotating perpendicular to the ground. An engine coughed. *Try something, anything, Chesterton,* I pleaded.

The little aircraft began to plummet downward, and I knew we were lost. The wind's irresistible force sucked me outward, away from the helicopter. I clung as desperately as ever, but felt my fingers slipping. I felt I might be torn limb from limb from the sheer force of the air rushing around me.

As I clung to the rim of the floor with my fingertips alone, Chesterton miraculously brought the helicopter out of the spin and we flew straight again. I hung on as Chesterton got the craft into a stationary hover. *How much longer could I do this?*

"Climb in!" I heard over my headphones. "Get his hand!" Sir Harold had come forward and was reaching out his hand from behind my seat. I had just let go with my right hand and was reaching for Westering's proffered lifeline, when the chopper tilted precipitously again to starboard. My right hand flew away from Westering, the fingers of my left hand slipping as the craft seemed to founder above me. With a combination of horror and resignation, I felt my whole body weakening.

At that moment of extremity I thought of Sarah. I didn't want to lose her, didn't want to miss life with her. And I couldn't let her lose me.

My mind seemed to clear a bit; I clung with all my might, telling myself to think of managing it for just one more second, then another second, and another. But the wind, gravity, and my own weight were determined to pull me away, the violent air rushing past my ears like a chorus of evil spirits. Through the fog of confusion, only one thing was apparent: Chesterton was "accidentally" doing a fine job of trying to kill me.

So why didn't I just let go? Perhaps it would be safer.

I looked down. He'd moved away from the rocky island, whether by force or choice, and was over the water quite close to shore. I would do what he *wasn't* expecting; I wouldn't give him any more chances to manage my death his way, if that was what he was doing.

I let go.

CHAPTER 11

I am part of all that I have read.

—JOHN KIERNAN

The wind whistled round me as I dropped. The helicopter had been so dangerously low that perhaps only fifty feet separated me from the water—though my free-fall seemed to go on forever. Above me I heard shouts of alarm.

As I plummeted towards the water, I smelled its fresh, pungent scent. I curled into a ball in an attempt to offer myself some small protection, and hit.

The impact was stunning, like smacking into solid ground. The breath was knocked right out of me. I plunged far below the surface of the waves. I'm a competent swimmer, but I felt the current tugging me down. I opened my eyes, but the water was so murky that at first I couldn't tell which way was up; I'd only just worked it out and begun to kick my way out of the current's powerful grip, when it slammed me into something hard.

The island?

I reached out with my hands and felt a smooth metallic surface. Then my fingers encountered a round wheel mounted on the metal. Hanging on to the wheel, I got my feet on it and pushed off, upward and away, trying with all my might to break free of the powerful current.

With relief, I broke into brighter water and then into sunlight. I hadn't been very far underwater, then, after all. What had that been—an underwater door into the island?

I heard shouts. A speedboat trawled nearby, waiting to ferry me—dead or alive—back to shore. I saw its hulk approaching, but not much more—my contact lenses had fallen out. My head throbbed disastrously as a strong arm helped pull me into the boat. From his all-white clothes and the gold on his hand, I knew it was the crewman from the yacht; he didn't speak as he took the wheel again and piloted us back to shore. I heard the helicopter overhead like a bad echo of my headache; it had regained its equilibrium and was smoothly wop-wopping back to the landing pad.

I didn't trust myself to have it out with Chesterton just then; I thanked the crewman, waved to my fellow members as they crowded round with congratulations and concern, and limped my way directly up to the castle. As I dripped through the door, Hawkes stopped and stared.

"Sir! What's happened to you?"

I didn't seem to have the energy to answer. I kept moving toward the staircase.

"Mr. Plumtree, sir. Let me at least get you a plaster. You've cut your head. Here—come with me." He steered me round to a back room, a sort of servants' utility room, I thought, and half pushed me into a chair as he opened a first aid kit. "Shall I ring for a doctor?" he asked, swabbing the cut. Again, I saw a forcefulness and calm competence in him that surprised me.

"No. Thank you."

When he'd finished, I thanked him again. I think I was a bit dazed.

"Mr. Plumtree." he said at the door a bit sharply. "Be careful."

"Right," I replied, and staggered on up the stairs. At least things were beginning to develop . . . although I honestly couldn't be sure whether the afternoon's life-threatening episodes had been accidents or deliberate attempts on my life. Surely the yachting incident could not have been deliberate, because the crewman worked for Trefoyle . . . who was supposedly helping me recover the Bedchamber book to hand over to the Iraqis. Presumably Trefoyle understood the importance of the book to them, because of his special relationship with the Middle Easterners. And as for Chesterton . . . I supposed he could have stolen the book, but . . . *the president of the Dibdin Club*? And again, the helicopter disaster had seemed just accidental enough that I couldn't be certain. After all, who can *plan* wind shears?

I got into my room, turned the lock, swallowed three aspirin tablets, set my travel alarm for half past seven, and collapsed onto the bed.

At some point I thought I heard pounding on the door. I rolled over. Two minutes later, or so it seemed, the alarm went off.

Just reaching over to switch off the alarm was agony. Sitting up was torture. The impact of my fall seemed to have bruised every inch of my body, and my head throbbed painfully. But I wasn't going to give anyone the satisfaction of leaving.

I mourned my contact lenses, lost somewhere in the old briny, but found the spare pair in my bag where I'd stowed them.

Woodenly, I began to prepare for the anniversary dinner. Using my brain was the only way out of this . . . and things could get far trickier. As I showered, trying in vain to keep the bandage dry on my forehead, I laboured to put the pieces together. My mind was far from clear; I felt more like a punch-bag than a human being.

But slowly some obvious bits slotted into place. There was more going on than just the theft of the Bedchamber book. Margulies was dead. I didn't feel confident, despite Trefoyle's disclaimer, that the cause of his death would be investigated. My old friend may well have been killed, as I'd nearly been twice that day.

Why Margulies? I stood under the warm stream of water in the shower and racked my aching brain. The new Boccaccio edition . . . the upcoming "life of Dibdin" novel . . .

But the Boccaccio was already out, to universal praise. And the Dibdin book hadn't even been written yet as far as I knew. Besides, why kill him over *that* book?

Dibdin . . . who cared about Dibdin? Then I remembered the moment of silence at "tea" the previous afternoon when I'd mentioned Haslewood's "legendary books" list, and said that Margulies wanted to work it into his book somehow, since Dibdin had been so fond of Haslewood and had inherited all his papers. I had surely sensed something, a tension in the air . . . perhaps it hadn't been coincidental silence, but people startled into rapt attention at the mention of Dibdin's name—or Haslewood's. But again—who would care so much about the founder of the Dibdin Club, or harmless old Haslewood?

Of course! Margulies's death *was* tied to the Bedchamber book. Van Vanderbilt had told me that night at the Chateaubriand that my incunable was listed in Haslewood's list of "legendary books." Perhaps someone didn't want word of the Bedchamber book to get out in any form . . . and a mention in Haslewood's list would lend credibility to its existence. Margulies and I had been about to publish that list for the first time. . . .

For a moment I had an eerie feeling that King Edward

IV's hatchet men had travelled forward in time, still ruthlessly obsessed with preventing all mention of the Bedchamber book. Was this a curse that would carry on from generation to generation?

I shook off a case of the creeps and officially dismissed my earlier shot in the dark that Margulies's death had been tied to old Lord Ashleigh's by their association with the campaign to eliminate hereditary peerages. It was much more likely—obvious, in fact—that the weekend's tragedies revolved around the Bedchamber book.

It also occurred to me that if someone's goal was forever to forestall the publication of Haslewood's list, I was as much in danger of being bumped off as Margulies had been. And that was in addition to my dangerous posture of pretending I knew the identity of the thief.

I plodded back into the bedroom towelling off my hair. I needed to ring Max again, have him track down the manuscript, whatever had been completed, at Margulies's flat. And come to think of it, Diana's facsimile had never arrived. Hardly surprising; someone was likely to have taken that as well. I pulled my mobile phone out of my sodden pocket, but it was absolutely dead. I'd have to find a telephone somewhere else.

As I threw the phone down in disgust, I stopped short. Since I'd entered the shower, someone had left a message on my mirror, brazenly scrawled in violent red lipstick: THIS IS YOUR LAST CHANCE TO LEAVE—ALIVE.

Lipstick?

I fought down fear at the sight of the stark red letters, and told myself I was making progress. Someone was very afraid. How, I wondered, were people getting into my room? Hawkes or Trefoyle could have, certainly. But instinct told me it wasn't either of them. Someone must have felt I was close to the truth, but they were still just trying to frighten me. If they'd really wanted to kill me, they could easily have done it in the shower.

Bollocks to them.

I drew a deep breath, summoned my reserves, and wiped the obscene scrawl off the mirror. My reflection showed that the flesh-coloured plaster obtained from Hawkes hid my cut nicely, along with part of the new and expanded bruise that was colouring the skin around it.

My plan was to find a phone while everyone was busy downing their first few drinks before dinner, and ring Max and Sarah. Then I would get through dinner as best I could, preferably alive. After dinner, I would do a bit of investigating. It was possible that if I made a physical inspection while people were out of their rooms, I might find my book.

It was a distinctly odd feeling, walking into Trefoyle's library and not knowing which of those eminent men and women planned to kill me . . . not to mention which of them had stolen my book.

"Plumtree!" I'd grown so used to hearing Chesterton's accent that I barely noticed any more it was *Plahmtreh*. "I've been looking for you. I knocked on your door earlier, but there was no answer."

Yes, I thought. *Perhaps you came in and left a note?* This was the great benefit of the stiff-upper-lip life-training programme: I could now, when I most needed to, look Chesterton in the eye and smile.

"Good God! Your face—did all that happen when you fell?"

"Slight accident on the yacht. Rather embarrassing."

He shook his head regretfully. "First Forsythe shot, then poor Margulies, now you. What a disaster. But listen, Plumtree. I couldn't do anything about those wind shears. And when I had to take my arm back, I—" His eyes actually grew misty, and very quickly too. Perhaps he'd studied at the Royal Academy of Dramatic Art at some point. "You know that I'd have done anything to help you, don't you?"

"Of course. Please, let's not speak of it again. But if you want to help, you might lend me your phone for a few minutes."

He looked delighted to be of assistance. Patting his pockets, he found the mobile phone clipped to his cummerbund, at his side.

"Here you are, my boy. Take it! Keep it! The number's there on the front, in case you want to receive calls. I'm just thankful you're alive." His eyes grew moist again as he gripped my arm and then brushed past me, back to work the party.

I moved out of the library, looking for a place to make my calls in privacy.

"Plumtree!" Young Ashleigh—now even *I* thought of him in those terms—came toward me at a trot. His rheumy eyes were desperately serious. "Could I speak with you for a moment?"

"Of course." Curious, I followed him round the corner into Trefoyle's deserted study. My second conference in there that day, I thought. Things were definitely hotting up. When he closed the door securely behind me and turned the lock, I became still more curious.

"Plumtree, there's something you should know." He lowered his bulk into one of the plush armchairs and sighed. "I understand you saw Trefoyle's heraldry book today."

News certainly travelled quickly in this group.

"My father, as you know, worked on that remarkable assimilation of information for twenty years. He uncovered new details, previously unrecorded families. One of those, I believe, you are now well aware of."

I nodded.

Sounding unspeakably weary, he continued. "My father also came across another family, whose details had been recorded improperly for a very long time. He shared this with me. And now I think you should know. I believe that this family found a way to kill my father. They could not bear for his book to reveal—"

The doorknob rattled. Ashleigh started in his chair.

Urgent knocks followed, then Trefoyle's voice. I raised my eyebrows at Ashleigh, went to the door, and unlocked it.

"I say! What's going on here?" Our host's bright eyes went from me to Ashleigh and back again.

Ashleigh said, struggling out of the chair, "Just sharing a bit of Dibdin lore with Plumtree, here."

"You haven't ruined our—er—surprise, have you, Ashleigh?"

"Good heavens! No," he said, affronted. He straightened his coat over his bulging middle and strode out of the room.

Surprise? I thought. *What surprise?* It was surprise enough that a *second* person had told me old Ashleigh had not died a natural death.

Trefoyle was waiting for me to leave. "Sorry, Plumtree—I need to use the telephone. If you don't mind."

"Sorry, of course." I came to my senses and departed. Ashleigh wasn't hanging about anywhere waiting to continue our discussion as I closed the door behind me. I decided to go make my own calls.

My thrice-battered body begged me not to climb the stairs to my room, so I settled on the back room Hawkes had used to bandage my cut. I left the lights off and the door cracked just enough to see the number pad on the phone.

As I finished pressing Max's number in, I noticed the number of the cell phone on a sticker adhered to its smooth black surface, then felt gooseflesh crawl: It was 0171 771017. The number Diana had given me from the British Museum phone records! It was *Chesterton* Bats had rung from his office that day.

I struggled to make sense of this as I put the already-squawking phone to my ear. "*The number you've dialled has been changed . . .*" The announcer's voice was cloying.

"Damn!" I re-entered the number and waited but received the same answer. "Damn and blast!"

Then I punched in the number at the Orchard. To my great surprise, I received the same notice. What was going on? I hadn't changed my number! With horrible certainty, I felt that something had gone badly wrong at home. I was just preparing to try Ian, when two voices spoke directly on the other side of the door.

"He tried to ring his brother, then his own house."

"But he didn't get through, right? You set up the call-forwarding to our message?"

"Yes." The other man sighed. "What a headache. Don't ask me to do *that* again."

Their voices—*whose?*—moved away.

Inside my hiding place I saw red. If they'd done something to Sarah, I'd *kill* them.

I flung open the door and looked for the two men I'd overheard; I saw no one. I hurried toward the library, where people were assembling for aperitifs, but saw no groups of two advancing into that room. Well, this was it. Involving Sarah and Max was the last straw; it was time to ring Graeme and tell him I had to abandon the weekend. But first I would find Trefoyle and tell him so.

"Plumtree! I've news for you."

The strident, affected voice of Jones-Harris called out to me as I stepped onto the parquet floor of the library. I couldn't ignore him, but I was in no mood for idle chat, especially with Jones-Harris. What I'd just heard in the back room had made my blood boil.

Eyeing my surroundings from a fresh but unpleasant perspective as I advanced to the territory staked out by Jones-Harris, I speculated that I was not unlike the rows upon rows of books surrounding us in the library. Hidden behind their quiet covers were stories of adventure, excitement, betrayal, murder, love, and unspeakable pain. But from the outside, one saw only the quiet exterior. The reader liked to think he had complete control of the book; in fact, that was far from the truth.

I'd learned that the hard way.

Chesterton's useless telephone hung heavy in my pocket, a reminder of the treachery of my "friend." "What news?" I asked Jones-Harris, burying my anger behind a facade that was as pleasant as I could make it. More flies, my father always said, would be caught with honey. Glancing at the gallery, I saw that a small orchestra had been hired for our musical pleasure that evening.

"Surely you haven't forgotten our bet?" Jones-Harris leered, smugness oozing from every pore. His smooth rosy cheeks and golden curls gave him the look of a child in a man's body.

His circle of friends in the club watched. The half-smiles on their self-satisfied faces told me they were enjoying my discomfort; it was entertainment for them as they sipped their drinks. Most unkind of them, I thought, considering they'd heard the bet the night before and knew the stakes.

I did my best to laugh but managed only a contemptuous chuckle.

"Right," I said sarcastically. "You expect me to believe that since last night at eight, you seduced my fiancée?" I shook my head and accepted a Scotch from Hawkes. At least it would be useful as a painkiller. "What do you take me for?"

"Oh, Sarah's not in Chorleywood at the Orchard anymore," Jones-Harris said, enjoying himself.

One of his friends, Marquette, I believe, said *"No, no, you berk!"* under his breath to Jones-Harris rather urgently, then hid himself behind his drink.

Disconcerted by his friend's correction, Jones-Harris ran a finger between his pudgy neck and his collar. His face blossomed red, as if his collar had suddenly tightened round his neck.

"Ah! Well, since you seem to know so much more about Sarah than I do, why don't you tell me where she is?" Grateful for natural inscrutability learned through careful observation of my father, I gazed at him.

He licked his lips and drank deeply from his martini. Finding his glass empty, he accosted a servant who took it away.

"I—ah—I really can't do that." He exchanged a look with his cohorts, who now looked away from him like schoolboys pretending they didn't share the same guilty secret. "Sorry," he finished lamely.

"Oh." This was fascinating. "Then, let me see. Perhaps I can guess how you managed this incredible feat. Is she here?"

Jones-Harris now looked distinctly uncomfortable. A servant brought him a fresh martini, to which he attached himself with immense relief. "Look. I can't tell you where she is, all right?" He gave off an exasperated air, along with his fear, and glanced round the library as if he expected spies.

"Fair enough," I said amiably. The Scotch was working admirably on my headache. It also made my tête-à-tête with Jones-Harris that much easier.

Hawkes raised his eyebrows slightly as he cruised past on drinks patrol. I dipped my head briefly, acknowledging our complicity, and relinquished my glass.

"Then at least persuade me that you have intimate knowledge of my soon-to-be wife." *Detestable as that thought may be,* I added privately.

Jones-Harris seemed to regain some of his composure at that. Casting me a nervous smile, he straightened his shoulders. "She has a m-mole, on her left—you know, there." He clapped his hand over his heart. Triumph warred with a guilty nervousness in him.

"On her left breast?" I smiled, not mincing words.

He nodded, relieved that I seemed to be taking it so well.

"You're right. But what does that prove? That you took her sunbathing?"

"Really, Plumtree. I can't believe you want me to go on."

"Oh, but I do, I do," I said, cruelly earnest.

Jones-Harris glanced at his companions, who seemed restless on their feet, as if they might abandon him at any moment. No doubt they sensed the lava beneath the ice.

He cleared his throat. "She has a scar—in a, um, private place."

Privately, I was stunned. How could he know that? For a moment I stood gazing at him, expressionless, then simply walked away. I couldn't remember a time when I'd lost my composure like that—not since childhood. I started off, heading anywhere that would take me away from Jones-Harris and his mates.

"There you are," Trefoyle said, spotting me and ushering me onto the lawn ahead of him. For some reason, I had the feeling everyone in the library was watching us. Perhaps my anger was not as well hidden as I thought.

"Do you mind if we walk?" I asked my host. "I need a walk."

"Of course, of course," he said, matching my brisk pace. "I'm a bit surprised you feel up to anything at all just now."

I saw him trying to study my face, which had no doubt already matured into even more ghastly bruises than the ones I'd seen in my mirror-cum-threat-notice-board.

"Good heavens," he exclaimed, wincing. "Alex, don't you think you should see a doctor? I really think you should. No one told me how badly you'd been hurt."

Still we walked on, toward the sea, as we had on the first day. That walk, on which he had misled me into thinking that Forsythe's life was in danger, seemed weeks, perhaps years ago.

"Chesterton feels abominable about what happened to you in the helicopter. Says he doesn't know how he'll ever make it up to you."

"I'm not so certain it was an accident," I said. We'd nearly reached the bench on which we'd sat the day before.

"What's that?" he barked. "What did you say?"

I stopped and turned to look him full in the face. "I said, Trefoyle, that I don't think it was an accident. It is quite possible that Chesterton, or you, to be honest, stole my book—at least you are the two people, as far as I can work out, who've tried to kill me. Furthermore, I think that the Dibdin Club has a very odd way of treating its new members. And now something's wrong at home; I can't reach Max or Sarah on the phone. It's all off, Trefoyle. I must leave immediately."

He nodded, almost as though he'd expected as much. "Yes, I know how you must feel," he said mildly. "But there's no need, really. Everything is fine at your home. All will become clear presently. Trust me."

He might have perceived that I did not trust him, looking away as I did toward the ocean with disdain. He chose to ignore the insult.

"Believe me, Plumtree. By the end of the evening you'll be laughing heartily at a little something we'll reveal to you. Do try to buck up. You mustn't leave now."

I marvelled at the poor taste of this group. First Clarissa Garthwaite as the Dibdin Damsel, somehow put in the position of maintaining that deplorable tradition. Then Margulies dying horridly with no one seeming to take much notice. And finally, the mockery of the unquestionably chaste person of my fiancée.

We were unable to discuss it further, as Hawkes came towards us at a run. "Telephone, sir. It's Whitehall. They said to tell you it's urgent."

A muscle twitched near Trefoyle's eye. He nodded once at Hawkes, but didn't speak to me again as he went smartly after his man to take the call.

Shortly after that the gong sounded for dinner. Gazing back at the castle, I thought of Sarah. I thought of Max. But there was something about the way Trefoyle had spoken to me . . . it almost seemed possible that things at home *were* all right, and I had somehow got the wrong end of the stick. Despite everything, I *did* trust him.

As I walked back towards the castle, heading directly for the great hall, I saw that there was an unusual sobriety about the group gathered round the banqueting table. Trefoyle stood at the head, looking grave, every bit the earl of the estate beneath the trefoil-decorated banners his ancestors had carried throughout history.

I found my place card at the head of the table again, this time next to Trefoyle on the other side of the table, on Chesterton's left. Desmond Delacroix stood directly across from me. Trefoyle clinked a massive sterling knife against a glass to get our attention.

"I'm terribly sorry to say that it looks as if things have come to a head in Iraq," Trefoyle announced. "They need me in London—you'll have to manage without me."

He looked directly at me, and seemed to want to say something further, but lifted his chin and looked away again. I interpreted the look as *We didn't manage to get the book in time.* "Chesterton will carry on for me and present my books." He raised a hand in farewell.

"Rotten luck!" the countess exclaimed.

"Good Lord!" Jones-Harris declared.

"Godspeed!" said Desmond Delacroix quietly as Trefoyle passed.

"Thank you," the harried earl replied, stopping to put a hand on Delacroix's shoulder. "Thank you."

Then he was gone, and we were left to celebrate . . .

. . . my failure.

CHAPTER 12

*Many another man would have wanted all of
them strung up, tortured, examined, and
interrogated. But in so doing, he would have
brought into the open a thing that people should
always try their utmost to conceal. And even if, by
displaying his hand, he had secured the fullest
possible revenge, he would not have lessened his
shame but greatly increased it. . . .*

—GIOVANNI BOCCACCIO, *DECAMERON*,
THIRD DAY: SECOND STORY

A hem." Chesterton stood, trying to regain control
of the table, which had fallen to verbal snip-
ing against war-mongering Yanks and towel-headed infi-
dels. "We shall carry on the tradition of the Dibdin Club,
as our predecessors have done through war, pestilence,
and privation."

Privately, I considered that the worst privation any of
our Dibdinian predecessors had experienced was probably
a shortage of cocktail olives. But I wasn't surprised that
Chesterton's rallying cry was business—and pleasure—as
usual. It was the only possible course these men and
women would consider. We could do little enough to help,
even if we abandoned our hedonistic pursuits. But there
was no escaping the tragedy of the fact that thousands of

men and women were leaving homes and families to risk their lives in the euphemistically named peacekeeping force, while we continued nonchalantly with our toasts.

In the next moment, however, Chesterton surprised me by making a concession to the extraordinary circumstances. "In view of this evening's developments, I would like His Grace the archbishop to offer a prayer for our nation— and the world." Chesterton sat as the clergyman rose to do his duty.

"Let us pray." In the momentary hush, heads bowed, chairs scraped, and delicate coughs rattled.

"Lord God, Heavenly Father, we beseech You to guide the world You have created, and all of humankind that You have given life, through this dark night in our planet's history."

I found it difficult to focus on the prayer. My mind raced along paths like some poor lost soul trying to find its way through a maze. But I wordlessly seconded the archbishop's plea for the Almighty to intercede in the sordid affairs of mankind—mostly to prevent a war and protect Sarah, but also to help me through the murky muddle in which I found myself at Castle Trefoyle. And as I tried to follow the prayer, I silently screamed desperate, furious petitions of my own.

Someone, presumably the person who had my Bed-chamber incunable, had twice threatened to kill me— though this was perhaps bluster, since I was still very much alive. *Why?*

"If it be Your will, prevent war among the nations. Preserve the lives of our countrymen and of our allies, and all peoples of the world."

Someone had gone to unbelievable lengths to prevent me from communicating with Sarah and Max. *Why?*

"Help us to resolve our differences with *words*, not weapons."

Somehow I was reliving selected stories from Boccaccio's *Decameron*. *Why? How?*

"Help the world's leaders to remember the lessons You have taught us through history and the experiences of mankind through the ages."

Someone had stolen my Bedchamber incunable. *Who? Why?*

"Grant them wisdom, that they might act wisely with all the power they possess. In the name of our Lord and Saviour Jesus Christ, Amen."

The room resounded with echoes of "amen."

We all sat in hushed silence, humbled by the forces of hatred and violence unleashed that night.

"Now, then." Chesterton stood and smiled his well-practised, pleasant grin. "On with the Dibdin anniversary dinner. First, the Loyal Toast."

"The Queen!"

And so we were embarked upon the same round of toasts as the night before, listed as before on a rolled-up sheet of paper at each place, with one difference. The final toast of the evening, I saw, would honor the newest member of the Dibdin, Alexander Plumtree, Esquire.

Dreading the focus of attention on myself even for the moment the toast would take, I steeled myself for it as Chesterton proceeded through the litany of renowned type designers, printers, and others so revered by the group.

But before he spoke that last excruciating toast, he trained his eyes on me with a look of—what was it? Mischief, almost.

Had the man no sensitivity at all?

When he saw the look in my eyes, his smile faded. "To Alexander Plumtree, our newest member."

"Hear, hear!" All members stood, as if on cue, and raised their glasses. With all eyes trained on me, I had the oddest feeling for a moment—the feeling that they all knew some secret about me, something even I didn't know about myself.

What on earth . . . ?

The toast was duly completed and Chesterton gestured

everyone to sit. With relief I felt the focus of attention return to the president. The empty seat between Chesterton and myself, where Trefoyle had been sitting, gaped like an open wound. As if in response to my thought, a waiter came and obsequiously removed the chair, passing it to a colleague behind him. He then gathered up Trefoyle's cutlery, crystal, charger plate, and table napkin. He placed them on a tray and passed them off as well, then fussily began moving my place up toward Chesterton's to close the gap.

"May I move your chair, sir?" he said softly into my ear as Chesterton watched.

"Er, yes—thanks." I stood and shifted the chair myself, feeling again as I did so that somehow this, too, had all been arranged. I settled myself again as the first course was delivered, though I never noticed what it was.

"Frightful shame about all this mess abroad," Chesterton said. "Thank God Trefoyle knows what he's doing. If anyone can forestall this conflict, even now, he can." He drank the champagne remaining from his toasts, his eyes roving round the table, keeping track of what was happening and taking note of the food being served. A man used to running things, I thought, accustomed to managing people and events.

"He keeps it very quiet," Chesterton went on, "but Trefoyle's actually quite chummy with our—er—friends in the Middle East. Did you know he's a book-collecting mate of the leader of what Trefoyle still likes to call 'Persia'? Gets his Arabian horses there too. Ships them right here to the castle." He shook his head. "Remarkable man. No one quite like him, I daresay."

He glanced at my untouched plate, then turned to Delacroix.

"I don't know anyone who is as well informed on the history of that region as Trefoyle," Delacroix pronounced carefully. "Most impressive. And it's no secret that he's more than a cultural attaché, as he modestly calls himself.

He's actually one of the principal negotiators for the West—the only one who actually knows the men in charge over there personally. I don't doubt that he'll be going a bit further than Whitehall tonight."

While Delacroix and Chesterton sang Trefoyle's praises, I decided that with my primary ally gone, I'd better get to work sussing out exactly what game we were all playing that weekend. Perhaps catching them off guard would work . . . not terrifically polite, but they might excuse it if it showed enough cleverness.

"Do you go to this trouble for every new member?"

Bingo. Chesterton and Delacroix exchanged a glance of barely concealed panic.

"What on earth do you mean, dear boy?" Chesterton answered, wiping the corner of his mouth with his napkin. He picked up the Sancerre that had been served after the champagne. I actually heard him gulp it down.

"This whole arrangement. The way you've planned everything that's happened to me since I arrived."

Chesterton's eyes went wide. His mouth opened, but Delacroix spoke first—quietly, circumspectly.

"Look here, Plumtree. You're the first to work it out. But don't ruin it for everyone else, all right? We know you're bright. Just play along, there's a good boy." Condescension oozed from every word. His tone suggested I was an ungrateful guest, not worthy of the effort being spent on the surprise party.

Ha! Perhaps I'd hit the nail on the head. This entire house party had been an elaborate ruse, and I'd borne the brunt of it for their entertainment—though poor Margulies Whitehead's death surely couldn't have been planned or expected.

Could it?

And there was still what Trefoyle—and young Ashleigh— had told me about Old Ashleigh's death not having been exactly what was reported in the papers.

I decided to press a bit, though I knew I was skating on thin ice.

"Does a member die each anniversary weekend?"

This time both men looked horrified. "Good God, man!" Delacroix glared at me with reprehension, giving notice that I had stepped out of line badly. His various palsies seemed to come and go; I wasn't sure if he was extremely angry or merely shocked.

"Listen, Plumtree." Chesterton leaned forward confidentially. The man to my left was engaged in an uproarious tale of some sort with his neighbour, and the archbishop on Delacroix's right seemed similarly occupied. "I'm sorry you've got wind of part of this somehow, but you've got it all wrong. Trefoyle told me you're concerned about your fiancée. Sarah is safe and sound, on her way here for the—er—dénouement. She's just been delayed a bit. We expect to hear from her at any time."

I felt myself turn to ice; recognised all the symptoms of serious, dangerous anger.

"The *dénouement*," I repeated, my diction frighteningly precise. I took the napkin from my lap and replaced it on the table. "If you'll excuse me." I stood, pushed back my chair, and walked the length of the great hall. I had to get home. The book didn't matter—war appeared inevitable anyway. Nothing mattered anymore if they had caused something to happen to Sarah. This was no game. This was sickness, insanity.

I heard footsteps behind me. If someone got in my way, he wouldn't be there for long. First to retrieve what remained of my possessions . . . then my car.

Only then did I realise how frighteningly well planned it had all been. They had the keys to my car, of course.

It didn't matter; I'd leave by boat if I had to. Or swim. As I crossed the hall past the library door, I heard Hawkes's voice behind me.

"Mr. Plumtree, sir," he called after me, his voice worried.

I didn't acknowledge Hawkes. Events had passed the point where discussion was useful. I continued up the stairs to retrieve my belongings, though I wouldn't have bothered with them if it weren't for the envelope of prints.

"Please. You don't understand. Mr. Delacroix asks you to please return to the party, and everything will be explained after dinner. Even the phone calls, about your fiancée, everything. If you would please just return to the banquet, sir. When this year's book is presented after the pudding, you will understand."

I slowed. Exasperated, I turned and looked at him. Behind him stood the muscular crewman who'd been on the yacht with me that afternoon.

Even then I couldn't tell. Was I being threatened, or merely toyed with?

"Hawkes."

"Yes, sir."

"Does this happen every time?"

He smiled. "Yes, sir. Only it's just worked out a bit differently this year. It's really not at all what you think. *Do* come back, sir, or you'll spoil the whole elaborate plan. They did try so hard to make it memorable for you."

Good Lord. I felt pulled in all directions. Was it really possible that these people had constructed some elaborate charade, complete with death threats, as part of the weekend's entertainment? Or some initiation ritual? From experience with my college fraternity, I knew such rites of passage could be brutal, but being chained naked to a tree at a neighbouring women's college overnight didn't hold a candle to this.

Surely Graeme hadn't designed the entire ruse about recovering the Bedchamber book for the sake of the weekend . . . ?

Slowly, deliberately, I descended the steps. Opposite Hawkes, I stopped and looked into the great hall. From the far end of the table, Delacroix and Chesterton peered back at me. I spoke to Hawkes. "I will see this through dinner. If my doubts haven't been assuaged by then, I will leave immediately."

"Of course, sir." He seemed to relax, and walked back into the great hall with me.

"All right?" Chesterton looked worried and relieved at the same time as I took my seat again. Another course had been deposited at my place.

With all the sangfroid I could summon, I nodded and took a sip of my wine. My stomach churned at the thought of what *might* be happening—to Sarah, to Max, to my book. . . .

Somehow I hung on through the endless evening. I made no effort to participate or even keep track of what was being said, and my dinner companions tolerated my silence, allowing me the dignity of retreat.

I puzzled through what I knew so far, tried to organise what information I had. Everything that had happened at the castle since Friday seemed veiled in a fog: What was pretence, what was reality? What I *thought* was real was as follows:

1. Some sort of elaborate deception had been planned in my honour that weekend.

2. Sarah had been part of the plan, but now they didn't know where she was.

3. Max had been nearly hysterical that morning when I'd spoken to him. I didn't know why, and he wouldn't tell me.

4. Trefoyle had worried about Denis deChauncey doing away with Osgood Forsythe to get access to his Boccaccio. But that had been either a deliberate smoke screen to distract me, or a serious mistake on Trefoyle's part . . .

5. . . . Because, instead, Margulies Whitehead had died under very strange circumstances.

6. I had seen in the new Dibdin Club heraldry book issued last year that Chesterton's ancestor had murdered King Richard I, if the Bedchamber incunable could be believed.

7. Young Ashleigh had taken me aside and told me that he thought someone had deliberately murdered his father over a heraldry issue. This person, given what I'd heard twice from Trefoyle over the dispute regarding the new heraldry book, would seem to be Chesterton. But Chesterton didn't know I knew any of this.

8. Max had wanted to get his hands on the Bedchamber book desperately. Again, I didn't know why.

9. Great Britain and other member nations of the UN had been forced to send a peacekeeping force to Iraq because I hadn't found the Bedchamber incunable. Things had got worse rather faster than expected. Trefoyle had some special relationship with the Iraqis, and was seen as an integral part of a diplomatic resolution.

10. Someone at the castle wanted to kill me if I didn't leave on my own—either because they didn't want me to publish Margulies's novel with the Haslewood list, or because they had the Bedchamber book. I had planted doubt in the minds of as many people as I could that I knew the identity of the thief.

A decameron of strange facts and possibilities . . . I closed my eyes in desperation. Now even my *suspicions* were organising themselves into Boccaccian form.

I thought I would go mad before the Plum Fool was served with its Bereich Bernkastel dessert wine, but at

last Chesterton stood and plinked his knife against a reso-
nant Waterford goblet. My watch said it was midnight.
Was it possible that the endless dinner had come to its
conclusion?

"Our host has asked me to do the honours this evening—
both of them." Chesterton and the entire group smiled . . .
at me. It was more than annoying; under the circumstances, I considered it an act of aggression. Every muscle
in my body had been tensed for hours. I felt ready to
jump to my feet, crash through the glass doors behind
me, and dive into the sea. Instead, I forced my body, if not
my mind, to relax. Surely this would all be over soon; they
couldn't expect me to stay for the Sunday as well, not after all that had happened.

"First, this year's book." He reached back to where a
waiter held a small package covered with a piece of brown
paper. Chesterton held it up, and with some drama, un-
folded the brown paper from around the volume. I saw
that it was a faithfully reproduced replica of the Valdarfer
Boccaccio.

I was rapidly tiring of everything to do with Giovanni
Boccaccio and Christopher Valdarfer.

Servants were moving down the table with trolleys, handing out the books to the members. I took the two allotted to
me, still wrapped in brown paper, with none of the thrill I'd
expected to feel upon receipt of my first Dibdin books.

Chesterton studiously avoided my eyes as he continued. "Trefoyle asked me to tell you that fifteen extra
copies have been made, for donation to the British Library and other institutions. As you know, you are en-
couraged to give one of your books away to a worthy
recipient of your choice."

There was applause, though Trefoyle wasn't there to
hear it. Opening one of my copies, I saw that Trefoyle had
done a good bit of editing himself, along with a preface
and a general introduction explaining why he'd chosen to
reproduce the Boccaccio in the original Italian rather

than in English. Other than the introduction and the members' page, the book was a nearly exact duplicate, errors and all, of the 1471 Valdarfer edition. Clearly, he'd spared no expense, down to the rubricated initial capital letters at the chapter heads. Since I'd joined the club too recently to have my name printed on the members' page, he'd written my name in by hand.

"Now to reveal a great mystery. Plumtree, you've had a rough time of it. Some of you may have heard that our newest member was involved in a yachting mishap today, and shortly thereafter in a nearly disastrous helicopter accident. Fortunately, he's still with us."

Laughter. Not malicious laughter, but "I'm pleased for you," surprise-party laughter.

"Plumtree has already worked out part of our little intrigue. He knows we have been re-enacting certain stories within the *Decameron* during his stay here, and I think he's twigged that this is a tradition for new members. A sort of memorable welcome, if you will—perhaps in this case too memorable. Delacroix?"

The old man put both hands on the table in front of him, allowed the waiter to help pull out his chair, then got to his feet with great deliberation. Lifting his chin, he looked up and down both sides of the table.

"I shall speak on behalf of our host. Trefoyle told me on Thursday that he would put Plumtree in the Madame Beritola Tapestry Room as the first hint of what was in store. This room, some of you may already know, contains a tapestry portraying the story of Boccaccio's most tragic creation, poor Madame Beritola. You may recall that having lost her baby and child in a shipwreck, she nursed goats, or roebucks—depending on your translation—seeking comfort in nurturing them after she thought she'd lost her family. If you recall the story, you will remember that her loved ones were restored to her in the fullness of time." He looked at me significantly.

I nodded to show that I'd taken his meaning.

"And on that note," Jones-Harris said, rising, "I pulled off perhaps the worst part of this deception. I made the same bet with Plumtree that Boccaccio's Abroginolo made with Bernardo about the fidelity of women. Like Abroginolo, I bet Plumtree that I could prove his fiancée had been unfaithful to him. Also like that character, I tricked him into thinking I'd won the bet by finding out certain *private* physical characteristics of her that Sarah herself was kind enough to provide. I must say, Alex, she's a frightfully good sport."

There was a murmur round the table as everyone absorbed this delicious titbit. I was appalled. For Sarah to be the butt of such a tasteless joke, and to *agree* to it . . . ? Still, men's parties were nothing if not fascinated by speculation about the physical characteristics of women. I glanced down to meet Dame Cleopatra's eyes. They burned with the same indignant anger I felt in mine.

Jones-Harris lifted his glass. "May I just say that Sarah Townsend, soon to be Sarah Plumtree, is every bit as virtuous as her husband-to-be—in reputation as in reality."

"Hear, hear!" the group chorused.

I felt the first hint of a smile coming on, but I wouldn't relax until they told me exactly where Sarah was at that moment—though it augured well that everything, even the threats, had been a charade.

"My turn," the countess said, still holding my eyes. She rose. "I took it upon myself, when I learned what we'd be doing to Plumtree here, who I must say has been *terrifically* sporting about all this, to re-enact Boccaccio's fifth story of the first day. Lady Monferrat, whose husband is off fighting for the king in the Crusades as one of his favoured knights, is renowned to be the most virtuous, beautiful, clever woman in the kingdom. The king decides to travel to her home while her husband is away fighting, and have his way with her. To his surprise, at the banquet she has prepared for him on the eve of his arrival, only hens are served, though that land was renowned for plentiful and varied game. Puzzled, the king asks, 'Madam, is it only hens that flourish in these parts, and not a single cock?'

"The virtuous Lady Monferrat replies very inoffensively, and I quote"—here she pulled a slip of paper from the pocket of her evening dress,—" 'No, my lord, but our women, whilst they may differ slightly from each other in their rank and the style of their dress, are made no differently here than they are elsewhere.' "

Touché, I thought. If all you want is to have your way with a woman, go and find her elsewhere, not here in the Dibdin Club.

Silence reigned. "You will have noticed that I and my fellow female member deem it a most deplorable disgrace that you take advantage of some young female each year—the bustiest of Bloomsbury, I believe is the term—to do your bidding in bed at this anniversary weekend. You should be ashamed. And what you did to the poor girl this year—having her find Margulies without telling her what you were about beforehand—that was unforgivable."

What they were about? I couldn't believe what I was hearing. They couldn't, wouldn't have killed Margulies for *sport*!

"Hear, hear!" Dame Cleopatra shouted, standing and clapping to second the countess's speech.

There was absolute silence from the others.

I rose and clapped with them into the silence of the hall, making a threesome.

"And I," Chesterton broke through the noise sonorously, showing no sign of having been chastened, "must report for Trefoyle on the Margulies Whitehead deception."

The countess, Dame Cleopatra, and I sat.

"This was yet another story from the *Decameron*, the eighth novella of the third day, in which someone is given what used to be so charmingly called a 'powder' to make him appear dead. Although in this case, Whitehead himself agreed to take the sleeping medicine as part of the game. Hawkes, will you bring in the honourable MP, please?"

Hawkes, whom I'd observed lurking pale-faced at the rear of the great hall, came forward. His shoes click-clacked ceremoniously on the stone floor. As he leaned over to speak in Chesterton's ear, I heard him say softly, "Sir, he hasn't returned to the castle. We can't find him anywhere. We even rang his flat in London; the police had some rather disturbing news. His flat has been burgled, and the police haven't been able to reach Mr. Whitehead, sir."

Chesterton didn't seem too troubled by this. "Rotten luck. Well, Whitehead must have been detained, or gone to stay with a friend . . . never mind. At any rate, Plumtree, put your mind to rest. Your author is not dead—no gaping hole in your trade list for next year, no corrections for your catalogue."

I was shocked. For all their confessions of high mischief, I couldn't get past my conviction that they'd really gone much too far. They reminded me of a group of adolescents I'd once worked with at my parish church. They, too, hadn't known where to stop with their practical jokes, and had to be reminded about such essential courtesies as common decency and respect for others. As far as I could tell, the Dibdin Club needed a little reminder of its own. Which, happily, I had in mind.

But first Delacroix stood, again, with the aid of a waiter, who helped pull out his chair. Balancing carefully on his long black wing tips, he spoke. "The final revelation, Plumtree, was to have been a lovely surprise for you. But I'm afraid there's been a bit of confusion. . . . Before I tell all, let me compliment you on recognising one of our little deceptions in progress.

"You remember the scene at the business meeting, beautifully acted by Forsythe, young Ashleigh, and Trefoyle, about the three Boccaccios. Jolly good work, Plumtree, remembering Boccaccio's story of the three rings and three faiths in—let me see . . ." The old man frowned in concentration, his brain sharp as ever. "The third novella of the first day. Oh, and let me confirm, Forsythe *does* have the only Valdarfer Boccaccio of 1471. Trefoyle and young Ashleigh only *wish* they had the original."

Delacroix nodded at Forsythe, who sat five people down from me. He waved gaily at me.

Ha-ha-ha, they chortled. But I laughed last; I had the second original.

"All right, Plumtree. You've been—well, actually, you haven't been very patient, but we'll forgive you that, considering you're about to be married to such a fine woman." Delacroix spoke to the rest of the table. "Plumtree here caught on to the fact that we were trying to keep him from speaking to his family today, because they were necessarily in on our little surprises. My boy, the final surprise was to have been the appearance of your lovely fiancée here tonight. But it appears she has not been able to make it in time; we know she was on her way earlier this afternoon but haven't heard from her since then."

Chesterton stood. "A toast to the future Mrs. Plumtree, and her sporting future husband!"

"Hear, hear!"

We drank, I for one immensely relieved about a good many things, though I felt deep malaise at the thought of Sarah unaccounted for since that afternoon. Still, I told myself I was worrying about her too much, as usual.

I heard cries of "Speech, speech!"

Smiling like a fool, I held up a hand to indicate that they could stop yelling at me. "All right, all right. I only hope that the clever so-and-so who added the death threats and stole my incunable knows the game is over. I didn't much like that part—and I haven't found *that* story in the *Decameron*. I'll expect my book back in perfect condition tonight, no questions asked."

The members looked from one to the other, wide-eyed. "*Death* threats!" Chesterton exclaimed. "That wasn't part of any plan." I noticed he didn't mention the stolen book not being part of the plan.

Delacroix looked at me, his mouth open and chin quivering, apparently shocked. But I was willing to accept that one of them had merely carried the joke too far. Now it was over.

"I don't know if I can actually *thank* you for what you've done this weekend. But I will say it's been an unforgettable experience. And I'll add that if any one of you ever *does* lay a finger on my fiancée, I'll deal with it according to Middle Eastern law. Which means, of course, that you'll be missing a finger."

There was much good-humoured—and drunken—laughter. When it subsided, I went on.

"In return for all you've done for me, I'd like to remind you of the first story of the second day in the *Decameron*, in which Martellino, who made an elaborate pretence like yours, paid for it dearly—though I won't make you pay with your lives, as he did. But never forget, in the words of Boccaccio: '*The deceiver is often trampled on, by such as he hath deceived*.' So beware." I took my seat.

The members dissolved into laughter and chatter. Chesterton leaned toward me and put a hand on my shoulder. "I've never heard such a good riposte in all my days with the club. I was a bit worried, earlier this evening, about how you'd take it all. You see, we've never quite gone this far before. Well done, Plumtree. Well done. Very sporting."

He stood and said, as if anyone needed reminding, "Drinks outside, everyone. On the lawn."

As everyone began to totter unsteadily out of the room, Hawkes touched my arm.

"Telephone, for you, sir. You'll have greater privacy in Earl Trefoyle's suite. Allow me to show you there." With what seemed to me great formality, he conducted me out of the great hall, down the corridor to the stairway, then up the tiny spiral stairs. At the door to Earl Trefoyle's chamber, he took out the same small key on a ribbon round his neck that I'd seen the earl himself use and let me in. He closed the door firmly behind us.

"No phone call?" I asked, half amused and half taken aback.

"No, sir."

"What is it, then?"

I watched in awe as Hawkes reached calmly into his jacket and brought out a black gun fitted with a silencer.

"Just this, sir."

CHAPTER 13

*[Boccaccio wove] tales filled with realistic
accounts of adventurous deeds, "l'estetica
dell'avventura" ('the aesthetics of adventure').*

—ALBERTO MORAVIA, ON BOCCACCIO IN THE ESSAY
"MAN AS AN END—A DEFENSE OF HUMANISM"

I stared down the long black barrel of the silencer.

"Er—Hawkes. If this is about your novel," I began . . .

But our conversation—or whatever it might have
been—was destined not to take place, for at that moment
Chesterton entered. Hawkes, still facing me, slid the
weapon back into his jacket before turning round, his expression unchanging.

"Yes, sir?"

"Good! You're both here. I've just had a most disturbing telephone call. It was Whitehall . . . Trefoyle still isn't
with them. It's"—he checked his Rolex—"nearly five
hours ago now, since he left." He shook his head. "I don't
like it."

Again, I had a very bad feeling that yet *another* person
had gone missing.

"Have you rung the police?"

"Yes. I also checked the castle car park—his Range

Rover is still here; so is the Ferrari. Were they sending a car for him?"

Hawkes knitted his brow. "I don't think so. His lordship usually drives himself. I'll have a look round," he said. "This isn't good, you know. Especially not tonight." He gave me a look that said *I've not finished with you.*

Still unsure whether Hawkes had intended to murder me or merely show me his weapon for some legitimate purpose, I felt myself looking a bit wide-eyed at Chesterton.

"All right, Plumtree? I say, you look all in."

"Mmm. I suppose I am a bit whacked. It's this partying from dawn to dusk." I smiled.

"Get some rest. It's a wonder you're still on your feet after today, my boy. You know, Plumtree, I must say, if we'd known there would be so many ghastly accidents— Forsythe's being shot, your helicopter near-disaster— we'd never have gone so far with the Boccaccio ruse."

Ah, I silently corrected him, but Forsythe's shooting *wasn't* an accident. Someone rigged it. And the jury was still out on the helicopter incident.

"Still, we all survived, didn't we?! You were brilliant at the dinner, Plumtree. Brilliant." He shook his head, still smiling. "If only your father could have seen you." He turned to Hawkes. "You will let me know, won't you, if you hear from Trefoyle? I'll be in my room."

Hawkes nodded. But before Chesterton got to the door, the telephone rang on Trefoyle's round table; the servant picked it up. "Castle Trefoyle, Hawkes speaking." He blinked, then said, "Yes, Prime Minister. He's standing right beside me. One moment, please." Hawkes passed me the phone.

"Yes, Graeme," I said. Chesterton, clearly stunned that I was on first-name terms with the PM, forgot for the moment that he was obliged to leave the room for a private telephone conversation. Flustered, he finally recovered himself and hurried to the door after Hawkes, who closed the door quietly behind them.

"Alex, I'm so sorry. There's no time to find a gentle way to say this. As you may have heard at the castle, things have gone from bad to worse in Iraq. They think we're deliberately withholding the book. And they've made sure they'll get it the only way they know: They've got Sarah."

He might have hit me over the head with a club. All my vague suspicions and fears had been for a reason. . . .

"Alex? Are you there?"

"I'm here."

"I'm so sorry, Alex. They've taken her hostage. Trefoyle knows; he was on his way to help us talk our way out of this, but he's not here yet—God only knows why. Now. If you can get that book to me here by five A.M., and so to Baghdad by their deadline, you'll have saved Sarah. You're the only person who can do it now, Alex."

"But I don't *have* the—"

"Alex, I won't mince words. This is absolutely vital. Now that Trefoyle isn't here to help us, we're in very hot water indeed. It could be that whoever has your book is someone who'd love to see this war erupt. So be careful, but for Sarah's sake, bring us that book! If you sense anything at all out of the ordinary there, you ring my private line. *Immediately*. Understood?"

Anything *out of the ordinary* . . . the entire weekend had been out of the ordinary. But the prime minister had far greater things on his mind. "Right, Graeme. I'll get the book to you. Good-bye." As I rang off, I vowed I would do it or die in the attempt.

Had Trefoyle left only to be ambushed along the way? Had he *ever* left? If his cars were still here, he might be in the castle grounds. I had a sudden vision of him lying injured or dying in his globe room, or on the rocks, pounded by the waves. I had to find him—and the book.

Above all, I had to save Sarah. Nothing could keep us from the rest of our lives together; I couldn't entertain the thought.

As I hurried to the door, it struck me that Hawkes

might be looking for me with his silenced gun—for whatever reason. I would have to watch out for him.

Opening the door quietly, I peered out. I wanted to get to my room to change out of my stiff evening clothes and shoes, and get my bag. James Bond might manage to roam about the castle grounds in the moonlight, in full evening dress, but not me. Not a soul was about—perhaps Hawkes had gone straight outside to search for his employer.

But on the way, I thought, I had the perfect opportunity to do some serious snooping. There was no more time for niceties, such as respecting privacy and private property. While my fellow members were out drinking on the lawn, it was absolutely essential that I rummage through their rooms . . . not that anyone would leave the Bedchamber book lying about in plain view.

I'd seen Chesterton coming out of the room next door to Trefoyle's earlier; he, of all people, seemed to have the most to lose from having the book at large, and it was quite possible that he'd been trying to kill me in the helicopter. I knocked on the door and listened. No response. When I tried the knob, it turned; I entered quickly and closed the door behind me. The room was roughly twice the size of mine, as befitted the president of the Dibdin Club. *Where would someone hide an incunable?*

Where had I hidden my prints? In my false-bottomed sailing bag . . .

I went to his three leather bags and unabashedly searched them. They were completely empty; his quarters had the look of a hotel room with everything so tidily stowed. Either Chesterton's secretary had functioned as a valet, or one of Trefoyle's servants had unpacked every item and put it away in the antique cupboards and chests. I couldn't find any false or hidden pockets in the suitcases; in the next fifteen minutes, as my desperation increased, I tried everything from the linings of his suits in the cupboard to under the mattress to behind the picture frames on the walls. I checked for loose floorboards; I groped on the top of tall furniture. Nothing. Chesterton was a scrupulously orderly and meticulous man—or at least his servants made him appear so.

Move on, I told myself, and hoped the next room down would be the private secretary's. This was a bit of a risk, because he didn't always go to club functions. But if he hadn't heard me rummaging about in his employer's room, he was most probably not in his own. And there was a good chance, I told myself, that Chesterton would protect himself by making the private secretary keep the book in his room. Once again, I knocked; when there was no answer, I turned the knob and went in. Chesterton's private secretary, who had leered at me so unpleasantly as I'd escorted Clarissa to her room the night before, was an utter pig. Clothes had been tossed haphazardly over every possible surface, including the floor. No wonder the man always looked hopelessly rumpled. I followed the same procedure I had in Chesterton's room; no luck. It wasn't that I had expected it to be easy to find the book, even breaking into people's rooms like a common thief; but I now had to admit how distant the possibility was that I would find it.

The next room down the corridor was Margulies's; now, there was a thought. Who would expect anything to be in *his* room? Evidently, he had left for London and wasn't coming back. It would make a convenient place for Chesterton and his secretary to hide something if they wished. . . .

Not bothering to knock, I stepped into the room and immediately felt a ripple of excitement. This could be it! I checked between the mattress and the old bed frame, not really expecting to find anything in such an obvious place, and to my surprise pulled out a version of Margulies's Plumtree Press edition of Boccaccio's *Decameron*. Odd, I thought, unless he'd forgotten it there. Still, a strange place to put his Boccaccio edition . . .

Absently, I lifted the lid and riffled the pages at the front. To my surprise, they were the only actual pages in the book; beneath them was a hole cut to the precise size of the Bedchamber incunable, which lay nestled inside. I stood for a moment and stared at its red velvet cover, transfixed. Then I thought I'd better check; this might have been the facsimile Diana had delivered. A clever disguise, indeed, I thought. But the bulge was inside the rear cover, and its musty smell told me it was the genuine article. Restorers had not yet found a musty scent with which to imbue newly minted books.

Until I knew who had hidden the book inside the modern edition, I wouldn't know if it was safe to be carrying it around. Most likely it was Chesterton and his secretary I had to avoid seeing with it; otherwise it was an excellent disguise for the valuable book. With immense relief I tucked the whole thing into the waistband of my trousers so that the book stuck up my back and would be covered by my dinner jacket. It was no small volume, but it would do until I got to my room.

I had only just stepped out of Margulies's door and started down the hall, when I saw Chesterton's obnoxious secretary reach the top of the stairs and turn in my direction. I smiled. "Good evening," I said, and he passed me, yawning, with a nod.

I made it safely to my room, stepped inside, turned the lock, and breathed a sigh of relief. I'd leave the lights off in case someone looked beneath the door to see if I was there. Odd, I thought; I smelled leather. Must be the shoes in the closet. Stepping round the bed, I ripped off my tie, pulled my shirttail out, and had my jacket half off, when I sensed something moving.

The tapestry on the wall . . . in the moonlight from the window, I thought I perceived a dark form at its edge. I froze.

"Where is the book?" came a whisper from the tapestry.

"Tell me where the book is or I will kill her." I knew he meant Sarah. He'd kill Sarah.

I felt sick. Did I recognise the voice? I couldn't tell from the sinister whisper. The accent had sounded foreign; I couldn't place it. Then again, the accent could be a disguise.

"I don't have it," I lied. I had to buy time, had to work out if this man would—could—return Sarah in exchange for the book. I reached for and tightened my hand round the heavy crystal vase on the desk next to me.

A shot, silenced, thunked dully into the wooden surround of the window behind me. Hawkes had a silencer . . . was this Hawkes with an attitude? I cursed my abysmal night vision. I could see nothing of the man except to have a general impression of his height; he was perhaps five feet eight inches—like both Hawkes and the crewman from the yacht. I thought perhaps the man wore a face mask; there was no shine on his face from the moonlight. But there was a dull patch of light on his gun.

He's going to kill me.

"Where is the book, Plumtree?" This time the whisper was much colder, more businesslike.

Another shot thudded into the wall behind me, so close that I was certain it had grazed my shirt.

"Next time I will try to hit you," the horrible whisper rasped. *"Tell me where it is—NOW!"*

Without taking more time to think, I flung the vase at him and lunged for his weapon. He caught me in the ribs with a heavy boot as I came. I thudded to the floor at his feet, and felt the book against my back as I clutched my chest and groaned involuntarily. The pain was so intense that I felt sick.

But stronger than all of that was my desperation to save Sarah. I wanted to kill the man. But to help Sarah, I had to use my mind to find a way out.

"I'll tell you where the book is," I said through clenched teeth. "Don't shoot."

"*Ha!*"

He had the gun trained right on me; I could *feel* it.

"*Now. Right now!*" He knelt next to me and pressed the weapon into my hair.

"It's with Earl Trefoyle. He tried to take it to London tonight and never made it there. But I know where he might be . . . if we find him, you can have the book." *Over my dead body,* I thought. I'd find a way to knock him unconscious at some point, train the gun on him, and force him to tell me exactly where Sarah was.

I felt him stiffen, hesitate, and finally relax. "*Yes. All right,*" he said, still in that sinister whisper. "*Let's go. Out the window—quickly!*"

The gun still pressed against my scalp, he forced me to my feet. He shoved me roughly over to the windows, clearly intending that I should climb out through one of the tiny, ancient openings no more than two feet square. I slid my legs through first, ribs screaming in protest.

"*No tricks, Plumtree. If I shoot you, I'll have Sarah for as long as I like. Then I'll kill her too.*"

I struggled for control as I forced my shoulders out one at a time through the tiny space. Then, with a precarious foothold on the roof, I clung to the window and prepared to leap.

I would have only an instant to do it. After I jumped from the first-storey window, I would have to roll into the shadows, which he would almost certainly spray with deadly, silent bullets.

God only knew what would happen, but I had to try.

I jumped, wanting to scream as my body hit the ground. For just an instant the pain was too overwhelming. I couldn't breathe, let alone move. My body had seen enough spills.

He'll shoot, he'll shoot . . .

Every breath hurt, thanks to his well-placed kicks. I

steeled myself for worse and rolled back towards the rocky castle foundation. I needed only a second . . . and I got it.

Scuttling along the foundations as silently as I could, doubled over, I came abreast of a knot of my all-night-revelling fellow members.

"Look!" I shouted incredulously, standing camouflaged in the crowd as if I'd been there all along. "I just saw a man pointing a gun out of that window up there!"

Some of them were just far gone enough to shout and point, causing my tormentor to retreat into my room. Others, still more inebriated, laughed and called out to him, begging him to shoot them. I rejoiced at the unwitting cooperation of the eccentric Dibdinians.

I'd been lucky; the man wouldn't show his face there again, though he'd be hunting me down soon enough. What was worse, under that disguise he *could* be one of us—even I was using that odious phrase now—and I might think he was a club member until he was close enough to do me irreparable damage.

Aware of the frighteningly short amount of time I had to get to London with the book, I still felt the need to find Trefoyle. But I acknowledged the possibility that I might have to leave if I couldn't find him soon. Still, my vision of him lying wounded on the rocks wouldn't subside; with the book still hidden against the small of my back, I obeyed intuition and raced down to the rocky shore. Tall waves smashed against the base of the castle and sent spray across the rocks, soaking my clothes. I searched the rocks in the moonlight, knowing all the while that in a high tide like this, if something had gone wrong, he may well have been washed out to sea hours before.

Aware that my whispering attacker, and possibly Hawkes as well, would be coming after me before long, I hugged the shore, keeping my eyes peeled for them while searching for the lost earl on the rocks. It was almost hopeless. Dark shapes shrouded the tumble of rocks—

lichen, barnacles, lumps of seaweed, debris . . . and with my poor night vision, I felt I was unlikely to find Trefoyle even if he was there.

As I walked along the rocky edge of the castle land, I tried to think. Trefoyle had gone for one of his cars . . . of course! The cars. Though surely Hawkes had checked that too. I made my way to the car park, crept across to his Range Rover, and saw that my Golf was gone.

Relief swept over me. It was possible that the clever old coot had taken my car. Perhaps he wasn't lying injured somewhere. . . . Never underestimate someone older and wiser.

What could have happened to prevent Trefoyle reaching Whitehall? My car was well maintained. It seemed likely that disaster had befallen him on the way to London.

I made for the shadows again and thought about my situation. If the whisperer should find me again, was it up to me to try to negotiate with him?

As ever, I was having difficulty distinguishing fact from fiction.

Blending briefly again with the two-dozen or so revellers who remained out on the lawn, tirelessly served by three very long-suffering staff, I crossed to the formal gardens. At their edge we'd done our shooting; here Forsythe had been hit by deChauncey's pellets.

What had been the point of that in our weekend of Dibdinian debauchery? I wondered. Or had it just been an honest accident, like my apparent sailing mishap?

I found myself at the yew hedge, behind which Hawkes had worked on his novel and discovered the hand-throwing tool. Stepping inside, I saw something dark on the ground. I knelt carefully, afraid of what I might find, and saw that it was Hawkes, unconscious. I felt for a pulse in his neck; it was strong. I patted his coat for the menacing gun. It was nowhere to be found.

"Hawkes! Can you hear me?"

He groaned.

"Hawkes." I patted his cheek roughly. "Come on. Who was it?"

"Ummmf . . ."

I heard someone running, panting, right towards the yew hedge. Certain it was the Whisperer coming after me, I shrank back against the shrub as best I could and prayed. But the winded runner ran straight past. With Hawkes lying still before me on the ground, I peered round the edge of the greenery. I could just make out the countess's sleek white satin evening dress, and Osgood Forsythe's film-star profile. They disappeared without a word into the formal gardens.

"Sir?" Hawkes squinted up at me.

"It's *Alex*," I said. "Please call me Alex. You're not going to shoot me this time, are you?"

"No, sir. I mean Alex." I helped him sit up. He fingered the back of his head gingerly. "I was merely going to lend you the gun at the earl's suggestion. Did he—er—tell you that this might happen?"

"That gunmen would chase me round the castle lawn? No. No, he did not."

He groaned. "We knew there might be terrorist activity, particularly because of your Bedchamber book. I work for the prime minister, special assignments." He stuck out his hand. "Julian Jarrow."

I realised my mouth was hanging open. I shut it.

"Sorry about all that rot about the novel. Some of our people cooked that up to, er, establish a relationship between us." He laughed, rubbing the back of his head. "Not that you seem to need *my* help! You'd be more at home with us than behind some desk in a publishing house. You're a real card, Plumtree. Anyway, we'd best get on. I wish I knew just what he meant by this." He dug a box of Charbonnel et Walker mints out of the base of the shrubbery.

"I thought it was well known that Trefoyle indulged in minty sweets. . . ."

He shook his head. "The box has *your* book in it, supposedly—but it looks much too new for a book printed in 1471."

"The facsimile!" I exclaimed, and reached for it. Jarrow took a short, fine-point torch from his belt and trained a narrow beam on the box. I removed the white ribbon, opened the lid, and saw my Bedchamber book inside, safely cradled in a nest of tissue. "My friend told me she'd disguised it. But why didn't Trefoyle *tell* me it had come? It's mine."

"There are a few things I don't understand myself . . . like where his lordship is. And where the *real* book is."

"Oh. I have it."

"*What?*"

"Mmm." I lifted up the back of my shirt and showed him. "It's inside *this* book, believe it or not. I found it in Margulies's room. I need to get it to London, Jarrow. Right away."

"Follow me," he ordered, tucking the torch away again and pulling out his weapon. He tucked the Charbonnel et Walker box inside *his* waistband. "We'll ring Whitehall from down below."

"I hope the Whisperer didn't reach Trefoyle—you do know about the other man with the silencer, right?"

He stopped suddenly and turned. "*Who?*"

"The man with the silencer in my room—I told you about him in the garden."

"Tell me what he said."

"He wanted the book, of course. He said he had Sarah; he'd kill her if I didn't give him the damned book. I told him I didn't have it, because if I gave it to the *wrong* person, I'd never see Sarah again, would I?"

He stared at me, his sharp eyes completely altered from those of the complacent Hawkes. "Are you serious?"

"Of course I'm serious!"

He swore and continued on, motioning for me to follow. "He doesn't sound like one of them. We expected the

Iraqi terrorists, but not this mystery man." He came to another door and pressed a button on a handheld transceiver. "Whoever he was, he *doesn't* have your fiancée. We have her—or, rather, we're in touch with people who know where she is."

Before I could comment, he pulled out his gun, glanced quickly in all directions, then took off across the lawn. I followed—what choice did I have? But to my surprise, he raced straight for the sea. I ran for my life, knowing that someone with a deadly weapon was hunting for me. Though I was no more than ten feet behind him, at the edge of the cliff down to the sea he simply disappeared. I stood exposed on the edge, desperately searching for his outline on the rocks below.

"Down here," he whispered, the words echoing slightly. Now Jarrow's voice seemed to be coming out of the rocks themselves. . . .

Then I glimpsed a pathway between the huge boulders, so well hidden that I'd never have found it on my own. The path doubled back under the lawn through a whitewashed concrete tunnel. Jarrow pressed a button and a rock wall slid down behind us.

There was no time to comment on these fantastic surroundings—Jarrow was forging ahead.

"I hope you don't mind if I ask," I panted, hurrying after him. Bright lights in industrial-looking wire cages lined the passageway. "But what exactly is going on here?"

"By now you know that our friends in Iraq believe we are egging them on by publicising this magnificent little book you discovered. They want it. Very badly. If they don't get the book our peacekeeping force will have to face their chemical weapons. Trefoyle, along with some American intelligence agent, managed to think of using your book as a peace offering. They proposed this t⌐ Iraqis, who agreed to back down if they rec⌐ foreign secretary and prime minister, t⌐ the United Nations are all bankin⌐

Suddenly I had the feeling the tunnel was closing in on me, but Jarrow was moving briskly down the passageway. I struggled to keep pace with him.

"When things blew up tonight, Trefoyle was called to Whitehall. But he and his driver never arrived there. We had a guard on them; now he's gone missing too."

He hurried on down the close, well-lit tunnel to another wall, where he pressed a button like the first one.

As the door slid aside, the body of a man clad entirely in black slumped onto the floor in front of us. Jarrow swore and threw himself back against the wall, putting out an arm to restrain me. From his posture and stillness, I knew Jarrow believed we were in immediate danger.

We waited for a moment; no one was visible down the tunnel. There was no sound. Jarrow took a radio from his pocket and knelt over the fallen man. He shook his head. "Caldwell's down, in the tunnel," he mumbled into the radio. "We'll need help." Looking ahead, I could see I was now in familiar territory—we were at the far end of the hallway I'd tumbled into from Trefoyle's steps, beyond his private jewel of a library, beyond the globe room.

"No time to lose," Jarrow told me in a low voice, moving forwards. "That was Trefoyle's guard. There's a secure line down here—we'll send for help, tell them we've got the book. We'll take Chesterton's helicopter." He ran down the hallway to the globe room, took hold of the key round his neck, and turned to me. "If anything happens to me, trust no one. Get yourself to London as fast as you can."

I nodded.

Jarrow silently slipped the key into the lock and turned it, pushing open the door with his foot.

We waited; nothing happened. The room was dark; there was no sound. Tension thickened the air.

Then a flash exploded out of the darkened room, along with a deafening roar. I threw myself against the wall as Jarrow's body was flung back into the hallway. His gun skated across the cold stone toward me. It stopped on the Persian runner; I grabbed it as if in a nightmare. I recoiled from Jarrow's stunned, wide-open eyes and mangled chest; he could not possibly have survived the blast.

I pointed the gun into the globe room and pulled the trigger, sending several wild shots into the pitch-black, only to hear rapid return fire ricochet off the stone wall opposite Jarrow's body. I ducked: Soon, I knew, whoever was in there would come after me.

If I could just get the book first . . .

I pulled Jarrow over to me and groped with desperate fingers for the mint box. There it was . . . I yanked it out, stuffed it inside my absurd cummerbund. I saw the ribbon round Jarrow's neck and grabbed at it savagely, pulling it over his head. I pocketed the ribbon and key.

My instinct was to run back out the way I'd come, towards the ocean. But something told me that the high ground was better: get up, above him, around the sheltering curves of the staircase as quickly as possible. I ran past the globe room, clambering up the narrow spiral stairs in the pitch-darkness as fast as my feet would carry me. I heard someone scrambling after me, swearing as he tripped on Jarrow's body, the footsteps and words resounding against the cold, hard stone, but I was already around the first curve. . . .

I made it to the door of Trefoyle's suite, stepped into his alcove, and left the door open behind me. Flattening myself against the wall to the left of the door, Jarrow's gun pointed at the open doorway, I waited. The steps of my pursuer came closer and closer . . . I could hear him panting. The lights were off in Trefoyle's room; only the barest reflections of moonlight through the windows showed the outlines of the table, chairs, and walls.

Suddenly he was there, the evil black nose of his weapon appearing first through the doorway. My hand tightened around Jarrow's gun; I hated the thought of what I was about to do. To my utter disbelief, the yacht crewman's head popped out.

"Plumtree!" he exclaimed. "Wait—"

The roar of firepower filled the room. Stunned, I looked at my own hand, saw the young man crumple to the ground, a look of surprise on his strong face.

In the next instant, I saw movement across the room, near the door to the hallway. Trembling but determined, I aimed.

"Good God, man!" Chesterton's voice boomed. He tucked a gun into *his* cummerbund. "Put that damned thing down. Thank God I made it in time. He almost had you."

Stunned, I stared in amazement as the duke crossed the room and knelt over the crewman's body. "But he works for Trefoyle! What makes you think he's—"

"I know all this must be frightfully confusing for you, Plumtree. I suppose you might say a few of us are a bit more than we appear to be." He smiled self-effacingly and took the weapon out of the man's hand, adding it to his own cache. "And people *will* forget the last world war. Some things you never forget. Trefoyle had warned me that the enemy was here. He told me what to expect, warned me that I might be pressed into service if the worst happened. Clearly, Trefoyle has met with some form of treachery tonight." He stood and shrugged, as if he'd just killed a rather nasty insect. "You didn't find him, did you?"

"No."

He shook his head. "Still, we must carry on. I presume you know what we're about. Where's Jarrow?"

I noted with interest that he didn't call him Hawkes, which did seem to indicate he was as close to Trefoyle as he made out.

"Down there."

"Ah. I see. Do you have the book?"

I nodded. It was possible, I thought, that Chesterton had hidden it in Margulies's room. Then again, it was equally possible that he had not. Either way, I realised, he could fly me to London in the helicopter as Hawkes had planned. I looked at my watch; we still had two hours. It was the only way to get there by Graeme's deadline. I proposed this to Chesterton.

"Absolutely," he said. "I was just about to suggest the same thing."

We used the passage out into the rocks to get outside, and encountered no one as we hurried the two hundred yards or so to the runway. Chesterton had known the location and operation of each control in the tunnel, I reflected. This was encouraging, because as we approached the helicopter I noticed it had acquired a menacing air since that afternoon.

"Just a moment," I said, pulling out the cell phone. It was Chesterton's; I held it up ironically for him to see. "I'll just let Graeme know I'm coming—I never got the chance."

Chesterton nodded and climbed into the helicopter. I pressed the special number Graeme had given me long ago, which would get straight to his assistant. Five seconds later I was speaking to Graeme himself. "We've had some trouble here—your man Jarrow is dead. So are two others. But I've got the book. I'm coming with Chesterton in his helicopter—seems the fastest way to get to you. All right?"

"*Excellent!* Yes. Well done, Alex. See you soon."

As I climbed into the bubble-nosed craft, the night air was balmy, the breeze gentle. Much too perfect a night for such treachery. I pulled the Charbonnel et Walker box out from under my shirt in the front, and the modern Boccaccio that contained my incunable out of the back. Chesterton watched as I set them carefully on the floor at my feet. We closed our doors this time, and fastened our safety restraints; Chesterton switched on the ignition and started the rotors spinning. He handed me earphones again with mouthpiece attached; I put mine on as he donned his own. The only other lights visible, apart from the soft red backlit controls in the cockpit, were the moon and a canopy of brilliant stars above the black horizon.

The noise grew steadily louder as Chesterton concentrated on the indicators and controls before him, then pulled up on the hand-brake–like lever on his left, setting it to remain at a constant level. He pushed forward on the stick and worked his pedals, and we rose into the star-studded darkness.

As the helicopter ascended, this time without mishap, Chesterton spoke. "Are you all right, Plumtree? Why are you hunching over like that?"

Urgent chatter began to erupt from the radio before I could reply. He reached over and turned it off, at the same time changing course slightly.

"Someone surprised me in my room; I think it was the same person who killed Hawkes."

Chesterton shook his head grimly. "I don't think Castle Trefoyle has seen this much action since pirate days. What an unholy mess."

I scowled. "Chesterton, you spoke to Boswell about the Bedchamber book on the Monday morning after I found it, didn't you?"

"Hmm?" He looked at me, disconcerted.

I waited.

"Oh! Yes. Boswell told me of your find. But I do fear it's a forgery; I'm certain all the original copies were destroyed. Trefoyle told me you had anonymous buyers, people trying to snatch it from you left and right—Trefoyle had confided in a few of us, you know. Just his closest friends. What a *fracas*." He used the French pronunciation. "I would love to see the book at some point, if you don't mind."

I saw no reason why I shouldn't show him the book . . . after all, he was flying me to London with it. No doubt I'd be just as eager to see it in his place. I reached down and brought out the Boccaccio edition. As Chesterton glanced over, I placed it on my lap, opened the lid, and I lifted out the book.

"Thank you," he said, snatching it neatly from my grasp. I was so surprised that I didn't even resist—wasn't aware of the need until it was too late. "Actually," he said, reaching inside his jacket, "it's just as well that I take care of this now, as you seem to be growing a bit suspicious."

I saw in the soft glow of the instrument panel that he was pointing a gun—*yet another gun*—at me. Before I could do anything, a shot shattered the glass of the window inches from me into a violent opaque spiderweb.

So this was how it would end.

"Wait!" I shouted, desperate to buy time. I put my hands in the air to indicate that I wouldn't cause trouble if he would only let me live for a few moments longer. "Please! At least tell me *why* . . ."

He seemed to find this amusing. "Ha! Right. You Plumtrees never did lack nerve. Well. I'm surprised you haven't died of humiliation by now, after that Boccaccio affair. A malicious trick—but rather clever all the same." He gave a deep, rumbling laugh, all the while keeping the gun trained on my temple with surprising accuracy. A pity the air was so calm now, I thought.

"I'll have to make a long story short—only certain places I can put you out unnoticed, you know."

I thought of the lonely expanses of Bodmin Moor and Dartmoor, either of which we might be flying over soon.

"It's all your fault, Plumtree. You think you're well educated, but you know so little. When you announced to the world that you'd found this charming little book, you didn't stop to think about the *people* involved, did you?"

It was eight hundred years ago! I wanted to scream. All right; he knew I'd noticed his coat of arms on the kneeling knight. And if he didn't know, he couldn't take the risk that I knew his family's secret. But why did it matter so very much to him? The past was the past . . . the rest of the world would be willing to forgive his ancestor—why couldn't he?

But all the fascinating historical significance in the world couldn't change the fact of the weapon in his hand, pointed directly at me. *Could I move fast enough to knock his arm up and get the gun pointed away from my head, or would he shoot first?*

"You're not going to pretend you didn't *notice* . . . ?" He turned to look at my face, saw my tacit admission that I had.

I tried the voice of reason. "What does it matter now? It was so long ago. No one would hold it against you—in fact, if anyone knew, I doubt they would care."

"*I care!*" His voice boomed over the headphones. "You don't think I'd let the world find out that a Chesterton killed the greatest king in history just to get his lands back, do you? At this point the Queen of England wishes she had *my* name. I tried to get the book any number of ways, quite reasonably, back in London. Boswell did his best too, with the help of some rather unsavoury friends of mine—it's difficult to find people to do that sort of work. But you weren't selling. I'll bet you wish you had that half a million pounds now, don't you?"

I didn't answer; he fell silent. *Quickly,* I thought. *Keep him talking.* "So you hid the book in Margulies's room?"

I said it more as a statement than a question, but he turned to me in confusion. "What do you mean, Margulies's room? You didn't have the book all along?"

"No! I told you and everyone else the truth—that it had been stolen back in London."

"Yes, but I never thought you were serious . . ."

Now *I* was completely confused. If Chesterton hadn't put the book under Margulies's mattress, who had? He didn't seem to be acting. I wanted a word with Margulies, though it didn't look as though I'd ever get the chance.

Luckily, Chesterton went on, subdued over the confusion about who'd had the book over the weekend. "Until this came up, we thought we'd suppressed all the copies—burned a few in my own time, I can tell you. Hunted them down the world over, as did our Middle-eastern friends—for their own reasons. You might as well know who it was that printed this despicable little volume—if you don't already. It was a Plumtree, of course. Some irritatingly honest ancestor of yours took it upon himself to print the truth of the legend recorded by Boccaccio. My family knew about it; got Edward IV to suppress the book and your early printing ancestor, though no one could prove he'd printed it. But now there's *your* family copy. I can't let it happen."

He shook his head, as if at the irony of it all. "And to think I restored your family's title, in Ashleigh's heraldry book, forgotten for so many years. At the same time you were trying to destroy *mine.*" With a derisive snort, he finished, "*Au revoir,* Plumtree. Or, rather, *adieu.*" His fleshy hand shifted on the gun, seeking a firmer grip for what he was about to do.

"Wait," I said with all the artificial calm I could muster. My mind raced down the avenues open to me: If I told him about the facsimiles, he might be angry enough to shoot me. On the other hand, he might realise that he'd have to come to an agreement with me to keep the facsimiles out of circulation—something I could do only if I were alive.

"You do know there are facsimiles, Chesterton . . . and multiple sets of photographic prints. If you kill me, it won't change a thing."

He sneered at me, keeping the gun steady. "How big a fool do you think I am? It takes *months* to make facsimiles. You've had the blasted book for only a week or so." All the same, he did sound worried, and glanced at the mint box at my feet. It seemed to me he was breathing a bit faster.

I shook my head. "Once it became clear that the book

was in danger, Diana Boillot agreed to rush one through. It's already done." I didn't tell him it was the one in the mint box at my feet. "She's already begun to make three more."

He turned to look at me, checking to see if I was bluffing, but apparently saw the truth in my eyes.

"*Damn you to HELL!*" he roared, his face a dangerously dark, enraged purple. To my vast surprise, he let go of the stick, keeping the gun trained on me. Then, with his left hand, he opened his door a fraction and tossed my priceless incunable out into the screaming darkness.

Stunned, I watched my hopes for Sarah's safe return disappear.

"Hand me that other box!"

I hesitated.

"*Hand me the box!!*" he bellowed, pressing the gun against my temple.

Why he didn't just shoot me then, I'll never know. But I obeyed: I reached down and handed the Charbonnel et Walker box over to him. He tossed *it* into the night as well. As he pulled his door shut, I heard him draw a sharp breath. His eyes widened, as if he'd had an astonishing thought. The gun wobbled.

I had nothing to lose. I ducked my head, shoved his arm up, and heard the *ping* of a bullet ricocheting off the metal roof of the interior. At the same moment, my would-be assassin gasped and shuddered, then slumped forward onto the stick. *Had the shot struck him?* I heard the gun thud to the floor, out of his inert hand.

The helicopter plunged, dropping forward and down; at the same time I saw brightly flashing lights outside. Bracing myself for disaster, shocked and befuddled by the turn of events, I thought perhaps the lights meant we were heading for a building. But we were plummeting downward, too fast. . . .

One way or another, it appeared, Chesterton was going to kill me.

CHAPTER 14

There arose certain customs that were quite
contrary to established tradition.

—GIOVANNI BOCCACCIO, *DECAMERON:*
FIRST DAY: INTRODUCTION

I had to get Chesterton off the stick.

As the helicopter careered through the night, I reached over, grabbed Chesterton's jacket, and yanked him back into a sitting position. There was no gunshot wound that I could see, but his face was tinged blue. He appeared to be unconscious.

"Chesterton! Chesterton!" I screamed, pulling back on the stick in front of me. No response. We rose steeply; I'd pulled it too far. I pushed my stick back; we dived again. Too much.

"Dear God," I said, and clutched the stick with clammy hands, desperately trying to finesse the helicopter into level flight. As I seesawed the craft onto a more even keel, I become aware that the flashing lights seemed to be staying with me. It almost seemed they were attached to the helicopter despite my accidental aerobatics. Looking out into the blackness, I saw a helicopter next to me on Chesterton's side. I whirled to see one on my right as well.

The pilot closest to me was motioning urgently to his earphones.

My mind seemed to be working in slow motion. *Earphones . . . Radio . . . Volume . . . Up . . .*

My shaking fingers turned up the radio volume control—the same knob I'd seen Chesterton turn down not so long before. Immediately I heard a calm voice saying my name. *"Alex Plumtree? Mr. Plumtree, sir. Can you hear me? I repeat, can you hear me?"*

I looked out of the window to my right and made eye contact with the pilot. I nodded.

"Speak into the mouthpiece on your headphones."

"I—I can hear you." My mouth was dry as paper, but the rest of me was drenched with sweat.

"All right, Alex. You're going to be okay. You know we've got to get your package to London, fast. You're going to have to fly the helicopter."

Package? The book. They thought I still had it. . . .

I shook my head. "The—*package*—is gone. Chesterton threw it out, minutes ago."

There was silence for a moment as they dealt with this information. Then the copilot on Chesterton's side was back with me. *"All right. We understand. Are you injured?"*

I knew he was just trying to keep me rational, to help me ignore the horror of the dying man next to me. I couldn't fly a helicopter, and we both knew it, though somehow the thing was soaring evenly through the night at the moment.

"I'm okay. But I don't know how to fly."

"I'll tell you how. Just stay calm."

"Right." I had a wild urge to laugh, told myself to get a grip.

"What is the duke's condition?"

"He—I'm not sure. His gun went off; he may have been hit by a bullet, but I don't see a wound. He seems in very bad shape."

"*Understood. We'll land at Exeter and get him to hospital before taking you on to London. We're nearly there now.*"

"All right," I said, sounding far more confident than I felt. The many lights of what must have been Exeter already loomed ahead. I wanted out of that deadly bubble of an aircraft desperately. I felt as close as I ever had to panic, felt a fear in my gut so profound that it was nearly incapacitating. But my inner voice told me to pull my socks up and get on with it. I took a deep breath and looked at my coach. It sank in now that it was a military helicopter; the pilot was in uniform.

He said, "*You've already noticed that the stick takes you down if you push it forwards, up if you pull it back. You can leave the collective, that lever by your left arm, alone. We're going to maintain a constant speed and glide you in like an aeroplane. Now, look up ahead, sir. Do you see those parallel stripes of light ahead? It's the airport at Exeter. They're getting ready for us.*"

"Can't I just get over the airport, hover, and go straight down? Wouldn't that be safer?"

"*No time to teach you how to use the pedals and collective—juggling it all is a bit more complicated than you'd think. We've thought about the best way to take you in. Now, ever so slightly, ease your stick forwards.*"

I did as he said, and the nose of the helicopter dipped the barest fraction.

"*Good. Now a bit more. See if you can follow us, match our angle. As we approach, you'll see what we call VASI boxes—they'll tell you if you're coming in at the right angle. They'll be two boxes of red and white lights along the runway, one farther ahead than the other, both on your right. Each has a strip of red lights inside the top, white inside the bottom. When you look through the window into the box, you want to be at an angle so that you see red on the top and white on the bottom. Red on red, you're dead—too low—white on white, you're high as a kite.*"

I wasn't sure I appreciated his effort at humour—if that's what it was. "Right. I understand."

"Good, take it down a little more. That's fine. The instant you touch the ground, start easing the collective down. That will slow you. Got it?"

"Got it."

"All right. We're counting on you—I'll be right beside you. Now bring her down, sir."

The escort helicopters stayed on either side of me, though they now flew at a distance, at the sides of the runway. I could see a phalanx of emergency vehicles lining the runway ahead—yellow, red, blue, and white lights flashing in a frenzy. The spectacle looked like a Christmas display—and the foam spreading rapidly across the runway looked like a sudden snowstorm.

They expected me to crash.

I watched the runway rushing towards me with horrifying speed. *How could I possibly do this?* I *would* crash . . .

"Do you see the edge of the runway?" I was glad to hear my coach's voice. *"Not far now. Get ready to line up the VASI lights—red on the top, white on the bottom. All right?"*

"Right." I looked, saw red on red light in the boxes, panicked, and pulled the stick up too far. Now I saw white on white.

The perfectly calm voice in my ears said, *"A bit too much on the stick, Alex—get it back down now."*

I had to; I did. Miraculously, the red lights showed through the top window of the box, and white on the bottom.

"Hang on, you're there!"

I hit the runway with a grinding crunch and a bounce that set my ribs aching anew. The port skid crashed into the ground first; it bounced up as the other side rocked down. The starboard skid dug into the runway with a shriek of metal on concrete and ground along the surface. The next second I was sailing through a sea of white foam.

"Collective down. Collective down!" my teacher yelled.

I eased the lever towards the floor, and the helicopter began to slow. It stayed on its skids and ground to a halt in the foam.

Kind hands came immediately to help me out of the helicopter; I was pulled out and urged away from the helicopter towards the edge of the runway. I'd been there for only several seconds, and was watching ambulance men lift the duke out of the helicopter, when I heard the voice of my flight instructor, this time directly in front of me.

"Nice job," he said, grinning. "Perhaps you'll have to learn to fly one day." He stuck out his hand; I shook it. He pretended not to feel the tremors in it.

"Er, thanks, but I don't think so. Thanks for getting me down."

"You're wanted in London, sir—I'll take you now, if you think you're all right."

I went with him to his double-rotored helicopter just off the runway. As I strapped myself into a seat behind the pilot, I saw an ambulance whisk away the duke. The ride to London was a blur; I slept the sleep of the deeply exhausted and discouraged for much of it. When they saw I was awake again, the copilot poured me a cup of coffee from a flask. They didn't attempt conversation. Scenes played and replayed through my mind: I thought of Sarah at the Orchard, looking startled at my shotgun; the book hurtling through space; Jarrow dead in the underground corridor; the runway racing towards me; the helicopter sliding into the foam.

We landed not at an airport but in Whitehall itself. I was ushered without a word from a rooftop down some stairs, and into a plain vanilla box occupied by the prime minister and the defence secretary. The defence secretary rose and nodded briskly at me, excused himself, and left the room.

"Alex." Graeme rose and gave me a hug. When he

pulled away, his hands on my shoulders, he looked unspeakably sad. "I'm glad you're here safely."

Words wouldn't come.

"Sit down, Alex. Sit down," my friend said, motioning
me into a chair across the table from him.

From the way Graeme sighed as he lowered himself
into the chair, I could tell he had bad news. Graeme sat
forward at the table, clasping his hands over a discreetly
closed foolscap folder. He frowned at me in concern.

"What's happened to your face?" He wasn't looking at
my forehead; he was looking at my cheek.

I reached up; blood came away on my hand. Tiny bits
of glass from the shot-up helicopter window. "As you
might know, we had a problem in the helicopter," I said
carefully. "Chesterton tried to shoot me, and my window
shattered. But this," I said, touching the bandage on top of
the receding purple knot on my forehead, "came from an
accident on Trefoyle's yacht."

"Ah." The set of his mouth told me he'd already got the
news about the duke trying to shoot me. "I see. Trefoyle
told us to intercept the duke's helicopter when he heard
you were flying here with him—he thought Chesterton
might have meant you harm, though I must say I don't
quite see why."

"I can tell you all about it. But you've spoken with Trefoyle? Is he all right?"

Graeme nodded. "He was delayed getting here, that's
all. Had us worried."

"Good. Thank God he's all right. We thought the worst
had happened." I sighed. "Well. You need to know about
the incunable. It has significance to more than just the
Iraqis."

"Yes—the pilots told me Chesterton threw it out of the
helicopter. Why would he do that? And why did he try to
shoot you?"

"You remember the knight in the Bedchamber book,

kneeling at the bed of the king with the dagger in his hand?"

He nodded.

"That knight was wearing Chesterton's arms—the lion with the crown in its teeth. I just didn't know it, and no one else who'd seen the book had recognised it; Chesterton's ancestors had long since eliminated the crown from the family arms. But Trefoyle showed me the new heraldry book Chesterton had released last year for Old Ashleigh. Evidently, he thought he'd eliminated every copy of the book, so he thought it was safe to resurrect the authentic Chesterton arms for the volume. The historically accurate version is the lion rampant with the crown in its teeth; in our 1925 book, I think it's just the lion rampant. Anyway, the restored version was identical to the murderous knight's."

"Good Lord. A matter of family honour, then. Or, rather, dishonour."

"Yes. But this is the confusing bit: I found the book in *Margulies Whitehead's* room. It's a long story, so bear with me, but the Dibdin carried out the ultimate initiation rite, and led me to believe Margulies had died."

Graeme sat forward, horrified.

"Yes, I know. It's difficult to explain—the ruse reenacted a Boccaccio story, as did virtually the entire weekend. After I saw the knight in the heraldry book, I realised that Chesterton had reason to want the Bedchamber incunable to disappear forever. So when I had the chance, I searched Chesterton's room, and that of his private secretary. But Margulies's vacant room was next door to their rooms—Margulies had never returned after his 'death' Friday night. The book was there, under his mattress, cleverly concealed inside another book. But in the helicopter Chesterton genuinely didn't know where the book was all weekend. He was totally surprised when I asked him why he'd put it in Margulies's room."

"My God, this is *complicated*." Graeme, closed his eyes briefly. "What does Margulies Whitehead have to do with all this?"

I shook my head. "I haven't worked that out. I can't imagine him stealing the Bedchamber book from my desk at the Press. He's a friend, and an author of mine, as you know. We need to try to reach him. When the club members looked into his whereabouts, someone said he wasn't at the hotel they'd taken him to the night before, and he wasn't at his flat. Evidently, someone rang a friend to check on him. He wasn't there, and his flat had been burgled."

Graeme picked up the telephone immediately and ordered one of his assistants to find out whether Margulies had been found, and if not, to keep searching until they found him.

"Too many people want this book." Graeme sighed, his dread palpable. "I must tell you, Alex, we've received some very bad news from our negotiators. When the pilots radioed us that the original book was lost, we had to tell our Iraqi contact, of course, who told the Great Teacher. He took it as a deliberate provocation. As you know, we'd promised it him."

From the look on Graeme's face, I could see this was only the beginning of the bad news he had for me. Panic rose; instinctively, I knew it was about Sarah.

"I'm so sorry, Alex. While you were still at the castle we learned they had Sarah in Cyprus, where our agents were able to keep an eye on her. Now we don't know where she is—but we're working on it, of course. One group of people in Iraq is working very closely with us to recover her. They're doing their best to cooperate."

I said nothing. But behind my quiet exterior a deeply buried, carefully contained fury seethed. If only I could *do* something . . .

The prime minister fell back in his chair wearily. "The Iraqis tried everything, we've learned. They tried to purchase the book from your brother this morning, telling him Sarah's life was at stake. But they forbade him to tell you, knowing that you were already working to obtain it for them. Now." He leaned forward again, folding his hands on the table. "The one hope we have is the facsimile. Diana told us she sent it to you at the castle. Do you know where *it* is?"

So many disasters had taken place in the last few hours . . . "Chesterton threw it out too, Graeme. I do have photographs of the pages of the book, you know—did Diana tell you that? She has a set too. Perhaps that would help."

"No. Tried that already. They won't say why, but they're demanding the entire thing—binding, covers, and all."

We sat for a moment, overwhelmed by the way events had painted us—and particularly Sarah—into a seemingly inescapable corner.

"You should know, Alex, that Trefoyle feels responsible for Sarah being in jeopardy in the first place. Evidently, he'd asked her to travel to Castle Trefoyle to surprise you at the end of their beastly initiation ritual."

I thought of what Chesterton had told me about his ancestors getting Edward IV to try to get rid of the book and all associated with it; did the Chestertons of old have enough power to get the Arab world to do their bidding as well?

"From what Intelligence have found," the PM continued grimly, "many people have died before now trying to dispose of the secret. I don't have to tell you, Alex, that it doesn't look good for Sarah. Once more than a few days have gone by . . ."

To do him credit, his voice and choice of words showed that he understood the issue and was being completely honest. I understood what he was saying. He looked down at the table.

Closing my eyes, I shut out the thought. It was too

horrible to contemplate what might be happening to Sarah at that very moment; what might happen to her in the near future. My mind went on working but focussed on other things. Details that had troubled me clicked into place. Now I understood Max's strange behaviour. I remembered how he'd told me he needed the book, the near-hysterical note in his voice. He'd been trying to save Sarah but couldn't tell me. It must have been torture for him.

"At this moment," Graeme told me, "our men are out combing the moors for the book."

"It was hidden inside Margulies's modern Boccaccio edition—strange, I know. Someone cut out the inside of the book and fitted the incunable into it. If they should see it, it may well have lost its dust wrapper. Better tell them to look for a deep burgundy imitation leather cover with gold lettering on it. But, you realise, the incunable may well have fallen out."

My old friend picked up the phone again and gave this information to his assistant, so he could radio the searchers.

"Tell me, Alex," he said. Every muscle in his face expressed his struggle to comprehend our bizarre situation. "Did you see *anything* else in that book that might have made it so very dangerous to so many, besides Chesterton, over nearly a millennium?"

"No." I shook my head. Who would have thought that the story of how King Richard the Lion-Heart *really* died, and at whose hands, would be so terrifically threatening to anyone now? I still couldn't believe that the old murder could be the sum total of it. There had to be more. I said as much to Graeme.

"My people think so too, as does Trefoyle. We just don't know what it is." He sighed. "Alex, Trefoyle wants you to go back to the castle with him for the point-to-point. Make a fool of yourself asking questions if you have to, but help him find out what that secret is. He wants you to focus on young Ashleigh, Albemarle, and Westering. It would seem to be our best chance."

I squared my shoulders, hoping he couldn't see how dazed I felt. How utterly exhausted. And how desperate to do anything at all that would bring Sarah back.

"Yes, of course," I said, focussing bleary eyes on Graeme—though how Ashleigh, Albemarle, and Westering would know the first thing about the secret of the Bedchamber incunable, I couldn't imagine.

Still, the very thought of being able to do something, anything, was a lifeline. My powerlessness in the face of Sarah's disaster was unbearable. At least here was a *chance* . . .

Graeme glanced at his watch and stood. "You'd best be off; you'll need to get some rest. Trefoyle should be back at the castle by now; he's agreed to stick with you on the course. I daresay he'll be of some help. Do be careful, Alex." He put a fatherly hand on my back as I walked toward the door.

On my way out of the room, I tripped and fell flat on my face. Graeme's assistant picked me up, handed me a polystyrene cup of murky tea, and I was on yet another helicopter back to the castle by seven A.M.

I fell asleep and woke only as the aircraft descended onto the landing pad, blinking at the grey rock of Castle Trefoyle shining in the brilliant early morning sun. As we hovered closer to that spectacular sight, I hoped that Earl Trefoyle was safely ensconced in his bastion after the horrors of the night before.

At last the helicopter touched down, first one side and then the other, as if testing the ground before committing itself. I waved thanks to the pilot and ran out of the violent blast of the rotors.

I made my way straight to the garden door, intending to tidy myself up a bit and then have a word with Trefoyle. A butler opened the door. "All right, Mr. Plumtree?"

With a start, I realised he was probably Jarrow's

replacement—in all likelihood, another secret agent of some sort. "Is, er, Hawkes—?"

He lowered his eyes and shook his head. What a price this book had exacted, from so many people.

"My name is Pemberton; please feel free to call upon me at any time."

"Thank you." Weary to the bone, I trudged up to my room and took a welcome hot shower. Then, clad temporarily in jeans and polo shirt, I made my way to Earl Trefoyle's suite. I knocked; there was no answer. I checked my watch; the point-to-point was to start in just under two hours. As host, Trefoyle would surely be up and about by now. I knocked again more loudly. When this knock, too, went unanswered, I began to worry. Remembering Jarrow's key still on the ribbon around my neck, I looked both ways down the hall. No one. I pulled the key out and furtively inserted it into the lock. The key turned smoothly; I opened the door and stepped hastily inside, closing it behind me before anyone could see.

Trefoyle's bed was made, no sign of anything unusual in his suite. Remembering the crewman Chesterton had shot, I shuddered and spun round to look at the alcove door. No trace of blood or struggle. I frowned. It didn't make sense. If the crewman had been the one shooting at Jarrow and me, then why, assuming Chesterton was opposing Trefoyle and the government in the effort to get the book to London, had he shot the man?

Fingering the key, my hand trembling from fatigue, I crossed to the alcove and fitted the key into the lock. Then I made my way cautiously down those irritating little steps and into the hallway where I'd last seen Jarrow.

I slowed as I approached the doorway to the globe room. Every last surface was spotless, eerily devoid of any trace of the carnage of several hours before. The ancient stone wall showed not a single nick from the cascade of wildly ricocheting bullets. The stone floor and its carpet runner revealed no stain. Someone had done a disturbingly thorough—and swift—job of tidying up. It made me uncomfortable; everything had been swept under the carpet too quickly, as after Margulies's death. Britain's secret forces at work, perhaps?

I hurried further down the Oriental runner, silent in my stealth. I don't mind admitting that I was afraid of what I might find. Rounding the curve I remembered from the night before, I saw where Jarrow and I had entered the passage from the rocks above. But there was also another door, heading—could it be?—straight towards the water . . .

Trefoyle's island. The door I'd felt when I'd fallen from the helicopter!

What on earth did he do down here? I had to find out.

There was a pressure pad next to the door, allowing someone to open it using a code of numbers one through nine. Jarrow's key would do me no good here. I thought about Max's security system at Watersmeet; it had a pad like this that locked up after three wrong tries. The worst that could happen, I supposed, was that I would set off the alarm.

I thought of the security codes I knew. My computer password was a combination of letters and numbers; the computing magazines claimed it was safest to use a combination. But Trefoyle's pad bore only numbers. . . .

A door opened behind me, perhaps from the castle to the underground passage. "Trefoyle?"

Silence.

Panic galvanised me into action.

Hurry.

What numbers were significant to Trefoyle? The date of the Duke of Windlesham's sale, when he first acquired the Boccaccio? 17 June 1812. I pressed the numbers *17, 6, 12*. Nothing happened. I tried *6, 17, 1812*. Still nothing.

Now the unmistakable sound of muffled footsteps

came down the runner. There was time to flee through
the door on the left to the rocks above. . . .

My heart beat in a terrified syncopation as I frantically
punched in the next number that came to mind, the year
the Valdarfer Boccaccio was printed: *1471.*

The door slid open; I dashed through and pushed a
button on the other side—the door slid shut quickly. It
had been virtually silent; now, if only the person I'd heard
in the passage wasn't coming *this* way . . .

I sprinted down a flight of concrete steps and into another whitewashed tunnel. The island was perhaps a hundred yards through the water from the castle. I covered
the passage quickly, and came upon another doorway.

Inwardly, I groaned. *Another* combination to work
out . . . I tried *1471* again, and to my surprise, the door
slid open. Perhaps, I thought, Trefoyle was less interested
in security than a sealed door to contain the water, in case
of a leak or even a complete breach. I advanced into an
officelike area surrounded by shelving filled with files,
and boxes with squiggles of Arabic script. Of course—
Westering and Jarrow had mentioned that Trefoyle im-
ported products from the Middle East for his personal
use. No evidence of shipping operations involving guns
from here . . .

As I glanced about, I thought I heard movement—not
behind me this time, but ahead, in the far corner of the
warehouse space. Rats? Having satisfied my curiosity
about the island, I had turned to retreat through the passage, when I heard an unmistakable human groan.

Picking my way through the shelves, I moved toward
the shadowy rear wall. "Is someone there?"

"Plumtree . . ." a weak voice answered. "Thank God!"

"Who—" I strained to see in the dim light.

A scraggly grey beard and dark, sunken skin beneath
the man's eyes told me this was no ghost.

"*Margulies?!* Are you all *right*? What on earth—"

"Please! I don't know when he'll come again. You must get me out of here."

I went to work on the thick rope that bound him to the steel beam. His lips were cracked; he seemed very weak. "Who? Who will come again?" I asked.

He tried to lick his lips. "Chesterton's ... secretary ..."

I got the rope untied and started to work on the one binding his wrists. The poor man had been there since Friday night, I suspected, without food or water. "I did hear someone down here as I came," I warned him. "He might not have come this way, but we mustn't waste any time getting you out. Can you walk?"

I slid the rope off his wrists at last, noticing that his skin was raw and bleeding.

"I think so," he replied. "Do you know about Van?"

"Know what?"

"He's dead. Car accident Friday night, in London."

"Van Vanderbilt is dead?"

Margulies nodded. He wobbled as I helped him up but stayed on his feet. "I called a friend of Van's early Saturday morning, after we played that ghastly trick on you. I'm sorry, Alex. I can tell you the sedative wasn't very pleasant to recover from either."

I waved off his apology to show I would hold no grudges.

"I've been thinking about it," he went on. "They're the only papers that actually document the existence of the Bedchamber book. Someone is hell-bent to make all traces of that book disappear."

"Yes," I said. "I worked that out too. It was Chesterton. It's his family coat of arms on the knight kneeling at Richard's bedside. His ancestor killed King Richard over a personal dispute, not only to recover his family title and lands, but so that he, as a distant relative of the king's, would be further up in the line of succession."

Margulies gazed at me in disbelief. "That's just insane

enough to be true." He shook his head again. "I have the feeling this indistinguishable fact and fantasy in Boccaccio has carried over into real life. . . ."

I took his arm and led him through the shelves. "Chesterton is out of commission just now—ill, I think. The main thing is to get you out of here, and as quietly as possible, in case Chesterton's private secretary is about. He can be up to no good."

"He was the one who did this to me," Margulies said as I opened the door. "Right after the call about Van. Came into the pub in the village, where I was staying after my little act, and asked me to come with him. He brought me here."

I shook my head. The passageway was clear; I tried to hurry Margulies, but he couldn't seem to move any faster than a shuffle. "I'm going to get you outside and go for help; there's someone I can trust here. His name's Pemberton; he's disguised as a servant, and extremely capable. He can take you round via the rocks until you reach the yacht harbour. There's a power tender moored there; Trefoyle leaves the keys in. I'll ask Pemberton to get you safely away."

Margulies nodded. We reached the door at the far end, and I entered the combination again to exit. After a quick look, I saw that the corridor back to the castle was empty, as far as I could see.

"Let's go!" I urged, hurrying him to the door near the rocks Jarrow had brought me through the night before. I grabbed the key round my neck and inserted it as Jarrow had on the outside. The door slid open and daylight streamed in as Margulies, blinded, put up a hand to shield his eyes. "Up you go," I whispered. "Come on . . . onto these rocks." I closed the door behind us. "Wait here for Pemberton; you'll be all right now. Everyone's preparing for the point-to-point on the far side of the castle. I'm sorry I can't go with you—I've got to be at that race."

He gripped my arm. "Thank you, Alex . . ." he said, and sat heavily on the rocks.

I made no reply. I was perilously close to being late for the breakfast and the race. I couldn't fail; Sarah was at stake.

I encountered no one as I jogged painfully across the lawn, into the castle, and up the stairs. I had barely locked myself inside my room and begun to take off my sweaty clothes, when I heard a perfunctory knock on the door. Before I could make myself decent and get there, it was unlocked and opened.

"Good morning, sir," a gentle voice said. I stuck my head round the corner of the bathroom; it was a servant carrying the early morning coffee. I still found it disconcerting the way people so easily popped in and out of my locked room. "The breakfast at the stables begins in half an hour, sir. I thought I'd let you sleep as long as I could. . . ."

I longed to laugh, but my sleepless night was not this man's fault. "Very kind. Thank you."

The man backed out of the room and closed the door silently. My head felt padded, thick, as if it were swathed in cotton wool. As I poured myself a cup of coffee, not bothering with cream, I was filled with dread at the thought of the race before me. Riding in a point-to-point was beyond imagining this morning; it was a torturous exercise at the best of times.

Had I been at all interested in self-preservation, I'd not have returned to the castle. But Trefoyle seemed to feel that chatting to several of my fellow members, before, during, and after a hellish fence and ditch course was the only way to decipher the Bedchamber incunable's secret. And discovering that secret seemed to be the only way to see Sarah again.

I would not fail her.

CHAPTER 15

All cats are grey in the dark.

—G. H. McWilliam, Boccaccio scholar

Somehow someone had found me a jacket, appropriate shirt, and riding breeches. They hung in my closet. Black riding boots of exactly the right size, soft, supple, and polished, waited on the floor. Amazing. I donned the traditional garb and started down to the stables.

As I stepped off the main staircase I'd run up so angrily the night Margulies had "died," I noticed that the castle seemed deserted. Still a bit early for the Dibdinians, I thought. Even as I walked through the corridor that passed through to the side of the castle away from the sea, I saw no one about, heard nothing but the gentle creak of the boots I wore.

As I walked, I made connections that I should have seen before then. In the rough draft of the article Van was writing for *SF* magazine about the San Francisco Dibdin Club, which I had invited him to expand into a novel, he'd included a box entitled *Have you seen these books?*

Just for fun, he'd listed the books on Haslewood's "rumoured to exist" list. I'd mentioned it at "tea" on Friday afternoon. Now I thought it quite likely that my idle chat had cost Van his life.

I walked in the direction of the stables, struggling to believe, even after all I'd seen, in Chesterton's obsession with eliminating all traces of the Bedchamber book. On Friday afternoon, shortly after Chesterton had arrived, he'd brought up the issue of the San Francisco club. Something about suing them because their widely publicised bad behaviour was affecting the reputation of the original Dibdin Club. Now I understood.

As I crossed the lawn, rather slowly due to my disturbing thoughts, I was caught up with by Sir Harold. He walked with me towards a tent that had been set up a discreet distance from the stables, far enough to be out of reach of flies and unpleasant horsey odours.

"Looking forward to this," he said with a smile, presumably referring to the point-to-point. Unfortunately, all of us who were beginning to drift across the lawn were obliged to follow the unwritten—and absolutely unbreakable—rule of not conversing before breakfast. I would have to wait to ask my questions until after we'd eaten, or they'd *know* something was up.

As I approached the breakfast buffet laid out upwind of the stables, I saw Desmond Delacroix helping himself to sausages ahead of me in the queue. I knew that any one of my fellow Dibdinians might prove to be the man we sought.

Trust no one, I reminded myself.

"Morning, Desmond."

"Morning, Plumtree."

A long, white-clad table had been laid opposite the buffet. After filling my plate for appearance's sake—food was the last thing I wanted—I carried it over and sat next to Desmond, opposite Sir Harold. I revised my lines in preparation for shocking someone into reacting to my statements about the Bedchamber incunable. Graeme had told me Trefoyle would send word to the castle that Chesterton had been called to London, in case news of his illness would affect the other matter we were pursuing.

Lord Peter Albemarle sat on my left, nodding a greeting. Perfect, I thought. Couldn't be better. Someone poured coffee and tea, and the reduced cast of riders gradually assembled at the table. For five minutes we ate in silence, occupied by food, coffee, and the bustle of the stable lads kitting out the horses. The dogs yapped near the stables; their harsh bark set my teeth on edge. I felt more than a little fear, as well, at the thought of jumping fences and tearing through the countryside at breakneck speed—even without playing the worm on the end of a line.

Lost in these thoughts, it was a moment before I noticed that Lord Peter was jabbing something into my side. Surprised, I looked down to find that he was offering me his silver hip flask—liquid strength for the point-to-point. It was customary to have a tipple before riding events of this sort, so I smiled my thanks as best I could and took a swallow. Brandy. All round the table, little silver flasks were flashing out of pockets and up to lips, and discreetly back into the inside pockets again. I seemed to be the only one without my own flask, duly engraved with family crest.

"Thank you, Lord Peter."

"Not at all, my boy." There was steel behind his mild exterior. "I should think you've had quite an unnerving weekend. Any news on your fiancée yet?"

I gritted my teeth. "No." *But there will be by the end of the day,* I wanted to add.

He tut-tutted, and I noticed that little snippets of conversation were beginning to erupt down the table. People were coming to life a bit, perhaps with the assistance of their flasks. "Lovely cool morning," someone said. "Looks as if they're nearly ready," said another. "Who's in charge, then, if Trefoyle's gone?"

"Where is Trefoyle?" I asked, all innocence.

"Don't know. But word was waiting this morning that I was to take over if he wasn't up and about by half-past nine," Sir Harold answered.

"Should make a change from your little ponies in Wiltshire," Colin Jones-Harris said tongue-in-cheek. Westering was known to be an indulgent grandfather; he'd purchased his grandchildren a gaggle of miniature ponies so they could start off riding safely. I hated it that Jones-Harris would mock him; indeed, I almost hated Jones-Harris himself. He and his little circle made up nearly a third of the riders. I vowed to keep my distance from that lot; they'd be falling out of their saddles with drink before long.

Sir Harold replied gamely, "Yes, indeed. Quite a change, young Jones-Harris. But never fear, I know the lie of the land. I started hunting here with Trefoyle—hmm, let's see—some ten years before you were born, I should say." He allowed himself a smile.

Lord Peter offered me his flask again. I appreciated the gesture and told him so, but declined.

"Go on, everyone needs a nip before a ride like this." He thrust it at me. Either he'd had a healthy dose of brandy already, or he was feeling extremely friendly that morning. I didn't want to seem rude. I took another small sip and passed it back with a smile.

"Lord Peter, I was wondering." I had to be careful, had to remember what they *didn't* know. I'd come up with a question for each of my targets that would tell me if I'd struck gold. "You know more about book collecting than almost anyone. This might seem an odd question, but can you think of any reason the book might be of interest to Iraqi buyers? I've been contacted by several; they've each offered exorbitant sums. They seem absolutely desperate to get it. But I can't imagine why."

"Nor can I," Lord Peter said earnestly, "unless that reference to Saladin makes it intriguing to them. Sometimes people are keen to collect things that pertain to their history."

"Yes, perhaps that's it," I murmured. Nothing. No twinkle of excitement in his eye, no flicker of suspicion. A reasonable answer.

I was aware of a small commotion at the end of the table; the countess had arrived with Dame Cleopatra. "Just coffee," the countess ordered the servant behind her. "Alex Plumtree! Bloody marvellous. You're still here," she said, and giggled. "Haven't scared you off yet, then?" Next to her, Dame Cleopatra smiled benignly.

I honestly couldn't discern the meaning behind the countess's words. Was she acknowledging in a light-hearted way the hell they'd put me through—though, of course, no one knew exactly how hellish the night had been—or was she being cruel? I couldn't forget her words in the library on the first afternoon. I merely smiled, and I then saw Sir Harold rise and fling his napkin down on the table as if it were a gauntlet.

"Well," he said cheerfully, "let's get on, shall we?"

This is it, I told myself. The last opportunity to be with the Dibdin members until the next meeting. Whatever I would learn, I had to learn right then.

I'd only just pushed my chair back and got to my feet when the world began to spin, the blue sky overhead turning in woozy circles. I steadied myself on the table, and after several seconds the sensation passed. I hoped the dreaded flu hadn't got its claws in me. That would be the icing on the cake.

I followed the others to where the lads had massed the horses. Ashleigh waddled up to me, then, sliding his hip flask into his pocket. " 'Morning," he said.

"Ah, Ashleigh. I was hoping to see you today. Do you mind if I ask a question?"

"Of course not. What is it?"

"I wondered . . . would you know why my Bedchamber incunable has such attraction for Iraqi buyers? Is there another legend about it that I don't know?"

He snorted. "No, but if I were you, I'd watch for Chesterton trying to get his hands on it. That, or the Committee for the Preservation of English Artifacts. They're ruthless, you know, in pursuing items relevant to English history."

I certainly knew about Chesterton. But surely Ashleigh didn't think Sir Harold and Lord Peter's *committee* would actually steal my book . . . ?

"Plumtree," Sir Harold barked, taking charge of matching riders to horses. "Here, you're a big, strapping fellow—you take Attila."

Terrific, I thought. A horse named Attila could possess only one overriding characteristic. The stable lad led the horse to me and held out the reins. I stared in disbelief at the huge, angry black beast that was to be mine for the next two hours, watched him stamp impatiently on the field with rolling eyes and ears flattened against his head. The lad looked at me with sulky eyes, then looked away again almost guiltily. . . . Or was it accusingly? Perhaps he suspected that I wasn't equal to the beautiful horse in his care.

There was nothing to do but carry on. As I took the reins from the lad, Attila reared up on his hind legs, achieving a terrifying height. I hung on to the reins grimly, somehow managing to stay out of the way of his flailing hooves as they thudded back to earth. In the next instant the animal bucked, its muscular hind legs kicking backwards as if jet-propelled. The countess, who was in the pucker stage of giving Osgood Forsythe a kiss on the cheek, was perilously close to the deadly hooves. Forsythe flung her out of harm's way with considerable drama as I fought for control of the beast, all the while doing what I could to save myself.

"For God's sake, Plumtree!!" Forsythe spat out, full of disdain. "Can't you control that animal?!"

"Sorry."

Forsythe shot me a look that told me I was a hopeless prat. But it didn't matter to me anymore. I led the horse a short distance away, speaking to him gently. I stroked and patted his withers, trying to exude calm control as he jerked and strained at the reins. No matter what I tried, the horse remained skittish.

The others mounted, and I saw with horror that the opportunity to dangle my bait was passing all too quickly. Once the race actually started, it would be too late. I got one foot in the stirrup and stepped into it. The instant my weight was on him, the beast went utterly berserk, snorting and screaming as it reared and then bucked. As I clung to his neck, holding on desperately with my knees, it seemed a very long way down to the ground. I'd never met a horse so mean-spirited, unless . . .

I stepped out of the stirrup when he'd come back to earth, and clutched the reins. He seemed to calm a bit, though he still danced about nervously as if prepared to buck at any moment. "Let's have a look, old boy, shall we?" I spoke to him quietly as I loosened the girth.

I ran a hand beneath the blanket and saddle, feeling the warmth of his massive back. My fingertips struck something hard, metallic. In disbelief, I reached in and pulled out one of Earl Trefoyle's heavy sterling forks. Some sadist had put it there with its tines pointing downward, sticking into Attila's back, and tightened the girth. When I'd stepped into the stirrup and put weight on the saddle, the sharp tines had driven him mad.

"Poor boy," I murmured. "Poor old boy. You're all right now." Without fuss I slid the fork into my inner pocket and took a quick look around. Who on earth . . . ?

I saw Colin Jones-Harris snap his head back toward his mount, then climb up into his saddle. He'd been watching me, there was no mistaking it. Well, I'd start with him, then.

"There, boy. We're all right now," I told the horse, and

climbed up on Attila, who now would have been better suited by the appellation Sweetie Pie. I guided my placid mount toward Jones-Harris, only to see him start away from me. I called out to him, but he ignored me, obviously deciding a quick turn round the meadow to warm up his horse was preferable to chatting to me. I was about to pursue him, when Sir Harold drew up next to me on an impressive chestnut.

"Got him well in hand now, have you?"

"Yes, fine, thanks." But as I answered him, I realised that everything was *not* fine. My hands were clammy, and my clothing was damp with sweat. I'd have considered it nerves, but I felt distinctly odd—distant from my own body. Perhaps the flu really had caught up with me. Or— and here was a horrible thought—Lord Peter's gin had been drugged. Perhaps he hadn't drunk any—it had looked as if he'd raised it to his lips, but I couldn't be sure. If he was the one I was looking for, and I'd let him put me out of commission so easily, all was lost. I couldn't think of any Boccaccio stories to that effect, though I hadn't read them all. . . .

But why Lord Peter? Even if there were a grain of truth to Ashleigh's wild idea about the committee, surely Lord Peter wouldn't need to kill me. Unless he was finally showing his wrath over my article in the *Bookseller* . . .

Kicking myself for trusting Albemarle, but more determined than ever, I vowed to stay on the horse if it killed me. I forced my eyes to focus on Sir Harold as he began to trot, warming up his mount, and said in a confidential tone, "Sir Harold, are you the one to ask about the, er, the real significance of the Bedchamber book to my potential Iraqi buyer?" Clumsy, but the best I could manage. If this had anything to do with his committee, perhaps he would show a hint of something unnatural.

His eyes narrowed as he studied me, but as with Albemarle, I saw no guile in them. "I'm not sure what you mean, but we might discuss it after the event, if you like. You know, you don't look at all well, Plumtree. I should be careful riding if I were you." Then he nudged his animal forward and was gone.

Threat or kind consideration? No time to think . . .

I had to dangle the bait before the others, just in case . . . *quickly.*

"Forsythe, Countess," I said, edging over to them on the now-angelic Attila. They looked at me as if I were an annoying fly, then exchanged a glance and broke into a canter, unquestionably trying to avoid me. But I urged Attila into a canter too, and when they saw they couldn't avoid me, they slowed to a trot.

"I do realise this is a rather inconvenient time to ask, but—er—I could be leaving directly afterwards. Is either of you the one to ask about the real significance of the Bedchamber book, especially to my Iraqi buyer?"

"God, Plumtree! What are you on about now?" Forsythe stared at me as if I were mentally deficient. With a roll of his eyes he nodded to his mistress in a way that said *Let's get the hell out of here.*

As they started off, the countess squinted at me. "Did you have a bit too much to drink last night, Plumtree? Your face is the most *ghastly* shade of white." Her smile was cruel. "Do you really think you should be riding with us today?"

Without waiting for a reply, they urged their horses forward. I heard the countess's rippling laugh and Forsythe's mumbled ironic aside, ". . . or *any* day?" as they moved away.

I didn't care what it took. Their horses could trample me, their helicopters pitch me into oblivion, and their yachts knock me silly again before I'd stop trying.

Denis deChauncey was just ahead; I clucked and nudged and got Attila abreast of his horse. I slowed to a trot and blundered into my question. "Denis. Are you the one who really knows about the Bedchamber book—what it might mean to an Iraqi buyer?"

He eyed me critically. "I say, do you feel all right?"

I nodded, but the bright morning had indeed begun to spin again. "Yes," I heard myself say quite normally as things came back into focus. "Thanks."

"All right, then . . . no, I'm sorry to say, I don't know as much about incunables as I'd like. And next to nothing about Middle Eastern book buyers." He smiled in self-deprecation.

Ah, my first clear answer. He probably *didn't* know, unless he was a superb actor. "I see," I said. "Well, thanks anyway . . ." I turned away and rode over to Jones-Harris's little knot of cronies. Nearly done now . . .

" 'Morning," I said. They still looked terrified of me, as on the night Jones-Harris had pretended to have the bet about Sarah. No doubt they would rather have been anywhere but there with me approaching at that moment. I lowered my voice as if sharing some vital secret. "Sorry to intrude. But I'm rather curious . . . does anyone here know the real secret of the Bedchamber book? Especially to the Iraqis?"

All stared at me blankly, until one of them guffawed and said, "Are you barmy? The 'real secret'? Is this a joke?"

But on the edge of the circle I thought I heard Jones-Harris murmur "Good Lord." I looked at him; his eyes were filled not with anger or disdain as I might have expected—but with terror.

Jones-Harris?!

At that moment Sir Harold used a megaphone to announce the order of things. I was last, of course—judged the least competent rider, most likely to hold up the others. This was to be a very informal point-to-point, he told us, the goal being merely to enjoy the ride while, of course trying to finish first. The course, he added, was filled with lovely obstacles of all sorts. He handed the megaphone to one of the stable lads and began the event, nudging his own splendid horse into an easy canter.

Jones-Harris's friends took off as if jolted by an electric shock, obviously grateful for the reprieve from me, and eager to forge ahead of Westering. Jones-Harris brushed past, leaning over as the other horses thundered by. "You're out of your mind, Plumtree. He'll *kill* you," he said. I was astounded that he was capable of such intensity and concern. His voice even sounded different, more serious. I glanced at his face and saw the warning in his eyes. Perhaps I had misjudged the tea heir, the all-too-obvious Hooray Henry. . . .

Urging his horse forward, he mouthed an urgent *"Get away from here!"* to me over his shoulder, and was off. I hesitated only a moment before nudging Attila after him. Jones-Harris didn't realise that was the whole point; the only thing that mattered to me now was to antagonise the culprit enough that he—or she—would expose himself or herself, most likely in the attempt to kill me.

I found myself riding in a rough pack with deChauncey, Lord Peter, and Dame Cleopatra. From the start we had to pay close attention; it was an extremely challenging course. This was undoubtedly part of the land used for the Trefoyle Hunt. We came upon a tallish fence first, which Attila took beautifully, like magic. He landed and seemed exhilarated by it, clearly wanting to go faster. But I pulled him back; if anything went wrong, in a close cluster we'd have a chain-reaction crunch-up. Besides, I had to give someone room to have a go at me. It was extraordinary, waiting for someone to attack me, actually *wanting* someone to do so. Attila took a tall hawthorn hedge with perfect grace, seeming to stay airborne forever. We were now well back from the group, through my continual reining in of my mount. I did let the horse go at his own speed as we approached the obstacles; he knew how to take them far better than I did.

Alert as I was for knives in my back, I couldn't help

noticing that the ground was springy green, as perfect for a ride as anyone could ask. The flowering bushes were blooming, wafting fragrance as we flew over several hedges in succession. I had an odd feeling of detachment from these surroundings, as if I were in the world but not a part of it.

And despite the circumstances, I will never forget the feeling of flying through the air on such a graceful creature. We rode on for perhaps twenty minutes—and then the wooziness seized me again. I clung blindly to the horse's neck, letting him take his head as I blinked back the blackness. It was getting worse as the morning wore on. At last the feeling began to pass, but Attila tossed his head and seemed confused by my lack of direction.

I suddenly noticed we were coming up on a wide ditch, almost a ravine, with a fence on the other side of it.

Hang on. This is for Sarah—for keeps.

I gave Attila his head, knowing he'd have to build up considerable speed for such a difficult jump. As he pounded towards the ditch, now muddy and churned up by all the hooves that had gone before, it happened.

Attila was just launching himself into the air, and I had just hunched low onto his neck to survive the jump, when a sharp crack sounded quite near us. It all happened so quickly and unexpectedly that at first I wasn't sure exactly *what* had happened. Attila screamed in what I thought was panic at the noise, and seemed to lose his balance. It was then, with my face pressed close to his neck, that I saw the spurt of dark liquid across the glossy hair, and the tragic hole in Attila's otherwise perfectly smooth neck.

I didn't have time to think that the shot had been intended for me.

The next few moments passed, like a slow-motion film clip, in which I saw each tiny component of the disaster with painful awareness. Attila had been caught by the bullet just after taking to the air to jump the fence. On his way back to earth, he clipped his front left fetlock against the stout rails. Before his front hooves could hit the ground, his rear hooves slipped on the muddy edge of the ditch just before the fence. The beautiful beast fell, still in slow motion, with me clinging to his back.

Had I been a more frequent and experienced rider, I would have known to get myself out of the way. As it was, I landed hard on the ground, in the mud, the water of the ditch inches from my face. Stunned at the impact, it was some time before I became aware of a crushing weight. I was pinned from shin to upper thigh by the horse's bulk.

Attila struggled to get up, whinnying pathetically, panicked. I tried to pull myself out from under him, but he was simply too massive. From my avid reading of Dick Francis novels, it came to me that a horse the size of Attila might weigh more than a ton. I clenched my teeth, desperately trying to endure until help came. *If* help came . . . but I'd been the last to ride.

"Plumtree!"

"Trefoyle," I murmured with relief. He'd returned and started late in the point-to-point. Thank God . . . otherwise no one would have had reason to come back and find me. "I'm so sorry . . . your horse."

He hurried over to me. I could think only of the blessed moment when he would help pull the dying horse off my leg.

He came close, knelt, surveying the problem, and looked into my eyes. "I'm more worried about you than him, Plumtree. We must get this beast off you straightaway. Hope he hasn't done too much damage."

Briefly, Trefoyle eyed his proud horse, unable to rise to its feet and rapidly losing strength. "Don't worry. I know exactly what must be done." He stood, but to my surprise didn't try to shift the horse. Instead, he went somewhere behind me and began to tell me a story, of all things.

Doesn't he understand? I thought. *The horse . . . get the horse off me . . .*

"You know, Plumtree, this very thing happened to my older brother—though not during a point-to-point. We were out for a ride." I heard him grunt, evidently struggling with something heavy.

"Trefoyle, *please*," I gasped. Didn't he understand how excruciating, how damaging, each second of the horse's weight was on my leg? The agony was unbearable.

"It would have taken too long to ride back for help. I had to get a fallen tree to lever the horse off him."

So that's what he was doing! If he would only hurry . . .

"Sadly, he didn't make it. Most unlucky."

He didn't seem to be wrestling with the tree behind me any longer; all was quiet.

"*Please . . .*" I breathed through clenched teeth. Why wasn't he helping me? Nausea and dizziness returned with horrible intensity.

Then, with relief, I heard him directly behind me, doing something with a thick fallen tree he'd dragged over, and a small boulder. I thought I understood. He would use the rock as a fulcrum, put the tree on it, and slide one end under Attila to lever him off me.

With difficulty I craned my neck to see Trefoyle behind me, fighting not to fade away . . . not to . . .

Attila still scrabbled pitifully with his hooves at the slippery mud, now moaning in a desperate plea that was pure torture to hear. I didn't think I could endure it much longer.

I wondered if I was imagining things after that. I heard the sudden pounding of hooves close by, and an oath from Trefoyle as he struggled to get the heavy rock into position.

"My God! What's happened here?" It was Jones-Harris's voice. I heard him drop down out of his saddle and come near.

Oh no, I thought through the mists. *Anyone but Jones-Harris...*

Jones-Harris swore, sounding squeamish. "Bloody hell!! Is he dead?"

"Not yet," I said, anguished. "Help me!"

Jones-Harris came and looked at me more closely, then spoke to Trefoyle. "Here, perhaps if we have a go together..."

Trefoyle said nothing. I heard them straining, felt poor Attila fighting as if to help them. Jones-Harris might have shifted the animal entirely by himself, but all I could be sure of was that the pain in my leg grew much worse, then eased. I could no longer feel the horse moving against me, though I could still hear its pitiful noises. I felt myself drifting further away; the feeling of detachment intensified.

"Plumtree needs medical attention," Trefoyle said. "God! What a mess. Listen. You ride back and call for an ambulance. I'll stay with him." He sounded heartbroken.

"No, I—I don't feel well." Jones-Harris did indeed sound queasy. Perhaps it was the sight of blood. "I can't ride back."

"Lord," Trefoyle mumbled irritably. I heard him mount up and ride off; Jones-Harris crouched in the mud next to me. He gripped my uninjured hand with surprising kindness.

"I'm sorry, Plumtree. Just hang on. Everything's all right now. You've done well."

I wondered what he meant, but suddenly felt very tired. At some point, I heard lots of people round me, felt the sting of a jab in my arm, knew I was being moved. Then I was blissfully unaware.

CHAPTER 16

*In all of the stories of the Second Day except
the last, Fortune is an impersonal and
capricious force, against whose operations the
individual is incapable of any response other
than an attitude of stoical indifference.*

—G. H. McWilliam, Boccaccio scholar

From the second I awoke each day in the week following my equestrian escapade, I was keenly aware
of Sarah's fate, and what Graeme had said about each
passing day lessening the chances of her return. I sta-
tioned myself at the Orchard, in a constant state of readi-
ness for the phone call that would tell me she was coming
home.

The flu hit me hard; Albemarle hadn't drugged or poi-
soned me with his gin after all. Between the fever and my
somewhat battered body, I was a bit under the weather
for the first few days. Poor Attila hadn't actually broken
my leg, it turned out, but had bruised it badly. The beautiful horse himself, I learned, was put out of his misery
shortly after they'd taken me away.

Max and Lisette took care of me with great kindness.
Both of them brought food and cheer as best they could.
Max had taken the train down to Cornwall upon receiv-
ing a call from Jones-Harris on Sunday, and drove us back

in my Golf. I had yet to ask Trefoyle whether he'd taken my car on Saturday night. Max was shocked by my story of the weekend.

"You should know, Alex," he said as he pulled out of the car park of the hospital on Sunday afternoon, "that someone rang my house yesterday morning. He told me I could save Sarah's life by giving them the Bedchamber book, but if I told you, it was all off. That's why I was behaving so strangely on the phone to you."

"I know," I'd said. "Graeme explained."

The Duke of Chesterton hadn't been hit by the ricocheting bullet from his own gun after all; he'd suffered a massive stroke. He survived it, though he couldn't speak or move his right side, and was confined to bed. I was haunted by the memory of his purple face after I'd told him about the facsimiles, just before the RAF helicopters appeared. I would never know if one or the other of those two shocks had driven his blood pressure up to an unsustainable level, or if the stroke had been inevitable.

By Tuesday the flu and headache were mostly gone; by then I'd also learned to cope with nearly everything else. The only things that didn't improve were Sarah's continued absence and the utter lack of information about her. We were no further along than before the disastrous weekend at Castle Trefoyle. No one in our government knew where Sarah was now, and we had nothing more with which to negotiate.

Suffice it to say that at every moment I was aware of standing by helplessly as Sarah suffered.

Graeme rang me every day. Iraq and the Western nations were still posturing. "Surgical strikes," as the Americans like to call limited bombing raids, had shown the West's determination to take action against Iraq's intransigence. So far there had been only those few forays and no loss of life on either side. And for that, everyone was grateful.

A cavalcade of visitors came through my door in the next three days before the truly stunning event occurred. Margulies came to the house on Tuesday afternoon and thanked me for saving his life. We discussed his new book, and his plans to dedicate it to Van Vanderbilt.

Shortly after Margulies left, Trefoyle arrived unannounced and agreed to stay for tea. When we were settled in the library, he fidgeted a bit in his chair and said, "You know, Plumtree, I never meant last weekend to be such an ordeal for you. Really, it was all supposed to be good fun. I'm terribly sorry about the whole thing, especially what's happened to Sarah."

I nodded. "No one could have known."

As we were sipping our tea, Lisette arrived with dinner from the Indian takeaway. I introduced them, and Trefoyle seemed inordinately disturbed that our visit had been interrupted. But Lisette wasn't giving any ground; I think she wanted him to leave me in peace, especially after what he'd put me through. She saw him out despite my protests that he needn't go.

"Lisette, you're too much," I scolded gently when she swept back into the library, all graceful bustle and efficiency. As usual, the scent of her perfume followed her about. "You're really spoiling me, you know."

"Yes, I know," she answered, slightly out of breath from the urgency with which she'd carried out her errands. "But, to be honest, I 'ave just been laid out with the flu for three days myself." Lisette's English had never achieved native idiom. "And George spoiled me rotten. It was wonderful. And you 'ave 'elped me through more than one scrape, as I recall."

She bustled about, turning on lamps in the library as if she thought I might not do it myself. "I am sorry I cannot stay; George is taking us out to dinner tonight. We would love to 'ave you join us, Alex, but I do not think you are quite up to snuff yet."

I smiled.

"We will do it next week when you are back to yourself, yes?" As an afterthought she came close, put the palm of her hand flat against my forehead, and felt for a temperature. "Perhaps a bit below normal. You will go to bed early tonight, yes?"

Secretly, I loved it that Lisette mothered me. Not only was it comforting, but it diffused any awkwardness about spending so much time with each other. This way, she was just family.

On Wednesday I had visits from the police, and from quiet, grave men without titles who worked somewhere in Whitehall. I received more phone calls than any human being ever should. In the end I turned off the ringer and answering machine, and answered only my mobile.

Early on Wednesday evening, Jones-Harris brought a massive gift basket of assorted family-brand teas; I thanked *him* for helping to save *my* life.

"I must apologise for playing that trick on you," he said, his smile fading as he looked down at his feet. "You know, the wager à la Boccaccio. I hope you can forgive me." I noticed that everyone but me, and Ian, studiously avoided using Sarah's name. It was almost as if she were already dead. But I couldn't blame them; the outlook was, after all, quite bleak.

Still, all this wasn't Jones-Harris's fault. Trying for a light tone, I said, "If you hadn't helped get that horse off me, I'd never have forgiven you."

He laughed.

"Stay for a drink?"

"I'd love to. But you should know, Alex, I'm not the hopeless sot you think I am. Believe it or not, I had a purpose for being at that weekend. Graeme asked me to keep an eye on you."

Very much surprised, I poured each of us a double whisky and we settled in the library for a chat. I studied him across the coffee table, noticed now his quiet athleticism, the steel behind the facade. I remembered his odd comment on the point-to-point course as we waited for the ambulance—that I'd done well.

"I had no idea," I said, hearing the insulting shock in my voice but unable to prevent it.

"That's exactly what I'd hoped," he said, smiling. "You weren't supposed to know."

"If you don't mind my asking, how exactly did you come to be the guardian of justice at the Dibdin Club anniversary weekend?" I asked, intrigued.

"I couldn't bear the thought of spending my life dealing in Darjeeling."

I smiled and sipped my drink.

"Nor do I fancy playing tricks with money. Besides, if I worked, I couldn't be in the Dibdin, could I?"

We both knew there was simply no point in his working—and no need.

"If only we were all as clever as you, Plumtree"—he raised his glass to me—"we'd be working out a way to sail yachts for a living."

Sometimes I did long for my former life. But then I'd never have come back to London and re-established my friendship with Sarah. As I thought of her again, the magnitude of the disaster struck me, and I fought off another wave of despair.

"Anyway," Jones-Harris continued, "I went through the proper channels and offered myself up for service to Her Majesty's government. They thought someone with my background might prove useful in certain cases, and I've been enjoying myself ever since. From time to time, of course. As the need arises."

I tried not to let on that I found it shocking that he *chose* to involve himself in such lethal matters. We found that otherwise we had quite a lot in common, and by the time he left we were friends. "Watch your back, won't you," he called on his way out, "until this is over." He was quite serious, but I couldn't imagine who he thought might have another go at me, or why.

Max interviewed me when he brought dinner that night; I let him have the story for *The Watch*, the newspaper he'd worked for before leaving to sell books. Graeme's experts thought that if an article were published documenting the fact that the Bedchamber book had been lost out of a helicopter, it might help persuade the Iraqis that we hadn't just made up a story in order to keep the book for ourselves.

Naturally, I omitted any mention of the contents of the volume that might give offence to the Great Teacher or others of his belief or nationality, and I left the prints of the book's pages well hidden in the secret behind-the-bookshelves compartment with the Valdarfer Boccaccio. But I saw no harm in revealing the historical significance of the book regarding Richard the Lion-Heart's murder. It felt much too cruel to be the one to point out that a Chesterton was responsible for the dirty deed, however, especially with the duke lying half paralysed and speechless in the hospital. So I left the identity of the murderous knight for someone else to reveal.

Max went straight back to his house, Watersmeet, to write up the article and e-mail it to the paper for the following day's edition. Max's editor valued his freelance copy highly; few men had a brother who got into such sensational scrapes, and with such frequency.

On Thursday I decided the barrage of telephone calls must surely be over, and turned the ringer back on. The next instant, the phone rang. I groaned, but reached over and picked it up all the same.

"Is that Alex Plumtree?" The voice was gruff, with a distinct Cornish accent.

"Yes." I stifled a sigh. Now that I'd picked up, I couldn't very well hang up on the man.

"I saw the article about you in *The Watch* today. Don't usually read that rag, you know, but the wife's brother showed it to me—because of the book, you see."

"Ah." I wondered how I was going to get rid of him. Chatting to the entire nation, one by one, about the book that had shattered my future, was not my fondest desire.

"What I wanted to know is, what did the outside of this book *look* like?" my caller asked with admirable straightforwardness.

"Um,—Mr—?"

"Tregurthen. Arthur Tregurthen."

"Mr. Tregurthen. May I ask why you want to know?"

"Oh! Didn't I say? I think I've found your book! Here, on my farm. The one about the Royal Order of the Bedchamber . . . the one that was lost out of the helicopter."

I froze. "You—you *have* it?" The original? Or the facsimile?

"Found it bang in the middle of my field, wrapped up like a baby in that polythene bubble wrap. Thought it was a bit of rubbish at first—nearly tossed it in the bin. But my grandson does fancy hopping on those bubbles—they make those popping noises, you know—so I brought it home. When I untaped the mass of stuff to lay the bubbles out on the floor for little Jack, I saw there was something inside. The wife picked it up like it was gold, had a look at it, then said all quiet-like, 'Oooh, Arthur, this is no ordinary book.' And then the wife's brother saw your article in the paper. So, you see."

If it was true, there was hope after all.

"Mr. Tregurthen," I said. "You are very kind to call. The book is extremely important to me." It might buy Sarah's life back if I could work out its meaning . . . and if Mr. Arthur Tregurthen didn't decide finders were keepers. "I'd very much like to have it back, and I'm certainly prepared to pay you for—"

"Never! Won't hear of it. Shall I stick it in the post?"

I felt equal measures of relief that he should relinquish the book so willingly, and dread that it should ever be "stuck in the post."

"Er, *no*, thank you—I'll see if my brother can come down and fetch it. Can you tell me where you are, please, Mr. Tregurthen?"

And so it was that the next evening Max arrived at the Orchard, book in hand, fresh from exercising his BMW in the fields of Devon. He returned *without* the giant roll of bubble wrap I'd instructed him to deliver with thanks to one Master Jack Tregurthen age four, of Moor Farm.

"It's a wonder it didn't land in a pond somewhere, or wasn't chewed up by a cow," Max said, unwrapping the book before an audience of eight. I'd rung Graeme—and his team of four experts—Diana, and Ian after Mr. Tregurthen had delivered his bombshell, and told them to keep it under their hats. They'd come directly to the Orchard to be present for the unveiling.

Max handed the now-familiar book to me as the others looked on; I suppose he felt I'd suffered most for it. I looked at the blank cover and passed it to Diana. Ian stood silently at my side. The look on his face since he'd learned about Sarah was painful to see.

"What I want to know," Diana said, "is if anything's been inserted behind the velvet of the back cover. I remember Boswell feeling for something, as if he were expecting it. We never had the chance to investigate." Gingerly, she lifted the rear cover and ran a finger over its inside surface. Her eyes flicked to mine. "There might be something in here. I could go back to the office for my tools . . . or I could improvise."

"Please," I said urgently. "Improvise. I trust you."

She nodded. "I'll need to steam this off; if someone would please put the kettle on . . . and a clean surface in the kitchen would probably do best."

We all proceeded to the kitchen, our steps quicker, our

anticipation palpable. Max put the kettle on; I meticulously cleaned and dried the worktop near it. Ian spread a fresh tablecloth over the surface, and Diana placed the book in the middle of it. The whole process had acquired the solemnity of a church service, with the book on its worktop altar.

When the kettle clicked off, Diana carefully aimed the steam at the edges of the bit of velvet that covered the inside of the rear cover, as if wafting incense from a censer. Gently, she worked the velvet loose from the board with a clean butter knife. There was a collective gasp when she pulled a small folded bit of dried paper from beneath it.

She handed it to me. With nervous fingers I opened out the square of brittle papyrus; I'd read about bits of ancient papyrus literally crumbling in the hands of those who had discovered them. Clearly, this scrap was even older than the incunable before me. What I saw handwritten on the papyrus made no sense to me at first.

Jeo Richard cuer-de-lion, a Saladin, sultan de Babylone, vus dun, en cest jur li 15 novembre, en l'an 1186, la ville de Londres, en change de quoi recevrai la ville de Jerusalem et le saint sepulcre.

The others read over my shoulder. There was silence as we tried to take it in. Some of the words seemed more English than French, but then, Richard had been an Anglo-Norman king. Translated, it said: *I, Richard the Lion-heart, give to you, Saladin, sultan of Babylon, on this fifteenth day of November, 1186, the city of London in exchange for the city of Jerusalem and the Holy Sepulchre.*

"You don't suppose it could be genuine . . . ?" Max finally ventured into the silence.

Ian left the room abruptly. Worried, I handed the paper to Max and told them I'd be right back. I limped after

Ian to the library and watched as he drew a book from the reference shelf.

"What is it?" I asked him.

As he opened my *Oxford Illustrated History of the British Monarchy*, he said, "Something I read about Richard the Lion-Heart and Saladin . . ." After briefly studying the index, he flipped through the pages until he found the short biography of Richard I. His finger flew down the page, then came to a stop. "Yes! I was right. It doesn't prove anything, but do you see? It says here that Richard was French at heart, and claimed he'd have willingly sold London to finance his Crusade to the Holy Land if he could have found a buyer."

"But, Ian, even if the papyrus is authentic, why would Iraq be so horrified at the possibility of its discovery? Why come to blows over *this*? Surely after all this time, such an agreement is meaningless." I was aghast at the outrageousness of the pact. "No one is ever going to surrender Jerusalem. And we'll never hand over the Square Mile."

Ian frowned and gazed out through the French doors. "Perhaps it's become the stuff of legend; as the Christians and the Moslems fought, the rumour of the pact's existence changed—as in a child's game of telephone. Each side decided the message was a blasphemous curse against them, or some damaging secret about their leader. Let me see," he said, turning again to the index of the history book.

"Second Crusade . . . ah, here we are." He found the page noted, scanned it quickly, then paraphrased for me. "Richard and Saladin respected each other highly, and even became friends—you already know that from the incunable. They reached a truce, but Richard became impatient waiting for Saladin to deliver his part of the bargain. There was a delay in releasing the Christian prisoners, handing over the 'true cross of Christ,' and paying a sum of money. Richard slaughtered all the Saracen pris-

oners held by the Christians on the plain, in full view of
the city, and attacked. Saladin, wounded by this treachery,
fought back. Richard lost Jerusalem in 1187, the greatest
failure of his life."

"So you're saying they might have drawn up the agreement during the period of the truce."

"Exactly."

"And when things went wrong, they each spread rumours of the other leader and his treachery."

"It's possible. I wonder who spirited away the scrap of
paper."

"Presumably someone in the Royal Order of the
Bedchamber . . ."

Ian and I stared at each other. Why did I have the feeling he already knew what I was about to tell him?

"Ian, I learned something at Castle Trefoyle—Trefoyle
himself told me. My ancestors fought in the Crusades,
were given lands and titles by Richard I. One of them
even served in the Royal Order. I can't get it out of my
head that a Plumtree might have told the story to Boccaccio, who wrote it down in the fourteenth century. What if
this scrap were handed down through my family until the
Plumtrees began to print? Otherwise, why did Max and I
find this book in our library? And otherwise, why did my
father give you the Boccaccio with the scrap of paper in
the back to keep for us?"

Ian nodded. "You could well be right. I don't know the
history of the books, but I do know that your father felt
the weight of responsibility for these historical artifacts
very keenly. Most people would give their right arm for a
title, but your father felt differently. He was very much
ashamed of the fact that your ancestors had gained lands
by killing people in the name of faith. He understood that
sensibilities were different then; but he was appalled by
the bloodshed in a so-called 'holy' war—the mere occu-
pation of land in the Middle East. I think he hoped you
would never know about your Crusading ancestors."

"Let's tell the others," I said. As we stepped back into the kitchen, Diana was speaking to Graeme and his experts.

"Yes," she said, cheeks glowing with excitement—or perhaps from the steam of the teakettle. "The papyrus they would have had in the Middle East, the Anglo-Norman dialect—and you say this is Saladin's signature at the bottom?" One of the men nodded. "From all appearances, I think it really *could* be authentic."

We left Graeme in the library, alone with his experts, to ring Cholmondeley to see if it made sense to him from the historical point of view. Then he said he'd ring the Iraqi negotiator in London and invite him over to see it straightaway.

As I closed the door and left the library, Graeme said, "Alex."

I stuck my head back in.

"Let's hope this works."

I knew what he meant. All I could do was wait and see.

When Graeme emerged, he told us there was much hushed excitement over the mediaeval bargain between Richard and Saladin. Everyone agreed that it was a desperate secret, and that neither party should breathe a word.

The flurry of faxes and e-mails and emergency telephone conferences culminated in a parade of cars travelling secretly to the Orchard at five o'clock that afternoon. The first car held the highest-ranking Iraqi negotiator here in Britain and his bodyguards; the second held the negotiator's experts.

Graeme and I welcomed them all to the Orchard, where Diana, Max, and Ian waited in the library. Graham introduced me to the head negotiator for Iraq, who, to my vast surprise, was about my own age and looked familiar. He was dressed much as I was, in suit and tie, and spoke with an English accent.

His eyes twinkled as the prime minister introduced us. "It is a pleasure. Mr. Plumtree. I believe we've met before . . . weren't you at Magdalene ten years or so ago?" Then he grinned and clapped me on the back.

I laughed and stuck out my hand for a hearty shake, barely able to believe that this was Mohammed Hussein from my college at Cambridge. I'd studied there for only two years, earning a master's degree. With a start, I remembered his speciality had been Boccaccio.

"What a very small world it is, Mo."

But as I looked into his dark eyes, I saw the same sort of dread I'd heard in the prime minister's voice when he'd told me Sarah was missing. Pleasant memories of shared evenings at the pub were instantly dismissed; our smiles faded wistfully as we got to the business at hand. I knew he would need to see the book and the papyrus before I could have a word with him in private. Both entourages followed me sombrely as I invited them into the library. I had placed a cloth over my desk, which still held my wedding invitation clutter.

Mo, Graeme, and the others followed me to my mother's desk, where I'd spread the book and the papyrus scrap on a cloth. Mo's experts clustered around it like bees around a honey pot poring over each page silently to the end. One of them, on the final page with the bed curtain engraving, pointed eagerly at the jumble of small patterns I'd noticed upon first opening the book. Nearly letters, or numbers, but not quite. They conversed briefly in hushed but excited tones in Arabic, then moved on to the papyrus scrap. One of them spoke, translating the text from French into Arabic, I thought. The men nodded earnestly. The PM's experts studied the paper side by side with the Iraqi contingent, then turned to Graeme for a hushed conference, pointing to something on the papyrus. More emphatic nods.

Mo spoke first. His voice was unemotional, civil. "My experts believe this paper to be authentic. Naturally, we would like to take it with the book to show to the Great Teacher and others."

Graeme looked at me; I nodded. Of course I would let them take the papyrus. I needed them to bend where Sarah was concerned.

But I knew full well that once they had the book and the papyrus, people less calm and restrained might destroy them. Then they could forever claim the historical document had been a blasphemous piece of treachery, which we had used to escalate hostilities.

"May I take some photographs first?"

Mo acquiesced with a nod.

I went to the cupboard where I kept my own camera, and handed it to Diana. I looked at Graeme and then glanced at his bodyguards while she clicked, flashed, and whirred. "These photos and negatives should be kept very safe," I said.

Graeme nodded; he took my meaning. When Diana had finished, I removed the film from the camera and passed it to the bodyguards.

I folded an old soft cloth carefully round the papyrus and placed it in yet another box lined with bubble wrap. Then I picked up another box from the shelf and handed both boxes to Mo. "The papyrus, and the Bedchamber book."

Mo inclined his head in her direction, then turned to me. "I am grateful, Alex. You have acted honourably."

I spoke to Graeme. "Would it be all right if Mo and I spoke for a moment in private?"

"Of course," he replied.

"There's tea in the dining room, if you'd care to help yourself." I'd prepared a large pot of tea and laid out some biscuits.

Mo issued a command to his men, and Graeme and Diana led them out of the room. As soon as Mo and I were alone, I said, "I need your help." I heard my

own voice as if it were a stranger's; I sounded astound-
ingly calm.

"I know. I only wish I could give it to you, Alex. Unfortunately, you know there are people in my part of the
world—as in yours—who are impatient. They act apart
from our official government. We cannot control those
who have been pushed too far—at least that is how they
see themselves. You cannot imagine this, but they believe
the West has committed unspeakable crimes against them
and their women. They will not wait for justice through
conventional channels."

My heart sank, though what he said didn't come as a
surprise. I'd known; but I'd still hoped.

"I can tell you one thing, Alex," Mo said. "Sarah
Townsend is alive. Please believe that I am doing my best
for you under the circumstances. It is . . . difficult."

"You're certain? That she's alive?" My eyes filled unexpectedly, overflowed.

Mo looked at the floor and nodded. "I don't know how
long I can guarantee it. I sent someone out to work with
the group that is holding her, to see if he could help keep
her safe. But it is difficult . . . and naturally, he cannot
communicate with me. I don't know if he's been able to
manage it. Please; do not mention this to anyone."

I nodded acknowledgement. I couldn't bring myself to
thank him.

"I'm sorry, Alex. Please tell no one what I have told
you, or my position is compromised. Thank you for letting us take your book and the papyrus."

We were finished. As I ushered Mo to the dining room,
I asked why his people felt the message was so important.
Was it what they'd expected?

"No. We thought it would be something quite different; I'm afraid I cannot tell you exactly what. There will
be those who will not believe me; they will not believe
that this settles the issue, even when they hold it in their

own hands." He shrugged. "I will do my best." After another handshake, he and his men departed. Diana left with them, promising to ring me later.

Graeme and the others stayed. "Our experts feel the paper is authentic," he said. "I think you did the right thing, Alex."

After they'd all gone, there was a quiet knock on the door. It was Diana. She handed me a gold box tied with a white ribbon, then gave me a quick hug. "I almost forgot, with all the excitement. It's still a wedding present, but you can open it now if you like."

Touched that she would convey her confidence in Sarah's return with such a thoughtful act, I slid the ribbon off and lifted the lid.

It was a replacement facsimile of the Bedchamber book. If the Iraqis knew we had another one . . .

"Shhhhhhh," Diana whispered, putting her finger to her lips with a smile, and trotted away to her car.

Fearful and profoundly grateful at the same time, I went directly to the bookshelves and slid it into the compartment, whence all our troubles had come.

CHAPTER 17

*And besides, by holding his tongue his honour
remained unimpaired, whereas if he were to talk
he would make himself look ridiculous.*

—GIOVANNI BOCCACCIO, *DECAMERON*,
THIRD DAY: SECOND STORY

I'd have forgotten all about the Friday meeting of the
Committee for the Preservation of English Artifacts if
Sir Harold Westering hadn't rung that morning.

"*Plahmtreh*," his sonorous voice boomed down the
line. "So sorry, I'm afraid I forgot to tell you where we're
meeting today. We'll be at Boodles, my club. In St. James's
Street. Half past twelve for drinks, lunch, and meeting after. Cheerio, then!" And in the breezy manner of aristo-
crats, he hung up before I'd said another word.

I put the phone back in its cradle and looked at my
vacant desktop. It was my first day back at the Press;
everyone had been painfully solicitous. Lisette had made
sure I wasn't overwhelmed by the pile of work waiting for
me, but this abnormally blank slate was worse. I couldn't
wait for people to start being irreverent again.

And I wanted my messy desk back.

Secretly, I was grateful for Westering's call about the
meeting. It would keep people from thinking they had to

invite me to lunch. Lisette had been tying herself in knots trying to make sure I didn't spend too much time alone ever since I'd returned from the castle. This normal activity would relieve her no end.

As noon approached, I decided to take a taxi to Boodles. I'd never been to that particular club before, and didn't want to waste time on parking. At the door of the august establishment, I gave my name and that of the committee to a snooty hall porter, who ticked my name off on a list and grudgingly allowed me to enter. As I passed, he eyed me coldly and told me the meeting was in a private room down the corridor, through the double doors, and to the left, the fourth door. His tone made it sound more like a warning than a set of directions.

Westering was already there, puffing on his cigar, along with Albemarle, Margulies, and "young" Ashleigh. The other dozen men in the room looked up when I entered; I didn't know them, but recognised some from photos in the papers. I'd thought I was a bit out of place in the Dibdin, but at least I was from the same world as those men. Here I was in an entirely different galaxy, as I learned shortly after Westering came to greet me.

"So glad you could join us, Plumtree. Delighted to have you. Let me introduce you to the others . . ."

The names of my fellow committee members were nearly all known to me as the nation's benefactors; theirs were the names memorialised in streets, museums, collections, and buildings all over London. Here again, I thought, I was one of the few untitled—but then I remembered. I did have a title, if I chose to use it. But what exactly was it?

At lunch I nearly felt I was back with the Dibdin Club; the club waiters plied us with multiple courses of vast amounts of seafood, shellfish, and meat, accompanied by endless wine. After Chesterton's sudden stroke, the main topic of discussion was auctions. At first I thought the members were talking about national treasures they'd collected for their own personal pleasure; then I realised the committee's mission was to purchase everything they could at a given auction, within the price range allocated by the committee, and turn it all over to an English museum. It was a moneyed force of secret agents, with assignments to buy, buy, buy British. I enjoyed the sense of intrigue associated with it; the members approached their duties with a sense of mission, and organised themselves to attend every significant sale.

Even with this background it came as a surprise to me when Sir Harold announced that I was first on the meeting's agenda. I glanced at my watch and thought of my faithful employees at the Press as the pudding was cleared away and coffee brought. It was nearly three o'clock; clearly, most of my fellow committee members did not work for a living.

"You've all met Alex Plumtree by now. Alex, we owe you an apology. I do hope you'll be able to forgive us."

I shifted in my chair and did my best to maintain a pleasant visage. *Not again!* I thought.

"Word got out at the end of last week that some wealthy foreign buyers were after your Bedchamber incunable. Well, of course it was irresistible to us, considering the book's historical significance. Then there were all sorts of wild rumours flying around that people had attempted to steal it, which wasn't surprising, considering its value. But we weren't about to lose this one. We didn't want to actually *buy* it—it's yours, of course. And at that point none of us knew you—you wouldn't have understood if we'd tried to purchase it. So we decided to take extraordinary measures to ensure that it stayed in this country for the duration, and to ensure that you didn't lose it."

"You *stole* it," I finished for him. Sir Harold flushed a deep crimson and looked chastened. It had been the only remaining part of the puzzle, aside from who fired the shot at me and Attila. It was almost a relief. And, although I did feel a flash of anger, I sensed that it wasn't at all appropriate to leave the table and ring the police immediately.

"You stole it for my own good?!" I added, and smiled. "You're a band of *cultural* terrorists." To my alarm, I began to laugh—at first merely a chuckle, but then uncontrollably. Soon I was hiding behind my napkin, laughing so hard, I was crying.

The aristocratic guerrillas round the table regarded me with distinct malaise. The silence was absolute. I recovered enough, with an effort, to ask a question. "How on earth did you know"—I stifled a residual laugh and tried to pretend it was a cough—"it was in my filing cabinet?!"

Westering looked down the table at a man about my own age who'd been introduced as St. John. His face reddening, he waggled a finger at me. "I can answer that one for you. Your brother is a friend of mine. I rang Max when I heard about the book, and he said he'd just spoken to you. He was worried about the book's safety, not to mention yours. He said you had it at the back of the filing cabinet in your office, could I believe it, and it was a wonder someone didn't steal it."

I stared at him in disbelief. St. John, of all people, who I'd just read in the *Times* had donated a handwritten Elgar score to the British Museum. Now I wondered if he'd stolen that too.

"Then it was Lord Peter's turn," Sir Harold interjected quietly.

I whipped my head round at this new surprise. "Lord *Peter*?"

Albemarle lowered his head as if to compensate for the weight of guilt. "I take full blame, credit, whatever you care to assign, Plumtree. As you may know, Ian Higginbotham is an acquaintance of mine. I rang him and asked if he could recommend a firm for printer repairs for my London office. From there it was easy. I just didn't feel you had enough experience handling a book of that magnitude, and through no fault of your own, you might find it had been taken from you. By the—er—*wrong* people. It's happened before now."

Bitter murmurs of "too true," "we've seen it before," "remember the Farnsworth etchings" wafted round the table.

"Hang on," I exclaimed. "This is really extraordinary. Aside from the fact that you are unafraid of prosecution in the criminal courts, you really feel you did me a *service* by stealing my book."

Continued discomfort round the table.

Dear God, I thought. They would never know what they had nearly cost me—if I hadn't recovered it by stealing myself—from Margulies's deserted room. Into the silence I asked Sir Harold, "Did *you* hide the book under Margulies's mattress?"

"Yes, Margulies was to have taken it with him, to return to you when the fuss died down. He has a safe in his flat."

I thought about my author's burgled flat; had word got out that Margulies would be keeping my book there?

"But, of course, he disappeared unexpectedly," Sir Harold went on. "He was to have returned for the anniversary dinner on Saturday night. We couldn't take the chance that he'd come back for the book and not find it there as arranged, so we left it. We would have taken it with us, on Sunday to lock it up in a safe deposit box. But then, of course, it was gone."

"I still don't understand. Why did you take it on the weekend at all?"

Sir Harold ran a finger around the inside of his collar as if it had suddenly grown too tight. "I know that must seem outrageous to you, since, I must admit, it was stolen in the end anyway. But, Plumtree, let me assure you, we will make good on—"

Again I laughed openly. I remembered Sir Harold's

surprised look at the luncheon on the castle lawn when I expressed interest in the committee; he'd been thinking of the book they'd stolen from me. The stunned silence round the table was audible; no doubt they thought I'd lost my marbles.

"Don't worry," I said. "*I* was the one who found it under Margulies's mattress and took it back, though I'm sorry to say it was stolen again shortly thereafter. Just as you'd feared. So we're back where we started."

They would never understand; I could never tell them. Best left this way.

When Sir Harold saw that I wasn't angry—rather, the opposite—he smiled. A chain reaction began around the table. The sixteen men first dared to smile, then couldn't contain what I assumed was relief. We were undoubtedly the only case of mass hilarity at Boodles that day; I wondered if the Queen could hear us at Buckingham Palace down the road.

At the end of it all, it was four o'clock. After a quick call to the Press, I raced to the BBC studios in White City for an appearance on *Talkabout*, the nation's most popular chat show. The programme was scheduled to be taped at five that afternoon for broadcasting later that evening. Max agreed to come on the programme with me, which helped somewhat, except that he was angry I didn't arrive in the studio until exactly when they'd asked us to, at half past four.

"Where have you *been*?" he demanded, standing from the waiting area bench. "What have you been doing?"

I didn't have the energy to explain it all to him. "I'm sorry, Max. I should've tried to call you."

As makeup artists dusted soot from our faces and covered them with powder, I thought back to the day before. Graeme's people had arranged our appearance on *Talkabout*, and the PM rang me personally to ask me if I would be a guest on the programme. I'd expressed surprise; I was hesitant to do anything that might offend the Iraqis, although we'd done all we could to cooperate with them. But Graeme told me his spin control specialists were firm on this: If we sent the Iraqis a message showing we were prepared to keep sensitive matters permanently secret, they might relent as far as Sarah was concerned. I couldn't help but note that none of us had any idea yet what those sensitive matters might be; it was as if we were blind but had to reassure them continually that we couldn't see— all the while apologising for our handicap.

They had to acknowledge we'd given them everything they'd asked for; after all, they now had the book and the papyrus, for whatever they were worth. And they had Sarah.

The Great Teacher had agreed, after hearing that the book was his at last, that he would do what he could to free Sarah. He would do this as long as he was convinced the *secret* contents of the book remained unknown. And, he pointed out, that was only if the fanatical group still had her. Uncertainty layered on uncertainty like a lop-sided wedding cake.

In my opinion, Sarah had become a pawn in a pointless chess match between the American President and the Great Teacher. It all looked like posturing; no one wanted to actually fight. So they used Sarah instead. As the days went by, the American government made more and more of her hostage status, flashing her dazzling photograph on news screens with increasing frequency. She'd become the symbol of Iraqi treachery, the missing daughter of the Western world. I didn't know if it would ultimately help or hurt her.

The plan, according to Graeme's experts, was to establish the *sole* newsworthy characteristic of the book as that of Richard the Lion-Heart's murder. The pact between Saladin and Richard would thus remain secret forever.

Mimi Reed, the BBC's bright and still-rising star of

prime-time news programmes, shot me a sympathetic smile as we prepared to go on camera on the set. But I could see right through it—all the way through, in fact, to several months before. On that occasion she'd hauled me over the coals in front of the entire nation for something I hadn't done. Understanding Mimi was simple: She would do anything to rise to the top.

"Welcome, Alex and Max Plumtree. Many of us are already acquainted with Alex, publisher of Plumtree Press, and Max, proprietor of his own antiquarian bookselling business. The two brothers were fortunate enough to find a book in their library, hidden behind larger volumes apparently for centuries, that changed history before tragically becoming lost once more. But first—Alex, you're limping. What's happened to you?"

I smiled. "Rather embarrassing, I'm afraid. A riding accident. I wish I could claim something profound—like the bookshelf toppling over on me, finally released from the weight of the secret behind Richard the Lion-Heart's death."

"And a great secret it was," Mimi said earnestly, her eyes opening wider. She turned away from us and shifted towards the camera. On the monitor I could see that the cameraman had focussed on her perfect nose and brilliant white teeth.

"Let me try to summarise this remarkable story for our viewers. An untitled book was found by the Plumtrees in their family library. It describes what life was like for those who protected the monarch, the Knights of the Royal Order of the Bedchamber. And it actually reveals for the first time that King Richard I was murdered by one of his protectors, a member of the Royal Order. The book shows a knight of the Order, Alex and Max tell me, kneeling by the king's bed, holding a dagger.

"The history books," Mimi went on earnestly, "have been proved wrong. For centuries they have told us that the Lion-Heart died from a wound sustained from a common poacher, during a struggle with a peasant over some old coins."

As she spoke, I reflected upon the PM's cleverness. What Mimi said, of course, was absolutely true. No one had any reason to suspect further intrigue behind the rare book.

Mimi shifted in her chair; a different camera came in and caught her from the new angle. She lifted one eyebrow provocatively. "Alex, what do you think of all this? It isn't every day that a book has the ability to change history."

"No, quite right. But the longer I publish books, the more I become aware of the awesome power of the printed word. A book is a living record of human experience, and once it exists, it forever affects real people with real feelings. We think we control books; we believe we can summon their magic at will, then put them back on the shelf. But a book will continue to affect people's lives as long as it exists. That's why this one, the only one of its kind before it, too, disappeared, was so carefully hidden away."

Mimi nodded and turned to Max. "What does it feel like to discover a book that has changed history?"

"Quite remarkable," Max answered. "A bit sad, of course, now, to have lost it—I am sorry about that. But a great privilege nonetheless. This particular book was meaningful because of when it was printed, not just by virtue of its contents. Any book printed before the year 1500 is considered an early example of printing, or an incunable—from the Latin for the 'cradle' period of printing."

"Can you tell us a bit more about the book, please?" she asked me.

"Yes, of course. It was really quite beautiful; the oak covers were covered in red velvet, and there were five really spectacular detailed woodcut illustrations of the king's bedchamber, the emblem of the Order—things like that. The text was written by the fourteenth-century writer Giovanni Boccaccio, judging from certain similarities to his style in the *Decameron*, and printed much later by someone else. This is in accord with the legend passed down about the book, preserved in a nineteenth-century list of books rumoured to exist."

I didn't tell them it had been printed and perhaps bound by a Plumtree; I wasn't about to get in deeper still.

"Would you like to hear the contents?" I asked. "We've reconstructed them for you."

Mimi said yes she certainly would, not a surprise, since she'd specifically requested this just before the cameras rolled. Max read the story from the cheat sheet we'd created, as a precaution leaving out the bit about Richard and Saladin's friendship.

"Absolutely fascinating," Mimi said, then managed to change expression in the blink of an eye. I'd known this was coming, had been dreading it. She turned doe eyes on me, and managed to look profoundly sympathetic. I sat up straighter and squared my shoulders. The subject she was about to broach was the *real* reason she'd wanted me on the program, not to talk about my book.

"Alex, we were all sorry to learn that your fiancée, Sarah Townsend, an American, disappeared this last weekend. She was staying at your home in Chorleywood, visiting before your wedding in August. We know from the news that the Americans think she was taken hostage by the Iraqis. Has there been any news of your fiancée at all?" She shook her head, as if to indicate it was just too tragic for words.

I hated her for it.

When I didn't speak, Max glanced at me and answered himself, brusquely. "No. Not yet, but Sarah's a strong and resourceful woman. We hope for the best." The dismissive finality of his last words warned her not to push further.

"We're all hoping for her safe return. Alex, Max, thanks for being with us tonight."

You could have cut the silence in the studio with a knife after she signed off; I knew the driving beat of the programme's theme music was thumping through sitting rooms all across Britain, but we couldn't hear it in the studio. Mimi rose smoothly on her high heels, unabashed in spite of the fact that she had just used my personal tragedy for her own gain and the entertainment of others.

"Best of luck," she said, reaching out for my hand. She ushered us to the door, flashing us one last sad smile. "Thanks again."

We obediently set off through the door, flung out of her busy orbit like so much cosmic debris. Before the soundproof door could seal completely behind us, I heard her voice drifting out from the backstage area. She wasn't speaking loudly, but it was loud enough.

"God, that's pitiful," she sighed. "He'll never see that poor woman again . . . Stephen, let's tape that promo for tomorrow. I've got to get away early."

The soundproof door snicked shut behind us, two seconds too late. Max let a burst of air out through his teeth as he stopped and gripped my good arm. "All right?" His eyes betrayed his anger at Mimi, his sorrow for the brother for whom he used to feel only jealousy and resentment. Now he knew *he* was the lucky one.

Before I could come up with some way of reassuring Max that I wasn't going to crumple at his feet, my mobile rang.

"Let's get out of here," I told him. We moved away from Mimi's door as I pulled the phone from my pocket. Max wiped his eyes surreptitiously as I pushed the on button and said, "Yes."

"Alex—Graeme here."

I froze.

"Thanks for doing the programme," he said. "I'm sure

it wasn't easy. I've just been in touch with Mo and told him the programme is about to be aired. But I'm sorry, Alex, I—I have bad news."

I closed my eyes and waited. I could feel Max watching me intently.

"There was a raid on the splinter group that held Sarah—we think perhaps it was an American attempt at a rescue. Intelligence reports say three of the dozen or so members were killed. But as a result, the radical faction has moved, Mo says, and his people have lost her again. The only good news is that we can be quite sure she was still alive—er, quite recently."

I was silent, unable to form a response.

"Alex? Are you there?"

"Yes."

He sighed in frustration. "I'll let you know the moment I hear anything."

"Thanks . . ."

I was dimly aware of Max taking the phone from my hand as I told him what Graeme had said. I remember my brother accompanying me down the hallway and putting me in the car. The next thing I knew I was at home, and Max was clattering in the kitchen. I retreated, relieved to my refuge in the library. But when I stepped gratefully through the door, I was greeted by the sight of my desk, which I knew was littered with ivory wedding invitation envelopes under the cloth. Now the cloth looked like a pall to me, all too symbolic of what had become of Sarah's and my plan for a life together. Struck full in the face with the wreckage of it all, I turned away.

CHAPTER 18

Each had his past shut in him like the leaves of a book known to him by heart; and his friends could only read the title.

—VIRGINIA WOOLF, JACOB'S ROOM

I stood for a time, looking out through the garden doors. I thought of how bravely Sarah would be enduring her ordeal . . . if she were in fact still alive. I'd made an effort *not* to think of the specific circumstances of her captivity, to imagine what she might have faced. I thought merely of her sparkling eyes, her fearless spirit, and her strength . . . and began to hope again.

Perhaps there *was* something I could do. Perhaps there *was* another secret to the Bedchamber book, and if I could find it . . . well, would it do any good? I'd already given them the book and the priceless papyrus, and they hadn't returned Sarah. Still, I was in no position to stop trying.

I went to the bookshelves, lifted out the books concealing the compartment, and drew out the new facsimile of the Bedchamber book Diana had made. The Valdarfer Boccaccio looked a bit forlorn on its own; I remembered what Ian said my father had told him, that the two books belonged together, or were a pair—something like that. On a whim I pulled out the Boccaccio too, replaced the other books on the shelf, and took my treasures to the coffee table.

I'd only just sat down when my brother entered, bearing a fully stocked tray. "Dinner is served."

"Thanks, Max." I stood and slid the books onto a corner of my desk as he put the tray down on the coffee table. I didn't fancy spilling Jones-Harris's tea all over our priceless Boccaccio. "Mind if we watch the news while we eat?"

"Now *there's* a recipe for indigestion," he muttered, but switched on the set.

As I ate the ham and eggs with toast he'd prepared—breakfast food has no equal in a crisis—we learned that nothing had changed in the Middle East. Things were in a holding pattern, with limited acts of hostility and provocation on both sides, and the omnipresent photo of Sarah. No effigies of the American President burned in Baghdad tonight, at least, and the Great Teacher had made no more furious speeches. It seemed to me that everything had come down to "wait and see."

It was pure torture.

When we'd finished food and news, Max nobly carried our plates out. "How about a glass of port?" he suggested. "It might help you sleep."

"Good idea," I agreed. "Thanks." I checked the coffee table for grease and crumbs and had a quick swipe at it with my napkin, then picked up the books again from the edge of my desk. With a pang of despair I removed the cloth from over the wedding invitations and threw it on top of the coffee table just in case. Then I set the books down on it and sank back onto the sofa. Max glanced over as he poured from a decanter on the drinks trolley.

"All right?" he asked.

"Mmm. I can't stop wondering what bothers them so much about this book." I turned to the first page and stared at it, head in my hands.

Max set down the port at a safe distance from the book and seated himself at the other end of the sofa. "Would you mind," he said, "if I had a look at the Valdarfer Boccaccio?"

"Good heavens, no—it's as much yours as it is mine, remember."

We sat thumbing through our books side by side, like the near-identical brothers we'd become. I felt the comfort of it and stole a glance at him as he turned the pages. Max always liked to look at the front of the book first, the end next, and finally—if at all—the middle. He frequently hummed a bit as he did it—at the moment it was U2's "Pride In the Name of Love." Now he turned the front cover facedown and opened the rear board, exposing the irregular latticelike paper stuck loosely inside.

"You know, this really bothers me," I said.

He looked over at me, surprised. "I'm sorry, I'll stop."

"No, not the humming. This." I lifted the paper out of the book. "It must have some *purpose* . . . I mean, who would cut an intricate pattern like that into a perfectly good piece of paper for no reason? And then put it in the Boccaccio, and leave it there for five hundred years?" Max studied it thoughtfully as I shook my head and returned to the Bedchamber book, which I turned to the bed-curtain page with its kneeling knight.

Looking down at that familiar design, I had the sensation you sometimes get when you've been looking at a shape—a tree, a tall building—outlined against the sun. When you look away, you still see the shape of the object, as if it's been burned into your eye's memory. I looked back at the paper in Max's hand, and saw, unmistakably, the curves of the bed curtain.

"Max. Hang on a minute." I moved the smaller book closer to the big Boccaccio and slid the cut-out paper over the Bedchamber facsimile.

"My God," Max murmured. "I don't believe it."

We stared in silence at the answer to the puzzle. The

story of the long-ago treachery of Chesterton's ancestor hadn't been the significant secret of this book, nor had the papyrus inside the back cover. It was the message within the bed curtain.

The tiny shapes and forms that I had several times thought were letters *were* in fact letters—but in distorted form. The pattern of the screen eliminated the superfluous parts of the design, concocted to obscure the message, and left only the clearly legible letters.

In Latin, it read, as best I could translate it aloud for Max:

"May a great secret be revealed to those who read this, that Richard the Lion-Heart and Saladin's wife lay together on the night of the great truce. On that same night, Saladin lay with Richard's wife, Berengaria of Navarre. Saladin's wife bore Richard a son, and the great line of Saladin so came to carry Christian blood. Richard's wife also bore Saladin a son, and the child was safely hidden away in secret lest Richard's evil brother John do away with him. Eleanor of Aquitaine cared for the child and saw that he was brought up as a nobleman and provided with land and title in the distant West of the kingdom when he reached adulthood. At the time of the printing of this book, 1471, this secret has been faithfully kept and this branch of Richard's line lives on in a family by the name Eleanor of Aquitaine devised for it: Trefoyle."

The globes, the maps, the connections in trade with the Middle East—Trefoyle was living out his legacy as the child of both Middle Eastern and Anglo-Norman empires. The last, and childless, child.

Max and I looked at each other, then back at the stunning message that ran in curved lines over the folds of bed curtains on the page.

"I wonder if Trefoyle knows . . . he *must*."

A voice boomed from behind us, "Indeed I do."

Max and I jumped to our feet and whirled to see Earl Trefoyle standing in the doorway.

"Trefoyle! I didn't know you were coming. You gave me a fright."

"Sorry, Plumtree. I don't often pay visits to other people's homes; you must excuse me. My social graces tend to be a bit rusty in some respects."

"Please, come in. Sit down."

"Thank you, Plumtree, but I won't be staying long. I just wanted to thank you for working out the secret of that book for me. I knew you would eventually." He closed the library door behind himself, and I began to get an odd feeling. His presence was . . . less than friendly.

"How did you get *in*?" Max asked, a bit put out at being taken by surprise. My older brother, known in the past for his violent temper, held his arms away from his body, tensed and ready to fight.

Trefoyle chuckled. "It was surprisingly easy; you hadn't even locked the front door. Even in Chorleywood, times have changed. Oh, don't worry—I've locked it now. Really, Alex, you're much too trusting. And I see this is your ne'er-do-well brother." He eyed Max up and down. "Such a disappointment to your father."

"If only my father could see the shape of things now," I said. "He believed you were a friend."

Trefoyle said nothing, but reached casually into his lightweight linen jacket with fawn-coloured-gloved hands and pulled out a pistol.

Stupid, I thought. Stupid of me not to work this out . . . everything now made sense. The rifle on the point-to-point, and Trefoyle's prompt arrival at the scene of Attila's disaster. He'd been watching, I felt sure, if not actually behind the gun. I recalled his disappointment at having to be the one to ride for help. With a ripple of horror, I realised he would have killed me with the rock while Jones-

Harris was away. Jones-Harris had feigned nausea at the sight of the accident and said he couldn't ride. *Had Jones-Harris suspected?* He *had* told me to watch my back when he'd visited the other day. . . .

"Isn't it remarkable to think, Alex, that when I nearly had you on Sunday, you didn't even know this?" Trefoyle smiled smugly. "I couldn't be sure of that, of course, which was why I had to get rid of you. But you would have died for nothing. Now at least you'll die for good reason."

"But *why*, Trefoyle? Why do you and the Iraqis care so much about this—this triviality of ancient history?"

His eyes grew cold. "It is not a *'triviality!'* I've worked all my life to earn this position of trust in the international community. You've no idea what it's like to be accepted in Iraq by people who will speak to no other Westerner. I know their language, understand their culture, their religion. The prime minister values my contributions enormously. Think what I've done for him! Do you think I would let you destroy all that I've lived and worked for? If my Iraqi friends learn that I'm part of the sultan's line, I don't even like to think what would become of me. My former closeness with them would be seen as an act of treachery, of manipulation. Britain has prevented worse terrorist acts during this crisis only because *I've* intervened. No, Plumtree. I won't allow you to ruin it."

His eyes flicked down to the facsimile for an instant, with the screen resting on the bed-curtain page. There was a look of hunger in his eyes, undisguised greed to have the book in his possession. "You do know that it was a Plumtree who printed and bound the blasted thing, don't you? He managed to escape death when King Edward IV came looking for the printer and binder. Too clever for your own good, you Plumtrees, aren't you? And too truthful by half. I'll take that screen right now, if you don't mind—the Boccaccio and the Bedchamber facsimile too, please. I'm afraid you won't be here to enjoy them."

He advanced, gun at the ready. Max and I backed away with our hands in the air to let him approach the books. He looked as perfectly groomed and tidy as if he'd been on the way to his London club for dinner. I smelled mint as he approached and was repelled by it.

"What about the other facsimiles?" I asked, feeling sweat gather on my upper lip. "I think Diana's already given them to the Library."

"Good one, Plumtree." He kept one eye on us as he slid the screen back into the Boccaccio. Stacking the smaller Bedchamber book on top of it, he tucked them both under his arm. "Top marks for effort. But it doesn't matter anymore. No one knows that the screen's the key, do they? You know, there always was the rumour that one of the Boccaccios had the screen in it. . . . No doubt you've wondered about my faking the three Boccaccios—there was a bit more to that than a re-enactment, inspired as it was, of the three-rings story. I'd hoped you wouldn't be able to resist coming forward and saying that *you* had the other. I really didn't think you'd come on the weekend without bringing your own Valdarfer Boccaccio to show off. I could have snatched it over the weekend, and you wouldn't have known it was me. I wouldn't have had to kill you, then." He sighed and flipped the safety catch off his gun. "But you proved far more restrained and prudent than I would have expected."

He shook his head. "You really kept me guessing, Plumtree—now I know it was all accidental brilliance on your part. I've been watching you ever since; I had the people who repaired your house after the break-in— Chesterton co-operated in that—install cameras and listening devices. There's one over there, in your television set, and another in your kitchen. I had a great deal of fun watching you and the woman from the British Museum discover that papyrus."

"You *bastard*!" Max, whose emotions were always close to the surface, lost his composure. He charged at Trefoyle, ready to strike.

The sound from the old pistol was deafening; bits of plaster fell from the ceiling. Max shook with rage and fear but stayed where he was. The bullet had gone over his head. I gripped his arm, warning him not to incite Trefoyle to violence any sooner than necessary.

If only we had nearer neighbours, they might have heard the shot. . . .

"Now. As you know, I'm prepared to give you a sporting chance. The spirit of chivalry and all that. If you come out with me to your lovely garden—I've had a good look round—I'll show you what I have in mind."

He gestured in the direction of the French doors, and we walked ahead of him. I wondered what, exactly, a "sporting" chivalric execution would be like. Max unfastened the lock on the doors and swung one open. A slight breeze ruffled the new leaves on the trees and shrubs. An absolutely perfect evening, with the exception of the armed madman behind us. We walked meekly through to the garden, the remains of the rhododendron shrubs still studding the grounds with pink, red, and purple blooms. When I judged Trefoyle had started through the door, I swung it back, slamming it into his face.

"Run!" I bellowed. Max broke away from me, sprinting round the house towards the garage. I ran the opposite way, towards the front, where there was a tall, thick hedge at the side of the house to hide behind. But the leg bruised by Attila still didn't co-operate the way it should have, and as I ran, a protruding root of the giant oak now partially eradicated—like the one in Trefoyle's coat of arms— caught my toe. I went flying and hit the ground hard.

As I struggled to get up again, I heard a rustle behind me. I knew it was Trefoyle; I just prayed he wouldn't shoot me yet. When at last I got to my knees, hunched over and breathing carefully to ease the pain in my still-tender ribs, I lifted my hands to show I wasn't going to fight, and turned to face him.

A trickle of blood ran from his nose; I'd injured him with the door. His upper lip curled when he spoke. "Not very sporting of you. I'm disappointed, Plumtree. And I was trying to be so fair." A nasty smile crept up one side of his mouth. "I see your brother has deserted you . . . exactly as I'd expected."

I kept my eyes on Trefoyle but became aware in my peripheral vision, of something moving behind and above him. It was on the roof of the house . . . Max! With a supreme effort of will I refrained from looking directly at him and so giving away his presence. But what could he hope to . . .

The oak. It still leaned up against the house where it had fallen weeks before. Surely Max didn't think . . .

I didn't dare give Trefoyle a hint of Max's presence or intentions. It was nearly impossible to keep my eyes trained on him. The breeze cooled the sweat that now soaked my clothing, and made a sighing noise in the ancient trees at the back of the garden.

Trefoyle regarded me coldly. "I've refilled my pistol, but I put in some blanks. You won't know when I'm shooting with real bullets or harmless ones. More exciting, I think. And frightfully generous of me. Now I'm going to give you five seconds. Then I'll start firing."

In disbelief I saw him look down and open his gun. I chanced a glance up at Max, who perched precariously on the edge of the gutter, some twenty feet above the ground, straining to dislodge the tree. I thought I could see the grimace on his mouth as he pushed with all his might. It seemed to be wedged too tightly; he wasn't going to shift it. Not in time anyway. I could just hear the noise over the sound of the wind, a scraping sound as the wood grated against the brick. I hoped Trefoyle wouldn't notice. Thank God for the wind, I thought.

I had to stall. *Something, anything,* I told myself.

"Wait! Trefoyle!" He was suspicious.

"I just want you to know . . ." With a gargantuan effort of will I refrained from moving my eyes. Trefoyle seemed to sense something; in the next instant a deafening noise not unlike the ripping of cloth engulfed us. He looked for the source of the racket, and I lunged for him. The Boccaccio and the Bedchamber book tumbled to the ground like so much old paper as I wrestled with him for the gun. I heard the ancient tree coming, its remaining roots ripping out of the ground as it fell fast towards us. And something was moving on top of it . . .

Max. He had climbed onto the top of the tree to dislodge it from against the house. In the time it took the tree to fall, miraculously directly towards us, it flashed through my mind that whatever injury the tree did to Trefoyle, it would also do to me. I didn't get the gun from him, but at the last second I tried to scramble away, and Trefoyle's eyes widened in recognition of what was happening.

But it was too late. The next instant the tree was upon us, its dry branches brittle as old bone. I dived away, out from under the trunk as it knocked Trefoyle, who was perhaps ten feet away from me and directly in line with the trunk, flat beneath it. I saw it strike him across the chest, the massive cylinder of wood smashing him mercilessly to the ground as if he'd been a matchstick.

A network of heavy branches bit into my arms and legs, pinning me to the ground. To my immense relief, I found it was possible, with a bit of effort and ripping of clothes and tearing of skin, to slide out from beneath the outer branches. The ten feet which separated me from Trefoyle had bought my life, putting me securely in the range of spreading, lesser boughs. I scuttled out from beneath them and went to Trefoyle.

He lay unmoving under the massive weight of the trunk; his eyes were closed, his face slack. I left him and hurried over to where Max lay on the ground, writhing in distress. Fearing some horrible injury, I panicked. "Max! Can you hear me?"

I knelt and helped him sit up. "Trefoyle?" he rasped.

I looked over to where the earl lay pinned beneath the trunk.

Max's eyes widened in horror. "Did we *kill* him?"

"Only just before he killed us," I said. "Can you help me move the tree? We've got to try."

I helped him up; he winced as he stood. But together we tried our best to pull the bulky trunk off Trefoyle. The earl was unconscious; now his face was a pasty white. I felt for a pulse in his neck and hoped I felt the faintest thread.

The trunk wouldn't budge, even with both of us heaving at it. I suggested ringing for help; Max told me he'd done it before climbing onto the roof. Max and I fell into stunned silence at what we'd done. As we looked at Trefoyle and longed for the ambulance to arrive, I watched in disbelief as the earl's arm began to move. It slid out slowly from next to his body and stopped. I thought it was some sort of weird muscle spasm, but then saw that his hand still clutched the gun. In the next second, mesmerised, I saw that he had managed to point the barrel at me. In the instant before I shoved Max down and flattened myself on the ground, I saw his eyes open. He pulled the trigger.

It was as though someone had thrown a hot coal onto my shoulder; I felt the sting of the bullet but then heard it thunk into the side of the house.

With a startled cry Max lunged for the gun and snatched it from Trefoyle, flinging it into the hedge before he could send off another shot. Max came and bent over me.

"I'm all right. Really," I said, and staggered to my feet.

He looked at me as if I'd lost my marbles, then was off to meet the ambulance as its siren blared down Old Shire Lane. My mind ground away, working out how to handle this. It finally became clear to me that if word got out that

Earl Trefoyle had been shooting at the Plumtree brothers, his Iraqi friends would want to know why. They might suspect that we'd lied to them about the papyrus being the ultimate secret of the book. I decided I would leave myself the option of revealing the message in the bed curtain to them at some point in the future. For now I would pretend I'd never found it.

The ambulance men pronounced Trefoyle dead; I repressed the urge to warn them that they could never be too sure with this one. Speaking up first, I set the tone that it had all been a ghastly accident. Yes, he'd been a personal friend. Yes, Earl Trefoyle was a fellow member of the Dibdin Club. It was too horrible that I hadn't taken care of the tree earlier. Yes, I agreed, it was most out of the ordinary that this deadly accident should have happened as we walked round the property.

The police asked us lots of questions and reflected how extraordinary it was that the tree had landed squarely on him. But they looked at our cuts and scrapes and the blood soaking into my shirt and realised we hadn't escaped unscathed either. They seemed to assume my shoulder had been hurt when the tree fell. They did not see the spent bullet near the house, nor did they find the gun in the hedge.

When they had finally taken Trefoyle's body and gone, I stood by the fallen oak with Max. "The message in the book," I said. "We mustn't tell anyone. Not yet."

"No."

We heard the telephone ringing through the still-open French door. Max went off to answer it; I followed more slowly.

"Yes, Graeme. Just a moment please." Max handed me the phone as I walked in the door.

"Lock the doors and set the alarm, would you?" I asked my brother, and put the phone to my ear. "Hello, Graeme." In that moment I had to decide whether to tell Graeme the ultimate secret of the book, or let it rest for ever.

I decided to let it rest.

"Alex. You sound absolutely knackered. I don't suppose you've had much sleep."

"No—and I'm afraid something horrible has just happened here at the Orchard. You'll have to excuse me . . . I'm not quite myself." I related the extraordinary events of the evening.

"I'm terribly sorry," he said when I'd concluded. "What a ghastly thing to endure—as if enough hasn't already happened." He paused. "But I nearly forgot—I'm actually calling with news. Our friends in the Middle East have decided that the book represents no threat to them, Alex. They've sent word that they believe the legend must have become garbled over the years, that the papyrus had to be the book's secret."

I gripped the telephone harder. "That's *wonderful*!"

He drew a deep breath. "The Great Teacher has sent out a message ordering the end of the conflict. He has specifically asked that all groups release any Western hostages; he has urged them to honour the Prophet by doing so."

My shoulders fell; I sat heavily on the edge of my desk. "She's not coming back, is she," I murmured. It wasn't a question.

Graeme was silent for a moment. When his voice travelled down the line, it shook with emotion. "You mustn't give up now, Alex. You mustn't. Hostages *have* returned . . . and Sarah's chances are better now than ever."

No, I thought. *I won't abandon her now. The only thing to do is behave as if she might come through the door at any moment. . . .*

The wedding invitations. I walked deliberately to my desk, and looked at the partially addressed envelope on top of the stack and the pen waiting beside it. Yes. Much better to hope. And when she was returned to me, she would know that I hadn't been ready to give up on her.

I sat down and picked up my fountain pen, writing

Sarah's name on a spare scrap of paper to get the ink flowing. The pen scratched along the creamy white surface of the envelope; I watched the dramatic curves of black ink take shape. I was careful to use my best decorative script. After all, you got married only once . . .

If you were very, very lucky.

If you enjoyed Julie Kaewert's **Untitled**, the third book in the *Booklover's Mystery* series, you won't want to miss any of the adventures in this exciting series.

Look for the next, **Unsolicited**, at your favorite booksellers in summer 2000.

ABOUT THE AUTHOR

JULIE KAEWERT first indulged her fascination with book publishing by taking the Radcliffe Publishing Procedures Course in 1981. She then worked for book publishers in Boston and London before starting her writing career with a London magazine. Her series of mysteries for booklovers has topped mystery bestseller lists around the country, and she is at work on her fifth Alex Plumtree adventure, *Unsigned*.